SECRETS OF STONE

Book One of
A WOLF IN THE SUN

A novel by
Coltrane Seesequasis

KEGEDONCE PRESS, 2024

Published by Kegedonce Press
11 Park Road, Neyaashiinigmiing, ON N0H 2T0
Administration Office/Book Orders: P.O. Box 517, Owen Sound, ON N4K 5R1
www.kegedonce.com

Printed in Canada by Trico Printing
Art Direction: Kateri Akiwenzie-Damm
Design: Chantal Lalonde Design
Cover art by: Don Chretien
Illustrations by: Coltrane Seesequasis
Author's photo: Sharmila Chowdhury

Library and Archives Canada Cataloguing in Publication

Title: Secrets of stone / a novel by Coltrane Seesequasis.
Names: Seesequasis, Coltrane, author.
Description: Series statement: A wolf in the sun ; book 1
Identifiers: Canadiana 20240364759 | ISBN 9781928120421 (softcover)
Subjects: LCGFT: Fantasy fiction. | LCGFT: Novels.
Classification: LCC PS8637.E44548 S43 2024 | DDC C813/.6—dc23

For Customer Service/Orders
Tel 1-800-591-6250 Fax 1-800-591-6251
100 Armstrong Ave., Georgetown, ON L7G 5S4
Email: orders@litdistco.ca

We acknowledge the support of the Canada Council for the Arts which last year
invested $20.1 million in writing and publishing throughout Canada.

Canada Council   Conseil des arts
for the Arts   du Canada

We would like to acknowledge funding support from the Ontario Arts Council,
an agency of the Government of Ontario.

ONTARIO ARTS COUNCIL
CONSEIL DES ARTS DE L'ONTARIO
an Ontario government agency
un organisme du gouvernement de l'Ontario

*To everyone who encouraged me, gave me feedback,
and helped me on my writing journey, thank you.*

Coltrane

MAP OF THE NORTHLANDS
(The Mortal Realm)

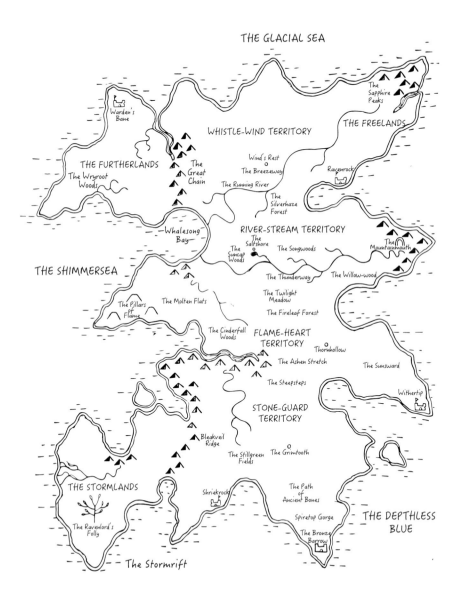

THE GLACIAL SEA

The Sapphire Peaks

Warden's Bane

WHISTLE-WIND TERRITORY

THE FREELANDS

THE FURTHERLANDS

The Wryroot Woods

The Great Chain

Wind's Rest
The Breezeway

Ravenrock

The Running River

The Silverhaze Forest

Whalesong Bay

RIVER-STREAM TERRITORY

The Saltshore

The Suncap Woods

The Songwoods

The Mountainmouth

THE SHIMMERSEA

The Thunderway

The Willow-wood

The Pillars of Flame

The Molten Flats

The Twilight Meadow

The Fireleaf Forest

The Cinderfall Woods

FLAME-HEART TERRITORY

Thornhollow

The Ashen Stretch

The Sunsward

The Steepsteps

Withertip

STONE-GUARD TERRITORY

Bleakveil Ridge

The Stillgreen Fields

The Grimtooth

THE STORMLANDS

Shriekrock

The Path of Ancient Bones

THE DEPTHLESS BLUE

Spiretop Gorge

The Ravenlord's Folly

The Bronze Barrow

The Stormrift

TABLE OF CONTENTS

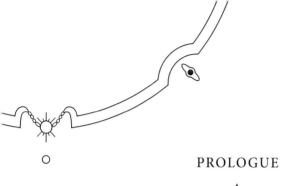

✦

A Broken Chain

"Keep up, or they'll catch you!" the grey wolf warned.

Swiftstorm followed the obvious advice. She darted through the malformed pines and jumped over outstretched roots, matching the speed of her partner despite the pain exploding through every paw. The savage laughter behind them stiffened her hackles. The exiles were getting closer.

"I wasn't exactly planning on stopping," Swiftstorm huffed, legs numb from sprinting as the stuffy air denied her a comfortable breath. "But thanks for the reminder, Greyhail."

Greyhail craned his head over his shoulder to smirk at her, eyes like amber sunsets in his broad and scarred face. "Had to make sure your focus was on the appropriate thing," he grunted, panting away his fatigue. "You always get distracted whenever you're near me for some reason. Must be my good looks, eh?"

Heat seeped into Swiftstorm's cheeks, but she forced herself to scowl until he turned around. "Ugh, you're so hopeless." She tried to hide a creeping smile.

"Not as hopeless as the situation we're in," he snorted.

The remaining stars glimmered defiantly against the thickening clouds, but like the moon before them, their light was smothered without mercy. Raspy voices cheered at the triumphant darkness, and the evergreens groaned and twisted in place, their roots below coming alive.

"Look out!" Swiftstorm yelped.

One of the roots tripped her partner, and he smacked his muzzle on the frozen ground. Before he could get up, tendrils of wood exploded out of the soil and entangled him like snakes coiling an unsuspecting rat. He thrashed and wriggled, but the choking prison never softened its assault. Slowly, the tendrils began to decay, emitting an odour foul enough to sicken even a vulture's stomach. They dragged him low and ignored his struggle.

Swiftstorm's nostrils curled. She blocked her nose and forced her mouth to suffer the unclean air instead. Even so, the sickening stench soured her tongue and wrenched her gut. "Greyhail!" She skidded to a standstill beside him.

"Argh!" Greyhail yowled, biting at his confines in between heaves. "Get them off!"

"Quit moving!" She braced herself and tore at the rotting roots, spitting out the sickening chunks of wood before they could slide down her parched gullet.

"Quit moving?! Really?!" Greyhail's forelegs broke free. "Oh, sure. I'll just relax while these roots BURY ME ALIVE!"

"Oh, be quiet, you bug-brained buffoon!" Swiftstorm growled, using her quick claws to sever the stubborn tendrils. She grabbed her partner by the scruff and helped him up. "Try not to embarrass yourself like that again. I'm getting tired of saving your sorry backside."

"Consider my sorry backside eternally grateful." Greyhail coughed and gave her a thankful nuzzle before stepping away from the writhing mass. "I definitely owe you the fattest prey I can sniff out."

Swiftstorm nudged him on the cheek. "For all the times I yanked your tail out of trouble, you owe me much more than a single meal."

The ceaseless barking of their pursuers reminded her of the danger they were in.

Ugh, to think this was supposed to be a simple scouting mission to see what the exiles were up to. Somehow we managed to attract the attention of every faithless mongrel in the Furtherlands instead! Some scouts we are.

Greyhail gave her a funny look before turning toward their destination. "I'll think of a fitting reward after we're safe in one of the cozy caves of the Great Chain. Deal?"

"Deal." Swiftstorm nosed him on the snout.

"Good. Now come!" He bolted in the direction where the summer sun would rise, kicking up clumps of frigid earth.

Several flea-bitten exiles bounded over the prickly undergrowth and snarled, fangs sharp and dripping saliva.

Swiftstorm whirled around and hurried after Greyhail, the banished wolves hot on her tail. Eager teeth snapped within a hair of her flesh, but they found themselves chomping on nothing but air. She maneuvered herself gracefully through the remainder of the forest, ducking under groping branches and hopping over slashing roots. Her muscles ached, her chest pounded, her throat burned, but the threat of death or worse forced her to keep going.

A line of mountains stretched high beyond the forest. It was the Great Chain, the sanctuary of the sentinels, her beloved home. The rocky ridge marched jaggedly until it met the distant sea—a lofty barrier separating the noble wolves from the savage outcasts. The memory of taking the sacred oaths to defend the Four Territories against the evils of the Furtherlands hardened her resolve. She was a jailor of the wicked and an enforcer of the Wolven Code! As a sentinel, she should've been the one doing the chasing! The Great Chain loomed ahead and beckoned her, promising safety once she arrived under its shadow.

Exiles wouldn't dare attack the line of mountains! Not even if the Heretic himself commanded it of them. The mere notion of the Heretic, the leader of the exiles, launching a direct assault on the home of the sentinels twisted her insides. *He would fail! The Great Chain has stood strong for countless seasons. Its stone is impenetrable even to wolves like the Heretic.*

Raspy laughter accompanied the growls of the relentless pursuers and caused a wave of chills to spike her fur. She pricked her ears and drained herself of fear, of worry, of all intruding thoughts. The currents of air created by her movements shifted and stirred, but disobeyed her command. The corruption tainting the Furtherlands was still too powerful. It blocked every attempt to weave even the faintest breeze.

A snowflake landed on her nose and melted. She craned her head skyward as more flakes drifted out of the brewing storm, calmly crowning the peaks of the Great Chain in white. The unnatural snowfall mocked the dawning days of summer. An uneasy pressure squeezed Swiftstorm's heart. This should've been a time for heat and growth, but the unwelcome blizzard now thwarted the delicate balance of the seasons.

Then she noticed it—a grinning face formed by the inky clouds, its deer-like shape stretched and twisted abnormally, its mouth exposing row upon row of sharp teeth. She recoiled and stifled a breath. Hollowed eye sockets stared right at her, and a tangle of antlers sprouted from its skull like warped roots snaking across the tainted sky.

She averted her gaze from the fiendish face. It was the Fallen Titan, the evil spirit responsible for the corruption of the Furtherlands. She was sure of it.

"I smell your fear, sentinel!" blared a ragged voice behind her. "Give up and accept your fate. You'll never make it to your precious mountains! The Fallen Titan's power flows through our veins."

"By the time we've finished tearing the flesh from your bones, the Warden herself won't even recognize your corpse!" another exile taunted. "And we'll slaughter her afterwards!"

"Motherwolf curse all you wretched scatfurs!" Swiftstorm yapped, her haste fueled by a desperate energy. The squirming pines cleared, and the earth felt warmer under her sore pads.

Almost there… almost there… almost there…

Greyhail jumped over a fence of sickly bracken, landing on the other side and barking for her to hurry. She pressed on her haunches and sprang into the air, her claws gently scraping the fronds before they crunched into the snowy ground beyond. The two bolted into the clearing, the mountains reaching overhead—an impenetrable bulwark against the vile and lawless wolves chasing them. Far above, spaced wide apart, were overlooks occupied by sentinels on sentry duty. Those who could see her and Greyhail howled to signal their arrival. She howled in return, pouring as much urgency as she could into her strident cry.

She emptied her mind again, focusing on the whisper of a stray breeze, feeling its gentle caress and touching its intricate pattern. She weaved it into a winding shield of air around her. The corruption of the Furtherlands was weaker here. Now she could defend herself properly. The ground rumbled beneath Greyhail, mimicking his low growl.

A horde of exiles leaped over the bracken and creeped forward, nasty snarls stretching their mouths. More sentinels above howled, this time as a warning to the dirty mongrels, their tones angry and ferocious. Some of the exiles fixed hateful glares on them.

"Stay back!" Swiftstorm bayed, lips parting into a snarl of her own. "Return to the Furtherlands and leave the Great Chain at once. We sentinels won't tolerate your filthy scents here!"

A din of jeers and growls challenged her warning, and aggressive laughter only emboldened the stirring thunder; the sky rumbled as if hunger had driven it mad.

"Congratulations. You made them even angrier," Greyhail remarked, crouching beside her as the enemy approached. "Also, you should really practice your snarl. You sound about as convincing as a pup trying to roar like a bear."

Her stomach fluttered, but she allowed none of the embarrassment to sneak into her expression. "Oh, I should've let those roots bury you alive."

"Come now." Greyhail bumped her shoulder. "Your life would be awfully boring without me to ruffle your fur."

"Awfully peaceful, you mean," Swiftstorm retorted, readying herself for the inevitable assault. "But still, I would prefer it if you refrained from dying tonight."

"Same goes for you." Greyhail hardened himself, body trembling as the earth shook beneath him. "Reinforcements should arrive soon. Let's stall the exiles some more."

The wind died, and with its death faded Swiftstorm's advantage. The barking and snarling ceased, and the unnatural twisting and turning of the trees abated. All plunged into complete silence. High in the sky, the mouth of the Fallen Titan gaped wider as if to swallow the mountains whole.

The stretch of bracken withered, making way for two large wolves. They stepped into the clearing as if it belonged to them. The exiles froze at the arrival of the Heretic—the ruler of the Furtherlands—and his loyal lieutenant, Rime.

The Heretic's grizzled fur was sleek and neatly groomed, and his icy green eyes spoke of an even colder soul. Like a black shadow, his lieutenant towered beside him, yellow glare fueled by a festering hatred for those who'd imprisoned him beyond the Great Chain.

The sky bellowed as the lieutenant huffed. "Ah, the little mice have finally been cornered. Unlucky how the Warden assigned you two to be on scouting duty tonight."

"Unlucky for YOU! Monster!" Swiftstorm hissed, but Rime merely sneered.

"Swiftstorm…" Greyhail whispered into her ear, his tone uncertain.

"Shh!" Swiftstorm released a steady growl.

"We can't win against—"

"I said quiet! I'm aware we can't win. I'm trying to stall them like you suggested!"

A flaming passion glowed in the Heretic's eyes, and his aged body appeared reinvigorated by the spirit of youth. "Monster? You see us all as irredeemable fiends, don't you? It amuses me how you sentinels use blind faith to justify your cruelty against us. You're so sure you're furthering a noble cause. Yes. Motherwolf must be so proud of you condemning us to suffer like wretches. You took our names and our freedom and stripped us of dignity because we dared to stand against the oppression you defend."

Within the rocky bowels of the Great Chain, the howling of battle-ready wolves vibrated through the stone. Soon Swiftstorm's fellow soldiers would pour out of every overlook and descend the mountainside to reinforce the front.

The Heretic turned his eyes to the angry storm. "The age of ignorance ends soon. If you understood the peace I would bring to the Four Territories, you would abandon your misplaced sense of duty and join me, sentinel."

Swiftstorm gritted her teeth, her fear churning into a whirlwind of fury. "If you think any sentinel would ever join you, then you're beyond saving. If it weren't for us keeping the peace and punishing code-breakers, wolves like you would take any excuse to do terrible things to the Four Territories."

"Sometimes terrible things are justified if the outcome leads to a better future." The Heretic flicked his tail, gesturing a command to his lieutenant, who closed his eyes and quivered. The clouds mirrored his trembling, and the face in the sky gaped its jaws ever wider. "Now, after countless seasons of withering away in this cursed place, I'll finally give the Four Territories everything they deserve. And I'll repay you sentinels for treating us so… unfairly. Do it, Rime!"

"Swiftstorm!" Greyhail's cry snapped her out of her fury. "Something's wrong! We have to retreat!"

Greyhail broke into a sprint as cracks of thunder shook Swiftstorm to the marrow. She followed her partner's lead and climbed up a ledge of stone, bristling alongside him, cowering at the monstrous visage that seemed to be getting closer with every blink. Greyhail smacked a forepaw on the rocky platform, and it lifted itself at the command, sliding upward like a reversed landslide. The exiles below howled for the storm to unleash its wrath as Swiftstorm craned her head to the closest overlook.

We're almost there!

A flash of crooked lightning streaked out of the gaping mouth, followed by an ear-splitting boom that eclipsed Swiftstorm's cry as everything collapsed. The mountain they were scaling crumbled and crashed into the hostile forest below.

Everything burned inside of her, and a foreign rage seared her thoughts and memories until even the most innocent ones perished in the pitiless inferno. Blind hatred scorched through every vein. Beyond the cacophony of the breaking stone, a crackling voice laughed at her demise, promising worse to come for those she'd sworn to defend.

The Great Chain was ruptured, and the exiles would now flood the Four Territories from top to bottom like an unstoppable tempest. She'd failed her mission as a sentinel. The Heretic had been released, and his desire for destruction would soon be met.

"Time itself shall soon be his to devour," her own distorted voice whispered to her from beyond the chaos.

No thrumming pain, no shattering of bones, no fear came the moment she hit the ground. All she could feel now was a deep, spreading numbness creeping into her core as the piling rubble sheltered her body.

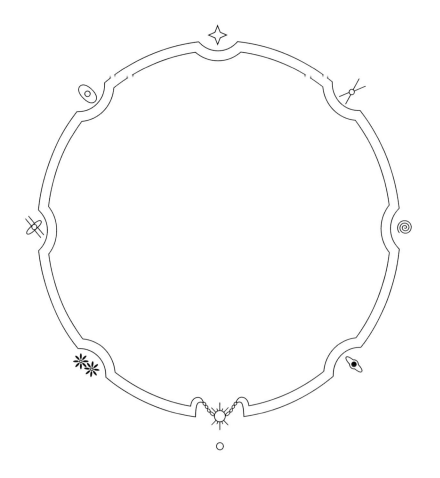

CHAPTER 1

✦

A Nearly Uneventful Morning

"I hate being a subordinate," Silversong groaned as he hunted for unsuspecting prey.

At least the black storm brewing where the moon was setting seemed to have no intention of coming his way. Foraging for food while getting drenched wasn't a fun experience. As if to reassure him, crimson rays lanced through the parting clouds to scorch away the faint layer of fog gathered at the forest floor, promising a hot day to come.

Though the morning was livened by birdsong and gentle zephyrs, Silversong would much rather have spent it lazing in his cozy lair until at least noon. He sighed, envying his higher-ranking packmates who weren't required to get up so early to begin their daily duties. His promotion couldn't come soon enough. The thought of remaining a lowly subordinate for another season sparked a shiver of worry. Pride at being the oldest of the *tail-tuckers* wasn't something he clenched his teeth onto and getting bossed around by wolves his age who now outranked him ruffled his fur the wrong way.

He should've been promoted to corporal ages ago, but because of his unremarkable feats and smaller physique, he'd been denied the chance to impress his leader and advance to a better position. The Chief had to see the sparks of eagerness flaring up inside him! If he could only prove himself, he wouldn't ever have to worry about keeping his tail tucked at all times or sleeping on an empty stomach. As a corporal, he would be allowed to eat whatever he wanted until his belly bulged like a blowfish!

And all I have to do is find a way to prove myself.

He buried all his doubts and fears in the deepest recesses of his mind until he could only think about his inevitable victory. The respect he deserved for lawfully serving the Whistle-Wind Pack would eventually be his, and any concerns his packmates had regarding his value would be discarded soon enough.

He strolled through the waking reaches of the Breezeway—a forest of proud pines and golden larches—and sniffed the moist air. He picked up a whirl of fresh morning scents: dew, earth, grass, and a whole assortment of equally uninteresting things. Not a single hare or squirrel dared peek out of their hidden shelters, and his ears couldn't detect any of the sneakier critters scuttling in their tunnels underground. The thought of hungry corporals punishing him for not filling the prey hollow only encouraged him to sniff harder.

After my promotion, I'll be the one doing the punishing if the other subordinates fail to keep my belly filled! He fantasized about barking insults at the more incompetent subordinates, but he promised himself he wouldn't be as mean as some of the senior corporals.

He added more weight to his steps, pushing deeper into the wet soil, cursing his failure to detect even a whiff of prey. He focused on finding medicinal plants instead, lifting his hind leg over each and spraying his scent on the ground there, which made finding them much easier for the corporals on harvesting duty later in the day. It took some time for his own scent to drown out the earthy fragrance.

At least they can't accuse me of being lazy.

Bladder emptied, he ambled up a slope littered with brown pine needles and tiny yellow mushrooms thriving in the morning's humidity. He ignored the pungent odour and climbed onto the Breezeway's upper levels. Taking in the clean air, he wiped off the soil wedged between his pads and yawned, blinking away a stubborn fatigue.

A rustle in the distance pricked his ears. Something on the breeze smelled familiar: wolves. Two wolves. One approaching faster than the other. He turned his head in time to see a white fuzzy shape hurling at him. Before he could even widen his eyes, it crashed into him, and he thudded onto the ground. Head rolling in circles, he tried to shake out his confusion.

Standing above him, tongue lolling and face puffy, was a snowy-furred wolf. Silversong snorted at his own scowling reflection caught in playful amber eyes. "Palesquall, even if you're excited to see me, you don't have to ram me into the ground like an angry goat!"

Palesquall grinned as he panted. "Shouldn't a member of the Whistle-Wind Pack always be alert and ready to move? *The breeze constantly shifts, and so should you,*" he whined in an elder's scolding voice. "Not my fault you're slower than a snail."

"Quoting the elders now, are we?" Silversong pawed his friend's face. "You going to give me a lecture or something? I'm already sleepy enough as it is." He yawned for emphasis.

Palesquall paused to feign consideration, scrunching up his eyes and wrinkling his nose. "Hmm… nope! Think I'll just gloat over my victory of successfully tackling your silver rump to the ground."

"My silver rump doesn't appreciate being tackled much." Silversong glowered, hind paws pressed against the arrogant subordinate's belly. While his opponent was distracted, Silversong poured all of his strength into his muscles and pushed, launching Palesquall into the air.

Palesquall landed on his spine and flailed in a panic. Silversong rolled over and lunged at his friend, using his forepaws to pin him before he could get up. "So much for being alert and ready to move, huh? How about this, bug-brain. Say I win, and I'll let you go."

Palesquall thrashed and showed his teeth. "Whistle-Wind wolves never surrender!"

"That so?" Silversong thought up a few ways on how to make the dogged dullard submit. "How about I—"

"PALESQUALL!" an angry she-wolf shouted. "WHERE IN MOTHERWOLF'S MILK ARE YOU?!"

"Uh, oh," Palesquall squeaked. "Let me go, Silversong! She's going to rip my tail off and force me to swallow it whole!"

"Oh, really? Sounds like a pretty entertaining thing to see, honestly." Silversong grinned. "Maybe she'll finally manage to muzzle you up for good this time, eh?"

"All right, all right! You win!" Palesquall kicked and struggled. Even though he was several seasons younger than Silversong and only slightly larger, it proved a challenge to keep him pinned.

"Huh?" Silversong teased, pressing his nose against Palesquall's. "I'm not sure I heard you. How about you say it a little louder this time? Maybe so the whole forest can hear you?"

Before Palesquall could declare anything, a mousy-furred she-wolf jumped over a cluster of brambles, bristling, green eyes so heated they could've melted a glacier. "There you are, you complete gullwit of a wolf!"

"Hey, Hazel. How's morning duty so far?" Silversong asked casually, still keeping Palesquall pinned.

"Oh, hey, Silversong. It's been fine, I guess." She gave him a pretty smile before glowering at Palesquall again. The way she could instantly shift from cheerful to angry was downright spine-chilling sometimes. "That deer I spotted would've been mine if you hadn't run off like a horde of hornets was at your tail!"

Silversong released his friend and whispered into his perked ear. "Heh. I can practically smell the fear wafting off you, Palesquall. Must've been quite the deer you frightened off to make her *this* angry."

"Oh, quiet," Palesquall retorted. "It wasn't even that big."

He tucked his tail deeper and deeper the closer Hazel came. A low growl enhanced her breathing as they touched noses, Palesquall crouching and quivering like a pathetic pup. "Listen here. You're going to track the deer you scared off and you're going to haul its corpse all the way to the den once I've killed it, understood? And if you dare take a bite out of it before I do, I'll sharpen my teeth on your hide! Am I clear?!"

"Y-yes, ma'am," Palesquall uttered, flattening his ears. "Clear as ice!"

Silversong smelled something musky on the breeze and turned to an opening between two huge pines. His amusement morphed into excitement. His mouth watered, and he panted. "Uh… Hazel, Palesquall?"

"Don't *ma'am* me!" Hazel snapped. "I'm a subordinate like you. Only lieutenants and Chiefs can be addressed as *sir* or *ma'am*."

"Hey!" Silversong pointed his muzzle at the hoofed beast staring blank-eyed at them, probably hoping if it were still enough, it would become invisible. "I think I found your deer, Hazel."

She turned to face her escaped quarry, its short fur glazed brown under the clearing sky. Her tail stiffened and her eyes widened.

Palesquall blinked at it, lips forming a goofy smirk. "Wow, this makes my job a whole lot easier, doesn't it?" He took a careful pace toward it. "Hey, why isn't it running from us?"

As if the deer had suddenly questioned that itself, it turned and dashed through the Breezeway, looking over its shoulder only once.

"Way to go, Palesquall," Hazel snarled. "You're a BIG HELP as always."

"Me?! But I—"

"After it!" Silversong charged, paws tingling, heart booming at the thrill of a chase.

His friends sprinted behind him as he drained his head of outer thoughts. He envisioned a strong gale that shifted, twirled, and danced to the cadence of his breaths, his movements. He connected himself to its potential, its power, its forever evolving pattern. Like a companion who would never abandon him, the wind embraced his body and buffeted his fur. He sprang after the fleeing beast, strides guided by the sudden draft propelling him onward. He focused on the smooth current, aware of everything it touched and everywhere it reached. All distractions were blown away, and he became the breeze itself, zipping through the trees and dispersing every leaf or pine needle in the way. Aided by the swiftness of air, he found himself a mere tail-length or so behind his target's pale backside. This chase would soon be over.

His prey craned its head around, eyes on the verge of popping. Its antlers brightened, shining green in the shafts of sunlight filtering through the forest roof. A deep hum vibrated within the pines and larches, and their branches swayed gently, but not because they'd been touched by the breeze.

Roots erupted out of the earth in all directions and slithered toward Silversong, threatening to strangle him. The radiance of the antlers lessened, but the roots continued to twist and slash, battering the steady connection between Silversong and the whirling air.

He struggled to maintain his quickened pace. Every time he touched ground, something sharp would prick him and attempt to entangle his limbs. He spared no look to whatever his prey had conjured. Instead, he pushed on his haunches and jumped, narrowly evading several whipping branches before skidding onto the rocky shore of the Running River. The deer halted before the fleeing waters, trapped and cornered. It darted its head around in hopes of finding something to use against its pursuer, but there were no trees or plants nearby for it to wield.

"It's over." Silversong panted, tail raised in triumph.

Hazel stopped beside him while Palesquall struggled to control his momentum. The air raged chaotically around him, and he tripped on a stone, smacking his muzzle on one of the pale boulders of the shore.

"Ow," he groaned.

Silversong snorted at his friend's failure and crouched, casting away all intrusive thoughts again. He connected himself to Palesquall's untamed whirlwind and pulled it close, willing it to manifest into swift currents around every paw. The deer released a screeching wail and veered toward the bending blue stretch cutting Whistle-Wind Territory in two.

Silversong's heart plummeted. "What're you... NO!"

The beast jumped into the river, disappearing under an explosive splash before resurfacing, head lifted above its submerged body. Steadily, it paddled the sparkling gap.

"No, no, no! Stupid deer! Come back!" Silversong bayed to no avail. He opened himself to invasive feelings once more, and the wheeling air around him dissipated, sighing away as if disappointed.

"Maybe if we try swimming after it?" Palesquall suggested. He got up and sleeked his fur.

"Don't be a gullwit," Silversong grunted. "We aren't River-Stream wolves. We'll exhaust ourselves in the current. But feel free to chance it, Palesquall. Just don't scream and flail like a drowning pup when you're swept out to sea."

"Hah! Wouldn't that be something to behold." Hazel licked her bared fangs.

The deer reached the other side and lifted itself onto the stone shore overrun by lichen. It shook off the water clinging to its fur and glared haughtily in their direction.

"Yeah, yeah, you beat us. Congratulations." Silversong grimaced.

His would-be prey released a burst of air from its nostrils and stomped up the rise of heather and gorse, the purple and yellow hues vibrant against the washed-out grass leading up to the crooked forest beyond.

Silversong exhaled a defeated breath while Hazel nagged Palesquall some more.

What a wasted opportunity!

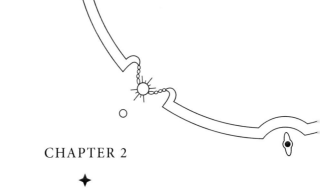

CHAPTER 2

✦

WIND'S REST

The sun had paled into a dazzling white orb by the time the three wolves returned to the den without prey and without pride.

"I still don't see how this is my fault," Palesquall muttered, tail drooping.

"No, of course you don't, Palesquall," Hazel whined as they neared the clearing in the forest. "You never see anything beyond your own muzzle."

"What's that supposed to mean?" Palesquall squinted his eyes and tilted his head.

"It means *be quiet before I bite your nose off*," she growled.

"Could you bite my ears off instead?" Palesquall smirked. "I swear you make being deaf seem like a blessing sometimes."

Before the irritable she-wolf could actually make good on one of her threats, Silversong let out a raspy groan. "Can someone please bite *my* ears off so I don't have to listen to you two bickering like undisciplined rookies all the time?!"

"He started it."

"She started it."

Silversong sighed, drawing it out so his annoyance was unmistakable. "Wow, I don't think I've ever made a more accurate comparison. Undisciplined rookies indeed." He paused until their scowls faded. "Moving on to more important things, we better come up with an excuse for why none of us brought any fresh prey to the den like we're supposed to."

"I wonder who's to blame for our failure." Hazel aimed a knowing eye at Palesquall, who retaliated with a toothy grimace.

"None of us is tossing the blame around like a salty bone." Silversong rubbed off the earth clinging between his claws. The grass was warmer here, all traces of dew scorched away. "We're all packmates. Start acting like it."

"Sheesh. Yes, sir," Palesquall whistled in a mocking tone.

Neither of them whined another comment or insult, which made Silversong's ears more than grateful.

The trees scattered and dwindled before a wide opening in the Breezeway. In the glade, a sward of clover-ridden grass circled a lofty mound of smooth boulders piled to the height of an ancient pine. The rockpile shone under the rays of the sun and beckoned the other subordinates who were also returning from morning duty, prey of varying sizes dangling from their mouths.

Wind's Rest. There isn't a more welcoming den in all the Four Territories.

The formation of boulders had six levels lessening in size the higher they climbed, each occupied by wolves of different standing. Between some of the boulders lay small grottos where packmates could enter to relax in the cool shade. The lowest and largest level was for the respected elders, the newborn pups, and the eager rookies. The second level was for the subordinates, dubbed as *tail-tuckers* by those higher than them. The third was restricted to the corporals, to those who'd proven themselves skillful hunters; their duties were to harvest medicinal plants marked by the subordinates and partake in border patrols whenever needed. The fourth level was given to the lieutenants, who organized operations and enforced the Chief's honourable commands. Above them were the Wise-Wolves, shrewd healers and counsellors to all who required their services, and the final platform—a huge circle of flattened stone soaking up the glare of the sun—was reserved for the Chief and his chosen mate.

"Looks like everyone is already up," Palesquall mused. "Maybe if we're sneaky, we won't get spotted for not dropping anything into the Prey Hollow."

Silversong surveyed the subordinates placing their quarry in the hole dug out at the lower end of the mound. Even from this distance, the scent of dried blood stung his nostrils, and his mouth watered. The Prey Hollow always smelled much stronger during the summer.

From the highest platform, Chief Amberstorm descended the levels and selected something to eat. Whether you were a subordinate or a lieutenant, and no matter how hungry you were, the Chief and their mate always ate before you. Always. His coat rippled like a grey wave in the stray breeze, sometimes outlining his large muscles and complementing his handsome face. He picked out two large hares before letting the lieutenants and corporals have their meals. The only ones who could contest them for food were the elders and Wise-Wolves. The subordinates were forever doomed to the discarded leftovers, which seemed unfair considering they were often worked to exhaustion for the gains of their betters.

But soon I'll be joining the corporals and won't ever have to go hungry again!

"Ugh, Palesquall, I think you jinxed our chances of not getting noticed." Hazel flicked her tail at the three corporals swaggering toward them.

"Oh, come on! Every time something goes wrong, I'm always the culprit." Palesquall bristled, making himself appear like a puffy dandelion ready to be blown by the breeze. In all honesty, he looked somewhat adorable.

Hazel grumbled, ignoring Palesquall and eyeing the approaching wolves. "Brace yourself, Silversong. Here they come."

Strutting in their direction were perhaps the three ugliest wolves in the Four Territories. Curled lips exposed yellow-fanged grins, and slitted eyes locked themselves only on Silversong.

His heartbeat quickened, and he tensed up on instinct. "Of all wolves who could've been promoted this summer, it just had to be those three."

"Gorsescratch becoming a corporal for his *leadership qualities* is definitely the joke of the season," Palesquall muttered. "I mean, really! I would rather follow a clumsy turtle into battle than *him*."

"Gorsescratch has been eyeing me ever since his promotion ceremony," Hazel snarled at the approaching corporal who snickered between his two friends, "like I'm his prey." She shivered in disgust, but her tail stayed low.

Palesquall grunted a chuckle. "Boy, is Gorsescratch in for a nasty surprise if he does actually gobble you up. You'll just nag him constantly while inside his belly until he vomits you out."

Silversong snorted. "Thanks, Palesquall, for giving me such a wonderful image. You've successfully crushed my appetite."

"And mine," Hazel added.

"Eh. More leftovers for me, I guess," Palesquall whined without shame.

"Looky here! If it isn't our favourite little tail-tucker." A gruff voice lured Silversong's attention to Gorsescratch's green glare and sandy fur. Beside him stood his two lackeys, each as unpleasant to look at as he was. "How'd the scavenging go this morning, puppy-eyes? Bring anything tasty to the Prey Hollow? I've been starving since morning."

Puppy-eyes. Silversong hated that stupid nickname. Out of all his grown packmates, he was the only one who'd retained the blue in his eyes. The juvenile colour clung to him like a determined flea he couldn't shake off.

Gorsescratch's tail curled above him, and a wrinkly scowl somehow made his face even uglier. "I asked you a question, puppy-eyes. You going to answer like a good little subordinate? Or do I have to force it out of you?"

Before Silversong could even begin whining a snide comment, Palesquall yipped. "We almost caught a deer this morning!"

Hazel looked as though she wanted to rip off Palesquall's whiskers one by one. Silversong wouldn't have stopped her if she pounced on the gullwit here and now. He really needed to learn how to keep his muzzle sealed!

"Almost?" Dustyleap twitched his ears at Gorsescratch's side, his grey face as unkind as his pale eyes. "I'm *almost* tempted to make you three eat grass for failing to complete your duty. As corporals, we can give you each any punishment we see fit."

Gorsescratch's gaze darted to Hazel for a moment, and something fiery ignited in his eyes, but he extinguished whatever it was and stared at the ground a breath later.

"Oh, come on!" Hazel barked, tail slightly tucked. "Can't you let us off just this once? We promise we'll deliver our dues to the Prey Hollow tomorrow."

"Quiet!" Tawnydrift growled at Gorsescratch's other side, brown hackles raised. "We haven't acknowledged you in any way, so keep your stinking muzzle clamped, subordinate."

Hazel showed as much outrage as she could without baring her fangs as Gorsescratch stretched his snarl wider. "Let you off? No. That's hardly good enough. One of you needs to be punished, and I'll allow you three to elect the unlucky mongrel. What do you say, puppy-eyes?"

I say you can all stick your ugly muzzles in your own stinking backsides, Silversong wanted whine, but stifled the urge. "There's no need for an election. I volunteer. Punish me however you like, Gorsescratch. Just remember this. Soon I'll be promoted to corporal, and then you'll regret ever having pulled my tail."

"Aww." The bully grinned. "Little puppy-eyes thinks he's going to become a corporal. How adorable." He lifted his muzzle and breathed into Silversong's ear, tickling the sensitive fur there. "You'll never get promoted, scatfur. You'll always be a subordinate living in the shadow of your sister. If I were your parents, I would regret not throwing you into the Running River as a pup. Now, onto your punishment."

Silversong's heart dropped at the biting insults, but a vortex of fury lifted it up again. Every paw prickled, a fire stirring within them, and his face heated up as he showed his untucked tail to the three bullies.

The air became distressingly still as the spectators backed away a couple paces, waiting for the fight to commence. Gorsescratch crouched, and Silversong hardened all his muscles.

I'll tear off your hide where you stand!

Just as he prepared to pounce, a cheery voice yipped. "Hey there, my favourite son—also my only son—Chief Amberstorm has summoned you to his platform!"

Silversong peeked over Gorsescratch's shoulder, and his tail swished from side to side. Approaching the scene were two lieutenants. One was a male whose grey coat bordered on black, and the other was a small she-wolf of snowy fur. He beamed at his parents, his rage submerged under a tide of excitement.

The Chief summoned me? Silversong panted at the growing anticipation. *Could this be about my promotion?!*

Palesquall praised Motherwolf for the interruption as Gorsescratch returned his focus to Silversong. "Impeccable timing," he growled. "You're one lucky tail-tucker, Silversong. But not lucky enough. You'll never leap out of your sister's shadow. You'll always be the lesser sibling." He leered at Hazel for a heartbeat before signaling his friends to follow him. They trotted away, tails proudly curled.

Silversong's anger resurfaced, and he bristled, running his claws through the grass, slicing off the blades.

Hazel spared no time to express her utter disgust at the bully. "Ugh, he's so needlessly cruel." She nuzzled Silversong on the cheek. "Don't listen to him, Silversong. You're every bit as great as Swiftstorm."

For once, Palesquall whistled in agreement. "Yeah. Even though the Warden chose to recruit her as a sentinel and not you, you're still our favourite silver scoundrel." Hazel scowled at Palesquall, who gave her an innocent look. "What? It's true!"

Silversong sighed heavily, letting the truth settle in despite the encouragement of his friends. "Oh, quit it. I'm no gullwit. How could I ever compare to Swiftstorm? She would've been promoted to lieutenant if the Warden hadn't chosen her to train as a sentinel. She would've been the youngest of the officers by far, too. We're the same age, but she's always been the shining pearl in the river while I was the common pebble." He let out a hollow chuckle. "She's still the pearl, actually, even though she's been gone for a while now."

"There he goes, brooding and making those awful comparisons again," Hazel whined. "I swear he does this every time he's sad."

Palesquall sleeked his fur. "I have to admit, it's a real mood-killer sometimes."

"Like you two never act all miserable from time to time!" Silversong gave accusing looks to Hazel and Palesquall.

Palesquall released a vigorous snort. "At least we're not as dramatic as you whenever we're unhappy."

"Dramatic?!" Silversong's fur spiked, and he bit his lower lip.

"See? Now you look as if a snake just bit your tail," Palesquall teased, making Hazel giggle. Silversong's face tightened even more.

Laughter bubbled inside his stomach, rising up and up and up, ignoring his efforts to keep it suppressed. After picturing how silly he must've looked, the heaviness pulling at his gut loosened, and the urge to laugh and nuzzle his friends took over.

They returned the embrace as Palesquall smirked. "Now there's the Silversong we needed to see."

"Shh!" Hazel hissed. "Don't ruin the moment."

Opening his eyes, Silversong stared at his nearing parents.

So the Chief summoned him, did he? Was it finally time for him to leap out of his sister's shadow? Was it finally time for him to prove himself?

Bring it on! He wore a determined expression, ready to challenge the sun itself if it was asked of him.

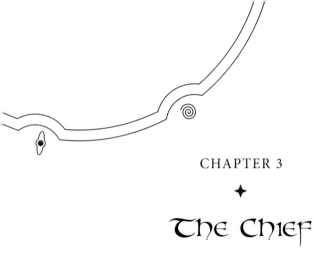

✦

CHAPTER 3

Ʇhe Chief

Absorbed in fantasies of leaving his life as a subordinate behind, Silversong barely had time to assume the correct submissive posture in the face of his parents. He followed the example of his friends, tucking his tail, flattening his ears, and crouching slightly as he waited for the approval of either one of the lieutenants before him.

"A little late on the reaction, son," his mother commented, green eyes scanning his posture for the slightest error. "Hmm. It's passable, I suppose." She flicked her tail, signaling for him to relax while she nudged his cheek in greeting.

His father shoved her to the side and licked his face as if it were drenched in the blood of his prey.

"Nice to see you too?" Silversong let the embarrassment unfold, unable to say whether he was flattered or annoyed. He returned one of the nuzzles, but wasn't too enthusiastic about it.

His mother's unamused eyes and growing scowl revealed more about her short temper than a growl or snarl ever could. "It still amazes me how I let myself be seduced by such a feather-headed buffoon," she grunted to herself.

Hazel and Palesquall snickered behind Silversong until his father finally relented the loving assault. "Sorry to interrupt your play-session with Gorsescratch. You two looked really into it, but the Chief needs to speak to you. It's not wise to keep him waiting."

"My play-session with Gorsescratch?!" Silversong recoiled his head so briskly it was a wonder it hadn't popped off. *Yeah, sure. Nothing says* play-session *quite like staring into someone's eyes while desperately wishing they would spontaneously explode!*

His mother sighed and bumped her mate on the shoulder. "Enough blithering like a talkative raven, Shadowgale. The Chief ordered us to escort our son. Let's be as quick about it as we can." She eyed Shadowgale's flailing tail. "And would you quit beating your tail like a horse trying to hit a pesky fly?!"

Palesquall choked on a laugh as Shadowgale sat on his tail to keep it still, his orange eyes lowered. "Right! Uh, sorry, Cedargaze." He got up and assumed a more respectable stance. "Let's go, son. Duty awaits!"

"Good luck," his friends whispered at the same time.

Cedargaze shook her head and padded toward the mound, unwilling to waste another breath on trivial conversation. Shadowgale waited for Silversong to follow her. He gave a smile to his friends before trailing his mother, tail tip quivering against his belly. Shadowgale trotted close behind, going on about some weird bug he'd seen in his lair even though no one was listening to him.

Silversong let his thoughts wander to his sister and how quickly she'd climbed to corporal. She was by far the fastest runner and the shrewdest hunter. An impressive combination. No wonder she overshadowed him even after she departed to become a sentinel. Rarely did the Warden leave the Great Chain to search for new recruits. Whenever she did, she picked only the finest wolves the Four Territories had to offer. The moment she chose Swiftstorm, Silversong knew everyone would expect the same greatness from him—a greatness he strived to leap for, but always failed to catch.

Maybe I'm not as gifted as her, but I'll prove I'm nothing to scoff at. His legs fizzled with energy.

Still following his mother, he sprang onto the lowest level of the mound as several elders gathered the mischievous rookies for their lessons of the day. Watching the youngsters fail at basic submissive and battle postures brought a wave of bitter nostalgia. As a rookie, he'd trained alongside Swiftstorm and others who'd since surpassed him. Sometimes he still had nightmares about the sterner elders barking at him for tripping over his own tail during posture practice or weaving the air in a dangerous manner. It took a lot of remedial training to improve his discipline and focus, but he got there… eventually.

After a dozen paces, they reached the bottom of the slate-grey stones rising up to the subordinates' level. From inside the hollow nook in front of him, the whimpers of spring's pups squeaked.

Only a few higher-ranking she-wolves were allowed to bear children every spring to avoid overpopulating the den. The ones begging for a milky snack belonged to Pinetrail, the Chief's mate, and they smelled of the she-wolves who'd helped in their rearing. Silversong wondered what names they would be given. As tradition demanded, the Wise-Wolves would gather them once they were old enough to chase prey and assess their personalities. At the end of the evaluations, they each would be given a name reflecting who they were.

Silversong resisted the urge to poke his muzzle into the nursing lairs and inspect his newest packmates. Instead, he followed his mother up to the second level.

Up, up, up they climbed, the mingled smell of wolves dwindling as they scampered onto the Wise-Wolves' level. A bossy voice sounded from around the circle of boulders. "Make sure you come see us if your headaches start acting up again, or if you need ointment for your scars! Are you even listening?!"

Elder Shrillbreeze—Whistle-Wind's former Chief who'd chosen Amberstorm to rule in his stead upon retiring—rounded the corner and scowled back at the Wise-Wolf hounding him. "Heh. At this point, I'll need something to purge your voice out of my head, Moonwhisper. I swear, every time I need your remedies, you always pester me like a stubborn flea afterwards. You should be quieter, like your assistant. If only all Wise-Wolves were like him."

Moonwhisper came into view, white coat flared up and misty eyes narrowed. "I'm pestering you because it's my duty to ensure your every ailment is cured, even those you're too blind to notice. Need I remind you of the time we were rookies and you caught a bad case of heart-fever? You thought it was only a cough until you started shaking like a bare branch during a storm! Luckily for you, I was there to haul your backside up to the experts in medicine at the time, and they saved your ungrateful life!"

Elder Shrillbreeze walked on without responding, his pinkish scars glinting in the sun. According to the stories, he'd gotten those wounds during his days as a lieutenant, fighting off a group of loners who thought they could steal prey from Whistle-Wind Territory.

"Fine. Ignore me, but don't come to my lair whimpering like a starved pup once you realize you need my cures!" The former Chief ignored her and smirked. Moonwhisper scoffed and turned around, disappearing behind a corner.

Shadowgale and Cedargaze bowed their heads to the elder. Silversong showed the same respect.

The grizzled elder flicked his tail and shook his head. "Wise-Wolves. Always sticking their snouts where it doesn't concern them."

I'm pretty sure your health does concern them, Silversong thought, not daring to whine it aloud. He couldn't count the times Moonwhisper had mended a cut or soothed an infection for him. Out of all potential Wise-Wolves, he was thankful she volunteered for the position and passed the qualifications. To become a healer, candidates had to succeed in naming every possible disease and its cure—a surprisingly tough challenge. After gaining their title, the training never fully stopped, as they constantly had to adapt their healing methods according to the weather and unforeseen factors. Every evening, corporals on harvesting duty brought them fresh medicinal plants marked by the subordinates, which they organized in their lair for future use.

After exchanging formalities, Elder Shrillbreeze sauntered off, and Silversong and his parents proceeded onto the crowning level of the mound. Chief Amberstorm waited for him there, standing proud in front of two slabs of stone leaning against each other, making room for a narrow lair at the centre of the platform. His mate, Pinetrail, smoothed her tawny fur and widened her leaf-green eyes.

Silversong slumped low, flattening his ears and making sure his tail was neatly tucked. He crept forward without staring, his heartbeat drumming a nervous rhythm. Once close enough, he stretched himself out and respectfully licked the faces of his superiors. The Chief cocked his head up, expressing satisfaction at the submissive display.

"Chief Amberstorm, Pinetrail." Silversong bowed his head. "You wanted to see meEEEE!" Something pricked him on the haunch, spilling fire into his flesh. He bristled and tensed every muscle, scowling at the hornet flying away innocently as if it hadn't just stung him. He growled as it buzzed away. *Way to ruin my introduction, you stupid bug!*

He turned to the wide-eyed Chief and his confused mate, embarrassment keeping Silversong's fur stiff as stalks. The Chief signalled for Shadowgale and Cedargaze to leave, and they lowered their heads before descending the mound. Alone before his leaders, all Silversong could manage was an awkward smile as he shrank in on himself, feeling like a nervous disaster.

"Now there's an interesting introduction if ever I've seen one," Pinetrail grunted.

"Indeed," Chief Amberstorm grumbled, his voice like stone grinding against gravel. "Swiftstorm's brother never fails to surprise me, for better or worse."

The Chief could've complimented him, and he still would've cowered like a cornered rat. "S-sir?"

His leader sighed. "At ease, subordinate. I've called you here because I think it's finally time you be given a chance to prove yourself." Silversong made an effort to keep himself from shaking. "Corporals on scouting duty reported a large group of deer grazing near the Freelands. While they're still within the boundaries of our territory, I intend to organize a hunting party and claim those we can. You'll be at the forefront, and if you manage to slay at least one of the deer, I'll see you promoted to corporal after everyone's fed."

"Y-yes, sir!" Silversong's voice quavered. *This is it! This is my chance!*

"Don't get too excited." Chief Amberstorm exhaled through his teeth, his breath strong and smelling of blood. "Before we begin, I need to ensure you're at least competent in your knowledge of our sacred ways, as any corporal should be. Remind me of the Wolven Code and its purpose."

Silversong composed himself before giving the answer every rookie had to recite before officially becoming a subordinate. "Uhm… it's a collection of sacred rules created by the one who founded the sentinels, the First Warden, and we're all bound to its—"

"Save the lectures for when you become an elder," interrupted the Chief. "Stick to the important things. Why should wolves of every territory follow the Wolven Code?"

Silversong scrunched up his forehead in deeper thought. "Because it ensures peace and stability between the different territories. It defines our ranking system, and it's why we always keep to our own and never allow rival wolves to weaken our loyalty to the Whistle-Wind Pack. Without those rules, we would be no better than lawless loners or faithless exiles."

"Good enough." The Chief lowered his head and turned to his mate. "Anything to add?"

Pinetrail gave Silversong a thoughtful look before whining, "can you give an example of how the Wolven Code ensures stability?"

Silversong picked one of the more obvious answers. "The Wolven Code says that if a Chief is to die without having chosen a successor, the corporals must elect a new leader from the existing lieutenants before the day is done. Without that rule, things would get ugly every time a Chief dies unexpectedly." He hoped this would be the end of the impromptu quiz.

The two leaders grunted in satisfaction, and Silversong exhaled a breath of relief.

Chief Amberstorm eyed one of the lonely clouds drifting across a vacant field of blue. "You better prepare yourself while the day is still bright, subordinate. We set out come evening. Dismissed."

It proved incredibly difficult for Silversong to keep his tail tucked while it begged to be wagged. As he hopped to the lower levels of the mound, all he could think about was Swiftstorm. He wished she were still here. He wished he could see her smile at his coming success.

I'll make you proud! A determined energy buzzed through him, and his fur lifted itself to stroke the breeze. His friends waited for him in the glade, wide-eyed and panting. Everything was about to change for the better, he could feel it. *One deer is all I need to win. How hard can that be?*

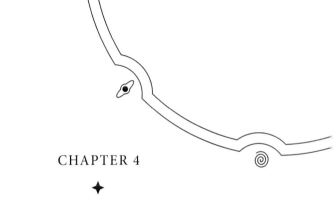

CHAPTER 4

✦

GORSESCRATCH

The hunting party padded alongside the Running River under evening's softer shades.

Gossip about Silversong's promotion had spread throughout the den like weeds in a meadow, but as the water rolled over giant egg-shaped stones, all Silversong could think about was proving himself as his sister's equal.

A bitter memory struck him. Several seasons ago, the Warden had visited Wind's Rest in search of potential recruits to join the defense of the Great Chain. Swiftstorm had been the only one worthy enough to gain her attention. As none could refuse the Warden's authority, everyone had stayed silent as Swiftstorm was stolen away. Always she comforted Silversong after a passing nightmare. Always she defended him against bullies. Always she made him laugh, until the day she departed to the Great Chain, and he sat beneath a shrouded moon whimpering like a pup.

I'll see her again one day. Who knows? Maybe I'll be chosen to train as a sentinel when the Warden needs new recruits. He released a raspy breath. *I hope you're doing all right, Swiftstorm.*

He buried worries about his sister and studied his surrounding packmates. Dozens of wolves comprised the group, led by Chief Amberstorm and his mate at the front. Silversong's parents had requested to be there, as had his friends. Luckily, the Chief had agreed, and Silversong beamed at their support. Among the corporals of the party, Dustyleap and Tawnydrift were cause for concern. They would cause problems for him given the chance, but at least the Chief hadn't been cruel enough to bring Gorsescratch into the mix. Thank Motherwolf he was on harvesting duty for the evening.

Silversong turned to Hazel at his side, her eyes locked on the forest of misshapen trees looming over the rise of heather and gorse beyond the river. Even from here, he could smell the humid fog permeating the distant woods. The slight trace of a putrid stench stung his nostrils.

"The Silverhaze Forest always gives me the shivers." Hazel bristled and scowled at the vile place.

Palesquall grinned at Silversong's other side before stealthily creeping up on Hazel.

"The creatures inside it scare me more than the forest itself," Silversong admitted, stifling a chill.

Palesquall pounced on Hazel, scaring the senses out of her. "Hah! You thought I was a spider!"

Hazel retaliated by biting him on the nose, making him shriek and causing annoyed corporals to glower at them. "If you EVER startle me again, I'll feed you to the spiders myself! Maybe if I make them an offering, they'll forgive us for driving them out of the Breezeway ages ago."

Palesquall grimaced. "I doubt I would make up for the humiliation the spiders suffered because of Whistle-Wind. Our founder invaded their home and claimed it as her own afterwards. You'll need to offer the spiders all the wolves in our territory for them to be satisfied."

Silversong's tail tip quivered. "We shouldn't even be talking about the spiders so close to their domain. Remember, their Empress lives at the heart of the Silverhaze Forest, and she likes to drink the blood of frightened wolves."

"I'm not afraid!" Hazel declared loudly. "If the spiders and their Empress try to reclaim the Breezeway, I'll remind them of Whistle-Wind's fury."

"Don't be silly," Palesquall chuckled. "The Empress sees everything. All your secrets you think are safe belong to her. She knows you better than you know yourself. She knows your deepest desires and your greatest weaknesses. If she thinks you'll make for a good snack, she'll dispatch her drones to imprison you in a silky cocoon when you're deep asleep. And once you wake up, you'll be trapped in her lair alongside other unfortunate souls waiting to be eaten alive. She's… she's… BEHIND YOU!"

Hazel glared at Palesquall, clearly unimpressed. "Nice try, gullwit."

Tawnydrift growled among the throng of corporals. "You three are worse than croaking ravens! Be quiet for once!"

Dustyleap came to her defense. "Yeah! You're giving me a headache here!"

Hazel and Palesquall tucked their tails on instinct, but Silversong let his rise even higher. He would be a corporal soon! No way would he ever submit to those bullies again!

The Silverhaze Forest breathed an icy chill onto him. He turned to the ashen trees, their writhen branches undisturbed, sheltered by broad leaves of a sickly colour. A dense layer of fog that smelled of fungus and death obscured everything within—a truly welcoming place to any vile creature.

The eerie lullaby Silversong's mother used to chant to him slithered out of a once forsaken memory to make the fur on his spine crawl.

Sneak out of your lair, little one,
and the spiders shall sneak too.
Stray far from our home, little one,
and the spiders shall eat you.

He never truly shook off the fear of those huge eight-legged monsters creeping out of their domain at night to drink his veins dry. At least they seemed to prefer the comfort of their ghastly caves and twisted tunnels, only venturing out into the open to sate their hunger for forgotten secrets and hidden knowledge.

Chief Amberstorm ordered the group to wheel into the Breezeway at a hasty gait, following the direction of the waking moon. Silversong detected the musky remnants of deer scent, and twinges of anticipation ran through his muscles.

The wolves padded over clusters of moss-eaten stones and cooled earth, following the slender shadows of the conifers pointed at the pearly moon. The Running River roared out of sight, but only its rising spray could be seen beyond the pines.

"The deer scent is getting stronger." Palesquall sniffed at the ground, tail swishing.

Hazel nosed Silversong on the shoulder. "You'll do great, Silversong. All you have to do is get at least one of the deer."

"Yeah," Palesquall whined encouragement. "Don't worry. You'll be a corporal in no time!" He licked Silversong on the cheek. "We believe in you."

"Thanks." Silversong smiled at the two of them. He was so lucky to have them by his side.

Shadowgale raved in hushed whines about his pride in his children while Pinetrail slowed her pace so she could pad beside Silversong, or so she could escape the blabbering lieutenant. "Subordinate. I trust you'll remember how the Wolven Code forbids the killing of prey too young to fight. And hunting tactics considered dishonourable won't win you any favours either."

Silversong tucked his tail as he addressed her. "No, ma'am. I won't forget."

Pinetrail sniffed the ground where the wolves in front of her had passed. "Good. A true corporal not only follows the Wolven Code, but understands why it was created and why it must be obeyed."

To prevent a calamity like the Rise of the Fallen Titan from ever happening again, Silversong recited the important lesson in his head.

Palesquall butted his head into the conversation. "Remember the games Swiftstorm and us used to play? She would pretend she was the Fallen Titan while she chased us across the Breezeway."

A heavy longing to see Swiftstorm again gusted through Silversong. "Yeah, I remember. She always started off as the innocent Forest Father, though. Before he became bad and turned into the Fallen Titan. It gave us enough time to hide from her."

"The creator of all prey, corrupted by his own hate," Palesquall copied the tone of an elder, earning him a scolding look from Pinetrail that he pretended not to see. "Your sister pranced around the trees and tried to re-enact the Forest Father caring for his creations. Considering how loud she was, she probably scared off all the prey in our territory instead." He laughed.

"I always hated those games you three played." Hazel shook her head in disapproval. "You shouldn't make fun of the Forest Father and the monster he became."

Palesquall's mischievous glare landed on Hazel. "Aww, you can admit you were scared, Hazel. It's all right," he teased. "Heh, even I tucked my tail whenever Swiftstorm acted out the Forest Father turning evil because of how our ancestors overhunted everything."

Silversong recalled the story every rookie had to learn. *Without a code to guide them, our ancestors overpopulated every territory and brought disease and death upon themselves. In his anger, the Forest*

Father turned his life-giving powers into a weapon of decay and began his mission to purge all wolves from the land.

Hazel showed Palesquall a few sharp teeth. "I wasn't scared!"

"You were too!" Palesquall smirked at how flustered Hazel looked. "Don't worry, Hazel. Our brave ancestors banded together and stood against the mean old Forest Father."

"You better quit whining to me like I'm some frightened pup, or you'll get a demonstration of how the First Warden killed the Fallen Titan." Hazel's claws pressed into the ground.

"It wasn't just the First Warden who killed the Fallen Titan," Silversong blurted out to loosen the tension. "She mustered a splinter faction of the strongest wolves willing to join her. They became known as sentinels, and they struck at the Fallen Titan together, slaying him and scattering his corrupted remains across the Furtherlands."

The forest dipped slightly, and the once sparse undergrowth now clustered closely together as the party passed over the ferny plants, some putting in more effort than others to make as little noise as possible. All around him, hushed voices blended together as efficiently as the rising moon blended into the dimming sky.

"And then the Wolven Code was finally created." Pinetrail's voice seemed to soothe the embers of anger within Hazel. "After being dubbed *First Warden* by her sentinels, she claimed the Great Chain as their home. And to make sure such a calamity would never happen again, she forced all territories to swear fealty to the Wolven Code and every Warden who succeeded her."

A shiver spiked up Silversong's fur. "And since the Fallen Titan's spirit never truly died, his corruption eats away at the souls of the exiled until they lose their connection to either the air, water, fire, or earth. It's the price they must pay for turning tail on our sacred rules."

Pinetrail gave him a satisfied smile. "I think you'll make a fine corporal, Silversong."

"You'll make a fine elder too if you keep up those lecturing skills," Palesquall teased. "*Elder* Silversong. Sounds fitting, doesn't it?"

"Not as fitting as *Corporal* Silversong." A thrill crackled through him. *No. Not as fitting at all.*

By the time the sun slipped toward a sound slumber and cooled itself into a circle of muted flame, the group arrived at the edge of the Breezeway. Silversong shifted forward to get a good look at one of the borders of his territory. The terrain flowed in a downward curve to a meadow of green. Thick briars flecked the waving grass, each shrub bearing blood-red berries that caught a glint of darkling light.

Beyond the vibrant pasture, a wave of foothills climbed into the Freelands, where beasts unbound by any law or code roamed. Far into the highland region, enormous trees reached for the pinkish clouds. Even from afar, their sheer size and majesty made them look like red spires crowned in green. Further still, the crisp outline of the Sapphire Peaks clawed into the fire-stricken sky, and from those lofty heights coursed the start of the Running River. It flowed in a great, shimmering arc and slithered across the meadow, curving away before returning to flank the Breezeway, its everlasting roar unchallenged as it hurried to meet the sun setting below the horizon.

The others weren't as entranced by the beauty as he was. Instead, their attention was rightfully drawn to where the moor descended into the Glacial Sea. Silversong followed their gaze and broadened his eyes. Nestled between two stark cliffs jutting out over the open waters was a throng of deer. They grazed near the hilly rise leading into the Freelands, blind to the watchful eyes observing them from above. He scanned the beasts one by one, panting as lines of saliva leaked onto the earth. His tail nearly hopped off his flank when he spotted the same deer who'd escaped him this morning.

Oh, you're not getting away this time! He locked eyes onto his preferred target.

"All right!" barked the Chief, catching the attention of all present. "I'll initiate the charge, followed by Pinetrail and the lieutenants. We'll funnel the deer between those two cliffs overlooking the sea."

"Yes, sir!" Pinetrail moved forward. Silversong's parents gave him a nuzzle on the cheek before joining her.

The Chief addressed the remainder of the group. "Corporals and subordinates, you'll charge in on either side of us and make sure no prey escapes into the Freelands. Don't chase after them if some do manage to flee. The bears won't appreciate us stealing prey from their grounds."

"Yes, sir!" everyone else barked, assembling along the edge of the forest, crouched and ready for the attack.

The Chief nosed Silversong before he took his place. "Remember. One deer is all you need to get your promotion. Make it count."

"Yes, sir." Determination flared inside Silversong as the Chief padded off.

"Don't mess this up, puppy-eyes," Dustyleap snarled before stopping beside Tawnydrift, who added, "yeah, this could be your only chance to become a corporal, after all." The two shared a mean-spirited laugh.

Hot blood filled Silversong's face. After today, he wouldn't allow anyone to bully him. After today, he would get the respect he deserved!

The strong smell of excited wolves dampened the forest's piney aroma. Silence broken only by the beating of many hearts increased the deepening pressure. Silversong emptied his head of negative thoughts, concentrating solely on his desire to be like his sister, to win where others expected him to fail. He immersed himself in the idea of victory and plunged into a state of utter focus.

The Chief swiped his tail in a brisk motion. "Now, my wolves! Make Whistle-Wind proud!"

Chief Amberstorm exploded out of the forest, followed by Pinetrail who called on streams of air to encircle her. The lieutenants charged, and a breath later, the corporals and subordinates followed. Silversong pressed on his haunches and bolted at the same time as his friends. Side by side, they dashed forward like gales blown from a mountain's peak. He connected himself to the breeze almost immediately. It coursed about him and enhanced his strides as he made his way toward his prize.

The line of wolves expanded in an arc to block off any escape routes, Silversong at the rightmost edge. No deer would flee to the Freelands if he had anything to say about it! His heart thumped life into him, and a sizzling energy ignited in his limbs. Nothing would impede his speed. The air surged around him, parting the high grass and thorny flowers. At the lip of the two cliffs, one of the more massive deer lifted its head and veered in their direction.

"Pricklethorn!" Silversong cursed.

The gigantic beast lifted its muzzle skyward. A shrill wail escaped its throat and echoed across the meadow. The hunting party sprinted faster and funneled the grazers into the protruding cliffs looming over the Glacial Sea, but the warning allowed the would-be prey to gather their strongest fighters to meet the assault head on. The deer formed a line across the opening between the cliffs, heads pointed downward, battle-scarred antlers sharp and ready. Silversong's chosen target disappeared behind them.

He skidded to a standstill, Hazel and Palesquall some distance apart. At least all escape routes had been blocked as planned, but the deer wouldn't give up their meat and blood without a struggle. Silversong scanned the defense, but nothing could penetrate the blockade of pure muscle. Someone had to incite a chase… or a panic from within.

The Chief twirled his tail, weaving a small twister in the air. Once the whirlwind was stable, he launched it at the defenders, but the attack merely scuffed them, leaving tiny gashes in their flesh. The scent of blood incited the wolves to keep pressuring the antlered beasts. Pinetrail exhaled blast after blast of condensed air upon her targets, snapping some of the weaker antlers, but the bodies never wavered.

The assault ceased as the antlers of the defenders turned translucent, emitting a bright green shine that faded an instant later. Something changed in the consistency of the air. The ground hummed as if bracing for an earthquake. Bees and other insects buzzed away from their flowers, and crows scavenging the ground for wriggly things took off toward the clouds.

"The Forest Father's uncorrupted power!" Pinetrail warned. "Get ready!"

The grass came alive and entangled Silversong and his packmates. Blades of green coiled around his limbs and pulled him to the ground. They were shockingly strong, obviously strengthened by the power that had invoked them. He bit at the groping tendrils, struggling to stand as terrified yelping pierced his ears.

Others succumbed to the grasp, Palesquall among them. Silversong barked to Hazel, who broke out of her confines and rushed to aid the white subordinate, digging him out of the hungry earth. The corporals strong enough to ignore the hostile grass helped those whose strength waned. The attack had failed. In the chaos, a few deer had darted through the line of wolves and escaped into the Freelands. Those remaining would soon charge once they found the courage, and the only reward awaiting Silversong would be broken bones.

He had to think of something! Above on his rightward side, one of the cliffs rose—a fat rocky head leaning over the water. If someone could scale the height and leap into the sea, the deer would have no idea a threat would be approaching them from behind.

The idea struck him like a crash of lightning. He bit off the remaining blades clinging to him and turned to Chief Amberstorm, who was locked in a struggle to keep the deer from charging. There was no getting his attention now.

"Hazel!" Silversong sprang, landed, then hopped again to avoid the clutch of the blades. "I'm going to incite a panic. Be ready!"

"Silversong?" Hazel whined, jumping so the entangling grass couldn't get her. "Now's not the time to do anything stupid!"

Refusing to allow Hazel's warning to sprout the seeds of doubt, he broke from his position and raced up the rightward cliff, pads pressing on pointy rocks.

"Oh, Motherwolf's milk, what's he doing?!" Palesquall shouted.

"Silversong!" Hazel cried.

"If I mess this up, Chief Amberstorm is going to rip out my fangs!" he muttered to himself, uttering a prayer for Motherwolf's guidance. "Oh, please let me succeed!"

A brief movement on the opposite bluff caught his attention, but he assumed it to be nothing more than a trick of the eye. A familiar scent snaked into his nostrils, challenging the musky odour of the fearful deer and the strong smell of his agitated packmates. It almost smelled like…

…*Gorsescratch?*

He shook his head, forcing himself to focus on the goal ahead. Everything depended on this moment.

At the edge of the cliff, Silversong released the air billowing about him, pressed on his haunches, and jumped into the deep blue. A smack to the belly, and frigid water swallowed him. He twisted upright and pushed, casting bubbles all around.

He poked his head out of the surface and paddled toward the flanks of the weaker deer, who stood still as pebbles on the coastline. This was it. This was the deed he would use to escape the shame of being the oldest subordinate! The thought animated his muscles and pushed him onward despite the fatigue gnawing at his bones.

The pale backsides of the smaller deer and their short, lifted tails faced him. He neared the shore and turned his fantasies of being as admired as his sister into a force that fought the frigid waters cutting through his flesh like tiny teeth. His eyes found his chosen prey—the same deer who'd made a fool out of him this morning. He would recognize those antlers anywhere.

"You're mine." Silversong's lips succumbed to a premature smirk of triumph.

His stomach dropped, and he gasped as his quarry veered around to stare straight at him, eyes growing wider and wider until they bulged.

"Nothing's ever so easy, is it?!" Silversong propelled himself forward, newfound energy replacing his fatigue. He salivated at his prey, his soon-to-be trophy.

More deer craned their heads around to stare at him, the scent of fear wafting, but it only encouraged his speed. He scrambled onto the pebbly coastline as the beasts scattered in every direction, abandoning control over their impenetrable defense.

From the front, Chief Amberstorm howled. "Wolves of Whistle-Wind, CHARGE!"

Among the discord, Silversong locked eyes onto his target and lunged. It bellowed and kicked, but he bounded sideways and leaped again as soon as he landed, aiming for the beast's throat. His fangs dove into flesh, and he tasted the tender blood encased within—the taste of winning.

Something heavy collided into him and knocked him off his prey. His forehead met the rough side of a boulder. Pain ricocheted from nose to tail. His vision looped in confused circles, and he shook his head, squinting to vanquish the blurriness. Unblinking green eyes glared at him, framed by a hateful scowl on an ugly face.

"Wha…" It took a long moment for him to realize who the sandy-furred wolf standing in front of him was.

Gorsescratch!

"I don't think you're ready to become a corporal just yet, puppy-eyes," Gorsescratch growled.

Heat boiled in Silversong's chest, rising to scorch away the pain in his head. He hadn't come this far only to lose to sabotage!

Gorsescratch would pay! Snarling, Silversong prepared to pounce on the treacherous mongrel.

A panicked deer jumped over Silversong, kicking him square on the head before it landed. Gorsescratch rolled over to avoid it.

A sharp ringing sensation spread through Silversong like water on dry soil. His legs turned to weak stems as he crumpled to the ground. Stars flickered across his eyes, and the final thing he saw before sinking into a blurry void was the prize that would've granted him the respect he deserved fleeing out of sight.

CHAPTER 5

CONFRONTATION

"NO!" Silversong jerked his head up. Countless invisible spikes impaled his brain as punishment for the brisk motion. He clenched his jaws to avoid yelping as memories of a troubling nightmare faded, leaving behind only a chill.

The Wise-Wolves rushed to him, sniffing his fur all over as he lay in their lair. His nostrils widened at the mingled scents of many medicinal plants. They flowed up his nose and fought the lingering drowsiness.

"Keep still, Silversong." Moonwhisper gingerly licked his forehead while her younger partner, Mistyfur, fetched something from one of the large stones encircling the grotto.

Their cave was directly below the topmost level. Minerals glistened in the smooth ceiling like distant stars, granting the place an aura of calmness. Moonwhisper's gentle voice also helped soothe the nerves. "You took a hoof to the face like a champion. You're lucky to be awake only two days after the hunting party returned."

"The… hunting party?" Silversong moaned as he chewed on the flower bud Mistyfur had brought him, swallowing its bitter juices. Everything had been going fine during his hour of triumph until…

"Gorsescratch! The treacherous scatfur! I'll tear off his pathetic tail! Where is he?!"

The Wise-Wolves shared a worried glance, and Moonwhisper sleeked her snowy fur. "Why did you insist we feed him root sap?! There's no telling how many false memories he'll think are real now!"

Mistyfur grimaced, his handsome grey face burdened by wrinkles of annoyance. "Hey! You were the one who suggested the root sap, remember? Not to mention all those other plants we stuffed into him. It's a miracle he hasn't spontaneously combusted yet!"

Hearing the Wise-Wolves mention how he might spontaneously combust from their cures was hardly comforting. "These aren't false memories!" Silversong lifted himself up, head feeling like it was about to *actually* explode. Hopping black spots dotted his vision.

"You shouldn't be getting up, Silversong," Moonwhisper warned, ignoring her partner's accusing look.

"I'm fine!" Silversong closed his eyes, brain spinning in rapid circles. He focused himself and breathed in deeply, slowly opening his gaze. This time, the dizziness ceased, chased away by a swarm of violent notions. "Where's Gorsescratch?"

An elder stepped through the entrance of the cave, paling fur flowing around an array of scars, a series of coughs wracking his chest. His frosty green eyes refused to meet either of the Wise-Wolves.

"Oh, look who's here again." Moonwhisper's eyes narrowed on the stubborn elder. "Hello, Shrillbreeze. Sounds like you've got quite the nasty cough."

"Save it, Moonwhisper," Shrillbreeze rasped. "I just need something to clear my throat."

"Oh no you don't!" Moonwhisper snarled. "You're staying here until I'm sure you don't have a more serious condition. The Wolven Code implores you to listen to a Wise-Wolf's advice, so you better listen this time!"

Shrillbreeze swallowed in between coughs. He sounded like he had a toad stuck inside him. "I think I would rather be nipped on the throat than have you nagging me all day. But I suppose maybe you have a point." His coughs really seemed painful.

"Mistyfur, go take care of our former Chief." Moonwhisper flicked her tail, and her partner hopped straight to it, taking the elder to a quiet corner of the grotto so he could be inspected in peace. "Sometimes convincing someone they need a cure is harder than actually curing them," she muttered to herself.

"Silversong!" Hazel's yip made Silversong's ears shoot up. She and Palesquall charged into the grotto, enthusiastic tongues battering his face while their tails beat the air. He greeted them in the same manner, mouth numbed from whatever sour medicine he'd been fed. "The Wise-Wolves said you weren't going to wake up until tomorrow!"

Moonwhisper gave a loud snort and scowled at her working partner. "Mistyfur said that, not me. As always, his predictions are laughably false."

"Heh." Palesquall ignored the senior Wise-Wolf. "Glad they were both wrong."

"*BOTH*?!" Moonwhisper barked in outrage.

Palesquall leaned toward her. "Silversong's not..." he paused and gave him a funny glance, "... let's just say I hope his wit hasn't been kicked out of him. It would be tragic considering he had precious little inside his head to begin with."

Silversong nipped him on the cheek. Palesquall yelped and recoiled in shock. "Go chase your own tail, Palesquall," Silversong panted teasingly.

Hazel laughed. "There's your answer, bug-brain. Looks like he's still the same old Silversong."

"Any other way I can reassure you, Palesquall?" Silversong grinned in a playful manner. His stomach rumbled, and saliva gushed into his mouth at the acknowledgment of his hunger.

Palesquall nearly jumped at the thunder-like sound. "Hey. Your idea to surprise the deer from behind worked perfectly, Silversong. They bolted straight to us, and we chose our targets as they ran. You're the reason every belly is bulging at the den. There're still some leftovers if you're feeling hungry. The flies haven't gotten to them yet. We could bring you a haunch or something."

Silversong looked up to his friends. His hunger could wait. There were more important things to worry about now. A hopeful tide washed over him. "How... how did Chief Amberstorm react...? Am I...?" He swallowed and prayed silently for the answer he wanted to hear. "Am I going to be a corporal?"

They stared at him in pity. His breath stopped itself short, and his posture deflated. His beaten hope plummeted to the pit of his stomach and crushed all sense of hunger. He circled a forepaw on the ground, but whined nothing. He couldn't get anything out if he tried.

Hazel licked Silversong on the cheek. "I'm sorry. We tried convincing Chief Amberstorm to promote you despite you not claiming any of the deer, but..."

"The Chief dismissed us every time." Palesquall released a hushed growl. "Even though you're the reason we're all fed, he said the condition for your promotion was clear, and you failed to meet it."

Silversong's scowl bulged over his eyes, and his mouth stretched into a wide snarl. A searing sensation numbed every paw and spiked up his fur. "Gorsescratch. Gorsescratch sabotaged me! I had my teeth clinging onto the throat of one of the deer, but he pushed me off! He's the reason I failed. I would've made the scatfur pay then and there, but another deer knocked the lights out of me before I could pounce on him!"

His friends glanced at each other, but uttered not a sound. An awkward silence came over the grotto, broken by Hazel's careful whine. "Silversong, do you have any proof of this?" She sniffed him. "I can't smell his stench on you, and I've bumped into the mongrel several times since we dragged you here." Her face contorted itself in disgust.

Silversong ran his claws against the ground, creating an awful noise. "Dustyleap and Tawnydrift were in on this too. I'm sure of it. While all of us were trying not to get strangled by the grass, Gorsescratch watched me from atop one of the cliffs, and once I broke formation and made my move, he waited there until he found an opportunity to strike." A shaky laugh forced itself up Silversong's throat. "I'll make sure he pays for this!"

"Beyond baseless accusations," Moonwhisper cut in, "if there's no direct proof of this sabotage, Gorsescratch is innocent, as are his friends."

"These aren't exactly *senseless accusations*," Palesquall admitted. "Gorsescratch has had a hateful bone for Silversong ever since he and Hazel became friends a few seasons ago."

A strange sense of nostalgia overcame Silversong as he remembered a time when Gorsescratch merely teased him and hurled petty insults his way. It wasn't until recently—precisely after he and Hazel had formed a friendship—that Gorsescratch had adopted the role of a cruel nemesis.

"Moonwhisper is right." Hazel's tail drooped. "Accusing someone of a crime as severe as betraying the trust of a packmate is not to be done lightly. If you have no proof of Gorsescratch's wrongdoing, you'll be severely punished, as much as I hate saying it."

"Can't imagine the punishment Gorsescratch would get if he were actually convicted of this." Palesquall shuddered. "We haven't banished anyone to the Furtherlands in a long time."

"Oh, I can think of several fitting punishments." Silversong's eyes darted from Palesquall to Hazel. "You two must've noticed something. Please think. Did any of you see or even smell Gorsescratch after I caused the panic?"

"I don't think so." Palesquall managed a thoughtful look. "But Gorsescratch was suspiciously dirty after he returned from harvesting duty later that evening. Like he rolled in mud or something."

To wipe off traces of my scent!

Hazel shook her head in defeat. "It's not enough to convict him. We were all too distracted by the deer to notice anything. If Gorsescratch is guilty, we have to play it smart."

"Gorsescratch brought us many of the medicinal plants that helped heal you," Moonwhisper added.

"To make himself seem innocent!" Silversong smacked a forepaw on the ground, pain ringing up his leg. A wave of heat seared it away. "Hey, Moonwhisper. How would the Wolven Code punish someone who betrayed the trust of a packmate?"

Moonwhisper tilted her head. "It's up to the Chief to decide a fitting punishment. Chances are he would have the packmate in question decide the penalty for the betrayal."

That settles it. Silversong shook the pulsing numbness out of the forepaw he'd smacked. "Where's Gorsescratch now?"

"I spotted him following me near the Running River this morning. He tried to pretend he was out for a stroll." Hazel eyed him cautiously. "It's weird for a corporal to be up so early, and even weirder for him to be stalking a subordinate." She shivered and grimaced. "I haven't seen him at the den since then, so maybe he's still out there."

Silversong got up and started toward the cave exit, a violent storm raging within. He would make Gorsescratch pay if he had to search the entire Breezeway to find him! "I need some time alone. Don't bother following me." He ignored whatever his friends were yapping as Moonwhisper tried convincing them he'd imagined the whole sabotage thing. Most likely she would succeed—the case against Gorsescratch wasn't strong—but the truth would eventually come out. It had to!

The climbing sun stabbed his eyes, and he squinted, tail tip quivering while he descended the mound and hopped onto the field of grass and clovers, limbs weightless and unbalanced. He could sense the curious looks of his packmates locked onto him as he padded to the Breezeway.

"Silversong!" his father called from behind. Silversong stopped only a moment before continuing on. Shadowgale strode beside him. "You're awake! Good. Your strategy was impressive! I'm so proud! It's a move I would've expected from your sister, but I guess her hunting skills have finally manifested in you too."

Silversong could practically feel the stretch of his father's irksome smile. "Not now!" Silversong stifled a growl. Near the rim of the Breezeway, he spotted the bully's friends joking about something.

They're laughing at me! A buzzing energy streamed through Silversong's veins.

"Oh, don't worry about not getting promoted," his father yipped and pranced. "You can always try to prove yourself during another season. We can't all be as successful as Swiftstorm now, can we?"

Before Silversong spilled his boiling rage onto his own father, he broke into a sprint, chest pounding and stirring the roaring blood in his ears. His hopes, his chances of gaining respect, it had all been stolen from him by Gorsescratch.

He charged into the forest, catching the course of a swift breeze, willing it to thrust him forward through pines and over protruding roots. He wound through the woods, searching for the scent of his enemy.

He found it.

Following the trail led him straight to the bully. Gorsescratch was alone and moping about the forest, tail turned to him. Silversong bared his fangs and pounced. Everything surrounding his target blurred out of focus until only he existed.

Just as Silversong descended, fangs ready to tear into flesh, Gorsescratch turned around and dodged the ambush.

A mere sidestep was all it took for Silversong to lose balance. He landed on the earth and wobbled, head spinning as tiny thorns pierced his skull. "You're dead, Gorsescratch!" He forced himself to ignore his own weakness.

Gorsescratch widened his eyes, tail swaying side to side. "Oh, am I, puppy-eyes?"

Silversong clamped his teeth on Gorsescratch's muzzle, drawing blood and making him squeal in shock. The wretch shook himself free and bared his fangs. "You dare attack a corporal?!"

Silversong linked himself to the passing breeze and wove a winding shield of air around his body. Gorsescratch focused for a moment and summoned a whirlwind at his tail, lashing it at Silversong, but the blows merely cracked against the unwavering sphere. Just as Gorsescratch was about to strike again, Silversong exploded his windy blockade, staggering his enemy and sending him flying into a trunk. Leaping forward, Silversong caught the bully off-guard, sinking his teeth into the mongrel's scruff and using all his strength to smash him into the ground a few paces away.

Confidence surged through Silversong. He crouched and twirled his tail, feeling the quick motions stirring a lean vortex. He waited for Gorsescratch to stand up from the humiliation.

The bully groaned and shook himself off. "Y-you can't do this! I'm a corporal, and you're a—"

Silversong launched the conjured vortex at him, but his enemy ordered a sudden draft to zip him to the side. Earth and debris sprayed everywhere as the bully charged through the dusty veil. The air coiled around Silversong and yanked him away from Gorsescratch's deadly lunge. Silversong leaped forward again, seizing his target midair and biting him near the spine.

Silversong forced his victim to the ground and stood over him. "Submit! Or I swear by Motherwolf even your friends won't recognize your face after my fangs have finished redecorating it!"

A sudden chill cooled the forest. Branches creaked under a murky shadow veiling the once bright sky. Dew on the mossy earth and leaves blanched to a pale frost. Drilling woodpeckers hid in their hollows, and the wary scavengers returned to their burrows as everything succumbed to a windless silence.

Gorsescratch calmed his struggle, but his loathsome glower remained. Silversong pushed his entire weight onto his adversary, restricting the corporal to only the briefest of breaths. "Why? Why did you sabotage me?" Silversong growled. "Breaking the Wolven Code is a little extreme even for you."

The defeated bully managed something between a defiant scowl and a fearful expression. "Bite my tail, scatfur!"

Oh, Silversong bit him all right, but on the snout instead.

"OW! Okay! Okay!" Gorsescratch barked hoarsely. "If… if I answer, you'll let me go?" Lines of blood leaked out of his fresh punctures.

Silversong stretched his snarl to the limit and pressed harder on the bully's throat, forcing him to wheeze out trails of frozen air. "You better pray I like your answer."

Gorsescratch's face wrinkled into a pathetic look. "I… I…"

"Cough it up, gullwit!" Silversong snapped. "Now!"

"I… I like Hazel, all right?!" His voice was like a mouse's squeak. His breaths quickened. "I always have. Ever since I was a subordinate. But she's never paid any attention to me. Only you. She smiles whenever you're near her. She's cheerful whenever she looks at you…" he gulped as if hoping to swallow the remainder of the confession, "I-I thought if I showed her how incompetent you really were…"

Gorsescratch had done all this to him because of jealousy? The realization hit Silversong like a boulder. His breath stopped short. Legs shaking, he had to harden his muscles so he could remain steady. He wanted to lash out at the bully for being so utterly pathetic, but falling specks descended from above to cool his seething anger. He looked around, ears pricked, eyes going wide.

It was snow.

CHAPTER 6

✦

Snow

Snow? Snow during summer?! Silversong shuddered as the violent cracks of thunder threatened to shatter the sky.

Snow fell everywhere as the trees creaked in protest at the unnatural storm, their branches writhing like maggots as they attempted to shake off the thickening sheets of white.

He released Gorsescratch, but the corporal stayed on the ground, a look of defeat creasing his face. Silversong sniffed the freezing air. Something about it smelled off—like a corpse not yet rotting, but on the brink of it.

A tide of unexplained dread washed over him, heightening his senses. Every creak, every falling pine needle and leaf, every shivering branch sounded hostile to him. Everywhere he turned, he expected something to lunge out at him. Nothing came, but the fear still deepened until he thought himself paralyzed. It took a great effort to convince his limbs to move again.

"We…" he startled himself at how loud his whisper sounded, "… I think we should return to the den." He found it impossible to ignore the desire to be comforted by his packmates, his family. Here he stood alone, sinking deeper into the throat of an unseen monster. He needed reassurance. He needed to feel safer. The sense of danger tightened—an invisible coil constricting his body until he would eventually pop like a squished caterpillar.

He whirled around at the crack of a root, every strand of fur stiff as a thorn. Gorsescratch remained unmoving. Pale tendrils of frozen air drifted out of his mouth—the only indication he was still alive. Despite everything, Gorsescratch was still a packmate, at least for now.

"Come on!" Silversong nipped the bully on the ear in hopes of stirring him. "We have to go. Now!"

Gorsescratch yelped and got up, wasting not a breath before fleeing in the direction of the den. Silversong followed him through the groaning woods, emptying his head of burdens and focusing on the cool air surrounding him. He separated it into four winding currents, each billowing around a different paw, granting him the swiftness of a leaf travelling along the mighty swirl of a tornado. Roots of decaying wood grasped at him, but he was too quick to let himself be ensnared.

What in Motherwolf's mercy is going on?! He glanced at the clouds spreading like rotting tumors in the sky.

The darkness above thickened like congealing sap and spewed out a flurry of flakes, blanketing the forest in a freezing shroud. At the horizon where the sun always set, the soot-black clouds merged to create a horrid face—like a deer whose snout was far too large and whose teeth were far too sharp within gaping jaws. Antlers twisted out of its skull like crooked twigs, and it appeared to be grinning at him, its cruel expression unnaturally contorted. Even though it had no eyes, Silversong could still feel its hateful gaze burning a hole through him.

He decided against looking at it any longer and focused instead on the sharp, deep howling coming from the lieutenants at the den—the declaration of an emergency or an impending attack. Something in the consistency of the air changed, fogging his connection to the breeze, applying a cramped pressure to his head. He caught up to Gorsescratch and exploded out of the forest, hurrying toward the mound.

A frantic pattering of urgent steps drummed on every level as the wolves followed the proper protocol. The lieutenants sorted the corporals and subordinates into formation upon their platforms as the sharp scent of panic formed a disorienting miasma. The Chief himself failed to conceal his anxiety atop the den, shivering despite trying to look tough and ready for whatever was to come. It seemed the suffocating pressure was enough to unsettle even the bravest hearts.

"To your positions!" Chief Amberstorm howled before addressing his mate, who herded the rookies on the bottommost level. "Pinetrail! Take the rookies and our children into the

Breezeway and wait there while the elders and Wise-Wolves empty the den of essential medicine. Then return to me!"

"Understood, my Chief!" she barked and did exactly as instructed, collecting her litter from the nooks between the boulders forming the second level. The little ones whimpered as they were ushered away alongside the rookies. Silversong's parents gave him a worried glance before returning to their duties. He prayed for their safety under his breath.

Gorsescratch was already scrambling up to the third level, eager to join Dustyleap and Tawnydrift. Some of the elders who could still bite stayed on the lowest circle and rallied behind Shrillbreeze. As defensive measures were taken, the Wise-Wolves carried bundles of medicinal plants in their mouths and delivered them to Pinetrail in case their lair was pillaged during the attack. *The attack? Why did I assume there's going to be an attack?*

Silversong bounded up to the second level and found his friends among the throng of shaking subordinates. Soon only the strong remained on the mound, waiting for an unknown threat to reveal itself. Pinetrail returned once the Wise-Wolves and the weak were safe and settled in the forest, joining her mate atop the crowning platform. They exchanged gentle whines under the stirring tempest.

Palesquall nudged Silversong's side. "Soooo… I'm guessing there's a reason Gorsescratch looks like he bumped into an angry bear?"

Silversong coughed up a chuckle. In all the commotion, he'd forgotten all about the bully's sabotage and confession. He glared at Gorsescratch's blank face on the third level.

Did jealousy really make you go this far?

Hazel scowled and shivered at Silversong's other side. "Ugh, can you try to be serious for once in your life, Palesquall?"

"Hmm, let me think." Palesquall scrunched up his forehead in thought. "Nope! Life is way too boring to take seriously all the time. You should try out my philosophy, Hazel. It would do you some good to laugh once in a while. Maybe it would even loosen up the log stuck in your rear end."

"Beg your pardon?!" She bristled and snarled at the white subordinate struggling to contain his laughter. "Oh, once the storm has passed, I'll have you chasing your own tail if you don't apologize."

Palesquall's silliness undid some of the knots tightening Silversong's insides. He dared to let a shaky smile contradict his fear. "Never change, you two."

The lighthearted feeling winked out of existence the moment they allowed silence to have its way. To counter the oppressive pressure suffocating the den, all wolves howled, joining their voices as one despite not fully understanding the nearing danger. The triumphant sound thundered inside Silversong, pummeling his fright and instilling in its place a vicious desire for the blood of any who would dare threaten his packmates. He closed his eyes and lifted his head, merging his own voice into the mighty howl.

The trees groaned louder as the clouds vomited a hail of thick flakes. The fierce howling dwindled into uncertain yelping, and then to an uncomfortable quiet. The storm boomed and bellowed, and the entire den watched and waited. The pines stopped shifting as sleet gathered on bristled fur, but not a single voice dared disturb the tumult of the wrathful sky. As abrupt as a falling branch, all sound ceased as if the whole earth had stopped breathing in anticipation of this moment.

The air exhaled by Silversong's packmates drifted up in foggy swirls, and the strong scent of agitation inspired a snarl on every face. It smelled like the critical moment before blood was drawn, like fear and anger swirling together in a whirlpool. Between the still trunks of the Breezeway, from the direction of the Silverhaze Forest, they came. Two wolves strode into the frost-covered glade, one old and grey, one large and darker than smoke. Others followed behind them, eyes reflecting the hatefulness of the terrible visage tainting the sky.

"River-Stream invaders?" one of the subordinates asked.

"No. River-Stream wolves wouldn't look so hungry for blood," another hissed.

"The Wolven Code forbids rival territories from invading one another," Hazel whispered. "So who are they?"

Silversong joined the growls, straightening his tail and crouching, warning the filthy mongrels to stay where they were. The older intruder moved casually toward the den, green eyes undisturbed, aged fur sleek as the larger one followed, his coat matching the shadowy sky.

The old wolf stopped midway between the forest and the mound, surveying every snarling face. "It seems the seasons have favoured you, Chief Amberstorm. You've assembled so many strong and capable warriors." His voice was a landslide of gravel. "Impressive."

"HALT!" Chief Amberstorm snapped at the air. "You stand before the Whistle-Wind Pack, mongrel, and we don't accept strays or loners who've turned their tails on Motherwolf and the Wolven Code. Return to wherever backward place you make your den, or we'll chase you out ourselves!"

The grizzled interloper regarded him, eyes impassive as his subordinates flooded the glade and surrounded the mound as if it were prey frozen in fear. "I imagine you rehearsed that warning over and over again in your head, sir. To motivate your soldiers to follow you into battle and into death, even, your resolve must be hardened into a shield. Allow no regret, weakness, or doubt to wear away your conviction. Only then can you inspire your wolves to charge headfirst into whatever end." He narrowed his glare on Chief Amberstorm. "Sadly, I fear all three of those flaws taint your voice."

The Chief growled out his fury, but the intruder showed no sign of backing off. "Ah, look at you. Ready to give the order to have me slaughtered without even knowing who I am." He lowered his gaze to the wolves gathered on the mound. "All you sheep would see me dead because you were raised to believe anyone who doesn't follow your sacred *code* deserves only your cruelty. It's disheartening for me to see so many misguided souls living in a bubble of unchanging ideas, ideas buried into your heads at the youngest age to ensure your undying loyalty to them."

"Are you always so dramatic?!" Pinetrail hissed, her tawny fur risen in defiance. "Spare us your sanctimony! Who are you, vagrant? Why did you come here? You've insulted us and our way of life already, so I suggest you tread very carefully from here on."

"Hmm, I suppose the sentinels gave me an appropriate title after my old name was besmirched following my banishment." Silversong's packmates gasped among themselves, and the intruder gave a slight smirk. Silversong was piecing together who these mean-looking wolves were, hoping against all odds he was wrong. "I am the Heretic, the leader of the Furtherlands and the exiles you've all shunned for wanting nothing but to be free of the Wolven Code."

Silversong's mouth went dry, and his heart tried to flee his chest. Rage and fear wrinkled every face around him. *No! He's* bluffing! *The Great Chain and the sentinels defending it keep us safe from exiles! Nothing can escape the Furtherlands! Nothing! The sentinels protect the Great Chain! Swiftstorm protects the Great Chain!*

"Liar!" A lieutenant shouted from above. "The Great Chain keeps the exiles confined to the Furtherlands forever! Just as the First Warden intended!"

"The sentinels would never allow any exile to escape!" a corporal barked. "Never!"

Shrillbreeze tensed on the lowest level. "You make a dangerous claim, trespasser. Even should it be false, the Wolven Code won't forgive such insolence."

A crash of thunder silenced the heated voices as the huge midnight-furred trespasser stepped forward. "The Great Chain is broken!" he announced in a booming voice. "The sentinels are scattered in defeat like the wretches they are. I destroyed their home by harnessing the corruption you've doomed us all to suffer." He gestured to the Heretic. "Under our master's charge, we learned to use the Fallen Titan's corruption to our advantage rather than let it consume us. We accepted its power and waited until we were strong enough to strike at the very heart of those who wronged us! The sentinels were too blind to see us as a real threat. They failed to acknowledge the true potential of the corruption until I used it to break their precious mountains."

"Impossible!" Chief Amberstorm declared. "The Great Chain has stood strong since the Fallen Titan's defeat! How could you possibly break it?!"

"Fate and the relentless turning of time have a way of dismantling even the strongest things, sir." The stranger breathed out through his nose. "My lieutenant, Rime, speaks true. The Great Chain is shattered, as are its zealous defenders."

The den erupted into a fit of furious barking. A deep sadness overcame Silversong's heart, which pounded for Swiftstorm, for her safety. But there was nothing, not even the beginning of a deceitful smirk, to suggest the stranger was lying. A bubbling heat filled Silversong to the brink as he narrowed his vision on the leader of the trespassers.

If… if you killed my sister, I'll… I'll…

Memories of the times he and Swiftstorm had chased each other across the glade drowned his anger under a wave of heavy sorrow. The thought of her smile, once a comforting reminder of better days, now haunted him in the brief darkness of every blink. He imagined her mangled corpse crushed under a pile of rubble, the image becoming more and more detailed the longer he lingered on it. The drumming of his chest fuelled the heated blood rushing to his head. If his sister was dead, he would avenge her here and now!

The Chief looked like he was going to be sick, but he managed some semblance of composure. "If… if you are who you say you are, why are you here?"

The stranger's claims had to be true. Who could lie about such things without shame? Who else could lead a horde of wolves who all fit the description of vicious exiles?

Silversong's claws scraped against stone as the Heretic's eyes widened to take in all the wolves on the mound. "A good question, sir. You must have many more. Allow me to elaborate on a couple things before I reveal the reason for my arrival here. Firstly, my true name is Ironwrath. I was a member of the Stone-Guard Pack prior to my banishment, and unlike my followers, I've resisted the Fallen Titan's corruption and retained my ability to command earth. Also, after Rime ruptured the Great Chain, I journeyed to the Silverhaze Forest and did the *unthinkable*. I visited the Empress of Spiders in her very lair, and together, we struck a bargain that'll ensure my unchallenged reign over the Four Territories."

"The Empress of Spiders?!" Pinetrail and many more shivered at the mere mention of the great evil presiding over the Silverhaze Forest.

"Yes. The Mistress of Woven Plots herself. The dreaded Spider Titan." The Heretic seemed to relish in the fear and outrage of the wolves before him. "All beasts have heard the tales of her unmatched knowledge, but few are brave enough to seek her out. My presence in her domain eventually piqued her interest enough for her to grant me a private audience. We discussed many things deep underground: our hatred for Motherwolf, our desire to see the Wolven Code abandoned, our disgust at how free souls are treated in the Four Territories." His eyes swept over his creeping followers.

"Get to the point!" demanded the Chief, his voice breaking through the agitated growls of his soldiers.

The Heretic's emotionless stare never faltered in the face of so many angry wolves. "So be it. Once bonding turned to boredom, we struck a bargain under the Silverhaze Forest. She revealed to me the location of a forgotten weapon I'll use to free you all of the Wolven Code. Once this weapon is mine, I'll force your eyes open to the evil you've all been blindly following for generations. And to repay the Empress for the knowledge she gifted me, I've agreed to avenge the spiders who ruled the Breezeway before your founder drove them out."

Worried yelping and growls of rage merged into a chaotic din. Rime's broad shoulders tensed, his forehead mirroring the scowl of the deer-like face in the sky. "Before I shatter this pathetic excuse of a den, Ironwrath wishes to prevent unnecessary bloodshed by making you a generous offer." Silversong readied himself for battle as the huge exile bristled beside his master. "Any of you tail-lickers who're tired of following a worthless code may join us and live for a higher cause. Whether you're a subordinate or a lieutenant, we won't discriminate against you. All wolves are equal in the eyes of Ironwrath. He'll grant you the freedom you're so frightened to accept."

"You can't be serious!" Pinetrail hissed through bared fangs. "No Whistle-Wind wolf would ever join a faithless exile who would doom us all to lawlessness! The Wolven Code keeps us strong and prevents us from plunging the Four Territories into chaos. We'll NEVER allow it to be destroyed!"

Rime's nostrils flared as he pushed his forepaws into the ground. The grass around him browned into withering blades. "Your code is evil. But the true tragedy is that you're not able to see it. Forcing wolves to keep to their own, putting boundaries on who you can love, allowing potential tyrants to rule unchallenged." Saliva dripped from his teeth. "I look forward to the day we all forget the Wolven Code ever existed. Ironwrath is going to bring us there. He is your salvation as he is mine. Join us now or be crushed under your own ignorance forever!"

The Heretic stepped closer despite all the growls and snarls. "I understand this is a shocking proposal, but I'm willing to accept any of you brave enough to forsake the oppressive structure our ancestors have wrongly glorified. The bargain I struck with the Empress ensures your den's destruction. Once I'm done here, her spiders will claim whatever remains of your territory. Join my cause. Aid me in creating a better future for us all, and I swear you'll live to see the Four Territories flourish as they never have before."

None moved or dared utter a sound. Not even the rumbling of the storm broke through the barrier of sap-thick suspense. Silversong's thoughts raced, and he prayed for the safety of every one of his packmates, even Gorsescratch.

Rime quivered in place; he almost seemed pained by something. "Master… I can't… contain his fury any longer. The Fallen Titan… wishes… to… destroy."

The Heretic sighed and lowered his head in disappointment. "A shame. Perhaps in time, they'll see the truth and learn to accept me in place of their deceitful code." He locked eyes on Chief Amberstorm, showing no aggression at all. "Let wrath rain down on them, Rime."

Thunder cracked and boomed, and the mouth of the terrible face in the clouds gaped wider, poised to devour the mound in one swift bite.

"Chief Amberstorm! Pinetrail! Look out!" Silversong yelled.

A forked line of blinding light streaked out of the mouth of the fiendish face, crashing against the roof of the den in a *CRACK* so loud, the ringing in Silversong's ears was broken only by the sound of splintering boulders and squeals of pain. A blank sheet covered his eyes, and no matter how many times he blinked, he couldn't get rid of it.

He landed on his spine, the impact punching the air out of him. He strained to breathe as the icy shock spread throughout his body and imprisoned his breaths within his heaving chest. He writhed on the snowy grass, thrashing as a creeping panic settled. He kicked and flailed, unable to get a single breath into his lungs. After the struggle became an unbearable agony, he finally inhaled, losing himself in momentary bliss, but the relief was short-lived.

The blankness veiling his eyes faded slightly, as if he were looking through cloudy ice. The entire mound lay shattered to its foundations. Fractured pieces of stone were scattered about the glade, steaming and sizzling, some crushing the lifeless bodies of his packmates. Frozen talons seized him by the heart, stealing away what should've been another relieving breath. A metallic scent stung his nostrils as his stomach plummeted. He looked around frantically, brain pounding as if it had a pulse of its own. His vision fully returned and amplified the horror.

Tawnydrift dragged Dustyleap's halved body away while the exiles finished off many of the others.

"Corporals, to me! Fight for the glory of Whistle-Wind!" Gorsescratch rallied several corporals to his side and charged the enemy head-on. Blasts of condensed air boomed all around, and the bully disappeared in the bloody skirmish.

The surviving subordinates assembled in fractured groups, protecting the wounded against the ruthless tide.

Elder Shrillbreeze charged the Heretic, a whirlwind already raging around him. The former Chief lunged quick as a squirrel, but a terrible cough ruined his balance, making his landing easy to predict. The Heretic sidestepped, and one blink later, his teeth plunged into the elder's throat. Shrillbreeze released a ragged breath before going limp.

"A worthy effort," the Heretic remarked.

"No!" Gorsescratch yelled while lashing whips of air at his attackers.

Some subordinates let fear claim their senses, deserting the battlefield and fleeing into the Breezeway where the Wise-Wolves and those too weak to fight remained. Hazel and Palesquall stood tail to tail, drawing the blood of any exile who came too close to their fangs.

"Cowards!" Gorsescratch barked at the deserters. As his corporals successfully fought off a small party of exiles, the bully charged Rime, but the huge exile hurled him off without effort.

Rime turned to Silversong and bared his fangs, speeding toward him. Silversong's limbs wobbled uselessly, refusing to stand despite the approaching danger. Before the Heretic's lieutenant could deliver the easy deathblow, Hazel pounced and chomped on the exile's throat, forcing out a shriek. Rime maneuvered himself around and grabbed Hazel by the scruff.

Silversong forced himself up despite the pain streaming through every vein and bit Rime square on the face. "LEAVE HER ALONE!"

"Argh!" Rime snarled. "Get off me!"

No matter how deep Silversong dug his teeth into the exile's flesh, Rime remained mostly unphased. Silversong missed a bite, and it was all it took for Rime to use his monstrous strength to shove Silversong aside. The brute lifted Hazel as she kicked and screamed, bringing her up by the scruff and smacking her head on a broken boulder. She convulsed and tumbled over as if the life had been yanked out of her. Black, dancing spots hopped around Silversong's vision as he attempted to rise, but failed to stand.

"HAZEL!" Palesquall cried, launching a wave of air at Rime, throwing him off balance before he could finish Hazel off. "YOU WON'T TOUCH HER AGAIN!"

The two clashed, Palesquall utilizing his swift reflexes and smaller size to avoid the exile's savage blows. At the edge of Silversong's vision, Pinetrail got up from atop her unconscious mate, her body badly mangled compared to his. Had she sheltered him from the debris? She coughed out a spray of crimson, glaring at the Heretic, teeth bared.

"For Whistle-Wind!" Pinetrail attacked. Cedargaze echoed the battle cry and helped Shadowgale in fending off a trio of scarred exiles.

Though every muscle ached and pulsed, Silversong rolled into a crouch and joined Palesquall's ferocious assault on Rime, lashing, biting, defending and striking as he'd been trained to do.

The fight brought them closer to the Heretic, who never even bothered to change his careless stance in the face of Pinetrail's leap. He moved one forepaw sideways, and a fractured boulder hurled itself off the grass, impaling Pinetrail through the gut. A brief look of shock flashed in the Heretic's eyes as she got up, preparing to attack again, the air whistling around her. Drawing his other forepaw inward, the Heretic commanded another heavy stone to fly off the ground. Pinetrail would've slaughtered him where he stood had the boulder not smashed her into the earth.

Horror and anger fed Silversong's energy. He ripped and tore alongside Palesquall, but Rime rammed into him again, knocking him to the ground. The big exile rolled over, narrowly dodging Palesquall's strike before grabbing him by the scruff and dragging him away.

"Let me go!" Palesquall writhed and bit. "Silversong!"

Silversong found his balance and rushed to save his friend, but roots of rotting wood exploded out of the ground and entangled him as his mouth foamed. "Palesquall!"

"Silversong!" Palesquall barked, kicking uselessly in his captor's grasp.

The tendrils tried pulling Silversong under, but he fought to stay above ground. The Heretic prodded Pinetrail's corpse and lifted his muzzle, howling to the sky. "The deed is done! The price of the bargain is paid! Whistle-Wind is crippled! Leave the survivors to mourn their losses before the spiders arrive. Regroup in the Silverhaze Forest. Then we head to River-Stream Territory. And bring a few *offerings* to display our thanks to the Empress. Move out!"

"Yes, master!" Rime called off the assaulting exiles while still holding Palesquall by the scruff. He dragged him away into the woods as the face in the clouds dissolved. The exiles all trailed their lieutenant and their master, some hauling the corpses of fallen wolves before vanishing into the Breezeway.

The survivors quivered, cringing low as if the enemy would return at any moment. Gorsescratch organized a patrol of wounded corporals and subordinates, ordering them to circle the glade in case of another attack. The lieutenants still living gathered the others and formed a defensive line around the gravely injured.

The roots trapping Silversong returned to the ruptured ground, but he stayed where he was, dizzied and in disbelief, breaths short and dry. He hobbled over to where Hazel lay, her chest rising and falling on the frost-touched grass, eyes closed and locked in a deep slumber.

The storm dulled into a sullen grey downpour, and the heavy snowfall lessened into raindrops washing over the ruin of Wind's Rest. Silversong collapsed and gazed up at the sorrowing clouds, unable to process a single thought under the weight of everything.

He hoped and prayed for this to be nothing more than a nightmare he would soon wake from, but the sun never intruded on his dream to announce the dawning day. The rain only poured harder.

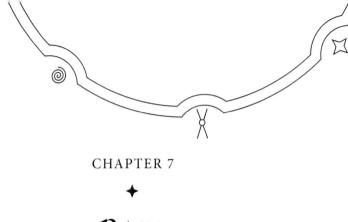

CHAPTER 7

✦

RAIN

The murky sky showered the broken mound and washed away the blood on its shattered stones. Hazel lay on the grass, the peaceful look on her sweet face too innocent for having experienced the cruelty of Rime.

Gorsescratch's breath got caught in his throat upon sighting Dustyleap's severed body. Tawnydrift limped toward the bully, burying herself in his coat. Silversong and Gorsescratch shared a brief glance void of hatred and disdain before the corporal took notice of Hazel. He froze, fur shooting up, green eyes widening. A moment later, he broke into a fit of whimpers.

Silversong's parents rushed toward him and sniffed his body for injuries, but he couldn't even bring himself to return their nuzzles.

"Oh, thank Motherwolf you're alive!" his mother whined while licking his face. "I can't lose you, not after Swiftstorm…" She wouldn't dare finish the thought.

His own heart dropped at the mention of his sister. He would never see her tender smile again or smell her comforting scent. The memory of who she really was would ultimately fade like a leaf drifting away from its native tree, and he would become more of a stain on her legacy. How could she have died and not him? If she were in his place, she would've saved Palesquall and fought off the exiles by herself!

A flickering hope shone against the deepening despair. Rime had said the sentinels were *scattered in defeat*. Maybe Swiftstorm hadn't died in the initial attack. Maybe she was still alive!

Shadowgale broke from the licking and nuzzling, eyes blank, his usual cheeriness drained. "I… I pray she's still alive. It would be just like her to pop out of the forest and come to our rescue now, wouldn't it?" he whined, voice cracking. "We… we won't let the Heretic break us like he broke our home! We'll rise from this stronger than ever! For Swiftstorm's sake."

"For Swiftstorm," Cedargaze whispered as if to herself. "No. She can't be dead. I refuse to believe it."

Silversong closed his eyes and uttered a prayer for his sister. He couldn't accept her death either. If there was a chance she was still alive, he had to believe in it. His sense of time slipped away, and upon opening his eyes again, he found himself alone overlooking Hazel's body.

The surviving lieutenants and corporals whimpered where Shrillbreeze and Pinetrail lay, some howling their sorrow. Wrapped deep within the layers of sadness and despair, the sparks of hatred and revenge blossomed, slowly burning their way to the surface. Heat filled Silversong's face, and his fur stiffened. His ears tuned out the sobbing, the howling, the rain and the hushing breeze until only the furious drumming of his heart could be heard.

The steady voice of Moonwhisper cut through his vengeful thoughts. "Silversong? Are you all right?"

"I…" it hit him how stupid the question was. "How can I be?" he grunted while gritting his teeth.

He stared at Chief Amberstorm and the wolves huddling around Mistyfur, who fed the fallen leader an assortment of flowers and minty leaves. "Is… is he…" Silversong couldn't muster the courage to ask.

"He's alive, thank Motherwolf." The tiniest droplet of relief settled into Silversong. "It looks like Pinetrail sheltered him from the impact. She was a worthy mate to our Chief, and she accomplished her duty to us without hesitation or doubt. The likes of her won't ever be seen again. Whether Chief Amberstorm relinquishes his position or chooses another mate to stand beside him and share the burden of leadership as the Wolven Code demands, we'll always support him."

Silversong growled at the deserters returning to the den alongside the weaker wolves. They rushed to the wounded, some helping to move the boulder crushing Pinetrail's corpse. The Chief's mate was entirely flattened, her coat drenched in red. Her body looked like it had decayed into nothingness, leaving behind a furry splatter to soak up the unrelenting rain.

Silversong stuck his claws into the earth, the tempest of hate rising up, up, up. Hazel's face was the only thing keeping his sanity hovering above the storm of blind rage. He licked her cheek, making her moan something inaudible. "Hazel!" He turned to Moonwhisper. "Is she all right? Please say she's all right!" He dreaded the answer more than anything else.

Moonwhisper lowered herself to inspect the subordinate, sniffing all around and prodding her here and there. "She'll live if she receives the proper care."

Bitter relief flooded him. *At least she's alive! Oh, Hazel, please wake up soon.* He nuzzled her softly, putting his ear to her chest. "I need you. We all do."

"I'll get the others to place the wounded atop the remains of the mound," Moonwhisper whined, pointing her muzzle to the flattened circle of bare stone which had once been the pride of Whistle-Wind Territory. "The dead ought to be carried to where the breeze flows the strongest. Let the wind cleanse their bodies before Motherwolf claims their spirits."

"The spiders are going to attack soon," Silversong grunted. "This was just the beginning of our end."

"Then I'll heal who I can before they crawl out of their cursed forest!" Moonwhisper bared her teeth at the heavens before stealing a glance at Shrillbreeze's punctured throat. "It's my duty to aid those who can't aid themselves, and by Motherwolf, I won't fail now!"

A biting draft sliced through the glade and would've toppled Silversong over were it not for the weight of his shame pressing on him, growing almost too heavy for his shoulders to bear.

He licked Hazel one final time on the cheek before trudging in the direction of the Silverhaze Forest.

"Where are you going?" Moonwhisper called out.

"I'm going to save Palesquall." Silversong's hackles stood up as a surge of adrenaline fought his sorrow. "I'm not going to let my friend die while I'm still breathing. And I'm not letting the Heretic off so easy! Swiftstorm would've done the same!"

Refusing to hear Moonwhisper's protests, he bolted through the waving grass, his prickling flesh numbing him to the lines of water running through his fur. He smothered the sparks of doubt before they could ignite, not wanting to think twice about his decision.

I'm coming, Palesquall! Don't you dare die before I'm there!

A powerful gale swirled toward him, but instead of crashing into him, he connected himself to its winding ferocity and willed it into an ally that pushed him toward his goal. He clenched his teeth onto the tiniest sliver of hope that he would succeed in saving Palesquall.

Shards of glittering water parted where he brushed the forest leaves. The melancholic howling of his packmates faded into memory as he looked only forward. *This* would be his defining moment—to save his friend and put an end to the Heretic! Being a corporal, being his sister's equal, came second to this new purpose.

The breeze whistled around him and encouraged his steps. *There's no time to waste! Palesquall could be sacrificed to the spiders at any moment!* He fought to keep himself motivated despite thinking about the consequences of his actions. *I'm breaking so many rules in the Wolven Code by leaving my territory without the approval of the Chief, but he's in no condition to approve anything. And I don't have time to wait around for the lieutenants to put this to a vote. I'm doing this for a good reason! Swiftstorm would've done the same! It's a greater crime to let my friend die without trying to save him!*

The thick trees granted fleeting moments of dryness, and it seemed an eternity before he reached the white stones making up the shore of the Running River. He stopped at the rim, gazing into the torrent gushing toward the sea in a roily brown surge. The Silverhaze Forest lingered on the other side, its presence ever hateful and taunting. He swore he could hear the laughter of the spiders echoing from deep within, plotting the final downfall of Whistle-Wind.

The clouds stopped pouring, but they never cleared for the sun beyond. They remained grey and broody, unsure whether to shower the land again or simply scowl at it. The wound hollowed out by the massacre wouldn't heal in his lifetime, if ever. No matter how bright the days shone, an invisible shadow heavy as a mountain would always loom over his packmates, drawing low every soul who remembered the foul storm and the destruction it brought.

I have to make sure this doesn't happen again! I have to bring the exiles to justice! The Heretic said the Empress revealed to him the location of a forgotten weapon. What could it be? A jumble of questions dizzied him.

He snarled at the stirring darkness swelling over the Silverhaze Forest like an evil eye. Rime and the Heretic were somewhere in there, no doubt gloating over their victory. A sizzling fire ignited in every paw. He needed to put an end to their plots before they could inflict more suffering on the Four Territories.

Silversong balanced himself across the water-rolled stones half-gorged by the racing current. He choked on a whimper at the thought of Hazel waking up only to realize he and Palesquall were gone. He ignored the roots of regret creeping into his thoughts. He had to do this! He had to try! The Heretic had offered a place under his reign for anyone foolish enough to abandon the Wolven Code. Maybe Silversong could feign loyalty to him and strike once Ironwrath's guard was lowered.

Silversong pulled himself onto the opposite shore and shook off the water clinging to his fur. On one side of the territory, the shadowy clouds were breaking into dappled smudges of black and grey floating amid an orange-glowing sky. But where he stood, standing below the crooked forest, the darkness endured in mockery of the sunshine beyond. He let go of his connection to the winding air and watched it evaporate before him.

He started up the slant of heather and gorse, losing himself in thought as the prickly plants and overgrown grass brushed his body. He blocked out all sounds: the whisper of a lonely zephyr, the rushing of the water behind him, the sound of something splashing in the river.

Something splashing in the river? Silversong jerked up and pricked his ears.

"Silversong!" a gruff voice stopped him before he crested the rise.

He craned his head around, blinking at Gorsescratch standing several paces away from the shore.

You followed me?! Silversong's drenched coat prevented him from bristling.

"Where do you think you're going, puppy-eyes?" Gorsescratch's face, for once, wasn't accompanied by wrinkles of hatred. "Are you deserting us or something? Your packmates need you at the den."

Silversong's tail swished restlessly. "There's never a bad time for a stroll now, is there?"

Gorsescratch narrowed his glare and stiffened. "Quit being a gullwit. We need to prepare before the spiders attack." He gulped as if not wanting to say more. "Hazel needs us. Let's go, Silversong."

"I'm leaving, Gorsescratch," Silversong admitted, feeling oddly good about it, "and I probably won't be returning for a while." He looked over his shoulder at the foul forest awaiting him.

Gorsescratch recoiled as if struck, and it took a while for him to get his thoughts out. "Did caterpillars crawl into your ears and eat your brain or something?! This isn't the time to go off gallivanting like a pup who finally stepped out of the nursing lairs. You have a duty to your territory!"

Silversong thought about what Swiftstorm would do if she were here. "That's exactly why I'm leaving. I'm going to save Palesquall and infiltrate the exiles, and once I've gained the Heretic's trust, I'll avenge all the lives he took today." He turned and continued onward, the foggy tendrils of the Silverhaze Forest reaching out to him.

Gorsescratch sprinted up the slant and blocked Silversong. "I'm a corporal, and I order you to forget this bug-brained idea at once!" After a long pause, the bully puffed out his chest and sighed. "Who do you think you are, anyway? Some hero who's going to save the day?! You're not your sister, Silversong! Accept it!"

"I've already accepted that." Silversong's admission was almost relieving in a sense, as if saying out loud how he wasn't anyone special was an advantage in the grand design of fate. No one ever expected the tiny breeze to become a raging tornado, after all. "I'm no hero, and I'll never be one."

"At least you're not as delusional as I thought," Gorsescratch snorted, tail flicking in unrest. "So don't leave. Hazel's going to need you when she wakes up. I've no idea how to even begin comforting her."

Silversong's lips curled into a wide snarl. "You can start by being less of an itch under her tail. Did you really think bullying me was going to win her over in the end? I don't even see her like you think I do. We're just friends, Gorsescratch!"

"Really?" The corporal stayed still as a tree trunk. "I…" he swallowed. "It just made me so angry seeing her pay so much attention to you while she never seemed to notice me at all. I thought if I made her think you were a failure, she would…" He examined his own forepaw circling the grass. "I even got Tawnydrift and Dustyleap in on it." His voice trembled at the mention of his fallen friend.

"Quit pitying yourself, Gorsescratch. It's pathetic." Silversong released a small growl. "You've got no idea how far out of your reach she is because of your own actions."

Gorsescratch stared straight at him, eyes quivering. "Hazel won't forgive me if I let you wander off to your death."

Typical Gorsescratch. Always thinking about himself. Silversong pressed his weight onto the wet ground. "Then say you tried to convince me to return, but I forced you out of the way. Which is exactly what I'll do if you don't move now."

The bully stepped to the side, head lowered and tail slightly tucked. "It's against the Wolven Code to lie."

"HAH!" Silversong's teeth begged him to rip into the mongrel's hide. "Like you care about not breaking the Wolven Code."

Gorsescratch gulped and bared his fangs, but not at Silversong. It looked like he was trying to keep something in, but the urge to get it out was winning. "I'm... I'm so—"

"Save your breath. I don't need your worthless apologies!" Silversong barked, towering over the crouched bully. "I'll never forget the things you did to degrade me, especially not the sabotage." He calmed his nerves by sighing deeply. "But you can try to make up for it all by helping Hazel and the others however you can." A sour pool welled up inside his chest.

Gorsescratch's stance deflated even more. "You're... you're really leaving then?"

"I have to." Silversong cleared his knotted throat, trying desperately not to imagine the faces of his parents once they realized he wouldn't be coming home. He turned the weight of his pain into his motivation to put an end to the Heretic. He walked past Gorsescratch, breaths unsteady. A sharp trembling claimed every lifted paw, but he pressed onward nonetheless. "Goodbye, Gorsescratch."

"Wait!" the bully called out, and Silversong whirled around to face the fire lit within Gorsescratch's eyes. "May the wind guide your steps, Silversong."

They shared a look of understanding, a look not between victim and bully, but between packmates, maybe even equals. Silversong gave a brief nod before turning around and hurrying his pace. He broke into a sprint, not once looking over his shoulder.

His old life was at his tail, dwindling further and further away. The road he'd chosen lay ahead, and he intended to follow it until the end.

I'm coming for you, Heretic!

The wind girdled him like an unbroken shell, and his thumping heartbeat stirred the tangle of emotions within him.

Don't doubt yourself. Keep pushing forward no matter what.

He parted the pale green blades, his breaths becoming quicker and quicker as he neared the cursed thicket of crooked branches and twisted boles—the domain of the Empress and her cunning spiders. The Heretic must've been desperate to seek her out. In the stories, none who laid eyes on the Empress were spared her fangs and mesmerizing whispers. He tried to suppress a chill, slowing his pace to a standstill and shivering at a cascade of rising fear. He sighed away a shaky breath and raised a trembling forepaw, carefully placing it into the clutches of the ashen forest like a fly buzzing willingly into a net.

The clean air dissipated, and the reeking fog reached out to claim him.

CHAPTER 8

✦

Shadow and Fog

Submerged in a sea of fog, Silversong padded forward, steps wary, eyes on the lookout for danger. Tiny tendrils of regret slithered into his head to challenge the strength of his resolve, but he gave as little attention as possible to the cracks in his courage.

I'm not leaving until the Heretic is dead and Palesquall is saved! I can't leave. Not while the Four Territories are still in danger. I owe it to my fallen packmates to keep going. He wasn't sure he had a choice now. Upon looking over his shoulder, nothing but a white, misty bar met his gaze—a barrier urging him deeper and deeper into the bowels of the twisted forest.

No matter where he sniffed, all he could smell was the humid, stuffy air tainting his nostrils, rotting away the memory of cleaner scents. How the exiles could stomach a place foul enough to clog their noses beyond repair eluded him. How the Heretic could willingly seek out the Empress of Spiders and her knowledge proved an even more frightening concept.

A denser layer of fog shrouded the lumpy ground, making it difficult to see beyond a couple tail-lengths ahead. Roots arched out of the moist soil, and the brownish barbed ivy scattered everywhere irritated his fur. He couldn't rely on his nose in place of his eyes either. In all directions, the stench of decay lingered, soaking into the air, disorienting his thoughts.

"Relax, Silversong," he whispered to himself, holding an avalanche of panic at bay. "These woods aren't so scary."

An eerie creaking noise forced his hackles up, and he whirled in the direction of the sound, trying to peer through the thick haze before him. "Nice forest… good forest. I promise I would make a terrible snack to whatever hungry creatures you're hiding. Yep! I taste absolutely horrible!" He continued on in quicker strides; there were no tracks for him to follow.

Every time he looked up, he could see the sun through cracks in the black clouds and the interwoven roof of the woods, but something was wrong. The light seemed to recoil as if afraid the writhen branches might snatch it out of the sky. He bumped his muzzle on a trunk and winced. Twice now this had happened—a tree seemingly appearing out of nowhere, perfectly camouflaged by the fog. He swerved his head in all directions. Something was watching him. Mocking him. A deepening hateful presence that wanted to do unspeakable things to him. Whether it was the sinister cravings of the trees or sadistic eyes peering at him from above, he couldn't say. The shiest strands of his fur remained upright, following the example of his hackles.

It makes sense why the spiders have a grudge against us. Our ancestors stole their land and forced them to live in this foul place. He gulped, praying his packmates still had time to prepare a defense against the nearing onslaught of eight-legged monsters.

Uncountable crawlers wriggled near the base of the trees, their bodies thick, black, and longer than most wolves from nose to tail. They curled into spirals whenever he approached and emitted a strong odour reeking of mildew. More insects too large for his liking chirped and buzzed in thorny bushes, lending their voices to the unsettling chorus of the woods.

"Keep moving forward no matter what," Silversong repeated to himself.

The boles had faces now, all deformed and screaming silently, and from their mouths trickled a sickly sap feasted upon by girthy grey caterpillars. Curious stone and metal objects poked out of the earth, sullied by patches of corrosion. He entered a gaping tunnel in a cracked and battered structure, stepping over barbed weeds until he came into a pillared field that reflected a time forsaken by memory. Carved shapes, lofty and wide, stood crookedly about him, their beauty dimmed into a rotting shadow of what once was. Silversong jerked up in a start. He was standing inside one of the ruins belonging to the Forgotten Ones.

He shivered, recalling the ancient legends about the Forgotten Ones. They stood two-legged without any fur to cover their hides, and they were a great threat that perished at the end of the War of Change. It was said the beasts and their mighty creators, the Titans, feared what the Forgotten Ones could become if left unchecked. Like invasive weeds, they'd spread through the land and felled every forest, conquered every grove, sullied every lake, and claimed every fertile ground so they could continue building their unnatural hives of stone and metal. The threat was clear, and so the Titans chose to eliminate it for the good of their mortal children. In swift waves, the forces of nature clashed against the Forgotten Ones and drove the remainder of their scattered armies deep into Stone-Guard Territory, where they ultimately disappeared at the climax of the war.

Silversong gulped and let another shiver have its way. Places like these were forbidden to enter for a reason. They belonged to an era better forgotten than remembered, an era when noble beasts were but nuisances at the mercy of a higher power.

He hurried through the decrepit ruin, leaving it to be claimed by time's steady decay.

The trees hemmed him closer and closer the further he walked, and the air thinned to a point where he had to force every breath to satisfy his straining lungs. Clumps of grey fungus infested the trunks now, oozing lines of clear and scentless liquid.

The crack of a branch and the ominous descent of a leaf made him crane his head to the coiling roof. Connected threads making up a ceiling of spiderwebs glittered, some vibrating as if stirred by unseen limbs. His hardened hackles pulled at his flesh, and he quivered at the feeling of fervid eyes watching him from the shadows, waiting for him to render himself vulnerable.

Stray far from our home, little one, and the spiders… NO! Quit scaring yourself!

Something shifted in the fog on either side of him. Instinct kicked in. His tail curled until it lay against his belly, and he lowered himself as the scent of wolves pierced the lingering smell of death. Two exiles emerged out of the whiteness and circled him, teeth bared, mottled fur erect.

I have to make them think I'm helpless. I have to convince them to take me to Palesquall.

"Who goes there?" Silversong deepened his voice and tried his hardest to envision himself as the hero of an exciting tale. He shrank a moment later, realizing how goofy he must've sounded.

"We go here," the exile of reddish fur answered, brown eyes slitted. He had all the characteristics of a former Flame-Heart member from the slender limbs to the larger ears. "Now who do we have here? A frightened pup all alone in these cruel woods?"

The other exile, his tawny coat scarred and mangled, squinted his stone-grey eyes. "Maybe he's come seeking the Empress' knowledge, or maybe he's come seeking revenge. Wouldn't that be adorable, Ripper?"

"Bonechew, he looks like that wretched sentinel we chased before Rime shattered the Great Chain, except he's got blue eyes for some reason." Ripper wetted his lips and inspected Silversong, sniffing him where his scent was strongest. "Smells a little like her too."

The sentinel you chased?! Silversong tried to remain composed, but his racing heartbeat revealed his anxiety. *Was it Swiftstorm?!* He had to bite his own lip to keep silent.

"Heh. He does look like a smaller version of her, except he's obviously a male, unless my nose betrays me." Bonechew grinned.

Silversong untucked his tail and stood as proud as he could, focusing on his mission to save Palesquall and thwart the Heretic. "I… I'm here to see your master, Ironwrath."

Bonechew laughed and bit the air a whisker-length from Silversong's snout, startling him. "Why would Ironwrath waste his time on an overgrown fox like you?" Bonechew glanced at his reddish-furred companion. "I say we tear out his eyes and bring him straight to Rime so our lieutenant can have something to bite on. Sound good, Ripper?"

Silversong flattened his ears and choked on his panic. "I-I've reconsidered your master's offer! After he attacked our den, I realized how powerless and foolish we were to trust in the Wolven Code and the sentinels. I… I see the truth now. They were never going to protect us. I would like to belong to a better cause—a higher cause. It would be wasteful to have me killed before giving me a chance to prove myself!"

Motherwolf, please forgive these lies.

"Hmm." Ripper's eyes darted from Silversong to Bonechew, his stance dominant. "I say we humor his request and bring him to our master. He'll decide his fate. After all, how much trouble can a little pup truly bring? If anything, he'll make another good distraction for the treacherous spiders. They took the dead Whistle-Wind wolves without hesitation and salivated at the thought of torturing the live one."

Oh, Palesquall, please be alive! Silversong's stomach bunched itself up.

"Cursed Empress!" Bonechew hissed. "She betrayed us the moment we gave the offerings to her mindless drones. We should've found another way into River-Stream Territory."

"I agree." Ripper licked his teeth. "Once the Empress has made use of a tool, she discards it afterwards. But who are we to question the master? He chose the fastest route into River-Stream Territory, so it's the one we'll take."

Silversong's heart thundered, his breaths shortening. *Don't be dead, Palesquall! I'll be there soon!*

"Come, Bonechew," Ripper grunted, tail swishing in brisk motions, "we've patrolled long enough, and I can feel the spiders watching us from above. Let's bring the Whistle-Wind pup to Ironwrath."

Bonechew released a groan and padded deeper into the forest, mumbling curses under his breath. Ripper bumped Silversong on the side, jolting him out of his thoughts. "Move your tail! You've convinced us to stall your death a little while longer, congratulations."

Silversong exhaled in relief and trailed Bonechew while Ripper followed from behind. All he had to do now was gain the Heretic's trust and save Palesquall. *He must be alive! I have to believe it!* Silversong clenched his jaws and refused to accept the possibility of his friend's death.

He almost laughed out loud for daring to think stopping the Heretic would be an easy feat. Nothing was ever so simple as the old tales of mighty heroes who saved the day and lived happily ever after.

Though his story was far from over, he doubted it would have a happy ending, but he hoped for it nonetheless. It was all he could do to keep himself moving forward.

✦

CHAPTER 9

The Heretic

"Move faster!" Ripper ordered, nipping Silversong on the haunch to motivate him, but it only begot a yelp. "Don't get too comfy around us."

As if I could ever get comfy around the two stinkiest scatfurs I've ever smelled! Silversong restrained himself from growling that. Being a lowly subordinate longer than most had trained him to keep his tongue under control when circumstances demanded it.

Ripper and Bonechew led him through a narrow gap between two interwoven trunks. On the other side, he froze before the hostile eyes of many scarred and mangy wolves, some licking their wounds alone, others helping one another by rubbing the juices of crushed flowers and leaves where flesh had been ripped or cut. The exiles were gathered within a small glade of pallid grass, and at its centre lay the piled carcasses of deer and unknown rodents, meat completely stripped from bone. Other remains were scattered about—corpses of at least a dozen spiders, their flesh wrinkled, their limbs curved inward, facing the roof of the forest. A tingle of disgust coursed along Silversong's spine. In place of eight black eyes, white, munching maggots filled their empty sockets.

An acidic taste stung his throat, and he let out a small whimper he masked as a cough. Maybe he shouldn't have come here.

"Silversong?" Palesquall's voice was faint like a cricket's chirp.

Oh, great. Now I'm hearing voices… WAIT! A buzzing energy filled Silversong to the brink as he turned to a corner of the glade where Palesquall stood. Silversong's ears perked up, and his eyes nearly popped out of his skull. Two crouched exiles guarded his friend, but he couldn't be bothered to let their snarls frighten him. "Palesquall!" His breath escaped his lungs, and he struggled not to leap into the sky at the sudden swell of relief. It took all his restraint to keep his tail from wagging.

Palesquall's gawking face lasted less than a moment as mixed emotions took over, lending him a confused expression. Silversong panted wildly, forepaws shaking and tail twitching at the growing temptation to wag. Palesquall's initial shock deflated, and he turned his head steadily to the one who'd killed Shrillbreeze and Pinetrail, the one who'd attacked Wind's Rest. He assumed the lowest of submissive postures.

Silversong followed Palesquall's gaze onto the Heretic, whose green eyes glowed menacingly under the shadow of the winding branches. A boiling stream bubbled through Silversong's veins as he stared at the remorseless wolf responsible for uniting the exiles and unleashing them on his packmates. He clenched his jaws so tightly he thought his teeth might shatter, and pressed his forepaws into the soil to keep from pouncing.

The Heretic strolled forward, grey fur smooth as his lieutenant trailed him. *Rime! I'll make you pay for hurting Hazel!*

The Heretic sniffed at the two wolves beside Silversong. "Ripper, Bonechew, who's this little lamb you've brought to me?" his commanding voice rumbled out of his throat.

Silversong glanced at Palesquall to remind himself his friend was still there. He swallowed his pride and rolled over, exposing his belly, inviting the Heretic to come inspect him while making himself seem as humble as possible. Laughter erupted among the exiles, but the former member of Stone-Guard remained unresponsive.

"Hah! Look here!" Rime's coarse grunt hushed the snickering voices. "This is exactly the type of pitiful behaviour we're doing just fine without. If we still followed the Wolven Code, we would be as pathetic as this brainwashed pup!"

Hot blood rushed to Silversong's face, but he stayed in the humiliating posture in hopes of appeasing the Heretic.

"Does he do other tricks?" asked a nameless exile, voice wheezy.

"Look at his pretty tail!" another exile rasped. "I hope I get permission to rip it off!"

"He looks an awful lot like one of the sentinels we buried beneath the Great Chain."

"Why's he got blue eyes? He a freak or something?"

Palesquall gulped audibly while assessing his captors, probably wondering if he could carry out a daring escape without leaving his friend behind. Silversong pleaded silently for him not to try anything stupid.

The Heretic studied Silversong as if he were a piece of fresh meat waiting to be savoured by a hungry mouth. "I remember sighting you on the subordinates' level. What's your name?"

Silversong calmed his risen fur and rolled onto his belly, pushing himself up into a crouched stance. "Silversong. My name is Silversong."

The Heretic loomed over him, eyes wide and focused. "A little uninspired, but I suppose your Wise-Wolves named you appropriately."

Rime grinned, yellow teeth smelling of unpleasant things. The scars on his face were freshly licked, and from the snort he gave, he recognized Silversong as their designer. "You're the one who pounced on my face and tore at it like it was a meaty haunch. Heh, I suppose my good looks had to be spoiled eventually."

The exiles laughed, and Silversong swallowed the urge to give Rime a dozen more scars.

"Silence." The Heretic's emotionless grunt quieted the yapping mouths, but his icy glare never strayed from Silversong. He doubted even Hazel could win a staring contest against the leader of the exiles. "Stand straight and untuck your tail. Let me get a good look at you."

Silversong obeyed and let his body be scrutinized by Rime and Ironwrath, their noses sniffing him as if searching for his every weakness. He found a flicker of courage upon meeting Palesquall's supportive expression. After the uncomfortable inspection, Silversong let the tension leak from his shoulders.

"Look at me." The Heretic's tone was without agitation, but it bore a power none could think of denying.

A whirlwind erupted in Silversong's core, its fury soaking into his bloodstream and prickling his fur, pleading for him to charge the Heretic and tear out his beating heart.

"Hmm." The Heretic refused to even twitch a whisker in the face of Silversong's anger. "Are you here to play the hero, Silversong? To slay the big bad *heretic* and save the day? I'm sure you could do it before Rime or any of the others had a chance to save me. So go ahead. Avenge your fallen packmates." He craned his head to

Palesquall, eyes brightening as if he suddenly found a better use for him. "Of course, I doubt your friend I spared would enjoy being ripped to pieces in retaliation, but it's your choice. A heavy sacrifice for the greater good is a price not many are willing to pay."

Palesquall shook his head briskly, the fearful wrinkles on his face cooling Silversong's rage. He gritted his teeth and cursed himself for all he was about to say. "Ironwrath, I've reconsidered your offer. I… I would like to join your cause."

The Heretic squinted, stepping forward a tail-length. At this distance, he hardly seemed alive at all; he looked more like an empty shell rather than anything living. It made his smile all the more unsettling. "Is that so, little lamb?"

Silversong firmed his muscles and forced his tail to rise. "Yes. I would like to be free of the law of the sentinels, free of the Wolven Code." The uncertainty plaguing his whine made him wince. *Gullwit! At least try to sound more convincing!*

The Heretic lowered his gaze to his own claws and sighed. "It's unfortunate you feel the need to lie to me. I'm afraid once an idea is shoved so profoundly into your skull, it takes a great effort to heave it out, no matter how foolish or ridiculous the idea is. Trust me, I tried to enlighten my own packmates about the flaws of the Wolven Code before my banishment, but I failed every time. Even as they escorted me to the Furtherlands to make me pay for my *heresy*, I tried to make them see the oppressive structure they were defending, but they refused to understand. They refused to listen." The Heretic's scowl added to the fierceness of his unblinking stare. "We're the outcasts, Silversong. We're those who understood. Those who listened. Those who acted on everything the Wolven Code forbids. We dared to think differently, and for this we were damned to suffer the Fallen Titan's corruption. A steep price for wanting nothing but freedom. Ironically, my followers have since absorbed the corruption and turned it into their means of achieving said freedom."

Palesquall yawned in an exaggerated manner. "Wow, does he always break into wordy speeches? I swear, I feel like I'm listening to an elder telling me the same story for the dozenth time."

One of the exiles guarding Palesquall nipped him behind the ear, making him squeal. "Silence! Or you'll lose your tongue!"

Please don't make things harder on yourself, Palesquall. Silversong prayed for his friend's safety.

The Heretic ignored Palesquall, eyes piercing Silversong to the marrow. "No doubt you think I'm insane. You think I couldn't possibly justify my hatred for the Wolven Code. After all, it has led us to great heights since the Fallen Titan's defeat, and you've personally never seen its flaws unfold before your very eyes. You've never seen how it corrupts Chiefs, how it instills fear in every heart, how it encourages wolves to see other territories as inferior to their own, how it keeps wolves confined to an arbitrary ranking system. You've willingly blinded yourself to the darkness beneath its shining promise of order."

"But you're also forgetting the peace it brought and the circumstances that created it." Silversong's tail tip shook like the end of a rattlesnake. "The First Warden thought an unbreakable code was the only cure to our chaotic nature. That without it, we were doomed to eventually repeat the same mistakes that led to the Rise of the Fallen Titan. Was she wrong?"

The Heretic took on a thoughtful look. "No. I suppose she wasn't wrong at the time. Unchecked, we spread ourselves from border to border, overpopulating every territory and overhunting every living creature we could stuff into our mouths. We brought disease and famine on ourselves and turned a noble being into a hateful fiend. I don't deny the peace the Wolven Code has brought. I deny its virtue."

"But why break it entirely?" Silversong demanded, sinking his forepaws into the soil. "Maybe there's a way to amend the Wolven Code, to make it less… strict."

Palesquall became still as ice, and Silversong almost gasped at his own suggestion. The Wolven Code wasn't supposed to be amendable! It clearly stated no one had the power to change its rules, whether subordinate or Chief.

"My goal isn't to return us to a state of chaos, little lamb." The Heretic paused as if reflecting on the things he believed. "It's to destroy an oppressive system and rebuild on its foundations. A balance must be struck between chaotic freedom and stern order, and I'll be the enforcer of this change."

Rime moved up to stand beside his master. "The Wolven Code created us, Silversong. It excludes wolves who think differently. It was only a matter of time before its victims banded together. *Never sully the pride of your ancestors by mingling with wolves of a different territory.* Bah! How dare some poorly thought up code decide who I should and shouldn't love?!"

Who said anything about love? Silversong thought.

"Not convinced?" The Heretic seemed to peer into Silversong's soul. "How about this. Why do you think I was banished from my territory? What horrible crime did I commit?"

Silversong scowled, showing a few of his teeth. "I'm sure you'll enlighten me."

The Heretic sniffed and gave him another uncanny smile. "Chief Bronzeblood of Stone-Guard Territory was always a bully. Nothing changed in his character from petulant rookie to incompetent leader, aside from his increased penchant for cruelty. However, one thing made him beyond dangerous, and it was his ability to make good-intentioned wolves behave despicably without them even knowing it."

Palesquall snorted. "Hah! If only I had this ability. I would be the Chief of the Four Territories in no time."

The Heretic waited for the angered exiles to cool off and continued his story. "Season by season, I watched as Chief Bronzeblood used my packmates to further his extravagant reign while the very soil beneath us dried out, while the prey he ordered us to overhunt dwindled until we were forced to seek out unsavoury meals. Even so, he continued to fatten himself and squash any hopes of resistance by using the Wolven Code against us, by saying he was the Chief—the rightful ruler of Stone-Guard Territory. He'd been chosen by the former leader, thus chosen by the Wolven Code. And my packmates never questioned him." Disgust spread across the Heretic's face. "How many newborns did he have to starve to satisfy his own gluttony? How many mates did he have to take on? How many innocents did he have to doom to a bitter death before someone finally found the courage to bring him to justice?"

"You had the courage, master. You exposed him for a tyrant and led a rebellion against his reign!" Rime bristled beside the Heretic and managed a prideful smile. The leader of the Furtherlands was an idol to him—the shining symbol of a misguided cause.

The Heretic growled and trembled like a violent earthquake. "I tried, Rime, I tried. But I failed. I gathered a small force of wolves loyal to reason and challenged the Chief to a duel. The winner would either stay or become the leader of Stone-Guard. To my surprise, my enemy accepted. I was about to win the duel, but I failed to predict how far the claws of blind faith had dragged my other packmates into the pit of ignorance. Their reason was beyond saving. At the Chief's command, they turned on me and my allies. I watched as my friends were crushed, beaten, starved and tortured until the life flickered out of their eyes. In the Wolven Code, it's forbidden to challenge a Chief chosen by the former leader of your territory. To the majority, I was the bad guy. I was the heretic, and so I was banished without a trial and without pity, stripped of my dignity and escorted to the Furtherlands to suffer the Fallen Titan's corruption. I've resisted it, of course, and I've chosen to keep my original name despite the sentinels cursing its memory. But still the taint of those woods scarred me in ways you'll never understand." He let out an empty chuckle. "I can't even dream anymore."

Silversong stood fixed to the ground, glued there by an invisible force. He thought if he tried to move, it would be like marching through sap. Why had he never considered how the Wolven Code could be used for evil? Would he have been able to stand against Chief Amberstorm if *he* were a tyrant? Silversong hoped he was brave enough to face the wicked no matter the weapon they used, but if the weapon was the Wolven Code—a thing as sacred to wolves as life itself—could he still stand on the side of justice, of truth?

The Heretic studied Silversong as if he secreted the answers to all life's questions. "You see now why I'm so desperate to change how we wolves live? This *order* we've subscribed ourselves to is as flawed as a rotting tree still standing upright, and we're ignoring the inevitability of its eventual collapse. The Wolven Code brings only ruin to those who see its imperfection. It should've been destroyed long ago. Sadly, only the future can be changed, and I aim to be its grand designer. Once the weapon the Empress spoke of is mine, I'll lead you all toward salvation. I'll erase any who resist me from existence until the only wolves remaining are those who see my truth. Then we can rebuild."

You're a monster! Even so, Silversong found it impossible to ignore the sway of the Heretic's vision. A future without the Wolven Code, without division between the Four Territories. Maybe… maybe it wouldn't be so bad.

The Heretic's voice was almost comforting. Like a rough stone grinding against a pebble that had been smoothed by a stream's steady course. "We were never meant to think. To reason. That burden belonged to the Forgotten Ones. Fate dropped it on us after we helped cause their extinction. Sadly, I doubt we can return to a time when we were simple beasts who found peace in lives driven by instinct. Given the power, I would even consider returning us to such a state."

"Sure, that doesn't sound evil at all," Palesquall grunted, earning him a few snarls.

The Heretic lifted his head and turned to his captive. "If I were as evil as you think, I would've fed you to the spiders alive and rejoiced at your wails of agony. But alas, mercy is a virtue I like to exercise, and so I'll allow you to breathe among us until you see the folly in following the Wolven Code." He shifted his regard to Silversong. "And you, if you truly seek to join us, I'll give you a chance to prove yourself. Welcome to my reign. While we journey to River-Stream Territory, you'll be placed under the surveillance of Bonechew and Ripper. They'll make sure you won't cause any trouble."

"You can't be serious," Bonechew groaned, muscles stiffening under his scarred flesh. He gave Ripper a snarl of disgust.

One glance from the Heretic made them crouch low. "You heard me. You're the ones who found him, after all." He craned his head to the chuckling exiles. "You all think it's funny, do you? All right, you'll all look after the other one." The Heretic gave a satisfactory flick of the tail at the sudden silence. "Now, if the treacherous Empress is to be believed, my prize lies deep within River-Stream's underground ruin. Within the Mountainmouth." His gaze encompassed Silversong and Palesquall. "You two, until I decide you're trustworthy, your lives are to remain under watchful eyes, understood?"

Palesquall whined a meek sound of agreement, and Silversong lowered his head respectfully.

Bonechew muttered something about how he should've killed Silversong, but Ripper only sighed in exasperation, probably having a few regrets himself.

The Heretic sniffed the air. "Good. In time, you'll learn to look beyond our crimes and rough exteriors and see that we're the noblest of wolves here." He lifted his head and addressed the entire gathering of filthy exiles. "Hear me! We head to the Mountainmouth at a trotting pace. We'll not sleep until we rid ourselves of these cursed woods. Though it took longer than I'd hoped, the bargain between me and the Empress proved a worthy endeavour. The sooner I claim my prize in the Mountainmouth, the sooner I can lead us all to salvation. Let's move!"

Through the murky forest, Silversong hurried alongside his new *packmates*. Bonechew and Ripper enclosed him on either side, their gruff, hostile breathing expressing their displeasure. Silversong dipped his head, but let his eyes wander to the Heretic.

Countless questions about the weapon the Heretic sought flooded Silversong's head, but Palesquall's nudge pushed them away. "Hey, fancy seeing you here, Silversong."

Silversong licked him softly, the fluttery feeling in his stomach tickling away his agitation. He sniffed Palesquall for serious injuries, but found none. Only his eyes carried the weight of having witnessed his home getting destroyed. "You gullwit. Do you have any idea how scared I was?! I thought I would stumble upon your dead body or something."

Palesquall nuzzled him on the cheek. "Aww, how cute. I never thought the broody and dramatic Silversong would care so deeply about me. I'm flattered." He gave a swooning look. As always, Palesquall used humor to temper his pain, something Silversong wished he could also do.

Silversong almost sneezed out his snort. "Don't get too flattered now. And I'm not dramatic," he added quickly.

Palesquall's silly face turned somber. "How's… how's Hazel?"

Silversong breathed out, wondering if he should prank Palesquall by making him be needlessly worried for a moment, then cringed at himself for even considering it. "She's alive, but in a deep sleep." Relief flashed across Palesquall's expression, and the tension in his body relaxed itself. For all the arguments the two had together, they were still friends to the core. "I decided to take the initiative to come save you."

Palesquall coughed out a chuckle. "Never took you for the gallant hero. Then again, you technically haven't *saved* me, have you? You've gotten yourself stuck in the same sticky situation I'm in, except I was dragged into it while you jumped straight into the mouth of the beast." His fur stood up as if startled. "Hazel's going to have a fit whenever she wakes up, and the only tragedy is me not being there to see it."

Silversong aimed an uneasy smirk at him. "She's going to have our hides, isn't she?"

"Yup," Palesquall almost yipped, but managed to keep control over his hushed voice. "Maybe I should actually join the exiles for real if they'll protect me from her," he joked.

Silversong nuzzled his fool of a friend, never giving a glance to the snarls of his jailors. "I'm happy you're alive, Palesquall."

"Yeah, I'm happy I'm alive too." Palesquall tensed and caught on to Silversong's sincerity. He failed to suppress an ear-to-ear smile. "Oh, don't make me feel all sappy, Silversong. Now isn't the time."

"Sorry." Silversong gave him a final nuzzle while they continued through the fog.

"So," Palesquall whispered, "I'm guessing you planned to infiltrate our enemies to get close to the big bad guy. So enlighten me. How're we going to save the day?"

Silversong hated admitting how unprepared he really was. "Uh…"

"Oh, we're so dead." Palesquall shook himself.

"Maybe not." Silversong squinted at Rime and his master, sizing the two up in his head, thinking up a dozen plans and discarding them a breath later. "I think we should wait it out. Play smart until the Heretic is vulnerable."

"You think we can take him on?" Palesquall's tail stiffened in shock. "He killed Pinetrail and Shrillbreeze without even blinking. Like they were nothing but pesky flies in his way. They were powerful fighters, but they never stood a chance."

Anger fumed in Silversong's core. "We'll find a way to beat him. We have to."

Maybe in the Mountainjaw, or whatever the underground ruin in River-Stream Territory is called, he'll render himself vulnerable somehow.

"Hey!" Bonechew's grunt startled them. "Quit squeaking together like babbling mice and be quiet!"

"Yeah," Ripper growled. "Don't give us an excuse to spill more Whistle-Wind blood."

"Sheesh! They've got bigger trees stuck in their rear ends than Hazel does," Palesquall joked, much to Silversong's dismay.

Before Bonechew or Ripper could act on their outrage, the Heretic halted. The others stopped too while their master sniffed the stuffy air, surveying the webbed roof of the forest.

Rime's muscles hardened, and the acrid scent of unnerved wolves overpowered all other odours.

Palesquall put his muzzle to Silversong's ear. "The Empress turned on the exiles after some of our dead packmates were offered to her drones. I think the Heretic even expected this move from her, and so he wanted his offerings to convince her to let him through the Silverhaze Forest in peace. It's the quickest way into River-Stream, after all." He swallowed bitterly. "I hope the Empress manages to claim the Heretic and his ugly lieutenant for herself somehow."

"Master?" Rime scanned the treetops, his breaths quickening. "More spiders?"

"Silence," his master ordered.

Silversong had to point his ears in specific directions to hear them, but sure as the fur on his rump, there were whispers chattering from the webbing above.

"They come from where the Fallen Titan was slain, from where corrupted bones were scattered by noble sentinels…"

"They turned the old deer's corruption into a weapon of decay and hate…"

"They sought to cross our woods without paying the price…"

"Now they flee to the Mountainmouth, where the Great Drowned One slumbers…"

"Where the golden circle spins eternally…"

"A weapon powerful enough to influence time itself…"

"They cannot wake the guardian in the deep; they cannot wake its fury…"

"They should remain here until their bones are dusty clumps…"

"Until the moon fades and the stars expire, swallowed by the hungry void…"

"Until the veil is broken. Until all is devoured by darkness…"

"Until existence itself is woven anew…"

"Until all things once living slumber under an eternal lullaby…"

"Reveal yourselves, you miserable insects!" The Heretic crouched as everyone assumed a defensive stance. Silversong followed Palesquall's example, tensing his shoulders, but there was no breeze to make use of here, and it would take too long to conjure a strong current because of the choking fog.

"Their blood is warm, warm as severed bowels!" An enormous spider leaped from unseen heights, hooked limbs pointed at Ironwrath's skull.

The Heretic dodged the dive and slipped a forepaw to the side, willing the earth to devour his attacker. More spiders descended, appendages rubbing against dripping fangs.

"Sinewy flesh to crave! Little beating hearts to drink dry!"
Another spider landed before the Heretic, but Rime plunged his forepaws into the ground, commanding festering roots to pierce the lunging insect. The spider thrashed and wailed, but the tendrils never yielded as they ripped and tore.

A dozen more spiders dropped all around and launched themselves at the exiles. In the chaos, Silversong signalled to Palesquall, and the two approached the Heretic as he bested his assailants one after the other, commanding explosions of soil to thwart every attempt on his life.

Silversong and Palesquall charged the Heretic, picking up speed as they ran, teeth bared and ready to strike. *This is where it ends!*

Palesquall peered over his shoulder in front of Silversong, gasping as his eyes bulged. "SILVERSONG! BEHIND YOU!"

They were so close to their target, so close to ending the true threat, but before Silversong could pounce, a sudden sting burned up his spine, wrapping his bones in liquid fire. It scorched through his veins until the hottest flame would've seemed cool in comparison. He teetered like waving grass and collapsed to the side. His muscles all constricted themselves at once. He opened his mouth to cry out, but no scream could do justice to the pain. His throat sealed itself as he tried to wriggle free, but the venom had already burrowed itself deep into his bloodstream and forced him to lie helpless like a fly in a net.

He gasped for a breath, but no air found its way into his lungs. A freezing panic prickled along his flesh like ants biting him through a sheet of numbing ice. He could feel his heart struggling to beat life into him as his vision darkened, brain pulsing harder than an untreated wound. Soon the beating slowed and slowed while a swarm of spiders wrapped him in a silky shroud. The added layers of his prison muffled the barking and growling of the fighting exiles, the howling of orders, the yelping of Palesquall.

Silversong couldn't struggle anymore. It was over.

His eyes closed, and he plunged into a black slumber where all he could hear were the avid whispers of his hungry captors.

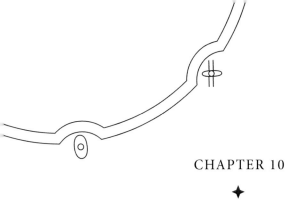

✦

The Fangs of the Empress

Silversong drifted in and out of a dreamless slumber, eyes leaden, vision blurry. He expected to see morning's tender rays reach through the entrance of his lair at Wind's Rest, welcoming him to stretch and prepare for a sunny day ahead.

Instead he found himself unable to twitch a single whisker. All but his eyes and tongue were stiff as stone, and he could hardly expand his knotted throat to welcome in the deep breaths he desperately needed. His heart thumped faster and faster, failing to unfreeze his muscles.

He looked side to side, squinting to adjust his vision, but he glimpsed nothing through the thick threads encasing his body. It all struck him in an instant—his chance to prove himself, Gorsescratch's sabotage, a snowstorm during summer, the terrible face in the clouds, a flash of white lightning, the attack, wolves dying, his friend stolen away, his foolish mission to infiltrate the exiles and save the day, the spiders, the sting…

Everywhere, the scurrying of many delicate steps made tapping sounds on wood and earth. Silversong managed a brief shake.

"*He wakes!*" whispered the spider carrying him under its fangs.

"*I can feel his little heart drumming,*" hushed another spider. "*Drumming faster now. Soon the music of his life shall fade forever.*"

"*Our beloved Empress shall delight in sucking his blood to the final droplet,*" a sinister voice giggled.

The tingly feeling of tiny thorns puncturing his spine erected his fur within the cocoon. His forepaws jerked up, freeing themselves from the once paralyzing venom. He could move either of them without much strain now, but the spiders had secured his prison tightly. He would have to wait until his whole body was responsive before he attempted an escape.

Looks like I'm not the gallant hero after all, Palesquall.

He closed his eyes and prayed the end would come swiftly if death awaited him wherever he was being taken, which it probably was! He envisioned his friends and his parents barking for him to keep fighting. Something about their imagined optimism summoned a dogged energy to surge through his body, diluting the stubborn venom.

The one carrying him moved nimbly over uneven terrain as he worked to liberate himself fully. After several agonizing tries, he finally managed to wake his hind paws. *Don't give up! Keep fighting!* Never would he have considered how frustrating and frightening it would be to have no control over himself, yet still be conscious of everything. Did caterpillars feel so trapped and helpless when they locked themselves in a cocoon? If he somehow broke free, he doubted he would become a pretty butterfly and take off in a merry flutter.

His eyes opened wide. A spasm inclined him into an awkward position, and invisible talons grabbed the insides of his stomach and wrung them mercilessly. His mouth readied itself to scream, but his sealed throat released no sound no matter the pain's severity. The sharpness faded after a while, leaving him free to move his jaws and tail now.

"*His body wakes!*" whispered the one carrying him. "*Spasms, cramps, shivers and twitches!*"

"*That's exactly how she likes them,*" laughed a voice above.

"*Bring him to the shrine! Bring him to the shrine!*" chanted the others, some near, some far. All it did was disorient him more.

His throat unclenched itself, and he rejoiced in every breath despite the unclean air.

"*Into the Whispering Hollow; into her lair,*" they murmured together. "*Where the old one struck the bargain.*"

The air cooled, and though his breaths now entered his lungs without toil, the filthy and sour stench stinging his nostrils made him regret having his throat unsealed prematurely. He snarled in disgust and gagged at the putrid taste tainting his tongue. It smelled worse than the Prey Hollow ever had during the hottest days of summer.

After another dry-heave, he deduced where he was. The enhanced sound of pointy limbs tapping on solid stone, the chilled and stinking air, the concentrated reek always lingering…

… I'm in a cave, and they're taking me deeper and deeper into its bowels.

A muffled din of rattles and excited whispers was all he could hear. Everywhere agile steps pattered like raindrops on dry earth. He thrashed and jerked, biting at his sticky confines. He couldn't die! Not here. Anywhere but here!

"Feisty he is," giggled the one bearing his cocoon. *"Our beloved Empress shall enjoy you, silver one, yes."*

He kicked and chewed at his prison, but not a thread came undone. "Let me go! Please! I'm no exile! I'm a subordinate of Whistle-Wind Territory! You can't do this!"

"A liar he is too. Tsk, tsk, tsk."

Their voices all sounded the same—a sharp wind piercing into his ears like pointy roots. Whether they came from above or from one side or the other, they never failed to feed the churning fear in his gut.

"I'm not lying!" Silversong struggled until his body gave in to exhaustion.

"Perhaps he lies, perhaps not. It no longer matters. You belong to our beloved Empress now, silver one. Her voice shall liquefy your senses until you no longer can resist her demands."

A heavy pressure deepened in his ears, followed by an aching *pop* as he swallowed. The air of the cave no longer smelled of rotting flesh, at least, but of metal and mildew. His captors dropped him on a solid surface, spinning him over and tearing off clumps of the cocoon.

"Hail! Empress of Secrets and Whispers in the Darkness!" the spiders chanted. *"Hail! Mistress of Woven Plots and Cunning Ambitions!"*

Hooked claws sliced the wrappings sheltering his face. His eyes needed a quarter of a breath to adjust to the unexpected light. Above him were the shapes of the huge spiders freeing him, and beyond them a massive net spanned the entire room. Eight orbs rested on the threads and glowed pale blue in the darkness, each as large as an acorn and distanced perfectly apart in a circle. Their striking beauty would've nulled his senses had the voices not continued chanting.

"We bring an offering whose heart is pure! Drink his blood and taste his essence! We failed to capture the one who bears the secrets of stone! Accept our apology, beloved Spider Titan!"

They tore off the remaining threads. Silversong rolled swiftly onto all fours and whirled around, teeth exposed. Every spider scattered like roaches fleeing the sun and crawled inside one of the many tunnels hollowed out in the curving chamber, creeping into darkness.

It dawned on him how he was as hopeless now as in the cocoon. A mixture of fear and frustration stirred inside his gut. He thought himself like an ant wandering on a lonely leaf drifting in the endless sea, or a salmon drowning on dry soil far from any stream or river.

"My, my, what a delightful specimen my subjects have brought me." A silky, alluring voice smoother than ice echoed behind him. "It almost merits forgiveness for their failure to bring me the old one who can still command stone. Almost."

His entire body tensed as if the venom had reignited in his veins. His hackles stood up, his eyes broadened beyond their sockets, and he turned to the source of the voice. At the opposite end of the cavern, positioned on the wet grey stone, was a spider much larger than any of the others. Eight amber eyes glared at him, and an enormous black abdomen spotted red at the centre rose to the net holding the shining orbs in place. Four rear limbs loomed up to press against the rocky contours while the front ones dangled loosely on either side of the monster's glossy fangs.

He flinched at the waves of shivers rippling across his fur, but no matter how deep the terror struck, he found his gaze glued to the godly creature in front of him. "Fear not, silver one. What your eyes see is merely an effigy of my true splendour, and what your ears hear are but whispers of mine echoing from far beyond your realm of mortality."

He uttered nothing. A prickling numbness soaked into him until he couldn't feel the ground anymore, but still he quivered as if frost coated his bones. He tucked his tail while the voice hummed through him. The eyes of the gigantic spider seemed to peer into his soul, plunging, searching, digging, claiming all the secrets he bore. "Say who I am, my little offering," she commanded, her tone serene and almost… pleasant. Like a mother's amused whine to her pup.

He breathed a trembling breath, making an effort to compose himself. "Y-you're the Empress of Spiders."

Silversong sighed at the delightful tingles accompanying every one of her laughs. "Yes, but like *Motherwolf*, the Titan you worship, my influence here is limited. However, through this effigy, my children whisper to me the secrets they collect. Their skill at navigating the darkness and the unseen has granted them great knowledge." She paused, but he could still taste the sweetness of her every whisper, sweet as honey on his tongue. "Here, under the shine of the stolen jewels, inside this shell of obsidian stone, I can see and feel you despite being realms apart. Come closer, silver one. Not since the War of Change have I tasted wolven blood as strong as yours surely is."

"So this is only an imitation of you. You're not actually here? You're not trapped inside your effigy?" His whine came out like a mouse's squeak.

"No." The effigy's eyes flickered angrily. "In a bygone era, I persuaded a faction of the Forgotten Ones to build this magnificent shrine in my name. So easily manipulated they were, the Forgotten Ones. You've only to anchor a single woven thread onto their emotions and play on their superstitions until they're lured to your bidding."

"But... how can you be in two places at once? How can you speak to me through this effigy if you aren't actually in there?" Silversong slurped up the drool leaking out of his mouth. "I don't understand."

"Of course you don't. Through enchantments unknown to you, I can merely fasten my consciousness to this construction." She paused, letting the heat of her eyes soften. "Though in a sense, I suppose I am trapped. Locked in a distant realm far from yours." Her gaze refocused itself on one of the eight orbs as if it were the place to which she referred. "No longer am I able to weave my beautiful schemes beyond my domain. The war against those two-legged barbarians yielded unforeseen consequences to immortal beings like me, it seems. We Titans disrupted the fate of your realm by exterminating the Forgotten Ones before their time, and thus we were punished accordingly by a force beyond even us. Sometimes I almost regret playing a role in the extinction of those furless brutes. Almost."

"I… I…" Silversong tried to make sense of the revelations, but they meant little to him. The more time he spent thinking, the more he longed to hear the Empress' whispers again. He needed to feel the vibrations; he needed to feel her voice slithering into his ears to caress his brain.

"Yes. Don't bother resisting. I can taste the sweet essence of your soul, and I seek to savour it fully. Come closer, and I'll share all the secrets you desire to know." Something about the smooth, seductive way she spoke evoked spasms of pleasurable tingles, and he panted to hear more.

He obeyed, thoughts melting into a confused mixture. He straightened his tail and brought himself forward. He wanted everything she could possibly offer him. He yearned to hear her voice, hungered for her knowledge, thrived for her promise of comfort. The closer he got, the more the need for her worsened. She was a disease he wanted to be infected by, an addiction he couldn't imagine living without.

He glimpsed something in her eyes now. A vision, he thought. Deep in the amber, wolves howled to the heavens as smoke and ash drifted out of the burning forests. Two-legged creatures covered in metal chased and killed their prey, but they never stopped to eat them or even gloat over their trophies. It was pure slaughter for the sake of it. Among the chaos, the Forgotten Ones wielded detachable claws of iron and other sinister weapons, fending off any beast brave enough to face their savagery.

At the grimmest hour, Motherwolf herself appeared out of the smoke to rally her creations. Her fur was a night without stars, but her eyes contained the swirling light of their fiery fury. Her battle cry shook the fear out of every heart and instilled courage in its place. A ferocious gale parted the flames and sought out Motherwolf's swiftest soldiers, imbuing in their bodies the power to weave the air itself. The ground rumbled under the wolves whose strength and bravery never faltered, and once the trembling ceased, they found themselves able to command the earth. Rain showered the loyal and the cunning, granting those wolves control over water. The flames themselves danced around the passionate and the caring without scorching their flesh. Fire would henceforth be theirs to wield in the coming battles.

And so the War of Change evolved. As Motherwolf's Blessings were given, other huge beasts emerged out of the nature still standing—an enormous grizzly bear, a deer whose starlit antlers shone blue and whose bellow rallied the roots and trees to his aid, a trickster raven who summoned shadows to his bidding, an eagle of golden feathers, and a black spider who looked exactly like the immobile effigy of the Empress. Many, many more answered the desperate cries of their creations, and together, they charged the monstrous foe. As the two forces clashed, the vision shifted out of focus.

Silversong watched the final remnants of the Forgotten Ones—led by a leader of ashen hair and pale blue eyes—flee across Stone-Guard Territory, through a gorge of towering spires, and into the belly of a massive ruin of bronze. He recognized the place from the stories the elders had narrated. The remaining Forgotten Ones disappeared there, vanishing from existence at the climax of the war.

Something hit him—a sense of urgency, a sense of duty. Why was he here again? The Heretic! Of course! How could he have forgotten?! He stopped moving toward the Empress, and the captivating vision in her eyes disintegrated to ash. "I-I shouldn't be here! I have a mission to accomplish! The Heretic has to be stopped. I-I was so close to killing him before one of your drones stung me! Please… it's not too late. You have to let me go."

Where's Palesquall?! Did he make it? Worry snapped Silversong to his senses.

The Empress giggled, and tremors of pure delight fizzled through his flesh and bones, dousing his panic and forcing him to come nearer. A blurriness shrouded his thoughts again. "Why bother worrying about the old one? He bores me. His schemes are so banal and predictable, and he's rather… unsightly. But you, my dear, you're far prettier, far younger, far tastier." Her glare brightened, and in it danced tongues of mesmerizing fire. "Come closer, and more knowledge I shall feed you. Or are there other things you desire? Do not hesitate. Any final request you make of me shall be considered."

He continued toward her on delicate paws, panting as if he'd travelled the entire stretch of the Running River in a sprint. "You revealed to Ironwrath—the Heretic—where he can claim a powerful weapon. Inside the Mountainmouth, the underground ruin in River-Stream Territory. What is this weapon?" His senses clung to him by the thinnest branch of sanity.

The Empress' eyes dimmed into orbs of wavering flame, and in their light another vision took shape. "To understand the origins of this weapon, you must understand the events leading up to the War of Change. For eons we Titans have watched over our creations, watched as the wheel of life and death turned, its constant motion keeping the balance of nature stable." The amber of her eyes morphed into beasts thriving among proud forests and lofty mountains, golden deserts and swaying prairies, winding rivers and depthless seas, and over them all a shadow bloomed. "The Forgotten Ones stood outside the wheel, watching it like vultures observing a dying animal. Their greed and selfishness, amplified by their intelligence and reason, made them a formidable threat. More and more, they disrupted the delicate balance required for nature to thrive. Like a pestilence, they infected the wheel until it was at their mercy."

As the looming shadow grasped every sanctuary and smothered them in one swift squeeze, the image changed to a mighty black stallion marked in coiling white patterns. He strode through a circular maze of twisted hallways and roads leading every which way, seeking something at the centre, something as unknowable as the void beyond the stars. "Although the threat of the Forgotten Ones concerned us, we decided not to take drastic action, at least, not yet. Only one of us was absolutely certain their continued existence would lead to the downfall of our creations. His name was Stormstrider, the Horse Titan, and upon hearing our decision to let events unfold, he set out to look for a way to glimpse the future, to prove to us the Forgotten Ones had to be wiped out."

In her eyes, the stallion found the centre of the maze, the black gloss of his coat glinting in the perfect darkness of the chamber. The contours faded away, leaving the Horse Titan alone in the empty abyss. No. Not alone. Countless inky eyeballs blinked at the stallion from everywhere, and in them even more eyeballs observed, and more within them, the pattern repeating itself forever. A maddening spiral. Silversong sauntered ever closer to the horrifying, beautiful image, ever closer to the Empress. "Stormstrider found something—an entity who'd been there since the beginning of existence, a traveller who watches events unfold from beyond the veil of reality, and it granted him the power to not only see potential futures, but to influence the woven threads of time itself."

Threads darker than midnight emerged out of the eyeballs and traced a golden circle before the stallion, its shine low yet blindingly radiant. Stormstrider bowed his head and swallowed it in one quick bite. "I can only guess at the price Stormstrider paid to be granted an object of such power. I shudder at even the thought. He returned to us bearing a piece of time itself, and he used it to reveal to us possible futures where we let the Forgotten Ones thrive: all of them were unkind to our mortal children. So we plotted to extinguish the two-legged beasts before they could evolve to heights even we couldn't reach. The War of Change began, but shockingly, during one of the battles, Stormstrider was slain by a Forgotten One."

A brief flash in the effigy's eyes showed the mighty stallion being pierced through the heart by a massive stick of thick wood and sharpened iron. "The piece of time Stormstrider had consumed was stolen by our enemies and taken to the core of the Mountainmouth. A bitter lesson: having the ability to see the future can't save you from your own demise. But by acting swiftly, we still won the war before the Forgotten Ones could use the weapon's true potential. Those of us who figured out where it was tried reclaiming it afterwards, but some things within the underground ruin are treacherous even to us Titans. Over the ages, the knowledge of time's physical manifestation faded from your realm. Until the Heretic's bargain."

Silversong couldn't believe the things he was hearing. It had to be a trick! "You're saying there's a piece of time inside the Mountainmouth?! And you gave this information to the Heretic?!" Silversong bristled, pacing side to side.

If the Heretic manages to use this manifestation of time against the Four Territories… Silversong shivered at the possible outcomes.

The Empress' unseen smile scorched his thoughts to cinders. "He bargained for it—a way to solidify his power and rule over the Four Territories unchallenged. He has only to consume time's physical manifestation to wield its potential." Her eyes glued themselves to Silversong's frantic pacing. "I admit, I hesitated giving him this information, but deemed our exchange a worthy bargain. It's a shame I couldn't capture him in the end, but if Titans couldn't pierce the underground ruin, how could he? And now, as we speak, a swarm of my subjects is crossing the Running River and shall soon reclaim their rightful property. Yes. A worthy bargain indeed."

A brewing heat burned away the need to hear more of her voice. Silversong scowled, letting a creeping snarl stretch his mouth wide. "I… I regret the actions my ancestors took against your subjects, but this isn't right. We've lived in the Breezeway all our lives, and we've called Wind's Rest our home for generations. You can't just take it from us. It's unfair!"

The flame in the effigy's eyes flickered and coiled into a wreathing pattern so captivating he almost wanted to leap in and relish in a fiery demise. "Unfair? It's no less fair than your wretched founder driving all my beautiful children into this foggy wasteland. A war she waged on my subjects, and now, centuries later, Whistle-Wind pays the price for the countless lives she took. Oh, I shall ensure your *packmates* suffer a prolonged end because of her insolence. Their despair is my delight."

The violent vibrations spawned from her voice wormed all over his brain, drying out the stains of anger. Why was he aching so badly to hear her speak again? Why was it so impossible to resist her? It was like maggots were eating away every rational thought he had. "I… I… I need to…"

"You need to face reality," she hushed him. "You can't accomplish anything. You're no hero. You're a failure. A lesser child. A disappointment playing at being something larger than he is. You won't ever be your sister. The only semblance in your fates is a gruesome end. You won't ever be anything to anyone but me. I am your destiny, the culmination of your mortal purpose. Accept it and surrender yourself to my fangs."

He whimpered at the faces of his packmates in her eyes, barking at him for leaving, cursing him for having failed his duty. The overwhelming weight crushed his chest and dragged his hopes into oblivion. "I… I'm sorry."

"Poor, pathetic child." Her sharp fangs glinted in the radiance of the orbs above. They were so shiny, so pretty. "Worry not. I can give your life meaning in its final, fleeting moments. Come closer, and don't look away, my dear."

As he peered into her amber gaze, he forgot his fears, his worries, his purpose. All he wanted now was to hear her loving voice again, to feel the tingling sensation of her whispers slither into his skull and fondle his brain.

He stopped below the glistening fangs, waiting to hear the Empress' commands. "Now, bow your head and prepare yourself.

Once my fangs descend, I shall feed you all the love and care you so desperately need while I savour your blood from afar. You shall experience a sharp pain, but it soon shall dissolve into utter bliss, and your only desire shall be to remain in my clutch until your body is a shriveled corpse fit only to be thrown aside."

He drooled, and his body convulsed at the chilling sensations she allowed him to feel. The room became so hot, all coolness seared away. He could taste the sweetness of her perfect voice on his lolling tongue again. It echoed through him and yanked at every strand of fur. His stomach tightened, and he shuddered, unable to imagine anything else but the Empress' welcoming fangs.

What harm can come from a single bite? He would only give her a few drops of his blood before pulling away, just enough to feel her loving touch before he escaped.

The brightness of her eyes was blinding as venom oozed from her fangs. "Let your very essence be mine to savour. Bow your head. Accept your fate."

"I… I…" He failed to form even a single coherent thought. He lowered his head a little, keeping his eyes fixed on the eight holes of wreathing fire. He wetted his mouth. *A single bite. Just a single bite before I escape and… and… why am I here?*

The alluring fangs lifted themselves slightly. All he cared for now was feeling her touch and drowning in her voice. A breath without hearing it was an eternity for him. Already he was starved for it.

"Yes. Bow, child of Motherwolf." The flames in her eyes scorched his jumbled thoughts. "The euphoria I offer is greater than the deepest delight, and the love I have for you is vaster than a thousand oceans. Give yourself to me, and let go of all the burdens of life."

Steadily, he presented himself for the fangs. "I'm yours, Empress."

Decaying roots entangled the shrine, and the Empress shrieked so loud it jolted him out of the trance. In an instant, all the love in her voice disintegrated into bitter ashes. His head throbbed as if countless thorns had stabbed his brain, and he recoiled a moment before the fangs descended right where he'd been standing, missing him by the slimmest hair.

"How dare you interrupt us?!" screamed the Empress. "Puppet of the Fallen Titan! May your soul be damned to the same torment he still suffers."

Silversong jumped around as the agony dimmed into an afterthought. Vision still blurred, he thought he saw two wolves crouching near one of the tunnels leading up the cavern. As his eyes adjusted, he bristled in shock. It was Bonechew and Palesquall! Friend and exile had saved him. Bonechew commanded the rotting roots twisting out of the roof above while Palesquall twirled his tail and conjured a scourge of air, lashing the effigy.

"On behalf of Ironwrath, we exiles thank you for your gracious hospitality, your majesty," Bonechew snarled.

The puncturing thorns inside Silversong's head had retracted themselves completely. He was free of the Empress' spell, free of the need to hear her voice and feel her *love*. Fear found his heart again, his eyes locked on his two saviours. "Wha… how… how did you…?"

"You going to stand there gawking like a pup until the spiders come for us?!" Palesquall growled over the screeching Empress. "Me and Bumchew—"

"Bonechew!" the exile corrected.

"Me and Bonechew got separated during the attack!" Palesquall blurted out. "I convinced him we should come look for you! And here we are!"

"Convinced?!" Bonechew wrinkled his face as he weaved the Fallen Titan's corruption. "More like hounded me until my ears couldn't take it anymore! Besides, I only came here to repay the Empress for her treachery. Move, Silversong! Or we'll all end up in cocoons waiting to have our veins sucked dry!"

Silversong had no time to even ponder the surprise of being rescued by his unlikely saviours. "Lead the way!"

He hurried after the two wolves into one of the tunnels. A shrill cry from behind tortured his ears as the darkness enveloped him. He focused on Bonechew's unclean scent and Palesquall's ragged breathing, the rocky ground beneath him cool and wet. His heart encouraged him to keep running until he collapsed, and so he did. A flood of blazing energy lit every fiber of him aflame. This was his only opportunity to escape. He had to make it count!

In the blackness, he heard the scuttling of spiders everywhere. They crept closer, determined to return an escaped prisoner to his jailor. They hissed while chasing him, the sound of their hurried steps tapping near his tail.

Bonechew barked, and the three of them veered into another tunnel, this one reeking of mildew. More spiders pursued them, some groping the fur of Silversong's tail. He inhaled deeply, lungs holding in a large amount of filthy air. To avoid gagging, he envisioned a swirling breeze above, dancing and gliding without any obstacle to thwart its course. He sensed a weak connection to the breath locked inside him, growing stronger and stronger the more he focused, the pressure in his chest increasing until it was almost painful. He turned around, blowing out a strong gale and sending the crawlers smashing against stone. Though his eyes failed to pierce the stifling darkness, the sudden stoppage of pattering sounds convinced him he'd delayed the chase for a time.

Silversong trailed his rescuers up narrow pathways and through cave systems where the bones of unlucky victims had been discarded. They came to a cavern where dozens of carcasses lay wrapped in cocoons suspended from tapering stones on the ceiling. Larger corpses rotted in wide, sticky spiderwebs at the corners of the rocky hollow.

Some of the cocoons jerked and twitched as Silversong passed by. *They're still alive in there!* He released a fragile whimper, shivering at the thought of waiting to die a horrible death alone here. He sprinted after Bonechew and Palesquall on the moist and misshapen floor, hurrying up a crooked hole that smelled of relatively fresher air.

At least the Whistle-Wind wolves the exiles killed were long dead before they were offered to the spiders.

The frantic pattering of angry arachnids disturbed his ears again, but it only motivated him to move faster up the twisting tunnel. As washed-out light struck his eyes, he exploded out of the Whispering Hollow behind the other two wolves and jumped onto the black soil of the Silverhaze Forest. Despite the hostile presence of the woods, standing below its crooked branches fostered an oddly welcome feeling after everything he'd been through deep below.

Silversong craned his head around and squinted at the lofty formation of uneven boulders rising out of the earth to form a tiny mound—a poor imitation of Wind's Rest and an unfitting home for anyone, especially those who'd been driven from the real thing.

Perhaps once this was all over, the spiders and the Whistle-Wind wolves could come to an understanding. Silversong's packmates had to survive the next attack first. He hoped they would flee far from the Breezeway. In a state of bloodlust, the spiders would give no quarter.

Several nooks and hollows dented the lopsided mound. At its stark peak, a malformed oak sprang, branches as sickly as the rotting leaves they bore. Bonechew must've commanded the tree's roots to entangle the Empress' shrine.

Out of the many entrances in the ugly mound, crawling shapes emerged. Silversong and Palesquall turned to Bonechew and sprinted after him through the ashen woods, down muddy slopes and up steep inclines until muscles burned and breaths became ragged wheezes. Silversong tumbled into a wide gully, the grimy water resting at the bottom soaking his fur. Palesquall settled himself beside him and rolled over, gasping for air. Silversong panted between coughs, throat hot and dry. He looked up only to face Bonechew's broad snout, wincing at the thorny shrubs poking him, their leaves gorged on by tiny black caterpillars.

"Get up," Bonechew snarled, pawing Silversong's shoulders and scratching into his dirtied coat. "We haven't escaped spider territory yet. The Empress must be furious. She'll dispatch a legion of her mindless drones to scour the whole forest in search of us. We can still catch up to Ironwrath if we're quick enough, so let's hurry!"

Silversong's legs wobbled as if his bones had turned to twigs. He collapsed every time he tried getting up.

Palesquall gave him a dire look. "You okay, buddy? Think of Hazel."

That only made Silversong's breaths even more of a struggle to take in. "The spiders, Palesquall, they're coming for them all."

Palesquall stood up in a start. "I-I'm sure they'll be fine!" He gulped, the uncertainty in his voice inspiring no comfort at all. "The Whistle-Wind Pack can't end like this."

Bonechew cursed. "Ugh, Fallen Titan take me. Why was I assigned to you?! I've been ever loyal to the master, and all I get for it is pup-sitting duty?!" He bared his fangs and pressed a forepaw on Silversong's head. "Get up! Or I'll tear out your heart and force your friend to eat it in front of you! Which means this whole errand I've been forced into will have been a complete waste of my time and energy!"

Palesquall blinked at the exile, unsure whether he was joking or not.

I can't let the Heretic reach the piece of time! GET UP!

Renewed thoughts of stopping the Heretic gave Silversong the motivation he needed. His dizzied head refocused itself on a single goal, and an eruption of anger and desperation produced the necessary strength for him to rise again. He hardly cared whether Bonechew was bluffing or not. Only Ironwrath mattered. Silversong yelped at the invisible blades shooting up his bones while he forced himself to stand. He shook like a brittle branch, but he looked straight at the exile regardless, challenging the mangy mongrel.

Bonechew pulled back in surprise, and an awkward moment passed before his scowl returned. "Hmph. Come on then. River-Stream Territory lies just ahead."

CHAPTER 11

✦

The Ruin
in River~Stream

The flight through the wicked forest was far from pleasant. In truth, there was no way to describe how awful it really was.

Every piece of Silversong ached and begged him to quit running. The blistering pain throbbing in his pads from small punctures made the whole ordeal even worse. The exile trotted close behind, eagerly waiting for either of his victims to stumble again. Dozens of fresh scars designed by Bonechew's teeth made certain places on Silversong's body feel as though they were being munched on by fire ants. A couple more tumbles, and he would start to look like a hardened exile himself, which would make him fit in more among his new *packmates*, at least.

By comparison, Palesquall had it a lot easier. The goofy subordinate who prided himself on annoying Hazel showed surprising resilience.

"Remember our game!" Bonechew grunted mockingly. "If you stumble for whatever reason, I'll bite until you get up again. You're not resting until we reach River-Stream Territory."

Palesquall slowed his pace so he could run beside Silversong. "Keep it up, buddy," he gave an encouraging whine. "Think of a nice tasty meal waiting for you at the end."

Silversong's stomach growled, then cramped up at knowing no reward awaited it. "Palesquall, you're making it worse," he rasped. "But thanks for saving me."

"I get kidnapped, and I'm the one who ends up saving my rescuer. Some hero you are." Palesquall chuckled lightly.

"Never said I was a hero," Silversong remarked, managing a weak smile.

"There's time yet to become one, eh?"

"Less chatting! More running!" Bonechew ordered stray roots to swipe at Silversong, but he copied Palesquall's maneuvers and dodged the blows.

Bonechew had already given Silversong wounds that would take a while to heal without the aid of a Wise-Wolf. Fighting the exile in a fatigued condition seemed like a poor idea, though, even if it was two against one. Silversong had to endure the bullying for now. If he could survive Gorsescratch's treatment of him, he could survive this too!

The air smells fresher here. We must be getting close. A circular pool caught golden sunbeams ahead as if drinking in their vibrant radiance. *A golden circle…*

"Palesquall," Silversong uttered, holding on to scrambled memories of the Empress and her revelations. "Time. Time is the weapon the Heretic is looking for. A physical manifestation of it lies at the core of the Mountainmouth."

"What?!" Palesquall released a confused yelp. "I don't understand."

"It's a long story." Silversong made sure his voice stayed low. "The Empress showed it to me, Palesquall. One of the Titans wielded a piece of time during the War of Change, but he got killed by a Forgotten One, and his weapon was hidden away in the underground ruin. If the Heretic manages to consume it, he'll be unstoppable."

Palesquall's eyes never blinked. "You're… you're not joking, are you?" He let out a frustrated growl, trying to keep it subtle. "But… but how's any of this even possible? I mean, a piece of time? Really?!"

"I'm not sure. But one thing's for certain. We can't let him gain control over the powers of time." Silversong's affirmation dulled the pain ringing throughout him.

He tripped on a lonely root and lurched forward, smacking his muzzle on the ground. He rushed to get up, but Bonechew was already atop him. The exile bit him on the flank. A sharp pain pushed itself through Silversong's flesh, and he yowled as the teeth found the extent of their reach. Palesquall begged Bonechew to relent, but the exile only crunched harder, forcing Silversong to cry out sounds he thought not even a suffering deer could achieve.

He yanked himself free and winced as a clump of fur tore itself off him at the brisk movement. He bolted and stifled his whimpers while the exile laughed and revelled in his own cruelty. "You taste good, little lamb! Much tastier than the loners of the Furtherlands!"

Silversong shuddered and hastened through the remainder of the harrowing woods. Bonechew willed thorny roots to prick him on the belly, further motivating his long strides. The Fallen Titan's power was similar to the way the deer influenced nature to do their bidding, but every time Bonechew used it, all he controlled withered into decay.

The ashen trees melded into an expanse of bushy oaks and colossal alders sprouting cone-like flowers from sturdy limbs. Green heads battled the sickly colours around them, dancing to the docile breeze. Snails slimed their way across a leaf-strewn floor, and singing jaybirds brought wriggling insects up to their nests. The oppressive gloom of the forest lifted into a gentler haze, and the air now smelled fresher, cleaner.

Fractured rays of sunshine warmed Silversong's wounds and inspired a dance of light on the ground. They were here. The edge of Whistle-Wind Territory. A chaotic tune of relief and anxiety drummed in his chest. He climbed a stone projecting like a tooth out of the earth and peered at the downward slope sliding into one of the territories below his own.

Finally! He stopped and panted, his muscles thanking him for giving in to exhaustion.

Bonechew and Palesquall padded to his sides, breathing raggedly. The exile's muzzle stank of dried blood. Silversong braced himself for another attack, but Bonechew merely glared at him and scoffed. "Took us long enough. We're at River-Stream's upper border. I remember trudging through this awful territory on my way to the Furtherlands, my guards biting and beating me whenever they got bored. Take a good guess at what my crime was."

Palesquall answered in Silversong's stead. "Hmm, let's see. You were too much of a scatfur, so they banished you."

"Hah!" Bonechew found the insult amusing, oddly enough. "Would've been as good a reason as any. But no. My crime was far more monstrous." He looked at Silversong and Palesquall expectantly.

Palesquall took one glance at Silversong's scars and growled. "Just end the needless suspense and vomit out your sad story. You've probably rehearsed it a dozen times already."

Bonechew lifted his head in a snobbish manner. "Fine. Before they banished me, I was a corporal of Stone-Guard Territory, like Ironwrath, except he got exiled before the Wise-Wolves even named me. After my promotion, I rescued a Flame-Heart trespasser and helped her escape into her territory. Chief Bronzeblood was about to execute her for unlawfully crossing our border. I understood she had to be punished, but I found it a little excessive to have her painfully crushed to death by boulders. But to question your Chief's honourable commands is to question the Wolven Code. The night before her execution, they put me in charge of guarding her, but instead I snuck her out of our den and let her go." Bonechew paused, staring off to the side while biting his lip. "The following morning, I was put on trial for helping an enemy escape. Some even accused me of *liking* her, which made my packmates hate me even more. And so, the Chief banished me, and those I'd once called *friends* brought me to the Great Chain and watched as I was thrown into the Furtherlands." He scraped his claws against the stone.

"Oh, come on. There's got to be more to the story." Silversong hoped Bonechew hadn't confessed everything. He hoped there was another reason to justify the exile's banishment.

Palesquall stayed silent, shifting a forepaw uneasily as he sniffed the air.

"You're terribly naïve, little lamb. Even Rime's crime of killing a River-Stream lieutenant because she discovered his *little secret* was justified." Bonechew snarled at the sky. "Evil is whatever the Wolven Code says it is, and to the Furtherlands for those who think otherwise!"

"Rime's *little secret*?" Silversong tilted his head and studied the exile's troubled face.

Palesquall snarled at the mention of the one who'd harmed Hazel.

Bonechew sighed as if not wanting to explain. "Before he called himself *Rime*, his name was Tiderunner of River-Stream. He was your average corporal. Proud, loyal, and sometimes prickly, but he hid a secret under the cover of darkness. When his whole pack was asleep, he would sneak out of his lair and cross into Flame-Heart grounds, where he would frolic with a young and pretty she-wolf. Good for him, I say. Thing is, they were wolves from different territories, and so they were committing a great crime by bonding together. Eventually, a River-Stream lieutenant caught on to his nightly outings and stalked him to the place where he and his *little friend* would always meet. The lieutenant revealed herself and threatened to expose them both as code-breakers, but distracted by her own outrage, Tiderunner killed her. He later returned to his den to confess everything he'd done, taking the blame for it all. He said he was the one who lusted after the Flame-Heart member and that she was only a victim foolish enough to have fallen for his tricks. In the end, she was spared punishment whereas he was beaten, humiliated, and exiled to the Furtherlands."

Palesquall coughed up an empty laugh. "Sounds to me like Rime deserved everything he got. Manipulating a poor Flame-Heart she-wolf and killing his own lieutenant because he was found out by her—ugh. He's a disgusting brute, nothing more."

Silversong grunted in agreement. "How can you say Rime's crime was justified?! He sounds every bit as evil as I thought he was. At least he had enough integrity to admit his crimes."

Bonechew scrunched up his forehead and narrowed his glare at the heavens. "Hmm. Guess this means I'm terrible at telling stories. Good thing I'll probably never become an elder." He shifted his gaze to Silversong. "There's a lot more to Rime's tragedy, little lamb. Stick with us, and eventually you'll learn the truth about his heart. Now let's move. We've wasted enough time here already."

The forest of oaks, alders, and other thick trees dipped along a broad slant gradually bending to meet even ground. From one side to the other, the slope continued as far as the eye could guess. The vibrant leaves of the woods shifted calmly, and far into the heart of the forest, where the treetops looked like tiny shrubs, a cluster of strangely shaped stones white as bone poked out of the green. And beyond, an unheard torrent of striking blue cut the territory in two. It looked like a younger sibling to the Running River, but a lot narrower, and more youthful and energetic in its passing.

Silversong inhaled through wide nostrils and tasted the unpolluted air of River-Stream. Never before had he stepped a paw inside another pack's territory, which was forbidden unless you were escorting a banished packmate to the Furtherlands or fleeing a calamity. Here he stood on the precipice. Palesquall tensed beside him, and a chill of uncertainty turned Silversong's fur into tiny spikes. Home and comfort were far behind, and an untold adventure lay ahead.

"The Mountainmouth lies in the direction where the sun always rises," Bonechew groused, his voice dampening the sheer beauty of the luxuriant forest. "We'll make for the white ruin over there and gather our strength under its shadow before we follow Ironwrath's trail again."

"Why there?" Silversong asked, regretting it the moment he glimpsed the contempt on Bonechew's face.

The exile bristled in annoyance. "Because River-Stream wolves fear anything even remotely related to the Forgotten Ones! Or so I heard from Rime."

"Or so you heard?" Silversong turned to Palesquall. "How reassuring."

Bonechew slammed into Silversong, pushing him off the side of the stone tooth. "Quit yapping and get moving already!"

"Oof!" Silversong landed on his side and winced at the pain stabbing through his ribs. He looked up at Palesquall who gritted his teeth, obviously angered at how the exile treated his friend. *Don't do anything stupid, gullwit. Now isn't the time.*

Silversong signalled for Palesquall to follow him.

The subordinate and the exile descended the stone and hopped onto the slanted ground where Silversong waited. Together, they pressed onward as the breeze flowed through their summer coats. Silversong nearly rejoiced at the fleeting coolness dampening the pain of his wounds. His bites and bruises needed a good licking, but he couldn't worry about it now. Sometimes the three of them had to maneuver around a few stark drops, but they kept up a good pace.

The fat leaves and strong branches minced the sun's blazing rays into countless sharp fragments, creating shifting shadows on the ground. The heat shortened Silversong's breaths and cooked his newer scars—a brutal reminder of summer's wrath. He pitied the wolves of Stone-Guard and wondered how they managed to survive the relentless season. According to gossip, they always suffered droughts during this period.

The group arrived at the bottom of the large slope, and Silversong panted to cool himself off. The trees stood closer together now, but not in a stifling way like those in the Silverhaze Forest. Here they rose side by side like dear friends fate would never dare separate, their proud wood reaching up to meet a shivering roof of shaded green.

Bonechew padded to the front of the group, sniffing his way through the unknown territory, ears pricked in alert and fur erect. He stopped before a mossy boulder and snuffled around it, flicking his tail at Silversong. "Come here."

Silversong gave Palesquall a questioning look before inspecting the boulder too. It bore the scent markings of a foreign wolf— strong, tangy, fresh. "I guess this is what River-Stream wolves smell like." He sniffed again. "It's a little saltier than mine."

"Indeed." An amused grimace spread across Bonechew's face. "Rub yourselves in it."

"What?! No way!" Silversong barked in disgust at the embarrassing suggestion.

"The odour of the Silverhaze Forest is fading, and your Whistle-Wind scent is going to stick out like a fox in a grassy field here." Bonechew tensed his muscles and swayed his tail impatiently, glancing at Palesquall. "You two should rid yourselves of it while you can."

Silversong scowled, bubbles of embarrassment already stirring in his gut. "And why don't you rub yourself in it too, then?"

Bonechew snorted as if the answer were obvious. "River-Stream wolves have no idea what we exiles smell like. They'll probably think I'm a stray coyote or something. Just do it and quit complaining!"

"You smell more like a dead rat than a coyote," Silversong mumbled as Palesquall choked on a laugh.

"Excuse me?!"

Silversong's fur stiffened. "N-nothing."

"Thought so."

Palesquall nosed Silversong on the shoulder. "I'll admit, I'm tempted to let myself be entertained by you two snapping at each other, but let's not give the smelly exile an excuse to give you more scars, all right?"

Silversong sighed, but agreed reluctantly.

He followed Palesquall's example and rubbed himself all over the marked stone, coating his fur in the foreign odour. Bonechew grinned at them, and Silversong thought of ways to tear the look of satisfaction off the mongrel's face. Once their Whistle-Wind scent was completely masked, they shook and cringed together at the ordeal.

Bonechew laughed. "You two are River-Stream wolves now! Enjoy your new scent. Oh, Ripper is going to love this."

"At least we still smell a lot better than you," Palesquall muttered.

Silversong grimaced and suppressed the urge to bite the exile. Bonechew turned, and they followed him through the vibrant woods, life thriving all around them. On the limbs of the melding trees, squirrels hopped, and spiky rodents dangled from the strong branches, every paw interlocked as they bathed in the cool shade. Clumps of ivy sprouted out of the soil and stretched in patches of light, and violet flowers were admired by the bees lending their buzzing tune to the forest's theme. Here and there, clusters of unmoving caterpillars the colour of twilight's sky huddled on the trunks, resting together as robins picked at them one by one. The abundance of living things and lively sounds was almost staggering.

By the time they reached their destination, daylight had dimmed ever so slightly, enough to bewilder the eye for a fleeting moment. The trees parted around broken structures of stone and metal as if they feared encroaching on them. Weeds, brambles, vines, and other nasty plants had no such reluctance. They crept up the eroded foundations battered by the passing of the ages, invading every crack and slowly eating away the memory of whatever this place had once been. The taller portions of the ruin stretched like mountains overlooking lesser knolls, their shapes unnatural, strange, wrong.

"Silversong," Palesquall brushed up against him, "we shouldn't be here."

"No. We shouldn't." Silversong nuzzled his friend for comfort. They stopped at the edge of a beaten road. "Remember how we used to scare each other by pretending one of us was a Forgotten One?"

A shaky smile parted Palesquall's mouth. "Hazel would always run off and whimper to the elders whenever I pounced on her during our games. *Grr! I'm the spirit of an angry Forgotten One who's come to avenge my comrades your ancestors killed!*" He broke into nervous laughter. "Never thought I would actually enter one of their ruins." He gaped at the arched entrance leading into the open belly of the ruin. It was a lot bigger than the one in the Silverhaze Forest.

"It's not so pretty to look at now. Just another reminder that nothing lasts forever." Bonechew groaned and sat for a moment, scratching off leaves and other irritants behind his ears. "According to some legends, there was a time we wolves lived in harmony alongside the Forgotten Ones. Before they learned to become more ambitious creatures. Before they began conquering everything." He stretched, then started forward.

Silversong and Palesquall trailed the exile on careful steps up to the main structures, all of which seemed more massive the closer they got. Despite Silversong's instincts telling him to stay outside, all three of them walked under the arched entrance still standing strong after the passing of countless seasons.

Within the heart of the ruin, a mossy road circled a figure of carved stone. It stood two-legged atop a polished base unbeaten by the cruelty of time and made of a material Silversong couldn't quite describe. The round platform was at times smooth as cloud and clear as ice, and the closer he came, the more he sensed a strange, otherworldly feeling sinking deep into his being. It had no colour— no—it had every colour, all of them curving around the structure like a rainbow dimmed of its former brilliance. Silversong broke his eyes away before the thing hypnotized him. Were the others also seeing this? Apparently not. Palesquall sniffed the ground here and there while Bonechew watched him suspiciously.

The stone figure itself was proud, lofty, and covered shoulder to ankle in a silvery substance. Its forelimbs were contorted in a manner that allowed its forepaws to clutch something at the chest—a small pillar lengthening to an intricate cross, and from there a sharp, tapering tooth of corroded metal descended to the multicoloured base.

Silversong gasped. The figure was almost an exact recreation of the Forgotten One who'd led the last of his kind to their disappearance deep in Stone-Guard Territory. The visions the Empress had shown him streamed through his head and dizzied his senses. A peculiar feeling wormed around his stomach the longer he stared. The figure looked so alien yet also so familiar at the same time. He turned to the exile who seemed rather bored. "Who do you suppose this was?"

"Huh?" Bonechew looked at him before glancing at the sapphire eyes of the stone figure. "Who cares? Some dead Forgotten One, nothing more."

"You ever wonder how the last of them disappeared?" Silversong's thoughts locked themselves on the mystery even the Empress had no answer to.

Palesquall gave him a blank stare.

"Does it matter?" Bonechew huffed. "What happened ages ago is of no concern to us. The future lies ahead, little lamb, and dwelling on the past only stalls our arrival there. The Forgotten Ones posed a threat to us, and the forces of nature purged them into extinction. That's that."

Silversong almost found it sad how the extinction of an entire species could be so casually glossed over.

Bonechew's grunt tore through Silversong's inner thoughts. "We belong to a destiny much larger than ourselves, Silversong. Ironwrath is the harbinger of our salvation. The future is his design. Once he has his weapon, he'll open all eyes to his truth."

Not if I have anything to say about it. Silversong exhaled and clenched his teeth onto the little hope he still had. Palesquall sauntered off toward a pool of stale water, satisfying his thirst.

Bonechew rambled on, "you're lucky the true power of the Fallen Titan weakens the further away we are from where he died. Otherwise Rime would've already shattered the Four Territories like he did the Great Chain."

Silversong trembled at the mere memory of the face in the clouds. "How do you control the corruption? How come it doesn't eat you alive like it's supposed to do? How does Rime… how does he corrupt the sky itself?"

Bonechew paused, clearly savouring his victory over the sentinels. "To resist the Fallen Titan is a futile battle. Eventually, everyone doomed to wander the Furtherlands succumbs to him. If you keep fighting him, he'll devour you from flesh to spirit. But if you accept his rage, his pain, if you promise to inflict suffering on his enemies, he'll drive his corruption into your soul, and you'll become more and more powerful in the weaving of death. The sentinels failed to predict just how powerful one could become. Rime showed them their error. But the Fallen Titan's strength does come at a price: Motherwolf's Blessings won't ever answer your summons again."

"But Ironwrath—"

"Ironwrath is an anomaly. He's the only one to have withstood the corruption for so many seasons and still retain his command over earth. Stone-Guard wolves are known for being difficult to break." The exile grinned as an old pride resurfaced. "To answer your other question, Rime bears the very spirit of the Fallen Titan inside him. He bears his true power. Like flies to a rotting corpse, their hatreds attracted one another and connected them together. Rather than use his own hate to corrupt living things like the others do, Rime knows how to channel the same fury and despair that drove the Forest Father into madness. The closer Rime is to where the Fallen Titan was slain, the more powerful the rage becomes, and the more destructive the potential grows. It's how he shattered the Great Chain but only managed to flatten your little den."

Silversong swallowed a growl. The image of Rime smacking Hazel's head on a broken boulder replayed itself over and over again, beckoning waves of prickling heat and causing a roar of blood in his ears. He steered his thoughts toward other things. At least Rime's power was limited, but Silversong still needed to thwart the Heretic before he claimed the weapon he sought.

I need a moment to think alone. How do I get rid of the exile?
"I'm… getting tired…" He yawned in an overexaggerated manner.

Bonechew muttered some unheard curses. "Fine. Get out of my fur and go sleep. I'll inspect the ruin some more and make sure your friend doesn't get into any trouble. Then I'll have a quick nap myself, I think. Don't try anything funny. I'm the only one who knows where the Mountainmouth is, and I can lead you there by the quickest routes. Without me, you're nothing but helpless prey to the River-Stream wolves. And trust me, their patrols won't even bother interrogating you before they rip you to pieces."

The exile padded off into one of the ruin's tunnels while Silversong hurried out of its grasp and returned onto the road overrun by thistles and other prickly things. He lay on his empty belly and curled himself up so his head rested comfortably on the ground, tail covering his muzzle. Fatigue found him again, and he realized how tired he actually was. He yawned truthfully this time.

He hoped to keep a much-needed slumber at bay by thinking about everything he'd learned today, but his muscles refused to listen to his commands to get up, and his body begged him to let go and recover from the exhaustion. The pain in every paw, the aching in every leg, and the burning in every open wound softened as his eyelids slowly slipped to cover his vision in darkness.

After a tiring struggle to remain awake, his consciousness fell prey to the lure of a shadowy dream.

✦

CHAPTER 12

Dreams of a Darker Road

Strands of fog groped Silversong's fur, their icy touch wet and desperate, as if they were begging him for companionship. Somehow, he could feel their sadness, their solitude, their utter emptiness which could only be filled by his eternal presence.

He strode through a forest of contorted trees black as death, wincing at the expressions of horror and despair carved in the trunks. Thick trails of blood-red sap leaked from the hollowed eyes of the wooden faces. The branches bore no leaves, and the breeze deigned not to enter whatever forsaken place he'd strayed into. Even the moon's sharp sliver recoiled its beams from the darkling woods, fearing its shine would be wasted on the void-touched earth.

He should've been afraid. He should've been running in hopes of eventually escaping the forest's shadow, but instead of the fear he was supposed to feel, instead of the sense of hopelessness that should've made him beg for Motherwolf's mercy, he allowed an invisible hole to expand inside him, sucking away all the happiness and sadness of all the seasons he'd lived, pulling pleasant and sorrowful memories alike into a whirlpool of nothingness—a meaningless abyss. Suffering and joy became one within the pit, and he rejoiced at knowing everything meant nothing in the end. He could only describe it as a horrifyingly comforting experience.

Between the trees, he thought he saw a wolfish shape grinning at him, eyes darker than the darkest void, fur smooth and black like threads of shadow. The longer he stared, the more a feeling of wrongness strengthened, but it was impossible to look away from those eyes, those terrifying, beautiful eyes—pools of perfect night. Within those pools writhed masses of tendrils each bearing countless blinking eyeballs, their depths profound, endless, hungering. He'd seen such a thing before, in one of the Empress' visions. Silversong yanked himself free of the lure, cringing at the sensation of insects crawling all over his flesh. The deepening feeling of wrongness faded, and he looked to where he'd been staring only to see nothing there.

A glimmer of mellow green stole his attention away from where the wolfish figure had been standing. He turned to a majestic deer, its fur shifting between shades of brown, marked in spiraling designs that emitted a gentle gleam. Its antlers were roots of pure starlight. He paced toward it, captivated by its perfect face, its eyes mirroring the vibrancy of a heavenly forest untarnished by anything that would dare sully it. If he were a deer, he would no doubt think the entity before him was the prettiest thing to have ever breathed.

The deer bolted, scurrying through the thicket like a leaf on the breeze. Silversong followed it as a heavy realization hardened every hackle—he was chasing the Forest Father! Around bulky roots and briars bearing glinting thorns, he pursued the irresistible beast as tongues of fog stroked his fur. The deer stopped within a glade of grey grass. Azure flowers dappled the stretch, their petals so striking not even the stars could rival their splendour.

The Forest Father approached another gigantic beast in the clearing—a glorious stallion: his body was a tide of rippling muscles, his coat smooth and black and covered with coiling white patterns. His shadowy mane flowed perfectly to one side, and his eyes were of a deeper blue than an ocean during a tranquil sunset.

"Stormstrider," Silversong exhaled.

The Forest Father bowed his head to the grand stallion, breath quavering. "My dearest friend, I feel so hopeless without you. I'm trapped within the Mortal Realm, and I can't depart to care for my domain beyond the sun. I feel… empty… scared… lost." He nuzzled the Horse Titan and buried his snout in the flowy mane.

The stallion never spoke. He stared coldly into the distance as if the Forest Father weren't even there. "I hope… I hope you still exist somewhere. I hope we'll meet again one day. Your creations are flourishing far to the south. You would be so proud of them." The Forest Father lowered himself, hooves quivering. "I've no idea how to go on. I feel our connection only in dreams; I feel you watching me, but I can't be sure of it. Wolves have taken over the continent where I now dwell, and they've begun multiplying like locusts. Their greed and gluttony spreads too. They've abandoned all the virtues of order in favour of chaos. Soon I fear they'll wipe out my children entirely if I don't act soon. It's like the War of Change all over again. The consequences of us interfering in mortal affairs still weigh on me, but I can't forsake my living designs. Not then. Not now. Especially not while I'm stuck in this realm. The wolves have already thinned my creations to a dire number, and I can't think of a future where their eyes are opened to reason. Maybe," his voice shifted to a darker tone, crackling like dying embers of a once roaring fire, "maybe they deserve death."

Silversong flinched, his fur stiffening. He tucked his tail as far as it could go, but he couldn't flee no matter how tempting the instinct was. A giant stick of wood tipped by an iron spike struck the stallion through the heart, and he rotted away while standing, maggots gorging on his eyes and swallowing gluttonous amounts of flesh until only bare bones remained. Even those evaporated into grey soot a breath later. The metal-tipped stick dropped to the earth, and the maggots morphed into huge flies buzzing about the grass and flowers, their presence causing everything to wither until nothing but death reigned.

Glacial shivers ran across Silversong's spine, but it was neither because of the demise of the stallion nor the abrupt decay: it was the Forest Father himself. The stag groaned eerily, flesh stretching, antlers darkening, eyes widening beyond a comfortable size until they ruptured, muzzle expanding, teeth sharpening into white thorns. His mouth contorted itself into a wicked smile, and Silversong recognized it as the one in the sky the day Rime had shattered Wind's Rest.

The Fallen Titan sniffed, the sound like a breeze gusting through rattling branches. He aimed his eyeless regard upon Silversong, freezing him in place. "Welcome to my dream, Silversong of Whistle-Wind." The ghostly snapping of countless twigs accompanied his voice, resonating from deep inside his throat.

Silversong couldn't even tremble. He was prey, helpless and frozen before a hungry predator. He wanted to run, but his rigid bones prevented the futile attempt of an escape. For some reason, knowing he was in a dream brought no comfort at all.

The monster of every pup's nightmare faced him, hollowed sockets spiraling to bloody depths. The Forest Father was a lot bulkier now, and his fur bristled like a bear's thick hide during winter. "I've drawn you here through Bonechew's presence. As he slumbers, the hatred festering in his heart lures you to me."

"Why?" Silversong backed away as the Fallen Titan approached, stifling a whimper once the dreaded figure loomed over him. The monster grinned as if he'd found the perfect prey.

"Because you intrigue me." The Fallen Titan exposed row upon row of pointy fangs, breath smelling of rot. "You've seen the flaws of the Wolven Code, and yet you still oppose the exiles oppressed by it. I mean to understand why."

Silversong lowered his muzzle and tried to keep his snarl concealed. "Isn't it obvious? The exiles aren't looking to fix anything. They're only here to destroy a system embedded too deep in our society to be yanked out so carelessly. The Heretic understands this, so instead he'll force his reign on the Four Territories by wielding the powers of time. I can't let him cause so much death no matter how *noble* his cause is."

The eyeless hollows in the creature's face broadened. "An admirable stance, but you fail to understand how these exiles of yours were forced into this position. The Wolven Code constricted their free souls until they saw no alternative but the destruction of the system itself and its supporters. All this strife and pain is the result of countless seasons of oppression building up to a breaking point. Now the hour of reckoning is upon your species, and the only ones at fault for it are yourselves."

"No amount of oppression excuses the deaths of so many," Silversong growled, a dogged energy pushing against his fear. "There must be another way to fix things! We can amend the Wolven Code if we all work together!"

The Fallen Titan released a bellowing laugh. "Bonechew did say you were naïve. The type of change you're aiming for takes time to achieve, and the patience of the exiles is understandably… thinned."

"Can you speak to Rime?" Silversong took a pace forward, tail tip shaking against his belly. "He can convince the Heretic not to swallow the piece of time. He can convince the Heretic there's another way. Please! You have to try!"

The monster in front of him stared off to the side, smile fading, teeth retracting. "No. It won't matter. Everything is already set in motion, and there's nothing you can do to divert the coming storm." An awful snarl parted his mouth. "And the truth is, I think I'll enjoy watching the destruction of the Four Territories."

"Why?!" Silversong bared his teeth and growled. "You already lashed out against us long ago! You invaded every territory in an attempt to wipe us out, remember?!" He recalled the nightmares he'd endured as a pup because of older packmates telling him stories about the Fallen Titan and his cruel deeds. "You corrupted entire forests against us! You moulded unspeakable evils into existence and forced many of your own creations to carry out your cruelty. All the pain you inflicted on our species should've already satisfied your need for vengeance, but you've fallen so far from the beautiful being you once were. You can't even be bothered to try and fix things. You're so consumed by hate you can't even imagine a better future for us all. You're a disease infecting everything you touch. Maybe I was naïve to think you could change, to think there's still some good in you after everything you've done."

"It's as I said. The circle of time is already spinning, and none can stop its course." The Fallen Titan looked away, his expression on the brink of sadness without being remorseful. "The good in me has long since rotted into who I am now. It's too late for anyone to save me."

"No! It's not too late! You still have the power to change things!"

The Fallen Titan peered at the darkened sky and sucked in a deep breath. "I admire your optimism, but I've chosen my fate. Hate has always been my weakness. During the War of Change, I charged headfirst into an ambush the Forgotten Ones laid for me. They'd captured many of my creations and were torturing them to lure me out. Stormstrider warned me against taking action, but in the moment, I ignored his wisdom and attacked. I would've died from one of the contraptions my enemies made if Stormstrider hadn't jumped in front of the projectile before it pierced my heart." A black liquid leaked out of the Fallen Titan's eyes and scorched the ground. "After I caused the death of my closest friend, I surrendered to my crueller impulses. Soon the Forgotten Ones were exterminated, and most Titans departed your homeworld only to be locked in the realm they entered next. You wolves took over the continent, and then you began culling my mortal children. I couldn't suppress my rage. I couldn't let your greed go unpunished, and as the sentinels swarmed me and tore at my beating heart, I thought maybe… maybe death would put an end to my suffering."

Sticky lines of sap dripped out of the Fallen Titan's mouth. "But my spirit is still bound here, and I'm unable to join my friend wherever he gallops. I believe he still exists somewhere. I have to believe it! Even if the price he paid for the powers of time was his soul!" Silversong could swear the monster in front of him was on the verge of whimpering.

The Fallen Titan stomped his front hooves on the ground, sending tremors through the black earth. The faces embedded in every tree screeched so loud it caused lines of blood to trickle out of Silversong's ears. He dropped to the shriveled grass and squirmed, begging for the piercing sound to stop.

The Fallen Titan's voice echoed above the intolerable squealing. "All I have now is my hatred, and my only purpose is to welcome it. Look for the Heretic if you're so sure you can change things. He's already entered the underground ruin. Your time is running short."

"Wait!" Silversong bayed as his surroundings shifted and blurred out of focus. "You can still change! There's still hope!"

But the woods themselves faded, and so did the Fallen Titan. Silversong found himself sliding, falling, plunging into a depthless abyss. It gobbled him up and absorbed all he ever was, all he ever had been and would be. As time slipped out of thought, he became a mere particle drifting among the vastness of oblivion.

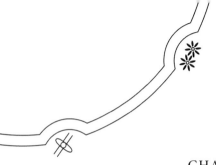

CHAPTER 13

✦

A Wolf Named Frostpaw

From far below, steady streams of light reached up to enfold Silversong and carry him beyond the realm of dreams. All feelings of loneliness and despair diminished into calming acceptance.

He opened his eyes to a yellow butterfly resting on his nose. The sensation tingled, and he braced himself for the coming of a sneeze. On instinct, he lifted his head and ejected a blast of air out of his nostrils. The insect took off, fluttering toward the forest too wary to encroach on the unnatural ruin. A lean vine uncurled from one of the structures and smacked the butterfly into a gunky splatter before wilting away.

Bonechew stood beside him, ears perked to the pinkish sky as Palesquall yawned some distance away from the exile. A crimson orb shyly hid itself behind a fleece of bleeding clouds. The dream was still hazy in the corners of Silversong's head, and he was starting to lose some of its details, but throughout the draining memories, one thing remained as palpable as the exile's scowl: fear.

The Fallen Titan spoke to me! He actually spoke to me! A tide of shivers puffed out his fur.

The thunder growling in his gut and the stinging pain in his cracked lips interrupted the cascade of thoughts. Hunger had drilled a hole into his stomach, a hole craving anything even slightly resembling food. It begged the obvious question: how long had they slept?

It can't be the next morning! How could it have been that long? But the sinking moon—silver against the bleeding sky—and the steady-rising sun contradicted his wishful claim.

"We've wasted far too much time here," the exile grunted, pacing side to side in a restless fashion, growling at nothing in particular. "Ugh, I can't believe we overslept! I promised myself I would only take a nap for a little while."

Palesquall shook off the dewdrops sticking to his fur and stretched nonchalantly. "Eh. I needed a good sleep myself."

Silversong's rumbling stomach attracted the exile's attention. Bonechew turned to face him. "Wait here while I fetch us something to eat. Then we make for the Mountainmouth at a trotting pace. Your friend is coming with me. Try not to attract any unwanted attention, little lamb."

"I am?!" Palesquall bristled.

"I'm not giving you a choice. I would be a gullwit if I trusted you two not to scheme behind my tail while I'm gone." Bonechew sniffed the air for a trace of prey scent. "Follow me."

"Wait!" Silversong barked, surprised at how gummy his mouth was. "I have to ask you something, Bonechew. Does the Fallen Titan sometimes… visit you in dreams?"

Palesquall tilted his head, and Bonechew gave Silversong a quizzical stare. "Since accepting his corruption inside me, since abandoning my inherited command over earth, I dream only of the place where he died. Sometimes, whenever I'm in a particularly foul mood, I can hear him whispering violent notions to me."

"And… is he whispering to you right now?"

Bonechew squinted. "Why, yes."

Silversong gulped. "What's he saying?"

"He's saying *quit answering this boulder-head's stupid questions!*" Bonechew grumbled under his breath and stalked off into the surrounding woods. Palesquall gave Silversong a reassuring nod before joining the cranky exile.

"I blame myself for falling for that," Silversong sighed.

He inhaled the air and tasted the wet, quiet morning on his tongue, still shaken at how quickly time had passed. On the eroded stone, brown slugs much larger than any he'd seen in the Breezeway moved like lagging waves, and little green critters that could've been mistaken for walking plants roamed in the bramble patches.

He craned his head up toward the Silverhaze Forest and Whistle-Wind Territory, envisioning Hazel and his other packmates fighting to free themselves from silky prisons while spiders slowly drained their blood.

They're alive! Chief Amberstorm must've woken up and rallied the others before fleeing the broken den. The spiders came after the survivors already left. I'm sure of it. He repeated that thought over and over until it quenched all stains of worry.

How were they faring at the moment? Would they ever recover even if the Heretic were brought to justice? An aching swell of shame pained his stomach and drowned his spirits. He pictured Pinetrail's impaled body jerking in its death throes and Elder Shrillbreeze bleeding out onto the snowy grass. Rage burned other feelings to cinders, but droplets of sorrow rained on the fire within, encouraging clouds of confused steam to dizzy him. He glanced at the yellow butterfly's crushed thorax and shook his head.

I won't become like the Fallen Titan. I won't let anger consume me.

Large dewdrops gathered on the vine leaves, and he lapped up all he could, vanquishing his thirst. Running his tongue along the sides of his mouth, he coated cracked lips in a mixture of saliva and water. He found a stretch of moist grass and rolled in it, dousing the bites and scratches all over his flesh. Upon inhaling, he pricked his ears at a strange yet familiar smell. His heartbeat raced, and he could feel his eyes broadening.

Another wolf?! I thought Bonechew said River-Stream wolves feared anything even remotely related to the Forgotten Ones! He veered to the forest and sniffed. Sure enough, the smell strengthened. *It's definitely a River-Stream wolf!*

"Oh, pricklethorn!" he cursed. Why was a River-Stream member awake so early? The sun had barely even stretched in the sky! *So much for not attracting any unwanted attention.*

He turned toward the ruin's main body and paced faster until he broke into a sprint, limbs still aching from yesterday's running. He skirted around the ashen-headed figure and charged out of another entrance. The broken homes of the Forgotten Ones here were made of fungi-infested wood. Clusters of white mushrooms, soaked in a viscous substance, emitted a pungent odour smelling of things that thrived on dead trees. He hoped the stink of the place would hide his scent trail.

From a thick veil of brambles and bracken in front of him, a large River-Stream male the colour of a deep blue lake pounced onto the battered road, snarling, hackles raised, crouched and ready to charge. He'd flanked him! Silversong whipped around in the direction of the rising sun and darted off. His pursuer was quick for his size, but the breeze was swifter. Silversong caught a stray current of air and connected himself to its sharp ferocity, willing it into a gale that guided his strides. He zipped through the waking forest, leaping over ferny plants, scurrying up steep slopes, then sliding down stark inclines while muddying himself up to his belly fur.

He halted in an open space of the woods where a small pool sparkled in the sun's ascending light. Invisible ants crawled all over his coat, and his heart dropped. He'd just given his pursuer a huge advantage! The water bulged into a see-through tendril and moved to squish him. He willed the air twirling around his body to slide him sideways, dodging the crashing water before it crushed him.

The large male emerged out of the trees, lips curled to reveal sharp fangs. Intense yellow eyes burned ferociously on an angry face. "Who dares trespass into River-Stream Territory?!" His voice was deep yet smooth.

"I dare!" Silversong slouched, tucking his tail as he eyed the wavy lines marking the male's sides, designed to resemble waves. He remembered Elder Shrillbreeze mentioning how River-Stream lieutenants used white mud on their coats to display their authority. This wasn't some stray subordinate of no importance growling before him, but a lieutenant!

Silversong sleeked his fur. "My name is Silversong. I'm a subordinate of Whistle-Wind! I'm here on urgent business. Listen. There're exiles lurking in your territory—"

Something cool and wet grabbed him by the scruff and yanked him up, shaking him like a misbehaving pup. He glanced over his shoulder, gasping as the tentacle of water suspending him over the glade froze into ice. He kicked and struggled, unable to do anything but look stupidly helpless. Embarrassment burned in his cheeks as he gulped. The stirred air around him danced away, obviously not wanting to participate in the humiliation.

The lieutenant approached in a hostile crouch, webbed forepaws brushing the soaked grass. "You've got until the moon is chased off by the sun to explain yourself, trespasser. Fail to give me a good reason for you being in my territory, and I'll take you to Chief Riptide, the honourable ruler of River-Stream."

Silversong tried to keep himself from bristling. There was no use in encouraging more agitation. He craned his head to the fading moon—a mere crescent slicing its way through the sky to flee

< 122 >

the scorching rays of the sun. "Umm, I may be more comfortable explaining things if maybe I wasn't dangling by the scruff."

The lieutenant scoffed and widened his snarl. "Whistle-Wind wolves really are sly talkers, aren't they? You're worse than ravens. Negotiating is only going to get you thrown into one of the boiling geysers at my den! Speak the reason for your intrusion, or we can get on to satisfying your death wish."

Anxious flies buzzed in Silversong's stomach, and he squirmed like a bee trapped in its own honey only to give up and droop loosely several tired breaths later. "Okay! Okay! I get it. Like I said, there're exiles in your territory. They escaped the Furtherlands, and they're being led by a former Stone-Guard member known as Ironwrath, the Heretic. His lieutenant, Tiderunner—I mean Rime—shattered the Great Chain by harnessing the Fallen Titan's corruption and unleashing it on the home of the sentinels."

At the mention of the Heretic's lieutenant, something flashed across his captor's eyes. Recognition, maybe? "Tiderunner," he almost growled out the name.

"Yeah. He also destroyed my den because the Empress of Spiders wanted her drones to retake the Breezeway. She commanded the Heretic to break us beyond repair." Silversong sucked in a breath, recalling the awful storm. "It's because they struck a bargain in the Silverhaze Forest. Ironwrath's goal is to bury the Wolven Code and become the ruler of all wolves. In return for crippling us, the Empress revealed to him where to look for an ancient weapon powerful enough to crush any opposition! The weapon is at the core of the Mountainmouth, but I'm here to make sure he never claims it. I'm on your side, sir! You've got to believe me!"

The lieutenant's eyes probed him for any trace of dishonesty. "You speak like an overexcited rookie who ate too many sugar berries. Start from the very beginning, and don't leave anything out." He ordered the tentacle of water to tighten, shooting a glance at the fading moon. "Don't worry. You still have time."

As demanded, Silversong spilled everything out. Mostly everything. He started at his failed chance to become a corporal, skimming over Gorsescratch's treachery and going straight to the attack on Wind's Rest. The lieutenant released a growl at the mention of Rime and his mastery over the Fallen Titan's corruption. Silversong explained the bargain between the Heretic and the

Empress in greater detail and why he chose to leave his packmates behind to save his friend and thwart the exiles. The River-Stream warrior flinched in surprise upon hearing of Silversong's mission to infiltrate the enemy, which led to his eventual capture by the spiders and his audience with the seductive Empress herself. He divulged all he'd gone through up until now, carefully omitting his dream about the Fallen Titan.

"Wow." The lieutenant's aggressive stance faltered. "Your story is too crazy to be a lie. Sounds like you've been through a lot."

"That's putting it mildly," Silversong released a sharp snort.

The frozen grasp around his collar melted into lukewarm liquid. He slipped out of its clutch and gave a brief cry before landing on all fours, shaking off drops of water. "Thanks."

"Like I said, no liar could possibly invent a story as crazy as yours." The lieutenant tilted his head, staring off to the side. "I'm sorry about your fallen packmates. They sounded like quite the fighters."

A bitter pressure squeezed Silversong's chest and made it difficult to breathe. He bit his lip to keep a whimper at bay.

The lieutenant waited a while before speaking again as if he too were immersed in a moment of sorrow. "You should've at least warned your packmates you were about to leave, and not just this *Gorsescratch* character. You broke so many rules in the Wolven Code by straight up abandoning your duty."

"This is my duty," Silversong affirmed, standing up to the larger male. "I shouldn't have to explain why I had to save my friend from the exiles."

"Fair enough." The blue wolf circled a forepaw around the blades of grass, sometimes shooting a brief look at Silversong. "So about your friend and your *caring escort…* we'll have to find them—"

Several thick roots erupted out of the earth and strangled the lieutenant as he yelped and squirmed. They wrapped around his throat and slowly putrefied into black strips, squeezing the air out of him. Bonechew padded into the open, a submissive Palesquall at his tail.

Silversong froze, his stomach twisting, his muscles hardening into stone. Bonechew and Palesquall neared him. An irritated scowl creased the exile's forehead. "I leave you alone for one moment, and already you've gotten yourself cornered by the enemy! Heh, at least we've found our snack for the day."

Palesquall and Silversong shared a panicked glance. The exile stopped beside the struggling lieutenant. "Finish this wretch and make it quick. If you're truly one of us, now's your time to prove it."

A frigid stream of fear washed over Silversong, paws numbing until it gave off the feeling as though he were standing on shifting clouds. He bared his teeth at the River-Stream member, whose eyes trembled within gaping sockets.

Silversong met Palesquall's gaze, and a moment of understanding passed between them. Silversong breathed in, emptying his head and connecting himself to the ever-changing pattern of the breeze. The instant of clarity granted him enough time to think. He needed Bonechew. He needed the exile to lead him into the Mountainmouth, but if it meant sacrificing an innocent life, could he do it? Lungs expanded to their limit, he envisioned his sister's pride-filled smile beaming bright on him.

Palesquall crouched as Silversong turned to face Bonechew, blowing out a condensed wave of air upon the exile, sending him flying into a nearby trunk. Bonechew yowled and crashed to the ground, snarling as he rushed to get up. Palesquall tore at the rotting shackles constricting the River-Stream lieutenant, helping him break free. Composure returning, the lieutenant hurried to stand beside Silversong. Together, they bared their fangs at the true enemy.

Saliva foamed around the exile's mouth, and his hateful glare revealed a frightening intent to cause pain just for the sake of it. He gave in to bloodlust and charged, leaping for Silversong. In the time it took to blink twice, the lieutenant willed the water of the pool up his body, solidifying it into frozen spikes atop him until he looked like a furry urchin. Frostpaw lunged beneath the exile and thrust upward just as Bonechew was about to land. Silversong cringed as the spikes impaled the exile, icy blades sticking out of bloodied fur.

The dripping blades melted into liquid unnaturally fast, slipping to refill the emptied pool. The lieutenant backpedalled, letting Bonechew tumble onto the grass. He writhed like a disturbed larva, cries of pain dwindling into sickly panting as death approached. After a futile struggle to cling to life, the exile calmed himself, accepting his own demise and wheezing sharply. "Heh," he coughed up a spray of red, "a poor choice you've made today, little lamb. The reckoning of the Four Territories is upon you, and you've chosen the side of oppression. Once Ironwrath… eats time itself… you'll see… you'll see…"

Bonechew's coughs became weaker and weaker until his body lay deflated in a pool of his own life-essence, tongue sagging, forepaws twitching. Silversong lowered his head. Despite everything, he'd hoped to redeem the exile in some way; he'd hoped for a better end for Bonechew.

Palesquall edged away from the punctured corpse to stand at Silversong's other side. "Good riddance."

The River-Stream wolf carefully strode to the exile's carcass and prodded it. He craned his head over his shoulder to look at Silversong. "Thanks."

"You're welcome!" Palesquall yipped before Silversong could respond. His limbs still shook like brittle bones.

The lieutenant tilted his head at the white subordinate. "I guess you also helped me." He turned to Silversong again. "For a moment, I thought you were on the exile's side." He nudged the corpse. "But it seems I can trust you, Silversong. My name's Frostpaw. I'm a lieutenant of River-Stream—"

"And I'm Pale—"

Silversong bumped his friend on the shoulder and silently begged for his silence. "I assumed your position from the painted waves on your sides, sir." He took in the strong scent of Frostpaw. Something about it smelled oddly familiar. His broad shoulders and defined muscles no doubt made him popular among the she-wolves, not to mention his handsome face and piercing yellow eyes. "I, uh, you're rather young to be a lieutenant, though. I'm guessing you're about the same age as me, maybe a few seasons older," he whined awkwardly.

Did I sound stupid? Oh, I hope not. He peered at his own claws so he wouldn't lose himself in Frostpaw's gaze. *My, those eyes are bright. It's like staring into the sun without the danger of getting blinded.*

Palesquall's snickering was hardly subtle. Silversong wanted to bite the cocky smirk off the gullwit's face.

"There's no need to refer to me as *sir*. We aren't packmates, after all." Frostpaw grunted a chuckle. "As for my age, I got promoted during winter for saving one of the Chief's daughters from a snowcat attack. Vicious beasts, those ones. And despite my

father's efforts to keep me as a corporal, I thankfully got promoted."
He trailed his nose along Silversong and Palesquall's coats, mouth
forming an amused smile. "Smart move, rubbing yourselves in my
scent markings to cover your true odours."

Palesquall shook his head briskly and snorted.

Silversong jerked his head up, fur puffed out as a flush of
heat rose to his cheeks. "The marking on the boulder was yours?!"
Upon catching the inquisitive look in the lieutenant's eyes, he
added, "I swear it wasn't our idea to rub ourselves in your—oh,
Motherwolf's mercy."

Palesquall grinned, his eyes lit by the spark of mischief. "Speak
for yourself. I, for one, love how oily his scent is. I'm sure rubbing
ourselves in it is going to attract so many potential mates."

Frostpaw broke into laughter.

Silversong aimed a heated glare at his friend. *Gross! He'll
think Whistle-Wind wolves are so weird now!* He dropped his gaze
in shame.

"I like your friend, Silversong." Frostpaw let out a couple more
laughs. "Palesquall, isn't it?"

"Yup!" Palesquall yipped proudly.

"Charmed." Frostpaw commanded the remaining water of
the pool to splash onto the three of them, washing their fur. After
shaking himself off, he walked to where the exile lay. "So, they came
through the Silverhaze Forest, you say?"

Silversong blinked at the blood-soaked corpse. "Yes."

Frostpaw snarled at Bonechew's body. "I can't believe they
managed to shatter the Great Chain. And here I was thinking my
usual morning stroll wouldn't be out of the ordinary. I have to
inform Chief Riptide about all of this."

"You do that," Silversong whined, pacing side to side. "But
I have to enter the Mountainmouth and foil the Heretic's plans
somehow—except you killed the only guide who could've taken
me there."

Frostpaw's white-tipped tail rose confidently. "I've been below
the shadow of the Mountainmouth before." He gave Silversong and
Palesquall a thoughtful, considering look. "Tide—I mean—Rime,
the Heretic's lieutenant. He's inside the underground ruin too?"

"I think so," Silversong grunted. "The Heretic keeps all his
followers close."

Frostpaw stared at the ground. "All right. I have an idea. I think we should—"

A growl from Frostpaw startled Silversong, and he tensed up alongside Palesquall, ears pricked and hackles stiff. But the lieutenant's fury wasn't aimed at them. Sniffing in the direction Frostpaw now faced, Silversong smelled two familiar scents growing stronger and stronger, one sweet and evoking a swell of pleasant memories, the other sharper and more bitter. Together, they blended into a conflicting mixture ruining the consistency of the forest's fragrance. A shifting in the nearby bramble patches silenced all other sounds. Time stopped, and Silversong's shoulders tightened until they ached.

Two wolves hopped over the lofty shrubs and into the glade, fur erect and fangs aimed at Frostpaw. It took several blinks for Silversong to believe his eyes. There in front of him stood Hazel and Gorsescratch, crouched and ready for battle.

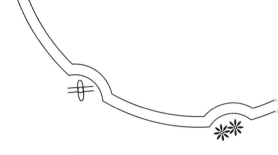

CHAPTER 14

CONFRONTATION

Windy projectiles met torrents of water. Silversong and Palesquall ducked to avoid the rain of serrated shards and deafening blasts as the two primal forces clashed in the name of chaos.

Frostpaw hurled blades of ice toward Hazel and Gorsescratch, but their shields of air cut the assault into sparkles of frost. Lashes from their tails struck at the lieutenant, who dodged and rolled to avoid every attack, getting closer and closer to the Whistle-Wind team. Swiping a forepaw sideways, he beckoned a line of spilled water to crash into Gorsescratch, breaking his defense and throwing him onto a trunk. The water froze and confined him there. Hazel erupted her winding shield. The blast stunned Frostpaw, making him lose balance. Hazel took advantage of the opportunity and jumped, teeth ready to plunge into flesh. But the River-Stream warrior lurched backward and summoned an icy spike to rise where Hazel was about to land.

"NO!" Silversong cried, the wind answering his desperate command and gathering at the tip of his tail. He wove it into a condensed string and whipped the spike, shattering it into countless fragments. Hazel landed, breath fleeing her lungs as she realized how close she'd come to getting impaled. "Hazel! Gorsescratch! Stop attacking! He's on my side!"

Gorsescratch struggled in his frozen prison. "As if I could attack from here!" He bit at the ice encasing him, but yelped every time his teeth smacked against the rigid surface.

Hazel's snarl returned, her glare fixed on the River-Stream lieutenant. "He almost killed me!"

Frostpaw ordered strands of water to slither like prowling snakes in her direction, tail still, teeth bared. "Hey! You're the one who attacked me like I'm some random exile!" He faced Silversong, keeping an eye on the other intruding wolves. "These your packmates, Silversong?"

"Yes, they are! Quit fighting, all of you!" he yapped, ready to leap in between Frostpaw and Hazel at any moment. The lieutenant calmed himself, but the water he controlled remained alert.

"Ahem," Palesquall coughed, tail wagging as he beamed at Hazel. "Bit of advice for you, Frostpaw. I recommend getting used to Hazel attacking you at random. Ruffle her fur even slightly, and she'll—"

Hazel rammed into him, knocking him over and licking his face as if it were a fresh bone. "YOU ABSOLUTE BUG-BRAINED GULLWIT! I THOUGHT YOU WERE DEAD! DO YOU HAVE ANY IDEA HOW WORRIED I WAS?!"

"Uh," Palesquall gave her a hesitant nuzzle, "sorry I got kidnapped?"

She broke into relieved whimpers and returned his affection. Gorsescratch eyed the two friends like an eagle eyeing a vulture who'd come a little too close to its prey.

You haven't told her. A twinge of pity for the bully pierced Silversong like a needle, followed by flaring frustration at having succumbed to pity in the first place. If anything, he should've been at least snarling at Gorsescratch if not outright growling at him! Someday he would confess his sabotage to every one of Silversong's packmates, and there would be a reckoning then. One look at Hazel returned Silversong to the here and now.

Silversong's heart couldn't take it anymore. He bounded toward his friends and piled atop them, knocking Hazel to the ground and licking her until his tongue ached. "Hazel! You're awake!"

"Great observation." Hazel's scowl would've made a starving bear think twice about attacking her. "I can't believe I'm saying this, Silversong, but you're more of a gullwit than Palesquall is! I get knocked out, and after I wake up, I have to learn from Gorsescratch of all wolves how you decided to prance off on some suicide mission?! DID YOUR BRAIN DROP OUT OF YOUR EARS ALL OF A SUDDEN?! IS YOUR HEAD FILLED WITH NOTHING BUT AIR NOW?!"

Silversong shrank in on himself. "That would explain why I feel so light-headed."

Palesquall choked on a chuckle. "Good one, Silversong."

Silversong peered into Hazel's leafy green eyes, his heart pulled into a pit of guilt by her worried, angry face. "I'm sorry, Hazel. I'm so sorry I worried you. But I had to save Palesquall. And I had to do something about the Heretic."

Her mouth quivered, and she buried herself in his fur. "Don't you EVER scare me like that again! Or I promise you the exiles are going to be the least of your worries."

Palesquall shivered at Hazel's promise. "Better be careful, Silversong…"

Frostpaw relinquished control over the snakes of water. "So, do Whistle-Wind wolves have no respect for the Wolven Code anymore? Are there any other intruders lurking in the bushes, maybe?" He sniffed around as if to make sure. "Next I'll learn your entire pack is wandering around somewhere in my territory."

"About that…" Gorsescratch whined, gulping as the lieutenant whirled to face him. Silversong almost hopped in surprise, and Palesquall gasped.

"Oh, Motherwolf's mercy, you've got to be joking!" Frostpaw stared disbelievingly at the four intruders. "I understand your den is destroyed and your territory is overrun by spiders, but was it really necessary to bring ALL the survivors here?! Couldn't you have gone to the Freelands or something? I mean seriously!"

The pounding in Silversong's chest was so loud it was a wonder it hadn't caused an earthquake. "They're in River-Stream?! Chief Amberstorm? Mother? Father? All of them? How are they? Are they okay?"

"How very considerate of you to ask." The look Hazel gave him almost knotted his tongue. "Don't even get me started on how worried your parents are. They're afraid Swiftstorm might be dead, and you still abandoned them."

Silversong looked away, his breath stopping itself before leaving his throat. He thought if the mildest breeze came by, it still would've tipped him over.

Thankfully, Gorsescratch released a few raspy grunts before Hazel could spill more of her boiling anger. "Chief Amberstorm regained consciousness before the spiders attacked. Upon assessing the situation, he organized groups of subordinates and corporals to come look for you and Palesquall. The lieutenants were tasked to protect the others on their journey here. Chief Amberstorm believes River-Stream and Whistle-Wind should become allies for the time being in the face of this calamity. The Wolven Code allows these temporary alliances if the situation is dire. I think we can all agree it is."

"Chief Riptide is to decide that, not Chief Amberstorm," Frostpaw grunted through a snarl. "For your sake, I pray my leader allows this infraction of the Wolven Code."

Hazel pushed Silversong off her and moved up to the River-Stream lieutenant as if she were his superior. "The sentinels are gone. Our den is shattered. The spiders have claimed our beloved forest, and you're telling us your *Chief* may have us killed for code-breaking?! There's no more Great Chain, so I assume a painful execution is the only punishment for code-breakers now. But we won't stand for it! Even though we've been driven out of our territory, Whistle-Wind won't ever be extinguished. Not while there're still wolves who share the values of our founder."

Palesquall screwed up his eyes and exhaled. "Wow. Riveting speech, Hazel. It really got my blood pumping."

Silversong gawked proudly at her, his sense of duty to Whistle-Wind and all it stood for rejuvenated tenfold.

"Admirable," Frostpaw mumbled, still uncertain about the rival wolves lurking in his territory. "But in the end, my Chief has the final say, as the Wolven Code dictates. Now, as I was saying before being unceremoniously attacked, we should discuss our course of action from here on."

"Yeah, we should." Hazel stared at the punctured corpse of Bonechew. "Good to see at least one faithless scatfur got his comeuppance." She turned to those she'd been tasked to look for. "Gorsescratch and I are to escort you to the River-Stream den. No excuses."

Silversong stiffened at the same time Palesquall woofed, "no way!"

Hazel's jaw dropped in outrage. "Yes, way! We've been given clear orders by Chief Amberstorm to bring you to—"

"I'm afraid I can't let you take them, Hazel," Frostpaw interrupted, the white tip of his tail twitching. "They're on track to bringing the exiles and their vicious leader to justice, and I aim to join their noble cause."

"WHAT?!" the four Whistle-Wind wolves exclaimed together.

"No, no, no, no," Silversong barked in rapid succession. "I'm going to the Mountainmouth alone. I'm not risking your life or Palesquall's. I'm the one who gained the Heretic's trust—or at least partly—so only I can get close enough to finish him."

"You're insane!" Hazel growled. "And what's this *Mountainmouth* of yours, anyway?!"

"It doesn't sound like anything good!" Gorsescratch grumbled, still trying to wriggle out of his frozen barrier.

"I'm coming too!" Palesquall yipped. "The Heretic thinks I can be turned to his side, so it makes sense for the two of us to go together, Silversong."

"Yes, it makes sense." Frostpaw narrowed his gaze and focused on something Silversong couldn't see. "But I figured out a way to greatly increase our chances of killing the Heretic. I'll pretend you two subdued me and act as your prisoner while inside the underground ruin. I can lead you there, by the way, and once the three of us corner the Heretic alone, we'll strike together."

"And Bonechew?" Palesquall asked. "We'll have to explain why he isn't guarding us like he was tasked to do."

"You can say the spiders got him. Or you can say I killed him, but you two bested me afterwards," Frostpaw suggested. "Either way, he's a flea flung from our fur."

Countless scenarios in which things could go horribly wrong played out in Silversong's head, but the lieutenant's suggestions couldn't be ignored. Frostpaw was now the only one who could lead him to the Mountainmouth, after all. But Silversong still had to rid himself of Palesquall, somehow. He couldn't allow his friend to put himself in danger. Not after he was free of his captors.

"I'll agree to your proposal, Frostpaw. On one condition." Silversong padded forward and put himself in the middle of the small gathering, away from the pool of water. He motioned for Frostpaw to come closer and whispered in his ear, "we go together. Me and you, or not at all. Do you understand?"

Frostpaw blinked twice before the look Silversong wanted to see spread across the lieutenant's face. He flicked his tail and inclined his head, scanning his surroundings, paying close attention to the trees and the stalks. Something stirred inside them.

Gorsescratch gave a few wide-eyed blinks. "Hey, puppy-eyes. How about you convince this fish-licker here to unfreeze me? I can barely feel my own limbs anymore."

"*Fish-licker*?" Frostpaw tilted his head to one side, unsure whether to be amused or insulted. "Why, I—"

"He does that." Silversong steered Frostpaw's attention away from the bully and toward more pressing things. "Once he decides a nickname for you, he'll stick to it until the sun and moon switch positions from which they rise. Now, we should probably shake off these other fleas from our fur." He hated referring to his packmates as *fleas*, but if they trailed him to the Mountainmouth, they would be stepped on by the exiles without question. He couldn't allow it. The thought of losing his friends drowned his returning hunger.

Hazel gasped, obviously catching on to Silversong's intentions. She prowled closer to him. "No! You're not leaving without us. You're not!" she growled, preparing to pounce on him.

The look in Frostpaw's eyes said he was ready, and Silversong crouched and smiled at his friends one final time. "I'm sorry you two, but… I'm not allowing the Heretic even the smallest opportunity to take your lives. NOW, FROSTPAW!"

Blasts of water erupted out of the trees and girthy stalks, entangling together like roots and enveloping Hazel and Palesquall before they could beckon the wind for protection. Frostpaw lifted them up to the surrounding trees, their heads poking out of the liquid shells before he froze them onto separate trunks. At least Frostpaw had imprisoned his friends in more comfortable positions than Gorsescratch.

"Oh, you've got to be kidding me!" barked the bully.

"I'm sorry," Silversong uttered again, heart racing, legs shaking.

"Silversong! Oh, by Motherwolf!" Palesquall yowled in his frozen confines. "Is this how betrayal feels? Silversong, why?!"

"SILVERSONG!" Hazel yapped, but he was too scared to meet her eyes. "ORDER THE RIVER-STREAM LIEUTENANT TO RELEASE US RIGHT NOW!"

Her risen voice ripped into the marrow of his bones and wrenched his stomach. "You'll be unfrozen eventually, don't worry. I had to make sure you wouldn't try and follow me." His whines quavered as he tried to swallow rising whimpers. "I promise we'll see each other again, and the day we do, I'll have beaten the Heretic." He forced himself to sound more certain than he was.

Frostpaw addressed the trapped wolves. "Once you're released, head to the Saltshore, the den of River-Stream, and inform Chief Riptide of my absence. I'm sure he'll understand. And if my father—" he stopped to stare at his own claws again. "Forget it." He turned and ran through the forest, signaling for Silversong to follow.

Silversong collected his scattered thoughts and sprinted after the lieutenant as Hazel and Palesquall begged for him not to leave. He blocked out their pleas and curses and clenched his jaws, refusing to look over his shoulder. *I put myself on this path, and now I must follow it until the end.*

✦

CHAPTER 15

Into the Mountainmouth

Although Silversong was far enough away now from where he'd abandoned his packmates, their cries of outrage and betrayal still haunted his ears. Hazel's furious face and Palesquall's wounded eyes were all he could think about as he trailed Frostpaw through the breathing forest.

The two rolled in an oily plant known as bleakthorn to hide their scents in case Hazel and Palesquall decided to come look for them once their icy prisons melted. Gorsescratch would probably give up. His laziness when it came to chasing prey was almost legendary; he mostly counted on others to do the chasing for him.

He still hasn't told Hazel why he was always so mean to me. Silversong dragged his claws through the soil, allowing old hatreds to sprout from where he'd scattered those seeds. *Gorsescratch seems to have changed a little, though. Maybe he really is trying to be a better wolf, but I won't even consider forgiving him until he confesses his sabotage to everyone.*

Silversong focused on the diverse sounds and beauty thriving around him, but the flood of regret swamped his already downcast mood. The roar of raging waters grew louder, but so did the ghostly barking of his friends.

"Beautiful, isn't it?" Frostpaw savoured a breath of clean air. Silversong did the same and tasted the sweet and strong aromas permeating his surroundings. "My ancestors named this place the Songwoods because you can hear a different sound each time you point your ears to the sky. I come here to get away from the bustle at the den. The forest has a way of helping you forget your troubles."

Silversong's ear fur stirred at the croak of a raven and the chirping of talkative jaybirds. "It does seem… liberating?" The breeze whistled through the branches and brushed the thick canopy of leaves shading them from the blistering heat. "Your ancestors could've called it the *Sound*woods, though. Would've made more sense if you think about it."

"Hah!" Frostpaw panted and bumped him on the flank. Silversong almost tripped over his own forepaws at the unexpected contact. "Good thing they were a little more inspired at naming things than you are." Frostpaw's nose wrinkled as he caught a whiff of the bleakthorn they'd rolled in. "I'll have to bathe us again before we enter the Mountainmouth. We smell like greasy crabs!"

A torrent of blue rushed in the opposite direction they padded, and in its course glinted tiny pearls lining the bottom. Silversong and the lieutenant slowed to a trotting pace along the river's edge. It wasn't as wide nor as deep as the Running River, but by Motherwolf, it was swift, its sides foaming as the current sliced a winding route to the sea.

According to Frostpaw, four streams broke out of the river's main body, each spaced far enough apart to tire any wolves who made the journey between them, each teeming with different species of crabs and fish. Sometimes, if hunting patrols were lucky, their keen noses would sniff out an extremely skittish type of deer known as *watersnouts*, which apparently had seaweed strips for manes and tasted similar to trout. Silversong wanted to see one while they travelled to the Mountainmouth not only because his stomach constantly reminded him of how hungry he was, but because it would be exciting to discover a new type of prey.

"She's quite feisty, your other friend." Frostpaw's deep voice made a few strands of fur stand at attention. "You're still thinking about her, aren't you?"

He stopped for a moment and considered how Hazel would react if he never came out of the Mountainmouth. Gorsescratch's tail would probably wag in celebration. Silversong gritted his teeth and continued forward. *I've come too far now to quit.* He squinted at the sun slowly dipping behind him, hoping his packmates would be granted refuge at the River-Stream den.

They padded for a while along the narrow shore rimming the river until the pain of regret dulled. Silversong couldn't remember how the conversation had started, but he found himself listening to the lieutenant flaunting his pride in River-Stream, unveiled patriotism clear in his tone. Silversong questioned how Frostpaw could think *his* pack was superior to the other four. Obviously Whistle-Wind had them all beaten! Silversong shook himself, recalling how the Wolven Code encouraged division between the territories as a way of ensuring loyalty only to packmates.

"Wait, wait, wait," Silversong interrupted the lieutenant on one of his tangents. "You actually teach your pups to swim when they're only a season old?!" *Motherwolf's milk! Won't they drown?!*

"We do!" Frostpaw yipped. "We need to familiarize them to water as soon as we can. The sooner you allow the water's touch to caress your body, the sooner you'll be able to wield its potential. Once this connection is achieved, whenever you're near a lake, a river, or an ocean, you'll feel the comfort of home in your heart. You'll feel the movement of the water within you as if you were the water itself. To command it, listen rather than feel. Listen to the nearby stream flowing on a steady course, listen to the waves crashing on a distant shore, listen to the motion of blood in every vein, every muscle, every heart. Water is the instrument of life, and if you respect the way it flows, it'll be your greatest ally."

Silversong strained his ears to listen like the lieutenant had suggested. He thought he heard something hidden in the raging of the river, in the current smoothing countless pebbles and stones. Music! No, a voice! But he banged into a barrier before he could hear it more clearly. It was like listening to an alien language so foreign he couldn't hope to understand it. Not if he had an eternity to study it.

They padded along the flower-ridden shore, petals of violet and blue captivating the eye. Leafy bushes sprouted near the rising earth, some bearing orange berries smelling of sour apples. Silversong also detected strange plants he'd never seen or scented before and wondered if they were used as medicine by the Wise-Wolves here.

He sniffed the shoreline, leaving deep prints in the moist soil where the flowers dwindled. For some reason, Bonechew clawed his way into his thoughts. "Hey. Do you… sometimes think the Wolven Code is… too stern on us?"

The lieutenant gave a snort as the river's spray sprinkled their coats. "It's not stern enough, apparently, since code-breakers everywhere still exist." His sharp eyes descended on Silversong. "Ah, don't worry. The First Warden was wise to establish rules for every territory to follow after she defeated the Fallen Titan—a problem our lawless ancestors created."

Silversong avoided looking at Frostpaw. "The Heretic seems to think the Wolven Code isn't so good. That it's imperfect, even evil."

"Hence his title." Frostpaw tensed beside him. "He thinks it's oppressive, so what?! It's ensured peace and order in all territories since the Fallen Titan's defeat. It's ensured morality and honour within wolves who follow it closely, and it's ensured balance— all things the Heretic threatens. It's clear he's the misguided villain here."

"Is it?" Silversong added more pressure to every step. "Maybe it's the tyranny of the Wolven Code that created him. Maybe because it's so intolerant, someone eventually had to take a stance against it."

The lieutenant screwed up his eyes in suspicion. "You think the Wolven Code ought to be amended? Even after all the good it's done?"

"I think as long as we keep banishing wolves who don't think like us, we'll create more conflict for ourselves." Silversong's heart banged against his chest, the blood in his ears pulsing. He shouldn't even be thinking about saying these things, but it came out before he could close his muzzle. The Heretic overcame all other thoughts. "I think we should strike a balance between chaotic freedom and stern order, between tradition and growth. Because if we continue like this without the necessary change, we'll stagnate into oblivion."

"Those thoughts are only going to distance you from wolves you care about, Silversong." Frostpaw released a heavy breath. "Better keep them to yourself."

"That only proves my point." Silversong contemplated the injustices done to Bonechew and the Heretic and countless other wolves.

The heat worsened, and they decided to take a short break, walking along a slender brook straying from the main current. Schools of salmon thrived along its clear length, their green-grey scales tempting Silversong for a bite. He hopped into the water like a fox leaping before diving into deep snow for a chance at catching unseen prey.

His teeth clasped onto one of the fatter salmon. He pulled it out and killed it swiftly, feasting on its tender and salty flesh, filling his empty stomach. He turned to Frostpaw for approval. Bees buzzed in his gut, and he realized his tail was wagging like that of a rookie hoping to please an older packmate.

The lieutenant blinked at him and swept a forepaw to the side. A breath later, the water spewed several salmon just as large as the one Silversong had caught. They piled in front of Frostpaw and flopped atop one another. He aimed a satisfied glance in Silversong's direction.

There's no way River-Stream wolves can ever go hungry if they're able to do stuff like that! Silversong tried not to look impressed. "Hmph. I'm still proud of my catch," he whined in a playful tone.

"You should be. That's an impressive dive you just did." Frostpaw panted, breath smelling of the sea. "As graceful as a fox. Heh, you even look somewhat like one from a distance."

"Thanks, fish-breath," Silversong teased. "Wolves like me have to put in some effort to catch prey."

The lieutenant's ears perked up, and for an awkward moment Silversong thought he may have insulted him. "*Fish-breath?* Ugh, you make it sound so gross. I would actually prefer it if you called me fish-licker or *sir.*"

"As you command, sir fish-licker," Silversong chuckled.

Frostpaw grimaced, dipping his forepaws into the stream and giving Silversong a playful glare, bright eyes glinting mischievously. "No, wait, I—"

A sudden wave smacked into Silversong, and he rolled onto his side, hurrying to get up as the freezing water gnawed at his bones. He shook until his fur puffed out like a porcupine's quills, deliberately spraying Frostpaw in the process. The breeze latched onto Silversong's tail, and he gently whipped the lieutenant's snout, careful not to cause him any real pain.

Frostpaw yelped lightly and backpedalled, laughing. "All right, we're even. Now let's dig in."

Though Frostpaw was a lieutenant, his youthful energy hadn't been stripped from him yet. He reminded Silversong of his father a little.

After their plentiful meal, they tossed the remains in the brook and continued on their journey. Soon oaks and alders were at their tails, and ahead, beyond a stretch of thick grass, climbed a jagged slope of rocky shelves descending from looming mountains above—a ridge of sparkling frost. Cutting between the stark rise was the violent beginning of the territory's river. It thundered through the snowy crags, never once tempering its mighty rage.

They loped through the grass trailing the edge of the forest and sprang onto the rugged rise beside the roaring channel, finding small platforms where they could stand without slipping.

Silversong moved in front of the lieutenant, scurrying upward as the icy spray chilled him to the marrow. He shivered, and his teeth clattered. The glacial temperature was almost unbearable. He wondered if Flame-Heart wolves could've conjured a blanket of fire to shield themselves from the river's frigid wrath. Frostpaw appeared wholly unaffected by it.

"Hey," Silversong whined to keep himself from focusing on the freezing droplets. "A twitch of my whiskers says you're not helping me because of some honourable sense of duty."

Frostpaw struggled as he climbed, slipping a couple times thanks to his size, but he always commanded the water to save him before he tumbled. "You're wrong. Duty is one of the only reasons why I'm helping you pursue these exiles."

Silversong stopped on one of the narrower shelves, muscles cramping. "You afraid your den is going to end up like mine if you don't do something? You got wolves to protect at home? Wolves threatened by the Heretic's ambition?"

"Heh. Who doesn't?" Frostpaw released a neutral growl.

"Friends? A mother? A father?" Silversong leaped onto another uneven surface, hoping to escape thoughts of his parents worrying about him.

"Friends, siblings, and a father." His whine was so silent it could've been mistaken for a distant echo. "My mother died when I was a pup. She was a brave lieutenant who always lived true to the Wolven Code, and she followed her sense of justice until the end."

Silversong flattened his ears and peered at the ground. "I'm sorry."

"Don't be," the lieutenant sighed. "Now she's howling alongside Motherwolf."

On one of the platforms, the smell of wolves was strong. Silversong sniffed harder, ignoring the frothing waters. The Heretic's scent was mingled there, and Rime's, and Ripper's. Frostpaw inspected the scents too, taking the time to memorize each. Silversong's heartbeat picked up its pace, and a tingly feeling wriggled in his gut. He climbed faster up the slope.

Sleet crunched under each paw as they pulled themselves onto the base of the ridge, its frost-touched peaks reaching far off, clawing into the clouds. Prints of varying sizes marked the snowy ground here, and patches of yellow stained the perfect whiteness in some places. They snuffled at each of them, following the pungent scent trail up to a gaping mouth carved into the face of one of the mountains.

A twinge of anxiety passed from nose to tail as Silversong turned to Frostpaw. "This is it, isn't it? The Mountainmouth."

"It is." Frostpaw squinted at the outthrust shape of the entrance, studying the symbols carved on its stone. They were crude and straight, never once curving. Silversong wondered if they meant anything.

They edged closer to the huge mouth that made the mountain look as if it were screaming in silent horror. Silversong stretched out his head and sniffed the murky darkness, detecting only a trace of metal and other bizarre odours belonging to the deep places.

A cutting breeze pushed them from behind, forcing them to lean unwillingly into the shadowy mouth. Was it the tug of destiny? Or was it the very lungs of the mountain drawing them into its forsaken bowels?

When I come out of the totally not-so-scary ruin, I'll be alive and victorious! I won't fail, and I won't flee!

A deep, resonating voice echoed in his ears and bounced off the inside of his skull, engulfing every other sound. **"You, who stand before my prison. I glimpse your thoughts. I glimpse your purpose."** His fur stiffened into thorns, and chills colder than the river itself cascaded along his spine. **"Come, child of Motherwolf. Come into the decayed bowels of carven stone. Come into the buried pride of those who once ruled this realm."**

Silversong crouched, tucked his tail, flattened his ears, and barked loud enough for the clouds to hear. "Who's there?!"

"GAH!" Frostpaw yowled and hopped in shock, bristling afterwards. "Who's where?!" He sleeked his fur and tried to look tough despite yelping like a scared little pup a moment ago.

The booming voice never answered. Silversong slowly recovered from his fright and inhaled deeply, fighting to banish the creeping tide of horror. "N-nothing. Thought I heard something, is all. It's nothing, really." He desperately wished his lie had been true.

He closed his eyes and prayed. *Motherwolf. If you're out there, if you're watching, if you care, don't take your eyes off me in the darkness. Light my courage aflame and keep all doubts at bay.*

As Frostpaw's fur brushed comfortingly against his, he forced himself forward. The lieutenant followed, and the gaping mouth of darkness swallowed them whole.

CHAPTER 16

✦

Ͳhe Forgotten Ones

Silversong sniffed his way deeper and deeper into the mountain's throat, his tail sometimes stroking Frostpaw's nose. Even though he wasn't a fellow packmate, he proved better than having no company at all.

There's another reason you're here, though. You're hiding something behind that heroic face of yours.

Silversong shivered whenever he lifted a paw off the cool, even floor, and though nothing could be seen beyond his own muzzle, he guessed they were walking in a massive corridor due to the consistency of the air and the faint echoes of their steps. His eyes eventually adjusted to the perpetual darkness, and he turned his head side to side, confirming his assumptions.

Walls of grey stone reached higher than his eyes could make out, and carved near the floor were squared hollows each a tree's length in stature and a tail-length apart. Pillars rose within them, intricately designed and bearing more of those markings he'd seen etched on the ruin's mouth. Of their significance or purpose, he couldn't say.

The rushing of the river outside, once a howling roar, now dwindled into a soothing hum that could only be heard if he pointed his ears in a particular direction.

"I'm assuming we're among the only wolves brave enough to enter here." Silversong's whine echoed throughout the seemingly unending chamber.

"Or foolish enough," Frostpaw whispered, but it was still shockingly loud. His voice cut through the silence like a draft blowing through a once still meadow. "There's a reason we're usually forbidden from exploring places like these. Many believe them to be haunted by the vengeful spirits of the Forgotten Ones."

Silversong grunted, trying to sound as tough as Frostpaw. "There aren't many ancient ruins in Whistle-Wind Territory, so my packmates don't have to worry about accidentally stumbling into one. Crows and ravens love them, though. Can't imagine why." The expansive emptiness made him feel alone, and anxious. Anything hidden in the shadows could be watching him—maybe even the source of the booming voice he'd heard outside—and so he hoped to postpone thinking about unseen eyes and the horror of utter isolation by filling the hungry silence with idle conversation.

"I have to wonder." Frostpaw gazed up as if trying to glimpse the ceiling masked by a staggering height. "According to the legends, the Forgotten Ones accomplished building wonders no beasts like us could hope to comprehend. If they could achieve such things, how did they perish in the end?"

Silversong remembered the tales the corporals had used to frighten him as a rookie. "No matter how advanced you are, nothing can prepare you for an army of angry Titans determined to destroy everything you've built." He sometimes dreamed he stood there, howling his pride alongside Motherwolf's generals—Whistle-Wind, River-Stream, Flame-Heart, and Stone-Guard—and fighting against the onslaught of two-legged monsters for the glory of the wolves. As a pup, he used to pretend he was Whistle-Wind herself, the *hero* who drove the spiders out of the Breezeway and claimed it for her loyal followers.

After a lengthy pause, Frostpaw's nose poked him on the cheek. "So, you got any *special friend* among your packmates?"

The question caught him off guard. "Hmm?"

"Come on, don't play the innocent gullwit." Frostpaw gently shouldered him.

Silversong tried to escape the lieutenant's regard but couldn't. The bubbles of awkwardness popped in his gut.

"So, is it Hazel who makes your tail wag without you noticing?" Frostpaw's yap had an amused tone to it. "You two seem to care a great deal about each other."

"No!" Silversong bristled, his cheeks on the verge of bursting into flames. "Just because we care about each other doesn't mean we're anything beyond friends! And to answer your stupid question, no wolf interests me. Not romantically, at least." A heavy weight nestled itself deep inside him. Hazel's smile plagued every thought. They could never be more than what they already were. It wouldn't feel right.

"If you say so." Frostpaw loosened his tensed shoulders. "I admire your restraint, but you're aware that even though you're a subordinate, it doesn't mean you're not allowed to love. You can't be a father, as dictated by the Wolven Code, but you can still have a mate. It's a bit like the sentinels, except I heard they imbibe a nasty concoction that permanently ensures they don't accidentally have litters."

Silversong fixed his eyes to the floor, focusing on its bland perfection. Peculiar twitches in his stomach thwarted any attempt at taking a normal breath. She-wolves and romance weren't exactly things he imagined himself chasing. Not during these times, especially.

"Oh, fine." Frostpaw released a defeated grunt. "Go on and play the brooding hero. You've got the perfect face for it. And who knows? Maybe you'll get swept away by the tide of love during your adventure."

Silversong chuckled, the sparks inside him cooling themselves. "Doubt it." He nudged Frostpaw's shoulder casually. "And you? You're a young and handsome lieutenant. I'll bet you've got many she-wolves eager for your eyes to take notice of them."

Frostpaw grinned. "There're a few potential suitors, I'll admit."

A few, eh? Silversong wrinkled his forehead, his stomach coiling itself into a sour loop. Any of the younger she-wolves of Whistle-Wind would've been swooning over someone like Frostpaw if he were their packmate.

Frostpaw continued, "but I'm not ready to make a decision yet on who I should burden for life," he laughed.

"Honestly, I'm grateful I'm not as good-looking as you. I don't think I could suffer all the attention she-wolves would be giving me." He stopped and stiffened, realizing he'd spoken his thoughts aloud. A searing heat numbed his face, and his tail tip quivered as it straightened itself out. Anger overtook embarrassment. *Gullwit! You can't feed the ego of a rival! He'll think Whistle-Wind wolves are nothing but tail-lickers now!*

Frostpaw's eyes were like orbs of sunshine lighting the darkness, and a satisfied smirk stretched his lips. Silversong gulped and looked away as if the lieutenant's gaze would blind him. "Heh, how flattering," Frostpaw whined. "She-wolves of River-Stream usually prefer leaner males, though. I think you would've been quite the popular choice if you were our packmate. Your blue eyes would certainly appeal to many."

"Really?" Silversong almost barked it out, eager to make the lieutenant forget everything he'd heard.

"I think so. Your eyes remind me of the lake overlooked by my den. A blue so striking it makes sapphires seem pale in comparison," Frostpaw whistled warmly, drawing Silversong's attention. The blazing yellow of Frostpaw's gaze seemed to encompass the reflection of Silversong's deep blue like sunstruck whirlpools surrounding lonely gemstones. For several heartbeats the two stood still, locked in time's clutches.

In the fiery confusion, Silversong couldn't shake off the feeling that all of this had already happened before and would happen again, as if his fate and Frostpaw's were woven into a circle spinning endlessly.

An outside draft cut through the moment of stillness. Frostpaw backpedalled slightly and swallowed, limbs shaking and fur standing erect, but Silversong had a feeling it wasn't because of the sudden coolness. The lieutenant stared off to the side. "We should probably get moving. Let's try and keep quiet from now on, all right? If the exiles are still lurking around here, it's better if we don't advertise our presence to the entire ruin."

"Agreed." Silversong averted his focus from Frostpaw, trying not to make his quivering too obvious. He breathed in and out to temper the heat engulfing his heart until dizziness took over. He found counting his steps to be another, less headache-inducing solution.

They came to a two-legged figure of stone standing proud on a raised block, shielded top to bottom in silvery coverings. It looked terribly uncomfortable. The creature's face was stern and smooth, and curly strands depicting hair sprouted around its mouth and ended near the throat. One forelimb was angled to a plated chest, and in its strange forepaw was clutched a small pole-like object fastened to a cross, and from it tapered a tooth of iron pointed downward. Its other forelimb was extended before the body, furless paw outstretched as if it were pushing something.

It wore a circle of silver around its head in which eight hollowed holes were dented, small enough for an acorn to fit snuggly in each. An image of the Empress and the pale blue orbs illuminating her lair outshone every other thought. Had her subjects stolen those jewels from this place?

The Empress said there're things treacherous even to Titans here. Silversong sniffed the darkness cautiously. *But so far we've seen nothing but emptiness.*

"This is one of them, isn't it?" Frostpaw stared in awe at the effigy. "A Forgotten One. Look at its pathetic muzzle and feeble claws! They must've been terrible hunters."

Silversong studied the tooth-like thing it grasped. "If they were as crafty as the Empress suggested, I'm sure they found ways to outmatch any claws or teeth."

"I suppose so." Frostpaw sniffed at the carved stone warily. "And I suppose they must've been pretty dangerous if the Titans joined forces to wipe them out."

To wipe most of them out. Silversong reminded himself about the remaining Forgotten Ones who disappeared deep in Stone-Guard Territory, within a ruin of bronze.

Behind the effigy, wide, flattened steps plunged further into unknown depths, slanting like the now apparent ceiling. Silversong lifted his muzzle and took in the stale air. The exiles had been here, but their scents had slightly faded. Something about the pit of blackness captivated the eye, like it was daring him to plunge into its embrace. He fought the notion and clung to his instincts.

Despite the dry trail, they descended the dusty shelves, dipping further and further into the abyss. The slanted ground stretched endlessly, and just when Silversong thought they might never reach the bottom, his paws landed on a level surface. He struggled not to tip over; the even floor was disorienting after being on an incline for so long. The blackness thickened here, and no matter how he screwed up his eyes, not a single strand of fur on either himself or Frostpaw could be seen. The lieutenant pressed against him, and the contact inspired a sense of safety. It reminded Silversong he wasn't utterly alone here. Together, they moved at an equal pace, relying on their noses to lead them over obstacles and through tunnels or narrow pathways.

For the length of countless breaths, they walked in the cold bowels of stone. Silversong wondered how the Forgotten Ones ever managed to navigate through their own maze of darkened hallways and winding tunnels. Maybe they had bat-like ears and used sound rather than sight to orient themselves. Though the black veil hindered his vision, other senses took over. Now he could hear the faint *tap*, *tap*, *tap* of falling droplets and smell an earthy scent wafting ahead.

The scent trail ended at the start of another passage. This one was dimly lit by blue-glowing critters of many limbs, each coiled around rocky columns hanging like teeth from the jagged ceiling. Drops of stale water dripped from their ends and formed small pools in the dented floor, and on the watery surfaces, the pearly shells of the insects above rippled like tiny flickering sparks.

At the far end of the eroded cave was a set of curving steps, this time leading upward, devoured by moss and cracked like the fissured ground before them. Another figure stood there, holding an outthrust tooth of metal. It stirred a familiar memory.

The smell of the exiles ended here, consumed by a rusty aroma and something akin to the reek of the Whispering Hollow. Silversong assumed the Heretic must've carried on through the abraded corridor. The pungent odour of the critters and the wet floor could've clouded his scent, and it wasn't like there was any other way forward.

Moving alongside Frostpaw, Silversong avoided the pools as the tapping droplets echoed all around. Mossy tendrils riddled every cleft in the ground, and an assembly of fallen pillars lay defeated at the centre, weathered by age or the wrath of the mountains.

Luminescent crickets hopped about whenever they came near a cluster of them. Silversong made sure his strides were careful and not too heavy. After an eternity of wary walking, they came under the regard of the figure standing before the steps. The effigy stood in a crooked stance, deprived of any former regality. Its lower limbs were submerged in a wide pool, its body below the head covered in rusted metal, and flowing to its shoulders was a mane of cracked clay.

Silversong gasped at the realization of who he was looking at. It was the one who'd led the remaining Forgotten Ones to their disappearance, the same one he'd seen in the Songwoods and in the vision of the Empress. It gripped the same tooth of metal, its tip pointed at the other end of the corridor as if it had challenged Silversong the moment he'd entered the place. Something about its smooth yet cracked face and the odd creases showing up in random places made the effigy seem like it had been built recently… or like it once wore another face prior to the one it had now. He couldn't quite explain it, but the figure appeared old and new all at the same time, as if it were a mistake and did not belong in the here and now. Its free forelimb was pressed against its thigh, and its expression appeared sorrow-stricken.

He wasted no more time studying the reoccurring Forgotten One and started up the flight of eroded steps, Frostpaw following. At the top, they continued onto a platform leading to a second hallway lit by a crevice in the distant roof. Silversong breathed in the renewed scents of the exiles and wagged his tail. Frostpaw huffed and panted, eager as Silversong to pursue their quarry.

They walked within a broad bar of sunshine filtering through a stark breach in the mountain's peak. In a straight file, on either side of them, rose a row of stone bodies sculpted to resemble the likeness of the Forgotten Ones. Each separate figure stood regally, and on every head rested a silver circle, eight jewels pale as a vacant sky glinting along the front of the ornament.

The effigies were encased in shiny metal coverings, and a silky fabric of blue flowed from their shoulders to their ankles. One forelimb reached above each of their heads, the strange paw at the end grasping the base of an iron blade risen in defiance of all below them. They reflected the splendour of a time before beasts ruled the earth, a time forgotten yet undimmed even in the darkest of places. The steady pour of dazzling daylight streaming from the crack in the roof seemed to shine in pity for all the noble figures of stone buried beneath the snowy ridge, never to be seen by worthy eyes. And so, the mountains themselves made the sky bear witness to such ancient glory.

Frostpaw sniffed at the bases supporting the effigies while Silversong moved onward, passing through the exit at the end of the magnificent hallway. He came to a crossroads, the majesty of the previous room still fresh in his thoughts. The trail became stale once more.

An enormous closed entrance of reddish metal rose before him. He padded toward it and sniffed, nose wrinkling at the rusty odour. He stood on his hind legs and used his forepaws to push the freezing surface. Not a budge. He returned to all fours and continued the search.

Frostpaw approached him, a look of bewilderment filling the profound yellow of his eyes. They explored their options together. On one side, a set of huge steps descended, ending on a low ledge overlooking a great abyss. Hanging from chains hooked to an unseen roof were surfaces of wood, and on each of them rested odd materials made of metal. Every platform dangled close together, but at different heights. Silversong doubted the exiles had been stupid enough to cross the gaping void.

On the other side, a narrow tunnel in the rising stone beckoned their attention. Glowing mushrooms speckled the burrow, and translucent slugs slimed across the mossy growths within. Silversong inspected the hole and snuffled around it. Nothing. He breathed in deeply, hoping the exiles had gone through there and praying it *did not* lead to a dead end.

Gesturing to Frostpaw, he swallowed his fear of getting stuck and eased himself into the clammy hollow. He extended his forelegs and wriggled his way forward like a furry caterpillar. He closed his eyes and thought of the forest surrounding his home to keep from panicking. Frostpaw squirmed behind him, his large build no doubt hindering his movements.

Please don't get stuck, please don't get stuck, please don't get stuck…

After a dozen stressful breaths or so, Silversong dropped out of the end of the tunnel and landed on all fours in an airy chamber. He yanked off the mushy slugs clinging to his fur and turned to Frostpaw, whose big head poked out of the hole comically.

"Hey! I think I'm stuck! Little help maybe?" The lieutenant struggled, grunting and trying to squeeze through to no avail.

Laughter brewed in Silversong's belly as he admired how helpless and adorable the lieutenant looked. "Why should I? You look quite comfortable in there."

"Guess who's not going to be so comfortable once I get out of here!" Frostpaw snarled, wiggling some more, but he made no progress at all.

"Heh, it certainly won't be me." Silversong paced side to side, tail waving. "You're the one who's stuck and at my mercy, after all."

Frostpaw released a flustered growl and gave up, dangling loosely. "Fine. You win. Now help me out."

"Sure thing, fish-breath." Silversong grabbed the lieutenant by the scruff and tugged.

Frostpaw yelped, "ow, ow, OW!" He thrashed.

"Oh, shush now!" Silversong grunted as he pulled. "My teeth aren't even that deep."

"OH, THEY FEEL PRETTY DEEP TO ME!" Frostpaw yowled, his voice filling the entire chamber. "OUCH!"

"SHH! You're being dramatic! Way to advertise our presence to the entire ruin, by the way. I'm sure even Motherwolf can hear you." Another tug, and the whiny lieutenant popped out of the hole. He landed atop Silversong, heavy forepaws pushing the air out of his chest. "Agh! Get off!" Silversong wheezed, but Frostpaw refused to budge.

"Why should I?" Frostpaw smirked and pressed his nose against Silversong's in a threatening manner. "After all the embarrassment you caused me, you deserve some discipline. I think I'll enjoy having a little subordinate at my mercy. I ought to put you in your place for mocking me."

Silversong laughed nervously and pawed the lieutenant's face. "Maybe later you can try. But let's not forget who our true enemies are. They should be around here somewhere. I wonder if your wailing scared the exiles into thinking there's a ghost haunting these mountains."

"Wailing?! I wasn't wailing!" Frostpaw got off him, muttering stuff under his breath as he shook off the slugs stuck to his fur, pride clearly shaken. "*Wailing*? Those were the cries of a tortured warrior!"

"More like the cries of an overdramatic doe." Silversong snickered at his own comparison, satisfied at the lieutenant's flustered expression. The joy evaporated at the realization of something. *Wolves from different territories aren't supposed to be friends. I should quit acting as if Frostpaw were my packmate.* He clenched his jaws. *No. The two of us are wolves. Why shouldn't we be allowed to have fun together? It isn't fair.* He gathered his thoughts and strode through the chamber, wondering if the Heretic's vision really was as bad as he initially thought it was.

They sniffed the cool floor in hopes of finding something to encourage their pursuit. A dozen entrances lay opened at the end of the cavern, but none bore the smell of wolves. Silversong poked his muzzle into the middle one and stared at the start of a winding flight of steps. This way looked more promising than the others. He signalled for Frostpaw to follow him and began the descent into the familiar darkness.

"Got any siblings?" Frostpaw's whiskers touched him, sparking a shiver. "I have two brothers and two sisters." His tone hinted at a complicated relationship.

The thought of Swiftstorm made Silversong feel as though a boulder were attached to every leg. "I have a sister." He tried to pour some strength into his quavering whine. "She was a sentinel…"

Frostpaw stiffened beside him. "Oh."

"Yeah." Silversong sighed, heart drowned under a heavy pressure. *Maybe she's still alive. Maybe—*

His forepaws landed on nothing but empty air. He yelped, slipping, chest lurching, stomach clenching itself as he tumbled over the edge. Frostpaw released a cry and tried to snatch him up, but the brisk movement launched the lieutenant into the pit instead. Without realizing it, the deceitful steps had ceased descending and had just decided to end abruptly. Silversong thrashed beside Frostpaw, spinning without control as the two of them plummeted to an unknown demise.

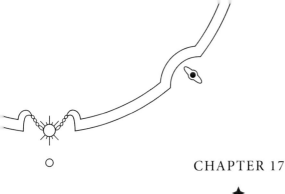

CHAPTER 17

✦

Ƈһє Ɗᴿᴏᴡɴᴇᴅ Ƈιᴛᴀɴ

Thwack!

Shock ricocheted throughout Silversong's body, the impact robbing him of air. Scorching pain compelled him to thrash as if fire ants were biting him everywhere. He released a breath that manifested into bubbles. His opened eyes stung, and he saw nothing but a murky blackness all around him. He kicked several times, rising higher and higher until his aching head popped out of the water. He coughed until he could breathe somewhat normally again.

Frostpaw emerged beside him, blinking rapidly and blowing a spray of droplets out of his nose. "Ah, so this is why I sensed the presence of water below us."

"You could've at least mentioned it!" Silversong glowered, trying to shake out the uncomfortable feeling of liquid in his nostrils and ears. "I guess we're lucky the water saved us from becoming bloody splatters."

"Lucky," Frostpaw mused, "or Motherwolf is watching over us."

I hope so, Frostpaw. I hope so…

The chill of the water drained the heat from Silversong's body, and he shivered violently, teeth clattering like rattling bones. Frostpaw closed his eyes and focused on something, forepaws undulating in steady motions. The frigid temperature rose to a more comfortable level as if flames had been ignited under the freezing surface. Silversong sighed in relief and paddled closer to Frostpaw.

"You River-Stream wolves are really something else." Silversong whined his thanks to the lieutenant, realizing if Frostpaw hadn't insisted on coming here too, he would've been doomed to become a frozen corpse.

Frostpaw motioned himself around in an elegant fashion—his wavy mud markings fading into the ripples—and moved like an eel under the submerged entrance of whatever structure they'd fallen into. Silversong paddled after him, his maneuvers nowhere near as graceful as his partner's. He ducked under the entrance and emerged on the other side, basking in the heat near the lieutenant.

Silversong's eyes widened at the gigantic cavern drowned beneath the mountains. No edges or corners could be seen anywhere except behind him, making the expanse seem endless. Other than the crooked pillars repeatedly poking their heads out of the surface, nothing disturbed the black lake stretching discouragingly before them.

The sheer vastness of the place staggered him, and it took a while for him to take it all in. He followed Frostpaw, paddling until fatigue buzzed in every muscle. Silversong found respite atop one of the pillars and stayed there until he regained some strength. The lieutenant waited beside him and gave out encouraging whines and nuzzles, never showing a crack in his stamina.

"Don't suppose you can wield the water and command a few fishy snacks to leap into my mouth?" Silversong joked, but his stomach failed to appreciate the untimely humor.

Frostpaw wore a solemn look. "There aren't any living things in the lake as far as I can sense, Silversong. At least, nothing close to where we are."

"Figures," Silversong muttered, relishing in another deep breath.

After giving himself the pause he needed, Silversong continued through the lake until his breathing turned to ragged wheezes again. He took another break, this time on the smooth top of one of the structures piercing the clean surface. The pattern of swimming and resting repeated itself beyond count.

We'll never reach the other side! Silversong panted during one of their breaks, the air expelled from his lungs leaving itchy trails of fire in his throat. *I'll collapse and die from exhaustion if I continue on like this.*

Just as the brief thought of giving up entered his head, he squinted, and in the far distance, a flight of enormous steps climbed up to the shore of the underground lake. His heart pumped faster, boiling the fatigue out of his body. The dense feeling tugging at his bones became lighter.

Oh, thank Motherwolf!

"Frostpaw! Over there!" Silversong pointed his muzzle at the distant shore.

The lieutenant yipped triumphantly and wagged his tail atop their shared platform.

Frostpaw plunged into the lake and splashed happily around. Silversong puffed out his weariness and dove in after him, ripples fleeing across the surface. The further he paddled, the more a subtle, orange-tinted light crept up his lower vision. He stopped swimming to glance into the deeps, curious to see the origin of the ghostly radiance.

Far beneath the surface rose numerous structures of neatly chipped stone, all soaking in the fiery glare of glassy orbs shining dimly atop rounded pillars. They stood one after the other upon the unbroken edges of the many roads intersecting the ruinous constructions, their pools of light revealing the grandeur and splendor of a long-forgotten age.

A yawning fissure halved the ruin and seemed to beckon him below to witness what the light feared to touch. The void returned his unblinking stare, its darkness deeper than a wakeless nightmare, so perfect in its eerie uncertainty, its horrific beauty enough to madden the sanest of minds.

If he listened carefully, he could barely make out the sound of a low, chanting voice echoing from deep within the cavernous fissure. The unearthly melody soothed his nerves and inspired a terrifying sense of wonder, and though he couldn't understand the singing, he was sure the voice was calling for him to dive into the chasm and join the eternal music.

Silence.

Out of the wondrous crevice came a massive ovoid shape. It blotted out everything from the submerged structures to the luminous orbs, plunging the entire cavern into darkness once more. Every bone in Silversong's body begged him to flee, but the shore was still too far away. His head darted in all directions, but always returned to the stirring thing below.

"Frostpaw! Over here!" he called out to the lieutenant, who stopped swimming some distance ahead and whipped himself around.

A gargantuan orange eye opened near the bottom of the oval shape, staring straight at Silversong, blood-red veins spidering to a black, round pupil many times the size of the tallest pine he'd ever seen.

"There you are." The deep voice beneath the lake thundered into his ears—the same voice he'd heard before entering the Mountainmouth, but it was a lot louder now.

His flesh crawled as if attempting to flee off his bones, and his heart tried to hop into his throat. He succumbed to terror's chill and shivered above the petrifying gaze of the enormous monster below. Without a second thought, he pushed himself toward the shore, hoping against hope he wouldn't be dragged under. If his destiny was to die here, he wouldn't go out without a struggle! "Go, Frostpaw! Now!"

The lieutenant took one look at the gigantic creature and let creases of determination settle onto his forehead. Instead of fleeing like any sane individual would, he weaved the water around him into a cocoon of bubbles, using it to propel himself closer and closer toward the eye.

"Frostpaw, you gullwit!" Silversong cried.

"I haven't requested your presence. Begone!" the monster commanded. A colossal tentacle reached above the surface and crashed into the water, forming a huge wave that swallowed Frostpaw and carried him to shore.

The heat the lieutenant once emitted dissipated, but fear convinced Silversong to keep moving despite the frigid temperature eating at his flesh and the exhaustion creeping into his core.

"Alone swims the silver one." The voice rumbled directly below him, shaking him to the marrow. "Your efforts are futile. You dwell in my prison now, child of Motherwolf."

Slimy black tentacles coiled around his body and dragged him under. His ears popped, and no matter how fiercely he thrashed, the choking grasp never yielded. One of the inky limbs snaked around his throat, preventing him from inhaling water. He kicked uselessly in the struggle as everything he'd lived through up to the present flashed in his head. Black spots flecked his vision, growing larger the weaker his heart became. In a final attempt to escape, he played dead, relaxing every muscle and going limp in the clutch of the monstrous thing.

"I can still feel your heart, little one. It drums to me the music of mortal life." The voice slithered into his ears and spiraled around his brain, drowning all thoughts in a maelstrom of horror. The monster shifted, but its eye always remained fixed on its prey.

Silversong tried again to squirm free, but the strangling tentacles were more powerful than his stubbornness. One of them touched his chest, and the surrounding water bubbled until he found himself encased in a large sphere of tepid air.

The monster released him. "Breathe now."

Silversong inhaled desperately, welcoming the feeling of satisfied lungs. Steady breaths broke into fearful gasps as the darkness spreading like a disease across his vision melted into clearness. In front of him, an immense eye glared unblinkingly, connected to an even bigger oval head. Some distance below the eye, the body of the creature splintered into countless, unending tentacles worming calmly about the cluttered lakebed. Some dragged against the ruined structures while others grasped the bases of the pillars. The thicker limbs reached straight into the open fissure, blending into perfect blackness.

The creature's upper body expanded wide as it breathed underwater, its gaze never straying from Silversong. "Hmm." Its speech flowed like a wave, changing into different tones, an ancient power thrumming within like that of the Empress or the Fallen Titan. "So, the tumultuous tide of fate has brought you to my lonely prison."

The flaming glare penetrated his thoughts. He closed his eyes, but the image of the monster still flashed before him, lingering no matter where he turned his head, its gaze stripping him of all secrets, burning its way to the very bottom of his soul and violating any sense of privacy he once had.

"STOP!" he yelled, fur feeling as if it had caught fire.

The searing sensation ceased, and he opened his eyes cautiously as the monster studied him more closely. "Ah, yours is an intriguing tale of wonder, sorrow, and adventure, but you have yet to be reborn in the crucible of pain. Few have witnessed the things you have, and fewer still grasp the secrets you've uncovered, secrets belonging to the one who evaded my summons, the one who seeks to wield the powers of time against you."

The enormous iris of the creature shrank a little. "Ironwrath, he is called. A heretic to his own species. He despises the code dictating the rules of your society. He despises the intolerant traditions leashing your lives. His ambition led him to seek out the Empress of Spiders following his escape from damnation, and she set him on the road toward the weapon once wielded by the mighty Stormstrider." The monster gave as close to a chuckle as its otherworldly voice allowed. "As I sensed Ironwrath and his lackeys entering my prison, I thought for a moment the Horse Titan's companion, the Forest Father, had sprung up from the dead and was accompanying them, but it was only the one called Rime carrying his corrupted spirit. Funny how a lowly mortal can be mistaken for a Titan under the correct circumstances."

"Who are you?" Silversong's meek whine came out as a fearful whistle.

"Hmm. As I've scoured your being to its deepest point, I suppose an exchange of names is fair." Tremors vibrated through him every time the monster spoke, but they weren't comforting like those of the Empress; they were intense and overpowering. "I go by many titles, little one, like your Motherwolf and the Empress who nearly seduced you to a gruesome end. More commonly, I am known as the Drowned Titan, the Lurker of the Deeps, the father of all who spurn the light."

"And," Silversong gulped, "why have you dragged me under?"

The black of the Drowned Titan's eye compressed itself. "Though I am loath to admit it to a mortal, I require your… cooperation."

"My cooperation?" Silversong's tail pressed itself against his belly.

"Yes. You are to free me, little one." Its tentacles slithered everywhere, almost excitedly, and its pupil expanded beyond measure, dwarfing even the widest of structures beneath it. "Long have I been trapped below these mountains, hoping a brave soul would become the tool of my release. And now here you breathe before me. The unlikely champion. I see the potential in you flaring bright to announce your worthiness. I would've forced the one you chase to do my bidding, but he and his followers have taken a different road, and now they come ever closer to their ultimate prize."

A sense of urgency struck Silversong on the head. "You have to let me go! The Heretic can't be allowed to consume the piece of time! You have to—"

"Patience," the Drowned Titan bellowed, its voice quaking through Silversong's bones. "Agree to cooperate, and you may continue your noble pursuit."

Silversong's thoughts searched for a way to escape this encounter, but finding none, they conceded. "Fine. I agree to cooperate." *It's not like I have much of a choice.*

"No, you don't have much of a choice." The Drowned Titan's grasp on some of the pillars tightened.

Silversong jerked up. A glacial chill ran up his spine and stiffened his hackles. *You can read my thoughts?!*

His captor ignored his surprise as if the ability were the simplest trick. "At the core of the underground ruin lies not only the piece of time, but also the Heart of the Mountains, an object of unstable energy powerful enough to tear my wretched prison asunder! You must bring it to me."

"All right. Heart of the Mountains. Got it." Silversong wasn't sure he wanted to free the Drowned Titan even if he could, but he pushed those thoughts away for now. "Who… who imprisoned you here, and why?"

"Ah, you are trying to see where I stand in regard to virtue and villainy. How admirable of you." A tentacle lifted itself off the lakebed and writhed into Silversong's bubble. He squirmed as it wormed closer. "Allow me to broaden your understanding."

The tip of the tentacle touched his forehead, and his brain froze and burned at the same time, the two opposite pains colliding, enveloping his head in a torturous vortex. Before he could scream, the agony dulled and faded into an unpleasant memory. He wasn't submerged in water anymore, but suspended in the air above it, blanketed by the heat of a blazing sun. A legion of weird constructions floated amid the endless sea, supporting many furless two-legged beings who barked incomprehensible commands at each other as spiderwebs made of woven threads were lowered into the abyss. They resurfaced a while later, bearing bundles of deep-dwelling creatures caught within.

They struggled and called for aid, huddled together and hanging helplessly. The Forgotten Ones, wielding detached claws of iron, cut into their prey and leaked blood into the waves as they cheered and celebrated on the floating vessels. Their victims cried out, unheard voices echoing across the cruel ocean, their pain unimaginable as some were thrown into round contraptions and boiled alive until their screams were swallowed by hissing steam. Far below, the sea rumbled and growled, trembling the wooden and metal surfaces the Forgotten Ones stood on. The water stirred, and enormous tentacles, angry and thrashing, coiled around the bodies of every structure, cracking them in two or pulling their entire weight under the ruthless tide.

The Drowned Titan's voice resounded like thunder foretelling a crash of lightning. "Unlike the Empress, I despised the Forgotten Ones from the very beginning. Their reckless sense of superiority tested my nerves. Never would I demand the hollow worship of those disgusting bipedal brutes as she once did. They disturbed my creations and used cruel contraptions to cook and slice them all in the name of untamed gluttony. And so, in return, I devoured those vermin alive, using their own rabid hunger against them. But my unchecked vengeance eventually attracted the attention of the one who trapped me here."

The vision shifted, and now Silversong watched as a more elegant vessel retreated from a massive creature pursuing it from below the waters. The one in command yelled at frightened subordinates. The swift construction swerved to avoid lashes from huge tentacles while waves battered it on all sides, conjured by the storm above. Projectiles from heavy weapons were flung into the monster's flesh, causing it to roar in anger. A range of mountains loomed ahead, and the commander pointed at the opening of a watery cave. They hastened toward it, the behemoth hot on their trail. Upon entering the cavern and leaving the wrath of the raging sky, the Forgotten Ones prepared a dozen cylindrical containers of blood-red wood, piling them atop one another.

The commander of the vessel grasped a smooth stick and lit the top of it aflame, waiting for the merciless hunter to enter the cave. The Drowned Titan surfaced out of the water, tentacles shooting for the commander, but the brave Forgotten One hurled the ignited rod at the containers. Only an instant passed before the entire construction erupted in a blinding explosion of fire and death. The entrance of the cave collapsed in on itself, trapping the remains of the vessel and its stalker alike beneath the mountains.

"I underestimated how clever and selfless my opponents could be… and so I slithered straight into their snare like a blind snake." The Drowned Titan spilled even more contempt into its already bitter voice. "And here I've remained as time flowed forward, trapped beneath the mountains, unable to escape, forced to use my voice as a means of retaining sanity. Eventually, the Forgotten Ones, ever ignorant to the consequences of their endeavours, started to build an underground kingdom above my watery prison. Ages passed, and slowly I spread my influence among those who settled directly above me, but before their descendants could be fully swayed to my control, the War of Change began. Battles raged on, storms engulfed the sky, the earth cracked and shook, and the fissure below us opened."

"I bet it was frustrating, not being able to participate in the war against the ones you hated so much," Silversong remarked coldly. "Why did the other Titans not free you?"

Silversong could feel the Drowned Titan trembling before him. "I was not very popular among my kin. They saw me as a dangerous nuisance who hungered for naught but power. They were partly correct, I suppose. I once dominated the seas, and all its denizens were forced to pay tribute to my glory. Stormstrider himself warned the others about the consequences should I be released during the war, and so I was abandoned here, aware of the victories and defeats of my fellow Titans yet unable to join their cause in the flesh. But times have changed. Our ability to travel between the realms has been taken from us, and all I desire now is my freedom."

The tentacle touching Silversong retracted and released him. He was inside his bubble again, brain numb and staring blank-eyed at the monster in front of him. "If I'm helping you escape this place, you have to promise me you'll return the favour."

If the Heretic can strike a bargain with a Titan, I can too.

The Drowned Titan glowered as if insulted. "Your boldness in the face of a Titan is as commendable as it is foolish. But if this is your price, then I accept it. I promise to return the favour one day before you die. By my own immortality, I swear it." A visible quivering overtook the huge creature as if the promise had branded its soul. "Now, bring me the Heart of the Mountains, but do not let yourself be vanquished by its fire, and beware the ruin itself. Since the end of the War of Change, something has haunted it and changed it in defiance of every law of nature, something even I cannot explain."

Silversong released the shakiest of breaths. "I'll bring you the Heart of the Mountains. Whatever it is. Now can you let me go?"

Before he could straighten out his tail, his bubble steadily rose to the surface.

"I'll be waiting here." The eye closed itself, and the Drowned Titan descended deeper and deeper into the wide crevice until its body melded into the murky shadows. The bubble popped once Silversong surfaced, and the haunting melody played on, as forever it would until he released the monster under the mountains. The delayed shock of the freezing water stole his breath as he kicked to stay afloat. Turning to the broad steps where Frostpaw barked frantically, he paddled, calling on all his strength and willpower to keep him alive.

His sense of time and direction slipped away, but he continued onward, panting, throat sore, eyes sluggish, heart struggling to siphon hot blood into his aching veins. Frostpaw's barking sounded so close... but also so far. Was he seeing doubles...? Or were there two Frostpaws now...?

That wouldn't be so bad, come to think of it... Confusion spread like maddening roots throughout him.

A surge of hot water gripped his body and pulled him toward the steps. His senses returned to reality as Frostpaw grabbed him by the scruff and lifted him up, laying him on his side. The lieutenant ran his forepaws along the length of Silversong, prodding wherever his temperature had dropped to critical levels. Silversong blinked and gasped at the sensation of heat returning to his core, reaching into every vein. "Fr-Frostpaw...?" He shivered.

"I-I thought you were gone!" Frostpaw whistled shrill whimpers. "I saw you get dragged under by something huge. I... I wanted to go back and save you, but... but..." His voice cracked.

Silversong nuzzled him on the cheek, teeth still clattering despite the renewed heat. "It's all right, Frostpaw. I'm fine." He stood up and flung off the water soaking his fur, the shivers returning to shake life into him.

"It's not all right!" Frostpaw scratched the floor angrily. "I should've dived in after you."

"Don't be silly. There's nothing you could've done." Silversong nosed the lieutenant, reminding him his ally—no, his friend—was still breathing. "Besides, I'm alive, aren't I?"

Frostpaw licked him on the face. "What happened, Silversong? You were gone for quite a while."

Silversong coughed up a nervous chuckle. "So, there's this huge immortal squid trapped beneath the lake who demanded me to free it. And if I do, it'll be indebted to me. Nothing too alarming."

He almost expected Frostpaw to laugh and demand the real story, but the lieutenant's eyes only widened more. "I guess it's only a matter of time before the Fallen Titan himself speaks to you too, huh?"

He already did. Silversong flexed his muscles to keep himself from shivering more. "We should probably continue our search. We already let the Heretic have a head start, so let's make sure he doesn't succeed, all right?" He gave Frostpaw a pleading look. The last thing he wanted now was to be reminded of the Titans he'd spoken to.

Frostpaw's gaze met the ground. "I'm… I'm happy you're alive."

A tingly spark buzzed within Silversong's heart and vanquished the shivers. "Thanks." He forced a smile. "And I'm happy you're here."

After an awkward pause of nothing but troubled breathing to counter the silence, they climbed up the steps and padded through another opening. A hallway of brownish metal curved before them, slanting upward, intersected by corridors leading to other rooms or tunnel systems. They moved through the main stretch, sniffing the ground for traces of the Heretic and his exiles.

They heard them before they smelled them. Silversong pricked his ears and tensed up as Frostpaw crouched beside him, tail risen and stiff. Behind the corner, heated voices spoke in guttural tones. Rime and the Heretic grunted above the gravelly growls, trying to lower the temper of their subordinates.

Silversong turned to the lieutenant, the anticipation flaring up. "All right, here's how we'll do things. You're my prisoner. Act like it. Palesquall and the exile you killed are gone. I haven't seen those two since the spiders attacked. I found you lurking around in your forest during the morning and surprised you. I bested you in combat and forced you to lead me into the Mountainmouth. Got it?"

"You're planning all this now?" Frostpaw looked at him like he'd suggested they stick their snouts in an anthill. Come to think of it, they were sticking their snouts in far worse than that.

"Better now than never." Silversong gave an uncertain smile, wiping it off upon noticing Frostpaw's unimpressed stare. "At least

I thought of something! Just do as I said, and we might still make it out of here alive."

"So we charge in and go straight for the Heretic. Got it."

"Frostpaw, this is serious." Silversong tried to make his glare more obvious.

"Okay, okay. I guess you're the lieutenant now." Frostpaw twitched his whiskers, standing up from his aggressive stance and flattening his ears. He tucked his tail and hunched his shoulders, scoffing. "Heh, I haven't assumed this position since I was a subordinate."

Silversong's scowl dissolved at the rise of an unexpected giggle. The lieutenant—who was as bulky as Chief Amberstorm—assuming an utterly pathetic stance was more than comical. Frostpaw's eyes were pup-like in their size, and Silversong struggled not to erupt into laughter despite the danger they were about to enter. "Hey, you should refer to me as *sir* while you're at it. Could make our act a little more convincing."

"Hah! You would enjoy that, wouldn't you?" Frostpaw grunted, nosing him on the cheek. "Come on. Let's do this."

Silversong exhaled and let his tail dangle. He turned the corner on shaking forepaws, twinges of anxiety knotting his stomach and strangling all emotions until fear oozed out of the squished bundle. Whatever happened now, his actions would decide the fate of countless lives. He had to win, or death would once again reign in the Heretic's wake.

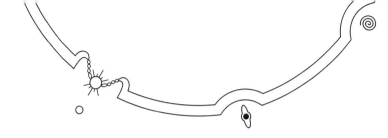

CHAPTER 18

✦

AN UGLY REUNION

"What in the Fallen Titan's prickly backside is this?!" Rime bristled and crouched into an attack position, wide glare focused on the *prisoner* at Silversong's side.

Confused eyes aimed themselves at him, fright-filled at first, expressions quickly morphing from shock to anger. The exiles were thinned in number, and some bore newer wounds that still needed a good licking. The smell of blood polluted the air, falling heavy on the expansive hallway. The Heretic tensed, taking a couple steps forward. Frostpaw never once stopped staring at Rime.

Silversong snarled as ferociously as he could at Frostpaw. "Submit to Ironwrath, and maybe he'll spare your life."

"Traitor!" Frostpaw growled quite convincingly, almost causing a startle. "You'll be punished by Motherwolf herself for betraying the Wolven Code!"

The exiles shifted their attention from Silversong to the false prisoner. Fangs bared, they wetted their mouths in anticipation, but they never moved in for as little as a sniff without their master's command.

"Motherwolf can't see us so deep underground, soldier of River-Stream." The Heretic moved within a tail-length of Silversong's face, dead green eyes peering into his. "I'll ask the questions no doubt plaguing everyone's thoughts. How did you escape the spiders? Where are Bonechew and Palesquall? How did you sniff us out? And who exactly have you brought into the Mountainmouth?" He squinted suspiciously at Frostpaw.

Silversong had to look away. The mere thought of standing still before the one who'd killed Elder Shrillbreeze and Pinetrail was beyond infuriating. Swiftstorm haunted his thoughts again, igniting the sparks of smouldering hate. He clenched his jaws and focused on the details of the large opening behind the bleeding exiles. It gaped hungrily, mimicking the entrance to the underground ruin.

He sucked in a breath, concentrating on his fabrications. "I woke up in my cocoon and bit my way out. I took the spiders by surprise and escaped. I ran until I reached River-Stream Territory, where I came across *him* skulking about during the morning." He flicked his tail at Frostpaw. "I pounced on the mongrel and subdued him, and once I was sure he would be obedient, I forced him to lead me into the Mountainmouth." He stretched his snarl and poured all his rage into his little act. "I thought maybe you would like to question him."

The Heretic remained emotionless, his eyes never conceding to a single blink. "You're forgetting Bonechew and your humorous friend, little lamb. How do they fit into your funny story?"

Silversong tensed, hoping he at least sounded mildly convincing. "I haven't seen Palesquall or Bonechew since the ambush. I hope they're all right."

The Heretic exhaled slowly. "So you say."

The exiles growled, and one whose jaw was crooked hissed. "I don't like the way the River-Stream cur is looking at us. His face needs a good biting!"

"Agreed, Brokenjaw." Ripper rallied the others into a fit of aggressive barking. "River-Stream wolves always think they're so enlightened compared to their neighbours. We should drown his pride so he can be properly humbled."

"The ruin's unpredictability has already claimed many of us," another exile grunted. "Let's have ourselves a little snack to regain morale."

Frostpaw flashed his teeth in every direction. "If any of you stinking scatfurs come near me, I'll give you each a bite not even the greatest Wise-Wolves can heal!"

Don't get carried away, Frostpaw! Silversong bristled and nudged the lieutenant, ordering him silently to get his nerves under control. *We'll strike together once we get a better opportunity.*

The Heretic only had to swipe his tail to silence the entire gathering. He moved closer to Silversong, sniffing as if to detect the scent of his lies. "Guide me through your story, little lamb. You're claiming you miraculously escaped the spiders and found your way into River-Stream Territory? And there you managed to beat a

warrior who looks like he could give Rime a tough time in a fight?"
Rime scoffed before the Heretic continued. "And you haven't even
seen Bonechew or your friend since the Silverhaze Forest? There's
something you're not telling me."

A prickly heat overcame Silversong, and his hackles hardened,
every strand wanting to flee his flesh. It took all his willpower to
return the Heretic's dead-eyed stare. "It's the truth. I swear it. I
ambushed my prisoner, and it was hardly a fair fight. Would you've
preferred it if I'd chosen the honourable route and gotten myself
captured or worse? And as for Bonechew and Palesquall, only
Motherwolf knows their fates now."

The Heretic creased his forehead as if considering the
possibility of the tale.

Rime pushed through his subordinates and released a
thick grunt. "We should take no chances. Something about his
story smells funny, and a twitch of my whiskers is warning me
of treachery. Look at this so-called prisoner! There's no scratch
or bite on him, and unless the Whistle-Wind pup nuzzled him
into submission, our newest member is a traitor and ought to be
punished accordingly."

The Heretic sleeked his fur, tail swishing calmly. "Your
whiskers are quite perceptive, Rime. It's true, the little lamb may
be feigning loyalty to us, in which case we'll make him regret his
betrayal in time. But for now, we'll give him the benefit of the
doubt. I still think we can open his eyes to my truth."

"As you command, master." Rime rubbed his forepaws on the
metal floor. "And the River-Stream mongrel? It's no use keeping
him alive."

The Heretic turned to Frostpaw, weighing the suggestion.

In a final attempt to get things under control, Silversong
barked as loud as he could. "He's not just any mongrel of River-
Stream! He's a lieutenant!" All heads whirled to face Silversong,
but he stayed put and showed no weakness, no crack in his facade.
"He's a lieutenant of River-Stream. Which is why I let him live and
decided to bring him to you. He may have information we can put
to good use. Distrust me if you like, but don't bury this opportunity
I'm presenting to you!"

"Smart move, gambling on the River-Stream warrior's position
to save him." The Heretic fixed an inquisitive glare on Frostpaw.

"Is it true, sir? I don't see any markings on your coat indicating your standing."

"There's an underground lake not too far from here. It's where we came from. His markings got washed off in there," Silversong explained, heart sinking upon noticing a hole in his story. "And… and the only reason I wasn't drowned by him is because… because he needs us to escape these mountains alive. Without us, he'll die here, and he knows it."

The Heretic's mouth was on the verge of grinning. "You're a talker, aren't you, little lamb? Your blabbering mouth is only going to dig you further into trouble, not out of it. But I suppose you're lucky if you managed to traverse the underground lake unmolested. The Empress hinted at who exactly was imprisoned there, and so I chose a different road which brought us to where we stand now. Unfortunately, my choices caused the untimely deaths of several of my followers. As you can understand, the survivors are quite agitated and would appreciate an opportunity to let out their frustrations."

Rime's guttural laugh echoed through the hallway as the others crouched, creeping toward Frostpaw, sharp teeth eager to bite. Silversong bowed his head in shame. Was it over? Had he gotten an innocent life killed because of his own incompetence?

Hazel, Palesquall, I'm so sorry.

Frostpaw's fangs aimed themselves at Rime's throat. "I've been waiting for this moment, murderer," he growled, ready to strike. "I've dreamed of killing you for a long time. I can't correct my mistake, but I can deliver justice!"

"For now," the Heretic's uncaring voice cooled the boiling tension, "you may live a little while longer. The information you carry about your territory could prove valuable even after I succeed here." He examined the River-Stream lieutenant's wrathful expression. "Your name is…?"

"Frostpaw. The Wise-Wolves named me Frostpaw."

The Heretic paused, but his eyes showed no more emotion than they always had. "Lieutenant Frostpaw, is it?" He craned his head over his shoulder to look at Rime. "And you say you don't believe in fate." He turned to Frostpaw again. "If you survive the unpredictability of the ruin and prove your usefulness, your future is yours to decide. Make things difficult for us, and we'll decide your future for you."

"One thing." Frostpaw abandoned his submissive posture entirely. "If I conform to your demands, I would like to speak to your lieutenant. Alone."

The Heretic regarded his prized lackey. "I'm sure Rime would love to hear whatever you have to say to him."

"I doubt it." Frostpaw trembled; Silversong could practically feel the storm brewing inside his partner. "I really do."

What's gotten into you?! Silversong brushed his flank against Frostpaw, trying to coax the anger out of him.

Rime stood rigid as a glacier, muttering something no ears could possibly hear. He and Frostpaw exchanged a look only old enemies would share. But how was that possible? Frostpaw would've only been a pup when Rime was banished for…

… for killing Frostpaw's mother! She must've been the lieutenant who found out about Rime's crime of seducing a member from a rival territory! The details of Bonechew's story returned little by little.

Silversong gasped, looking at Frostpaw from a different angle. *That's why you came! You're here to avenge your mother, aren't you?* Everything clicked together.

While the exiles studied the scene intently, the Heretic released a few sharp grunts. "Though I'm sure we all would like to see the outcome of this confrontation, it'll have to wait. We've wasted enough time here licking wounds and encouraging old hatreds, I'm afraid. The core of the Mountainmouth awaits us, and we'll soon be rewarded for our tireless efforts. Salvation begins once the weapon is mine. A new age of peace and enlightenment is soon upon us, and we are its harbingers!"

The exiles all yipped and jumped, except for Ironwrath, Ripper, Brokenjaw, and Rime, who sometimes stole a glance at the son of the mother he'd killed. No pity marred Rime's biting eyes.

Brokenjaw neared his leader in a crouched stance. "Master, we've all got wolves who were once close to us among our enemies. After you claim the weapon and launch your assault, are you going to spare the few we still care about like you promised? Even if they refuse to see the evils of the Wolven Code?"

The Heretic acknowledged the concern of his subordinate. "Once time answers to me, I imagine many who value their lives won't foolishly offer themselves to a futile cause. Those whose brains aren't completely muddled by the oppression we fight are sure to flock to me. Though we've evolved into more complicated creatures since the War of Change, the instinct to survive is still nestled deep in our hearts. I hope your loved ones come to their senses, Brokenjaw. If not, perhaps they'll listen to you."

Brokenjaw hung his grey head in defeat. "No. They hate me for being a code-breaker. But I don't hate them, no matter how desperately I try to convince myself I do."

The Heretic stepped closer to Brokenjaw. "Ultimately, it's their choice whether they live or die. But I hope for your sake they don't choose the latter. And if they do, we all have to make sacrifices for the greater good, don't we?"

Brokenjaw bowed in agreement and slinked away.

"Having second thoughts about coming here?" Silversong whispered to Frostpaw.

"It's too late for second thoughts now," Frostpaw snarled, eyes locked on Rime.

Are your other siblings this angry at Rime, Frostpaw? Or is it just you? There's something I'm missing here…

Ripper approached his superiors, a deepening scowl wrinkling his face. "Master, Rime, I suggest we give the River-Stream lieutenant a taste of the pain he'll suffer if he tries to hinder us."

Rime paused and entertained the thought, searching his master's eyes for approval. Upon finding it, he smirked. "Yes. Good thinking, Ripper. A *small* bite should suffice for now."

"Wonderful." Frostpaw tried to sound tough despite his wafting fear scent.

"I'll be the one to do it." Rime paced forward, yellow fangs sharp. "It'll bring back pleasant memories of me killing a certain inquisitive lieutenant who couldn't keep her nose out of my business."

"No," Ironwrath commanded before Frostpaw could unleash his fury on Rime. "Let the little lamb do the deed. If he goes easy on his prisoner, you've my permission to interfere however you desire."

"Heh. Sounds reasonable," Rime grunted as the assembly of exiles displayed their ferocious excitement. "You heard Ironwrath. Get to it!"

Fear knotted Silversong's throat and shortened his breaths. A sour taste tainted his dried-up tongue as he backed away from Frostpaw, eyes darting everywhere but at the lieutenant, head spiraling in a tornado of anxiety. Frostpaw placed a forepaw atop Silversong's and gave him a look of understanding. Silversong closed his eyes and growled at himself, disgusted at an action he hadn't even done yet.

There was no way out of it. The Heretic was too far away to attack, and so was Rime. This had to be done if there was any hope of coming out victorious in the end.

"Stalling only makes it worse! Do it already!" Rime barked above the riled crowd. "Bite him! Let's hear him wail! Or you'll soon discover the true meaning of pain."

"Little lamb! Little lamb! Little lamb!" the exiles cheered.

Frostpaw gulped and readied himself, eyes begging Silversong not to bite too deep. Silversong bared his teeth and clamped onto the lieutenant's shoulder before he could even think about refusing and making things worse in the process. *I'm so sorry!* The more the weight of his shame increased, the more he wanted to empty the contents of his stomach.

Frostpaw yelped as his blood soaked Silversong's mouth. He gagged and wretched while he chewed and bit, his whimpers muffled by the booming laughter of the exiles.

"I better see flesh being ripped off him, little lamb! Else you'll be wishing you never strayed from your broken den!" Rime taunted.

Silversong swallowed the coming of another whimper and tore off a chunk of bloody fur and flesh from Frostpaw's shoulder. The lieutenant yowled and dropped to the ground, writhing on his side, trying to extinguish the searing sting of his wound. Silversong could only imagine the pain.

His stomach convulsed, and saliva flooded his mouth, diluting the salty blood. He heaved as hot vomit gurgled up his throat, but he swallowed its bitterness and spewed out the red-soaked clump of flesh and fur instead. "Satisfied?!" He challenged the Heretic, ready to charge headfirst into his own demise if he was ordered to bite Frostpaw again.

"Do not let unchecked vengeance sweep you under its tide as it once did me." The Drowned Titan's voice pounded against the borders of Silversong's skull. **"Remember our deal. I need you alive to bring me the Heart of the Mountains."**

I haven't forgotten. Silversong allowed the winds of rationality to wear away at his hardened anger.

The Heretic's expression remained indistinct. He just stood there, studying the scene, eyes distant as ever. He noted the brief tail flick of his lieutenant and faced Silversong. "Yes. We're satisfied. Take care of your prisoner's wound. Make sure he doesn't bleed out on us."

Silversong wasted no time licking the pulsing tear on Frostpaw's shoulder, cringing at the taste. "I'm sorry, Frostpaw… I'm so…"

"Shh." Frostpaw gave him a subtle nudge. "They're watching us like vultures. Better I be harmed than you."

"No…" Silversong stiffened to keep himself standing. The bloated weight of his shame became too heavy for his shoulders to bear, and he stooped low.

"Fix yourself, subordinate." Frostpaw got up and winced, crimson lines leaking through clean fur. He fought to keep his voice low. "Now's not the time to feel sorry for yourself. You had to do it, or Rime would've done it for you, and I would rather have your fangs in me than his, trust me. Remember why you're here and let it feed your strength."

Silversong's bones became weaker than brittle twigs. He couldn't look away from Frostpaw's face even if he'd wanted to.

"You two done nuzzling each other?" Rime mocked. The exiles behind him laughed and sneered, some hurling slurs and insults.

Silversong gritted his teeth and let the fire in Frostpaw's eyes reignite the embers of determination within himself. He thought of all the wolves who'd died because of the Heretic, because of Rime and the other exiles. Fuming rage enveloped his shame, and he strode forward, heat returning to every corner of his body.

Frostpaw followed his lead, head low, posture submissive as he suffered in silence.

The younger exiles rushed to Silversong and lapped the fresh blood off his muzzle, but he paid no attention to their rough tongues and spiteful laughs. He narrowed his focus on the one who'd given him the order to bite Frostpaw, the one who'd allowed all this to happen. He peered into the green, passionless stare of the Heretic and promised himself he would close those eyes forever soon enough.

✦

CHAPTER 19

Che Maze of Madness

Silversong found himself surrounded by disquieted exiles as he walked through a grey corridor. Crude markings decorated the stone on each side, climbing to a ceiling so far up it blended into shadow. He focused on the etchings to keep his shame from avalanching onto him. Frostpaw's wound had dried, but its metallic stench still lingered—a constant reminder of why Silversong would never forgive himself.

Rime stayed at the front alongside his master, never tempted to look over his shoulder to lay eyes on the son of the mother he'd murdered. Did he feel no remorse for the crime? Or for seducing a poor, gullible Flame-Heart member? From the way Bonechew had explained things, she was an innocent victim whose only folly was being the target for Rime's manipulation.

Why did he confess, though? Maybe if he'd tried running away instead of taking all the blame, he could've avoided punishment. Silversong squinted at the scarred brute. *But then the Flame-Heart she-wolf would've been suspected of conspiring with Rime, and she would've been judged guilty; her scent would've been all over the site of the murder. There's no way the death of a lieutenant would've gone unnoticed. Rime's only options were to flee and hope to escape justice or confess. So why confess?*

Brokenjaw coughed out a spray of blood while another exile licked the cut on his throat. They talked about the ruin and how it was hostile to their presence, how blades of iron had sprung to life in one room and nearly sliced their party into pieces of meat, how more traps lay in wait, how the mountains themselves were determined to exterminate them like parasites. Silversong's ears turned to drown out the conversation as he stared at Frostpaw's wound, thorns pricking his heart.

He mouthed a quiet apology, meeting the lieutenant's eyes. Frostpaw gave him a nod and an uncertain smile as if trying to reassure him of forgiveness.

Silversong focused on the Heretic before the thorns pierced too deep, letting hatred smother sorrow and regret. His tail tip quivered, and his scowl tightened. Frostpaw glared at Rime, and though he was still in a feigned submissive posture, his hardened hackles betrayed the true reason he was here.

Silversong caught the stray whisper of an unnerved voice. "I can't believe the master let so many of us die to those traps so he could clear a safe way forward for himself."

"Would you've preferred it if he'd charged into those snares and gotten himself killed in the process?" Ripper snarled. "Who would've led us then? Would we've continued his mission for him? Would one of us claim the weapon in his place? Would we've even made it so far? A selfless leader is sometimes admirable, but a ruthless one is always necessary."

The only answer to Ripper's arguments was silence.

"I thought so," Ripper grunted. "So long as Ironwrath succeeds, the sacrifices he made along the way aren't in vain. He'll win because he's willing to make those sacrifices. All of us must be prepared to give up our lives for a higher cause, especially this one. Every life given for it is a steppingstone to victory."

"But the way the master so casually discarded them—"

"Is unsettling," Ripper admitted. Silversong could almost smell the uncertainty wafting off the exile. "But we've come too far to start questioning our leader. Take heart, Blackroot, we'll see the sun again soon enough."

The Heretic's ears perked up at the end of the corridor, and the whole group passed through an arched mouth of stone and into a chamber defying description. A gaping abyss stretched endlessly before them, which alone would've been worthy of a shiver, but it was the contours of the place that made Silversong cough out a tiny whimper.

Steps and winding lanes were paved up, downward, to one side and the other, all warped and twisted in every direction imaginable. Roads and tunnels turned the ceiling into a confusing labyrinth of pathways and intersecting routes. Everything was either flipped sideways or completely inverted. Nothing save for the narrow platform the wolves stood on was as it should've been.

The entire expanse from side to side and ceiling to unseen floor was a jumble of steps and roads, all overturned and flipped, disobeying every law known to nature. Silversong glanced behind him, gasping at the disappearance of the entrance he'd come through. A panel of stone containing the start of many lanes met his bulging eyes, each trail leading upward until they diverged drastically, melding into the maze of madness.

Silversong fixed his sight to the bland ground—the only thing that made sense among the sprawling insanity. "Motherwolf's mercy. What is this place?"

"Our greatest trial yet." The Heretic's answer carried a foreboding weight. "The Empress hinted at this, but I wasn't sure if she was speaking in riddles or not. It appears she wasn't exaggerating in the slightest. This is where all the Titans who tried reclaiming the piece of time after the War of Change got discouraged from their pursuit," he addressed his worried followers.

"Can't say I blame them. I would've been discouraged too, Titan or not." Silversong gaped at the utter absurdity facing him. An unwelcome feeling of familiarity struck him on the head. He couldn't shake off the impression that he'd been here before, that everything he was going through had already happened. Deep beneath the tide of confused thoughts, his own distorted voice seemed to laugh at him.

A sudden worry sprouted a cool shiver. He should've acted surprised upon the Heretic mentioning the piece of time. As far as Ironwrath was concerned, Silversong had no clue as to the nature of the weapon lying at the core of the Mountainmouth.

Too late to act surprised now. Silversong turned to Frostpaw who appeared to be having the same concern.

"And the deceit is revealed." The Heretic narrowed his fang-sharp eyes on Silversong.

Thankfully, Ripper cut off whatever Ironwrath was about to say next. "This is nothing short of madness!" Ripper's breaths shortened into panicked panting. "How're we supposed to continue forward if Titans couldn't make it through?!"

The Heretic faced his outspoken subordinate before studying the countless roads and upturned steps lining the dizzying ceiling, clearly at a loss.

"We press on the only way we can: we choose a road and follow it until its end," Silversong grunted on instinct before jerking up in shock. He'd said that without thinking, as if someone had possessed his body to answer Ripper's question. Again, a distorted voice he thought was his own laughed, a voice no one but him could hear.

The Heretic gave him an inquisitive stare. "I think you may be right, little lamb." He returned his attention to the maddening ceiling.

The Drowned Titan's voice thundered into Silversong's skull. He yelped, clenching his jaws so tightly it was a wonder his teeth hadn't shattered. **"You've avoided a great number of traps by choosing the way that led you to my watery prison, but I fear you'll be forced to confront this one. If your spirit is unbroken, fear not. The energies that distort reality slowly decay once exposed to time, and in your realm, time always ensures decay, even to itself. Your eyes may discover a crack in the once impenetrable maze, and sometimes a crack is all you need to break through. Think of those important to you while roaming the hallways winding in endless spirals, and you'll have your encouragement."**

"Thanks for the advice, slimy tentacle monster." Silversong stopped himself, realizing he'd whined that aloud.

"Beg your pardon?" The Heretic tilted his head, the action accompanied by a look of confusion as the exiles blinked and exchanged curious glances.

"Nothing." Silversong cringed, shifting his forepaws as the awkwardness settled.

The Heretic dismissed him, flicking his tail and keeping it lifted. "Let's each choose one of the roads leading up. It's better if we separate to cover more ground. I refuse to let the maze discourage me, even if I must spend an eternity inside it. Move out."

Blackroot barked, his whole body shaking. "No! This is beyond insanity. We'll never make it out of here!"

A couple more exiles also voiced their concerns, but Rime's growling shushed them. "Insubordination won't be tolerated. Look around you. There's no way out, so you have two options. Either you stay here until starvation devours you, or you swallow your cowardice and choose your road."

The Heretic's eyes swept over those who'd spoken up, finding nothing but defeated faces. "If it's any consolation, the Empress said the way out remained open for the Titans who dared to delve into the Mountainmouth, but for us it disappeared. It's as if fate needs us here. Every one of us is a crucial thread in the weavings of destiny. If we give up now, all the pain we've suffered would've been for nothing. This is where we're meant to be. This is where we win."

Despite a few frightened whines, the exiles wasted no time choosing their roads, sitting beneath them and trying to glimpse where they led. Silversong padded to one of the more innocent-looking ones, nosing Frostpaw on the way there. Silversong stared at the vertical line diverging under and over a ceaseless expanse of bridges and intersecting pathways leading to nowhere and everywhere. He shook the dizziness out of his brain and shared Frostpaw's uncertain look, managing a smile to try and cheer the lieutenant up, but his friend only bowed his head solemnly.

We'll make it out of here, Frostpaw. We have to.

"Everyone ready?" The Heretic turned to Rime, who looked around and gave a quick grunt of confirmation. "Good. Let's begin. Be mindful of your surroundings and keep searching for a way to beat the maze. May fate favour us all."

I hope it doesn't favour you. Silversong watched the Heretic placing a forepaw on his vertical lane. Silversong's eyes almost popped out of their sockets upon witnessing Ironwrath's body move in a way that made him now stand on the upright pathway as if he were glued to its stone. After a brief fit of gasping, the others also started on their chosen lanes, walking straight up like ants climbing a tree.

Frostpaw hesitated, coat bristling. Silversong found the lieutenant's eyes and managed a steady smile of encouragement. Together, they lifted a forepaw and placed it on their own pathway. Everything seemed normal so far. Silversong moved his other forepaw onto the vertical floor and walked up until his vision changed perspective. A whirling dizziness overcame him before his eyes quickly readjusted themselves. Staring to one side, he saw Frostpaw crouched upon his road, head darting wildly to assess his shifted surroundings. Silversong looked behind him, chills sliding from nose to tail. The platform they were previously standing on was inverted—a thick grey block acting as a barrier between him and the deep descent. The lane under him, once an upright line carved in stone, was now the only thing not abnormally altered.

He barked to Frostpaw, attracting the attention of exiles on other roads in the process. The lieutenant stopped glancing around like a frightened fox and stared at him, taking a breath to soothe his agitation. Silversong waited until Frostpaw was ready to go forward, determined to comfort his new friend for as long as he could. After another glance behind him, the lieutenant started along his lane. Silversong echoed Frostpaw's movements until the River-Stream member vanished from view, his pathway breaking into steps leading downward. He faded into the stone, and Silversong continued over a narrow bridge overlooking a steep pit. Soon the exiles also disappeared out of his vision, and he walked alone through tunnels and up coiling routes, the claws of complete isolation gripping his heart.

He imagined a black stallion walking by himself through an endless labyrinth, seeking something at the centre of it all. Come to think of it, this place looked almost exactly like the maze Stormstrider had gone through to receive the piece of time.

Silversong panted as panic settled itself within him. He could've sworn he'd already taken the road he now padded on, and he was sure he'd already descended those steps and climbed up those ones. He tried reaching out for the Drowned Titan, but the monster's booming voice stayed silent as death. He was alone… alone to contemplate the draining of his sanity.

I can't give up! I won't!

He slipped into a hallway of reflections, each one depicting a future he'd avoided. He watched his friends following him into the Mountainmouth and into their own demise. Palesquall sheltered Hazel while they ran from metallic traps and slicing blades. Sometimes they fought the exiles and even the Heretic himself, always dying in different ways, always breaking Silversong's heart into infinite pieces. It became unbearable to witness, and he used his own movements to conjure lashes of air, whipping the images until they shattered. More roads and steps and tunnels revealed themselves before him, all leading to the exact same room of undying torment, always repaired as if nothing had ever happened to it. The reflections now showed his packmates cursing him for leaving them in their hour of need, his parents wishing he'd never been their son, his sister renouncing him entirely and spitting on his memory. At least she was alive and healthy in the projections.

He trudged on as if through sap until the hallway of cruel reflections got bored of his whimpers. It shifted into a long corridor of bronze that sucked away all notion of time. He could've been walking for days or entire seasons without knowing it, but still he pressed on, his only motivation being the memories of Swiftstorm and of an innocent time when all he had to worry about was proving himself a worthy member of Whistle-Wind.

He thought of Hazel, of Palesquall, of his parents, and of… of… *who're the others? I can't remember their faces or their names! Oh, Motherwolf, am I going mad?! Who am I? What am I doing here? I have to go home! But… where is home?*

A silvery shape in the distance corrected his hazy vision. It pulled at him, tugged at his flesh and bones, lured him to its shine. He ran toward it, the metallic floor clinking under his hasty steps. A lithe male who looked to belong to Whistle-Wind Territory stood before a closed entrance sealed by stone. He skidded and stopped in front of him.

One of the stranger's eyes was missing, like something sharp had jabbed it out, but his remaining one was blue like a tranquil sky somehow robbed of vibrancy, and his silver coat, scarred and discoloured in several areas, was neatly sleeked. Some of the scars looked familiar, and his scent… he almost smelled like… *ME!* Silversong gasped and pricked his ears. A twinge of energy jolted every sleeping nerve awake. He was staring at himself!

"I think I've officially gone crazy," Silversong exhaled, sniffing the image of himself as if it were a stranger. Every particular place smelled exactly as it should've.

"Not yet you haven't," the image whined, and Silversong jumped backward, hackles shooting up. It sounded exactly like him too! "Oh, come on. Don't act like I'm the strangest thing you've seen so far." The image inspected him in return, sniffing him all over and scoffing. "Wow, I forgot how pretty I looked before everything happened." His one eye hinted at a lifetime of pain. "Frostpaw's compliments had some truth to them, after all."

"You… you… you're me!" Silversong drooled, trying to fathom how this all could be possible. It hurt his head to even think about it.

"I am, unfortunately." His double returned to the front of the closed entrance. There was something peculiar about the design on the stone—a circle dented in seven equally distanced spots, and in each inwardly curved nook rested a glowing orb. There was a gap at the bottom of the circle filled by the brightest orb of all, and it was linked by chains to the shape itself.

Eight orbs, eight stars. Silversong thought about the Empress and the stolen jewels shining in a circle above her shrine. It all meant something. It was all connected, but he couldn't fathom how.

"The Ring of Realms," his double sighed. "If I accomplish my duty here, I'll prevent you from ever seeing it up close. I'm you in the future if you haven't already guessed. More specifically, I'm you, but from a diverging timeline. I came here long ago, but also in the distant future, to knock some sense into you. I've been granted the means to shift and divert the course of all realities, but only within this corner of the underground ruin. I stopped the Titans in your timeline from claiming Stormstrider's weapon, and now I'm here to prevent you from becoming me, to save you from the pain. You stand at the crossroads. One way leads to suffering, and the other leads to salvation. Allow me to influence your decision."

"I don't understand!" Silversong barked at himself. "None of this makes sense to me!"

"Don't worry. I'll make sure you never understand the suffering I've gone through." The image let loose a subtle growl. "Don't question things you aren't meant to question yet. All you have to do is listen to me."

Silversong couldn't even think properly. It was like his brain had hopped out of his head and was dancing around it. He could do nothing but stare stupidly at his scarred imitation, wishing he could voice just one of the questions he had.

"Don't look at me like that." His double scowled.

"Like what?"

"Like that!" The image lowered his head and shook it. "Forget it. I know why you're here, Silversong: the piece of time—the weapon gifted to Stormstrider by the same entity who gave me my powers. You're hoping to slay the Heretic before he consumes it." He sighed again, his tone pained by the deepest sorrow. "I'll forever regret the day I set off on this foolish journey. All it led to was my own doom."

"Your own doom?!" Silversong pressed his nose against the snout of his older self. "What happens to me?! To my packmates?! To Frostpaw?!"

"Nothing good if you don't quiet your yapping muzzle," his beaten reflection snapped. "Listen. I'll keep this short. The sway of power won't lead Ironwrath to tyranny. He's the only one who can properly wield the potency of time without being influenced by it. You have to let him claim it. You have to let him break the Wolven Code and unite the Four Territories under his reign, or you'll lose everything."

"WHAT?!" Silversong growled, outrage stretching the snarl on his face. "No, you can't be serious! After everything he's done, you're telling me I have to—"

"Telling you about the potential future won't change anything. Trust me, I'll go through this routine countless times. I already have if you think about it." The one-eyed image craned his head to the captivating design carved so intricately at the centre of the sealed entrance. "You'll see the truth only after you witness Ironwrath's future for yourself. The course is set. You can't change it now."

The stone of the entrance flashed into a white panel, beckoning Silversong to enter. He'd never seen anything so perfectly bright. The lure of the light outshone all lesser desires, and yet he stopped himself short of striding into the blinding opening.

"Go on," his double urged him into the pure whiteness. "See for yourself the salvation Ironwrath offers should he claim the piece of time."

Silversong hesitated, his lifted forepaw shaking, his heart so afraid the older version of himself was telling the truth.

The Heretic is a dangerous lunatic, nothing more! I won't be swayed by a potential future no matter how good it is!

Drawing a deep breath, he stepped into the dazzling white entrance. The light enveloped him, its caress gentle, soothing, growing warmer as it soaked into every pore, slowly increasing in temperature until it reached an uncomfortable level. Silversong panicked, and his blood boiled into liquid fire. He screeched, but before he could scream his final breath, his body exploded into sparks, the heat searing him to the very soul. A fraction of a breath later, he disintegrated into specks of silvery ash.

CHAPTER 20

✦

A Good Future

Silversong floated within a blank void, the scattered fibers of his being linking themselves together again, forming bone and sinew, flesh and muscle, on and on until his body reconstructed itself. The process defied any measurement of time. One blink could've been akin to an infinite number of seasons or the shortest moment imaginable as he was reborn from his own ashes.

His body enveloped his hovering consciousness, and the pale emptiness transformed into a scene of vibrant beauty. The memory of burning alive faded, sinking ever deeper into a pit reserved for forgotten troubles. Birdsong livened the surrounding forest. His eyes adjusted to the springtime sun glittering at its highest peak amid a cloud-purged sky. He breathed the crisp air, finding himself atop a geyser-ridden shore overlooking an enormous lake so blue it would've made a sapphire envious, its surface a striking reflection of everything its gaze beheld.

Wolves played merrily around the blanched geysers, chasing each other and yipping as the day bloomed. A breath of surprise pushed itself out of him upon realizing the wolves weren't at all packmates. The paler colours of Whistle-Wind complemented the bluish and darker tinges of River-Stream, and the thinner coats of Flame-Heart clashed against the thicker hides of Stone-Guard.

Some of the youngsters had fur of different colours and patterns altogether. Silversong gasped, stomach dropping. They were halfbloods! Creatures whose very existence was an affront to the Wolven Code! A few of the rascals turned to him, ears pricked and eyes huge. Silversong noticed he was snarling and corrected himself, but his hackles still stood straight. Those of mixed blood wouldn't ever learn how to wield Motherwolf's Blessings, no matter how desperately they tried.

I… I shouldn't be angry at them. They have no control over who they are.

Paw steps pattered behind him, and he turned to see Hazel and Palesquall smiling together, joy-filled eyes bright as the sky. Silversong's heartbeat quickened, and a shaky breath escaped him as heavy whimpers climbed up his throat. He launched himself at his friends, nuzzling their faces and burying himself in their scents.

"Uh, you okay, buddy?" Palesquall let out an uncertain chuckle.

Hazel returned some of the nuzzles hesitantly. "Okay, something's gotten into you. You're never *this* affectionate with us."

Palesquall gave her a knowing nudge. "I thought only a certain lieutenant could get this reaction out of him. I guess our favourite silver scoundrel still has some surprises to offer."

Silversong swallowed the wedge stuck in his throat. "I'm… I'm just happy to see you two."

Hazel and Palesquall exchanged a curious look. Only now did Silversong see how different—how older—they were. From their taller statures to their more mature faces, he took it all in and grinned without control. Maybe things were going to get better after all.

"Hey, uhm," Silversong began, memories of a darker time shading the joyful present, "remind me of our old home, of Whistle-Wind Territory. I can't seem to recall how we got here. Everything's so fuzzy in my head all of a sudden."

Palesquall scoffed and wrinkled his forehead. "You're not getting senile already, I hope. Frostpaw has enough things to worry about as it is without having to take care of you."

Why would Frostpaw have to take care of me? Silversong wondered.

Hazel tilted her head and gave a worried stare. "Whistle-Wind Territory? It's been ages since I've heard the name of our old home."

"Ages?" Something heavy dropped to the pit of Silversong's stomach.

Palesquall mirrored Hazel's concern. "Since we abandoned our old den and settled ourselves here, we decided not to think about those darker days. Too many awful memories linger there for my comfort. The spiders can rot atop the shattered mound for all I care."

"Darker days?" Silversong shuddered, his heart on the brink of plummeting. *Please don't go where I think you're going.*

"The days before Ironwrath broke the Wolven Code and united the Four Territories as one," Palesquall confirmed Silversong's fear.

Silversong backed away, bristling, liquid ice streaming through every vein. "No. You can't mean it. The Heretic is evil! He slaughtered our packmates and—"

"The Heretic?!" Hazel hushed him, ears pricked in alarm. "Silversong, Ironwrath saved us. He showed us the truth about the sentinels and the Wolven Code, and he brought peace to all wolfkind. Yes, he killed many in the process, but it was a necessary evil. The blind Chiefs and their followers had to be culled for the oppressed to see things clearly. Sometimes I hate him for doing it. I hate him for executing all the remaining sentinels, the Warden, Chief Amberstorm and the others, but in the end, I always remind myself of why it had to happen, and I accept it. He's our saviour, Silversong. He led us to salvation. And I'll always be thankful he decided to spare your life and Frostpaw's after he swallowed the piece of time all those seasons ago."

"No, no, no!" Silversong couldn't keep it in anymore. Hazel's confession zapped the strength out of his bones, and he collapsed, whimpering and grieving for a future that hadn't yet happened.

His friends looked at him as if he were crazy, but after the initial confusion passed, they sat and tried to comfort him, offering leftovers from a different Prey Hollow of a different den. The thought of eating brought a sour taste to his tongue. He declined and stood up, searching all around for a way out of this dreadful vision.

"Maybe we should get him some medicine from the caverns beneath the Saltshore," Palesquall suggested. "He's acting awfully strange. It's almost like a previous version of himself took over."

"That makes no sense, gullwit," Hazel grunted. "Silversong? We're here if you feel like talking to us about whatever you're going through."

Silversong peered into her leafy green eyes, hoping to detect something—anything—that would indicate she wasn't as happy as she thought she was. The idea of his friends being content—even accepting—of Ironwrath's reign sickened him to the core.

Something beyond Silversong's shoulders caught their attention, and Palesquall smirked. "Now, there's someone who can cheer him up. Look who it is, Silversong."

Silversong turned to Frostpaw, who smiled warmly between two geysers, his eyes and face as striking as the sun itself. Silversong's spirit lifted itself a little, and his tail tip twitched. The lieutenant stood slightly taller now, and his strong features were more defined, but he was as handsome as ever.

Hazel nosed Silversong on the side, pushing him toward the lieutenant. "Go on. Looks like he's waiting for you. Try not to keep Ironwrath's second-in-command waiting."

Second-in-command?! Silversong's throat knotted itself again. *It can't be!* He strode carefully in Frostpaw's direction regardless, a troubled curiosity motivating his steps.

Palesquall whispered something to Hazel, the two giggling afterwards, but Silversong couldn't be bothered to guess whatever obscenities his silly friend had uttered. Upon reaching Frostpaw, the lieutenant licked him tenderly on the nose. "Hey, little fox. You okay?"

"I… uh." Silversong couldn't get anything out. His conflicted emotions clashed together, stirring a confused whirlwind of scrambled thoughts. "I'm fine, thanks. And you?" He took in Frostpaw's comforting scent, hesitating for a heartbeat before rubbing himself in the lieutenant's smooth coat. The wound on his shoulder was still there, but it looked a lot better now.

"I suppose I'm doing good after designating tasks for the day, but my job does get exhausting sometimes." He released a quick sigh, leaning to whisper into Silversong's ear. "Don't mention this to Ironwrath, but I sometimes miss the Wolven Code's ranking system. No matter how flawed and oppressive it was, it made the territories run smoothly." Frostpaw smiled, his longing for a break clearly satisfied.

It's only a vision, Silversong! It's not real!

Frostpaw licked him on the cheek this time. "Oh, by the way, the master wanted to see you. Care for an escort?"

Silversong stifled a shiver and accepted despite not wanting to, bowing low to the Heretic's second-in-command.

Frostpaw tilted his head and looked at him funny. "Why the submissiveness all of a sudden? There's no longer a need for such humiliating postures, remember?"

"Oh, right. Old habits, I guess." Silversong fought against the instinct to lower himself before Frostpaw. "Lead the way." He lifted his stature and faced Frostpaw as an equal.

Frostpaw took him around big and small geysers alike as the deep greens of spring shifted in the current of a smooth breeze. Catching the trail, Silversong inhaled the sweetness of blossoming flowers, the bitterness of distant mushrooms, the muskiness of migrating deer, the salty aroma of the shore, and the fresh fragrance of the lake all entwined in one complex scent.

A few familiar faces distinguished themselves among the lounging and playful wolves. His father was there, fur greyed and eyes pale, his youthful spirit finally withered by age, but still he smiled and wagged his tail as Silversong passed by.

Do you even remember Pinetrail, father? Or your Chief?

Every time he spotted wolves from different packs acting like mates, he turned away as if he'd witnessed something inappropriate. He focused instead on the exiles roaming openly about the strange den, laughing while bathing in the sun, their once mottled fur slick and their scarred flesh nearly fully healed. Ripper was there, chuckling at something a Flame-Heart she-wolf had said to him. Younger wolves chased Brokenjaw around spitting geysers, yipping as they played, and an older Blackroot sat beside Tawnydrift, the couple sitting at the edge of the shore, looking out into the singing Songwoods. Gorsescratch was nowhere to be found.

After everything you've all done, how can you act like normal wolves?! He struggled not to growl at the exiles.

Frostpaw's whine chased away Silversong's scowl. "So I've been thinking…"

"Yeah?" Silversong glanced at the lieutenant's perky smile, finding it more and more of a challenge not to wag his tail even after reminding himself this was only a vision.

"If the master allows it, I would like to explore beyond our borders, to see the wonders outside our home." Frostpaw gazed up at the clear sky, a pup-like twinkle lighting his eyes. "Silversong, Ironwrath used the piece of time to visit places you wouldn't believe existed! He spoke to me about it! Over a veil of mountains at the edge of our new territory, there's a valley so green it would make the leaves here look sickly in comparison, and further still, there's another continent dominated by great felines so bloodthirsty they would mangle you just for looking at them funny. He's seen everything, from golden plains to forests of mushrooms taller than the average oak, from ridges of pure ice to canyons steep enough to dizzy a soaring eagle, all inhabited by creatures so wondrous they would make your eyes pop out of your head! The only thing I wouldn't like to see are more ancient ruins. According to Ironwrath, they're abundant in those strange lands. At least I'll die happy knowing I'll never see the inside of one again."

A flood of unease welled up inside Silversong. "Sounds like quite the adventure."

Frostpaw looked at him expectantly. "Yes, but it won't be complete without you."

Silversong's eyes jerked away from Frostpaw to study the familiar oaks and alders surrounding the lake and shore. "I… I'll have to think about it." Guilt riddled his chest upon glimpsing the lieutenant's crestfallen face.

It's only a vision. It isn't real.

"You don't have to decide now, of course!" Frostpaw yipped quickly, tail stiff. "Just think about it, okay? I think it would be fun to explore the unknown together." His smile produced tingles as efficiently as bees produced honey.

Silversong tried to uproot the sappy feeling sprouting inside him, pondering how he and the lieutenant could've possibly grown so close. Some wolves gave them inquisitive stares while others assumed respectful postures as Frostpaw passed by.

Silversong perked up his ears at Frostpaw's joyful panting. "Why so cheerful?" He gave in to temptation and ran his tongue along the healed wound on Frostpaw's shoulder. The lieutenant giggled and nuzzled him in return.

"Oh, sorry." Frostpaw stopped and wore a more serious look, chuckling to himself. "I'm just happy everything worked out for us in the end. I still remember how crazy I thought you were in the Mountainmouth all those seasons ago, trying to convince me we had to let Ironwrath swallow the piece of time." He exhaled a relieved breath. "I'm thankful you managed to convince me to stand aside. If you hadn't, I probably never would've gotten the chance to challenge Rime to a duel and take his place, and we probably would've died in the underground ruin. At least we would've died side by side, but I prefer a future where we're alive and still young enough to enjoy life together, wouldn't you agree?"

"Yeah." Silversong's grunt was more like a squeak. The lieutenant smiled before continuing forward.

A sharp sting spread throughout Silversong, a sting colder than ice and more bitter than spoiled meat. He trailed Frostpaw and sealed his muzzle, smothering his desire to ask questions on how to achieve this future. At the edge of the shore, overlooking a gully of grey stones curving about the forest's rim, sat a brittle elder whose days of glory were far behind him. His fur was utterly blanched, patches of it missing in some places, revealing spots of dried flesh.

He emitted an odd aura Silversong couldn't quite explain, and it gave him a slight tickle as he came nearer. The closer he got, the more he could feel the old one's mastery over certain unseen threads binding existence together. The elder craned his head around, and Silversong crouched, hackles shooting up, teeth fighting to bare themselves as he stared into the dead eyes of the Heretic.

The leader of the exiles beckoned him forward and gestured to his second-in-command. "You may leave us."

Frostpaw dipped his head and gave Silversong a brief nudge and a tender smile before padding away. Silversong stayed there, legs shaking like twigs battered by a freezing gale. The Heretic commanded him forward once more. This time, he obeyed, caution guiding every stride until he stopped beside the bane of the Four Territories. *But these aren't the Four Territories anymore.*

"Sit and listen," the Heretic ordered. Though his voice was frail, it still contained enough power to caution against disobedience.

Silversong rested himself beside the one responsible for too many deaths to forgive. He struggled to contain the hot rage brewing inside him.

"My life is coming to an end, Silversong." The Heretic inhaled deeply. "Although time's decay clouds the certainty of the future, I still see my death as clear as the day is bright. On the eve of summer, I'll return to my birthplace and climb the highest mountain there, and as I ascend, I'll think about all the good I accomplished while I lived… all the victories I won. At the top, I'll lie under the moon and stars and wait for the conclusion to my story."

Silversong breathed sharply, his risen fur refusing to lay low, his stomach bunching up, his nerves fueling the growing heat within. But he released no growl. He only sat there and listened as if pulled to the ground by an invisible weight too heavy to fight.

The Heretic coughed, his hunched shoulders showing bone. "The physical manifestation of time has granted me clarity. I've scried every possible future in search of the one we now thrive within, and I've attained it by following the patterns your eyes can't yet see. I've expended the weapon's strength in the process, and now it's at its weakest state, and although its power is still great, I can't use it to prolong my life any longer. Death is inevitable. Entropy is inevitable. You'll never truly forgive the actions I took to achieve peace, but you understand their necessity. I see it in your eyes." He took a moment to compose himself, straightening up and sitting like a regal cat. "Silversong, throughout the seasons since my rise to power, you've shown the qualities of an exceptional leader. You inspire wolves around you to be their better selves and to never give up hope. I'll even dare to say you inspired me to truly follow the virtues of mercy. Silversong, once death finally claims me, I would like you to continue my legacy. Time's physical manifestation needs a body it can inhabit, and I think you should be the vessel for its remaining power. Use it to lead our enlightened nation to an even brighter future."

The Heretic's offer crushed Silversong. He wanted to scream, to decline, to rip his enemy's throat out and curse his rotten soul to suffer the Fallen Titan's corruption, but all Silversong could do was nod and accept.

"Good." The Heretic coughed again. "Yes… very good." He managed a weak smile. It looked so natural on his old, peaceful face. One could almost swear he wasn't actually a warmongering murderer. "Don't despair for the means I took to get us here, Silversong. Despair only for those who refused to accept salvation."

Silversong remained composed despite the chill in his bones.

The Heretic let out a raspy breath and lay on the ground, gazing in the direction of the Mountainmouth. "Now, go see Frostpaw. Enjoy his company while the day still shines, and consider his offer. I think you'll enjoy travelling together."

Time slowed to a standstill, and Silversong's own voice roared in his head. *"Do you see now the prosperity awaiting us if we let Ironwrath win? No more Chiefs abusing their power! No more oppressive rules dictating how we should live our lives! No more boundaries on friendships and love! No more meaningless divisions!*

We'll be free! Free of the veil of ignorance blinding our eyes! Free of the judgment of those too weak to think for themselves! Isn't it wonderful?"

Silversong shuddered and hoped against all evidence the vision was wrong. There had to be another way! This future couldn't be real! He wouldn't accept it!

"No. There is no other way," his own voice answered his doubts. "We all have to make sacrifices in the end, and this one is destined to be yours. Let go of your sense of justice and your desire to save everyone and accept a heretic's reign."

Silversong gritted his teeth and glowered at the sky. A falcon frozen in time sliced the sun's still rays into bright, unmoving streams. "I… I have to see the future where I don't let the Heretic win."

The voice in his head sighed. "So be it."

Silversong braced himself for whatever his one-eyed image would reveal. Time streamed forward again, and the sky turned black as smoke, clouds forming a snarling mouth reaching to gobble him up. Thunder boomed, and drops of blood wetted the ground where he stood. His packmates were tethered to the few sentinels who survived the breaking of the Great Chain, and they were drawn to a towering spire of obsidian jutting out of the earth to scrape the clouds.

Flames consumed a forest of crimson leaves, and the exiles clashed against the scattered forces of the Four Territories, death being the ultimate victor of the skirmish. Chief Amberstorm lay in a pool of his own blood, throat punctured, gasping his final breaths. Upon obsidian heights, Silversong listened to the anguished cries of Ripper as he melted from the inside out. Chaos engulfed anything remotely resembling order. Silversong watched helplessly as a hail of black stone crushed the life out of one he assumed to be the Warden. Frostpaw chased Rime, but the sinful murderer escaped the fangs of justice by the thinnest hair. Silversong tried to look away as sworn enemies fought for the soul of the Four Territories, but the movement only brought him to another horrific scene. He found himself frozen before Hazel's broken body, her bones shattered, her opened eyes telling of the horror she'd experienced in her final moments. Gorsescratch wailed over her corpse, crying out for vengeance.

Ripples in the vision brought Silversong to a circular room of bronze where the Heretic presented a rugged-looking version of Swiftstorm. Silversong tried leaping to his sister, but the more he struggled, the more the floor tightened its grasp around his limbs. No matter how violently he thrashed or barked, he couldn't reach her. A golden circle lit the intricate chamber, the threads making up the glowing shape weakening until they disintegrated into nothingness. In the darkness, a metallic spike formed under Swiftstorm and impaled her stomach, lifting her body, the tip forcing itself up through her spine as she screamed in agony. Silversong yowled and closed his eyes, trying desperately to block out the terrible image.

Does this confirm she's still alive in the present? Even the barest hope wasn't enough to bring comfort.

Opening his eyes made him regret not leaving them closed. He stood amid the aftermath of a massacre. An army of dead wolves littered a field of blood like leaves stripped from autumn's trees. Dozens of packmates lay broken on the rough terrain, and as the survivors huddled together and stared blankly at the unhealable destruction, Silversong caught a pair of icy blue eyes watching him from atop a grey ridge, warning him not to pursue his own doom.

A strike of lightning, and the vision shifted out of focus. Silversong dropped to the ground in a metal corridor, facing his one-eyed double, panting heavily. "No! There has to be another way!"

"Listen to yourself, gullwit!" his double scolded. "Heed my warning and let Ironwrath win! Or you'll lose your friends, your family, your—" he broke off and snarled at his own reflection on the floor, "—everything. You'll lose everything if you don't listen to me! If you don't listen to yourself!"

"Who gave you this power, huh?! What price did this entity ask of you?! How did you even find him?!" Silversong demanded, backing away from the future he refused to become. He wouldn't be a slave to time, to destiny or anything else. His choices were *his* to make!

"I…" Fear scent wafted from the pathetic image, and he cowered beneath the now closed entrance. "I'm not allowed to say, but if you listen, you won't ever have to meet him. I stopped Ironwrath from consuming the piece of time, and my mistake led me to this torture. Let your enemy win, and you can avoid your darkest fate. Please!"

Cracks of white spidered across one side of the corridor, chunks of it breaking off to reveal nothing but a sparkling shine beyond. Again, Silversong's own distorted voice laughed. He glanced from his double to the breaking metal. *But if I swallow the piece of time instead of the Heretic, I'll have the power to save everyone and change things for the better! I can amend the Wolven Code and bring unity to the divided territories! I can be the balance the Four Territories need! I can do it!*

"NO!" His double bristled at the cracks in the metal. "This isn't how it's supposed to be. The decay has reached us. It's too soon. You aren't yet persuaded. You can't leave! I must save this timeline before you make everything worse!"

Silversong crouched and twirled his tail until the motion created a swift current. Connecting himself to it, he lashed his scarred doppelganger aside and bolted toward the beckoning brightness.

"ARGH!" his lesser image yelped as an aura expanded from within him, the same aura Silversong had sensed in the vision of the *good* future. "I won't fail myself! You can't leave! Not now! Not ever!" Invisible threads started tightening around the corridor, threatening to keep Silversong ensnared in the underground ruin forever.

"Bite my tail!" Silversong jumped into the light, and it wrapped him in a brilliant cocoon. Muffled shattering sounds and distant screams reached his ears, but the impenetrable beams coiling his body reassured him of his safety. Where did this unnatural light come from? And how did he know it would protect him?

"Stay the course, and you'll have your answers." His warped voice was so faint he could barely hear it, but still it made him squirm, the safety of the cocoon compromised by something unknowable, something wrong.

"GOOD!" The Drowned Titan's voice rumbled outside the wrappings of light. **"You've found the crack in the maze and shattered it once and for all. The Heart of the Mountains awaits near the prize you seek. Bring it to me, and I'll be free."**

The white veil darkened into a grey almost like stone before spewing Silversong out like a snake spitting venom. As he plummeted into an abyss, he could almost hear the wicked laughter of the mountains echoing from deep within their shadowy bowels. Shutting his eyes, Silversong awaited whatever end fate had in store for him.

✦

CHAPTER 21

The Wolf Who Swallowed Time

A smooth surface of grey stone came up toward Silversong faster than a snake's strike at the moment of the attack. He yelped, but no pain followed. At his side, Frostpaw pushed himself up and stood stiffly on the dusty ground overlooking an expansive cavern. Silversong realized he was lying sideways and rolled over to get up too. He'd never been falling. He'd charged straight through the wound in the fabric warping reality, and he'd been placed wherever he was now. He thought it useless to ask himself how.

But the things I've been shown, were they real? Or was it all a trick? He hoped the latter was the truth. He turned to Frostpaw and lamented the future they had in the vision where the Heretic won. *But I can't let him win.*

He hurried to Frostpaw to remind himself he wasn't alone in this deceitful, sunless pit. Frostpaw bounded over to Silversong and nearly crashed into him, whining something about how he thought they wouldn't ever escape the maze. Silversong returned the passionate nuzzles and allowed himself to smile.

"Frostpaw?" Silversong broke from the tenderness. "Did you see anything strange in the maze? Anything at all?"

Frostpaw lapped Silversong on the cheek. "No. Nothing. I vaguely remember losing my sanity as I walked through endless hallways, but I can't remember anything else up until I saw white cracks spreading around me. I blinked, then everything shattered, and I was falling." He shivered. "Why? Did you see something else?"

"I broke the maze." Silversong stared at the floor, the pain of the visions nestling itself into his core. "Frostpaw, I saw—"

"You did it."

Their hackles hardened as they whirled around to face the Heretic and his scowling exiles. The two backed away from each other and stood apart on the large shelf. Ripper padded past everyone, making sure all were accounted for. Three weren't present. He signalled their absence to the Heretic, who whined nothing, but allowed his followers to grieve a moment for their departed comrades.

Silversong tried not to think about how they might've met their ends.

"A fascinating thing, the maze. I wonder who could've had the power to design it, and why." The Heretic settled his unfeeling eyes on Silversong. "A question for another time, perhaps."

"Master." Rime moved to the front, shouldering his way through the throng of exiles and to the Heretic's side. "These little rodents have exceeded their use." He cocked his head to Silversong and Frostpaw. "We should rid ourselves of any potential nuisances while we can."

"Try it, scatfur," Frostpaw growled. Silversong wished he had the River-Stream lieutenant's foolhardiness sometimes.

Ripper grunted, breaking the tension. His raspy voice travelled across the gigantic expanse overlooked by the huge steps of stone descending behind Silversong. "Where are we?"

The Heretic flicked his tail, which again was enough to silence the concerned voices. "We're at the core of the Mountainmouth, the place where the Forgotten Ones eventually took the piece of time after slaying its original wielder. Now the weapon lies at the heart of the ruin, according to the Empress of Spiders." He faced his loyal lieutenant. "As I've said before, the little lamb and his little friend are to witness my ascension."

Rime relented. "As you command."

You'll never ascend. Not while I'm still breathing. Silversong trembled, trying not to envision the future where the Heretic won, trying not to remember the peace, the prosperity, the beauty, the joy... *NO! It's a trick. I can't let a monster like him win!*

The Heretic's attention was drawn to a massive bipedal figure of black crystal stomping about the grey expanse below. Something within it flickered brightly—an untamed orange flame banishing all creeping shadows.

"You're so close now." The Drowned Titan's whispers pushed into Silversong's ears and bounced off his brain. **"The Heart of the Mountains lies ahead, as does the piece of time Stormstrider bargained for. It awaits a vessel through which its powers may be used. Seize it for yourself and thwart your enemy."**

The Heretic's sharp barking cut off Silversong's planning. "Everything is falling into place. A manifestation of time's nature awaits my grasp. Victory is finally upon us!"

The exiles howled, rallying in groups as the Heretic and Rime exchanged hushed whines. The banished wolves hopped onto the steps, starting downward, heading into the sprawling stretch of carved structures huddled neatly together. The odd and dangerous-looking constructions were parted by lanes cutting all the way to the centre, where the gigantic figure of black crystal patrolled, its heart shining like a shivering flame. The ceiling far above extended over the colossal ruin, and silvery minerals stuck in the rocky creases glinted like tiny stars trapped in stone.

Silversong strained his ears to listen to the conversation between the Heretic and his lieutenant. "After we question the River-Stream pup, he'll no doubt ask for a chance to settle the score for you killing his mother all those seasons ago. Before you came to me."

Frostpaw tensed, muscles outlined under his fur. He looked ready to pounce. Silversong thought about the two possibilities shown to him by his future image. In one, Frostpaw had challenged Rime to a duel and won fairly, assuming the murderer's place at the Heretic's side afterwards. In another time, Rime had escaped justice.

Rime gave the lieutenant of his former territory a malicious stare. "He can try. If the pup wishes to suffer the same fate as his dead mother, I'll gladly oblige."

"Hmm." The Heretic seemed almost troubled at the prospect of potentially losing his loyal servant. "Understood. Let's begin the descent. I would like to be rid of the ruin as soon as possible. Wolves aren't meant to dwell in the deep places."

Frostpaw's yellow glare stayed glued to Rime's shoulders as the huge exile passed by. Silversong could practically feel the tension hanging by the thinnest thread. The hatred seething within the two enemies pierced to the heart. Silversong nudged Frostpaw, hoping to soothe at least some of his boiling rage. Why was he so keen on shirking his duty as a lieutenant to pursue vengeance? There was another factor to Frostpaw's anger, Silversong was sure of it. He nudged him again, and the lieutenant straightened up, finally composing himself. Side by side, they descended the broad shelves, Silversong pondering the potential futures he and Frostpaw could have if they ever made it out of here.

The steps were impractically placed, their stark heights forcing all the wolves to leap every time the rim overlooked a steep descent. The journey to the bottom was long and quiet as everyone dipped further and further into the fading memory of a bygone time. After an uncounted number of tiring drops, Silversong and Frostpaw landed at the edge of the Mountainmouth's core, trailing the exiles through bowels of stone and rusted metal.

Strange contraptions of steel and other materials cluttered the expanse, some linked to chains, some broken by the ruthless passing of time, some still clutching desperately to their former glory, but all evoking a sense of unease, of wrongness.

Like stray moths, the group was drawn to the bright shimmer in the middle of the decayed ruin. Shadows cowered behind them, their blocky shapes quivering. Silversong's eyes bulged at the more impressive constructions. Some reached to incredible heights, but none ever dared to touch the unmoving ripples of the sparkling roof. The place had to be at least twice the size of the lake where the Drowned Titan slept. The strides of the giant patrolling ahead caused brief tremors as its weight struck ground, tempering Silversong's wonder.

"Remember your purpose, little one." The thundering voice resounded in Silversong's skull. **"Bring me the Heart of the Mountains, and I'll return the favour one day."**

I hope that day comes soon. Silversong convinced himself not to whine his thoughts out loud this time.

"Hey, Silversong?" Frostpaw's whisper startled him. "Sorry. I wanted to ask you something."

"Hmm?" Silversong faced the lieutenant's bright yellow eyes.

"Up there, before you broke the maze, what did you see?" Frostpaw's whine quavered as if he were unsure whether he wanted to hear the answer or not.

Claws of ice and fire gripped Silversong's chest, the memory of the horrifying visions causing a spasm of dread. "I-I don't…" He inhaled slowly to weaken his warring emotions. "Frostpaw, I saw things I never wanted to see—futures I never wanted to glimpse."

And then there was his distorted voice at the end of it all, but he refused to mention it for fear of its return.

His heart ached as Frostpaw gave him a questioning stare. "I don't follow."

Silversong forced his eyes forward, wondering if it truly would be better if he let the Heretic succeed. "I think maybe… maybe we should…" Ironwrath's victims stared at him from the darkest corners of his thoughts, saddened at the notion of never having justice. His sister stared too, blinking at him in disappointment. "No. Forget it. There's always another way."

Frostpaw's forehead bore wrinkles of confusion. Silversong licked the dried wound on his companion's shoulder, stealing a glance at the Heretic to make sure he wasn't listening. "We'll be fine, fish-breath. Don't worry about what I saw. It's not important. We'll beat the Heretic and leave the Mountainmouth alive. Nothing else matters."

That, at least, planted a small smile on the lieutenant's face. "I hope so, little fox. I hope so."

Memories of the kinder vision streamed into Silversong's mind and sparked a shiver. At the front of the group, the Heretic whispered something to Rime and turned around, pacing toward them. Silversong and Frostpaw distanced themselves a little, tails going stiff.

"Not even trying to hide your *friendship* now, are you?" the Heretic remarked, joining their slower strides.

"Friendship?" Frostpaw wrinkled his nose as if disgusted by a sour smell. "A true follower of the Wolven Code knows it's a crime for two wolves of different territories to become friends. It leads to confused loyalties."

Silversong's gaze plummeted. Something sharp clutched his stomach and pulled it low.

"Deny it all you like." The Heretic's unblinking stare intensified. "Deep inside, I'm sure you understand the folly of blindly obeying an array of oppressive rules. Maybe the Wolven Code would've prevented the Forest Father from becoming the Fallen Titan, maybe not. One thing is certain, though. The Wolven Code has destroyed more lives than I ever have. So many condemned without reason, without a proper trial. Can't you see I'm trying to change things? To make life better for us all?"

"You speak as though you get to choose the future for everyone." Frostpaw openly snarled. "How can wolves be morally good without a code to follow? Without something to guide us toward virtue?"

The Heretic laughed as if Frostpaw had barked the funniest joke. The sudden display of emotion coming from the dead-eyed monster made Silversong hide his tail on instinct. "If you can't distinguish good from evil by exercising your own judgment, you're more of a danger to the Four Territories than I'll ever be."

"And you think you're good for the Four Territories?!" Several exiles looked over their shoulders and growled at Frostpaw, but the Heretic allowed the River-Stream lieutenant to continue. "Even after all the pain and suffering you caused?!"

"The wise understand the need of sometimes delving into necessary evils." The Heretic took one look at the bristling lieutenant and sighed. "But I don't expect you to understand. Not yet at least. You're still young and naïve like I once was. I could've stopped a tyrant from leading Stone-Guard Territory into a depraved state. If I'd gotten rid of Chief Bronzeblood subtly instead of doing the honourable thing and challenging him, I could've saved so many. Instead, I took the virtuous route and doomed myself and those who counted on me. If I'd chosen differently, I wouldn't have been exiled, and I wouldn't have been forced to seek out the means to solidify my power over the Four Territories. Always remember, those who cling to evil act out of their own ignorance, nothing more. We exiles act out of hope, the hope for a brighter future."

The Heretic whined nothing more as they pressed on. Frostpaw growled curses under his breath only Silversong's ears could hear. Ironwrath padded to Rime's side again, tail proudly displayed. How he could so casually justify his rotten nature brought chills to Silversong's spine.

Pale flowers bearing no particular scent caught the eye as the group passed by. They sprouted in rocky nooks, their snaking petals resembling splayed ribbons.

The violent flickering and the brief tremors every time the distant giant's feet met the ground produced uncomfortable twinges—warnings of impending danger. Everyone padded shoulder to shoulder in an arched tunnel stinking of rusted metal. Shelled insects sometimes lurked on the ground or on the buildings themselves, their chittering limbs beating an odd rhythm to counter the oppressive silence.

Every so often, Silversong spotted skeletons in the distance or in one of the trenches littering the expanse. Squinting to get a better look revealed them as the bones of the Forgotten Ones. Frostpaw's lifted hackles and hidden tail communicated his unease.

The Heretic appeared unbothered compared to his jittery exiles. "Looks like not all the Forgotten Ones perished during the War of Change. Some obviously stayed here until starvation ate them. Bad way to go."

Frostpaw closed his eyes and inhaled deeply, settling his gaze on Rime. It was a smart strategy to drown fear under waves of anger. The miasma of sharp anxiety the exiles emitted dissipated after an eternity of walking. The party rounded the corner of a rectangular structure and started along the main road leading to the source of the ceaseless flickering. The bipedal monstrosity strode in circles around the centre of the ruin. A single, orange-shining eye at the middle of its squarish forehead beamed a constant stream of light, and deep inside its chest of darkened crystal, something flashed, then dimmed, then flashed once more, pulsing like a heart of unstable fire. Its wide, blocky body bore no scratch or imperfection. It moved as a smooth two-legged behemoth of shadowy ice, its posture slightly crouched.

Silversong let his eyes be drawn to the giant's heart, its mesmerizing shimmer too striking not to admire from a distance. "The Heart of the Mountains."

"Yes." The Drowned Titan couldn't hide his excitement. **"And below it lies the tool to defeat your enemy. Claim the weapon, and let its protector follow you to my grasp. Lure the behemoth to my prison."**

A twitch of my whiskers says this is a terrible idea, Silversong thought.

"If you're swift enough to evade the protector's fire, you've nothing to fear. Remember our deal."

Silversong whispered to Frostpaw his intention of stealing the piece of time from the Heretic. Frostpaw gaped and shook his head wildly. He clearly thought the idea was beyond insane too.

It's now or never.

They all stopped and hid behind a corner to avoid the giant's gaze. Under its shadow, even more remarkable in comparison, was a small golden circle, its rotating edge coiling in on itself in an impossible manner. It emitted an aura affecting the air surrounding it, pulling at invisible threads, weaving each into endlessly looping patterns. The shape looked so flawless in its smoothness and shine, so seductive, so tempting to approach, to smell, to touch. Silversong wetted his mouth.

There it is. The piece of time. Stormstrider's weapon.

Beneath the captivating shape lay the skeleton of a Forgotten One, bones still white despite the passing of the ages, covered in a deep green fabric. Its skull wore a golden ornament in which many round rubies and striking emeralds glinted.

The Heretic quivered in delight and approached the golden circle cautiously, tail wagging as he panted. "Now begins my ascension."

Seeing the leader of the exiles so alive yanked Silversong out of the trance. He remembered his mission, his purpose. While the others remained intoxicated by the motion of the golden circle, Silversong neared it too, prowling into its heavy aura. The giant stopped, its eye flaring up, a fire within threatening to incinerate the intruders. Silversong and the Heretic halted. Winding through the very fabric of the air were roads leading to futures where Silversong thrived, futures where he ruled over every territory as a benevolent Chief, futures where he amended the Wolven Code and brought undying prosperity to all, futures where he, his packmates, and Frostpaw lived in happiness and peace. He wanted it. He wanted it all!

And as he turned to the Heretic, he saw other futures bloom, futures where peace was built upon the bones of fallen loved ones, futures where destruction and death were needed to ensure Ironwrath's unquestioned authority.

I can't allow it.

The protector of time growled, its stone-grinding voice trembling through bone.

The Heretic whirled to face Silversong, green eyes like brilliant gemstones in widened sockets. "NO! You won't steal my destiny from me! The piece of time is mine!" He charged toward the golden circle, mouth open and ready to swallow it whole.

Silversong broke into the fastest sprint he could manage, currents of air whizzing about him as the protector lifted a heavy foot to crush its targets. They jumped out of the way to avoid getting flattened, the force of the stomp sending the two flying in opposite directions. Black stars speckled Silversong's vision as he fought the temptation to faint. A pulsing migraine forced him to clench his jaws. The Heretic willed buildings of stone to launch themselves in Silversong's direction, but he got up and ran to avoid the enormous blocks crashing at his tail, shattering into chunks of dusty debris.

The giant bellowed, its thunderous roar shaking the entire expanse to its foundations. Silversong had not even a moment to register the blare before it pounded against his eardrums. A shrill ringing sound burrowed itself deep inside his skull to embolden his migraine. Still, he ran straight toward the golden circle so bright it outshone the chaotic flickering of the protector's heart, so captivating it overshadowed even the instinct to survive.

A clenched crystal paw moved to smite him into the cracking ground, but he used his momentum to dodge the strike. Blindingly swift, the protector struck again, its other blocky forepaw poised to pummel him into oblivion. He pushed on his haunches and leaped to the side, cringing at the powerful impact behind. The floor ruptured and broke beneath him as a hail of stone and metal came his way. He jumped again, and time seemed to decelerate. He aimed his gaping mouth at the golden circle and braced himself. A blank sheet covered his eyes as he crunched on the physical manifestation of time, forcing it to slide into his throat.

Everything stopped. The universe paused its linear course. The chaos froze, and Silversong zipped in circular motions through a hole that had neither an end nor a beginning.

CHAPTER 22

✦

A Wolf in the Sun

Silversong whirled at a speed beyond measure into a maelstrom of memories spanning the length of time and space. A spinning current locked him in an unbreakable circle, the motion steadily slowing. Somehow, it all made sense to him. The looping shape, the winding course, the light of his timeline bending in on itself, everything clicked together. The end tied itself to the beginning, and the beginning to the end, the threads of time wrapping themselves around his formless consciousness.

A new sense of awareness sprouted through him. He was a passenger in the threads, an unseen onlooker yanked out of his physical body to witness unknowable secrets. He peeked through strands in the decelerated circle and stared at an enormous shadowy stallion, the coiling patterns on his body bright compared to the empty void surrounding him. No… not empty.

Everywhere, blinking eyeballs darker than death watched the stallion. Some even turned to Silversong. If he were here in the flesh, he would've shriveled in utter terror, but he wasn't, and so he continued spying even though the creeping feeling of wrongness only worsened.

The Horse Titan blinked at Silversong, or at the threads binding him in place. "This is it?" His voice was like the galloping thunder of a stampede, and yet it seemed weak as the stomping of a foal in the presence of whatever entity ruled this place. "It doesn't look like the weapon I asked for."

"It's your prize for finding me. And for your bargain," Stormstrider's own voice answered him in all the wrong tones. "Swallow it, and time's course is yours to glimpse and influence."

"Thank you, Traveller." Stormstrider bowed, his perfect mane shifting at the slightest movement. "After it's all over, I'll belong to you as promised. Body and soul."

The deep silence of a pause settled on the expanse, furthering the blooming sense of dread. Finally, the entity spoke again. "You can't escape the circle."

The infinite eyes of the unknown being shifted to Silversong, and the space between the threads collapsed, shutting the gap as the circle turned to reveal another memory within another narrow opening.

Ash drifted from the clouds to blanket the remains of a dead forest. Corpses of beasts and Forgotten Ones outnumbered the leaves littered about the ground, and the calming flames—once roaring infernos—exhaled trails of soot-black smoke, announcing the end of another battle won at too great a price to be considered a victory.

The sun blazed red at its zenith as if it had absorbed all the blood spilled today and was hungry yet for more. Shining unseen around Stormstrider's body, Silversong observed the devastation from the hilltop until the presence of another Titan tugged at his attention.

The Forest Father in all his grace stopped beside his companion and licked the fresh wounds all over his muscles. "Stormstrider? Is everything all right? Did you foresee something new?" Scars cut through some of the green spirals lighting his brown fur, and there was a dimness to his starlit antlers.

Ever stoic in silent contemplation, the stone-faced stallion made no sound.

The Forest Father sniffed the air. How his nose could smell anything other than the stench of blood and death was beyond Silversong. "More Titans approach. Stay strong, my friend. Another battle is won. We're close to ending this now. I feel it in my bones."

"This couldn't have been the road to the future you saw!" Nearing them was a giant she-wolf whose coat was deep as the void between stars, and whose eyes were pearly nebulas fit to shame a sunrise. "So many of our creations died today, so many whose lives have been thrown away." Sorrow deepened her marrow-chilling growl. "And no matter how much we try to convince ourselves otherwise, they'll only be remembered as nameless soldiers."

"Maybe it's better that way." A huge feline crested the rise alongside Motherwolf, his fur the shade of dried blood, his claws slick with it. Fine, curving lines marked his body and would've made a raven's feathers seem pale. He settled a pair of burning yellow eyes on Stormstrider. "If their names are ultimately forgotten, their deeds become who they were in life. And that is a timeless reward for their sacrifices."

"I never took you for a great thinker," Motherwolf grunted, swiping a bushy tail.

"I have other surprises in store," the feline grouched in a growly voice. Two long fangs protruded from his snarling mouth, one of them chipped halfway.

"Training your creations to become vicious beasts for the sake of this war was definitely a surprise." Motherwolf's disapproving scowl was grimmer than a thundercloud. "Not that they were particularly noble creatures before," she added quickly.

The cat rivaled Motherwolf's glare in intensity. "You care for your creations in your way, and I'll care for mine how I see fit. This is a brutal realm where only the strong thrive. I hope for your sake your mortal children remember that."

"But is it such a blessing to be strong? Other, more subtle qualities have ensured the survival of my loyal subjects for unnumbered generations." All Titans except Stormstrider whirled to face the Empress of Spiders crawling in their direction. "Don't look so perplexed. I agreed to aid you all in this little war of yours, did I not? Beyond simply ensuring *others* don't try to interfere in it, of course."

"Only for your own gain, no doubt." Motherwolf snarled at the Spider Titan.

"My dear, aren't we all doing this for strictly selfish reasons?" The Empress giggled. "We're participating in the extinction of an entire species because we're trying to ensure a future for *our* creations. You can try telling yourself you're following your own code of honour, in which case I'll remind you of the Titans who opposed this war even after receiving proof of the dangers of humanity, and I'll remind you of how we killed them all. At least we weren't desperate enough to consume their hearts and absorb their strengths, but we're no better off now that we're threatening the very balance of the realms by directly interfering in mortal affairs."

"Some rules you just can't break." The great cat lowered his stance solemnly.

"Yes," Stormstrider whispered too lightly for anyone but himself and Silversong to hear. "The balance is threatened. The Ring of Realms *feels* the torment we've inflicted here. It won't allow immortal beings to travel between the different homeworlds soon. All because of us."

All because of you? Silversong thought back to his one-eyed image and to the indented circle carved on stone. *The Ring of Realms. Everything is connected. But how?*

"Spare us your scolding, insect!" The Forest Father's hoof struck the ground in annoyance. "The strain of time weighs heavily on Stormstrider. He doesn't need you to start spreading the roots of doubt."

The flaming eyes of the Empress settled on the Forest Father, but he never allowed their promise of pain to affect him.

"Are his migraines getting better?" the feline asked, flicking a long tail, the thick fur at the tip forked like a fish fin.

The Forest Father gave his companion a somber look. "They come every time he tries to glimpse the far future. The weapon's potency diminishes after every use, and now he can only guess at potential outcomes, and the roads to them aren't always as clear as they once were."

"Time decays," Stormstrider whispered to himself again. "Time always decays."

"He must keep trying!" Motherwolf bristled, her fur sharp as quills. "I imparted the elemental powers bestowed upon me to my creations as he suggested. I tied the Blessings to their blood, but the action hasn't yet stemmed the tide of casualties. Whatever it takes, convince him to endure the migraines and search for a way to mitigate our losses."

"*Your* losses," the Empress murmured. "There goes your selfishness again."

"I won't put him through more pain than I can bear!" the Forest Father bellowed, and the roots beneath the grass stirred.

"We've put this realm through more pain than it can bear," Stormstrider uttered under his breath. "Entire forests turned to ash, lakes boiled, rivers polluted by rotting corpses. How many portals to the Ring of Realms have we destroyed? How many remain?" He craned his head to the blood-soaked sun. "If humanity ends, who then suffers the curse of sentience here?"

"There's no need to cause him more stress." The marked feline dragged bloody claws through the earth. "We're already winning. All we need to do now is keep the pressure on humanity's strongholds and exterminate the stragglers before they regroup."

"Your talent for complex strategies is inspiring, Bloodclaw," the Empress mocked. "I'll take care of these *stragglers* of yours. As long as my subjects remain vigilant, our enemies won't ever be safe from the fangs hiding in dark corners."

"I convinced those who surrendered to me to infiltrate the armies still standing." The Forest Father's glowing antlers dimmed, and he spoke as if giving a confession. "They'll cause chaos from within, believing I'll let them live if they serve me dutifully. Their betrayal should give us a better advantage."

"Ooh, how devious." Delight flashed in the Empress' eyes. "Are you sure my influence isn't rubbing off on you? Who would've thought the innocent doe-eyed deer was no stranger to cruel tactics?"

The Forest Father snorted loud enough for the Empress to hear his vexation in the act. "Honour favours the foolish in war, does it not?"

Motherwolf sighed and shook her head, obviously disagreeing without saying it.

"These petty quarrels are nothing but a distraction." Bloodclaw licked clean the thickest forepaw Silversong had ever seen. "We should rally our mortal children before the day is done. This war is far from over."

"How come Stormstrider of all Titans found the Traveller?" Motherwolf bared bone-white fangs. "If I'd pierced the maze, I would've bargained for something better than the piece of time."

Stormstrider's maddening whispers continued. "The Traveller found me, but *he* has his own plans in the grand scheme of destiny, and I'm but a seed in one of them. I should've bargained for more. I wanted so badly to save our creations. I should've given more to receive more in return. To history we'll be the victors, but the true conflict never ends, not until *he* collects us all. We can't escape the circle. We can't escape the circle…"

The mumbling of the mad Titan faded as the ever-present motion of time pulled Silversong into another memory.

Events flashed forward, and Silversong found himself completely wrapped in golden threads again, observing through a tiny gap the core of the Mountainmouth in all its former glory. Two male Forgotten Ones—he thought they were males, at least—argued on opposite sides of the piece of time. One had curly brown hair on his head while the other displayed an ashen mane, his frosty eyes framed by an angular face so pale it would make a ghost seem colourful. Silversong recognized the second one as the reoccurring figure he'd seen a few times now. The all-too-familiar tapering tooth of metal was attached somehow to his waist, and his elegant coverings outshone the cloth-wearing labourers toiling about the bustling expanse. In the distance, towering constructs brought together blocks of black crystal, the workers chipping and chiseling the shadowy minerals into more distinct shapes.

The drilling of stone and the constant metallic ringing made it difficult to hear the evolving argument between the two prominent figures, but Silversong caught it all, and though they spoke in a complicated, alien language, the piece of time allowed him to understand everything.

"We can't use an object we barely understand to win the war, Galdreth!" The ashen-haired one glared at the piece of time as if it were the enemy, his voice smooth despite his risen temper, his bone-white flesh lending him an almost sickly appearance. "The beasts and their makers could be trying to trick us into thinking we've stolen their advantage."

The one named Galdreth smoothed the deep green fabric sheltering his furless body. "We *have* stolen their advantage, Aelrion, and the greatest one to boot!" The gemstones in the golden ornament circling his head seemed to twinkle, contrasting the brown of his eyes. "I've seen it in the threads. The Great Stallion's sacrifice opened the doors of victory for us. We can win!" He focused on the threads of time and squinted directly at Silversong without seeing him. "If only we'd also been granted the opportunity to consume the stallion's heart, we would've absorbed its strengths and been unstoppable afterwards. The line between mortal and immortal would've been blurred, and the war would already have been won. Alas, time flows only forward."

"I don't trust it." Aelrion averted his gaze from the golden shine. "Nor should you. We've retaken many of our outposts without relying on this *thing*." He cocked his head in Silversong's direction. "Your innovations have granted us this chance at victory, not the weapon of the enemy!"

"And where do you think I got the ideas for those innovations?" Galdreth unstrapped from his shoulder an odd stick-like thing of wood and metal. He opened the lid of the lengthy object and placed a small metallic cylinder within it. After working the contraption a bit, he aimed the tube-like end of the *stick* at a solid chunk of stone. Pressing on a curved piece at the bottom produced a loud *BANG* and an explosion of white smoke from the top. Like fragile ice, the stone now lay shattered on the ground. Satisfied, he set the *stick* down. "Although the piece of time is weathered from use, I exercised all my focus and peered into the future where we won. I studied the apex of humanity and all its magnificent, terrible marvels. The new weapons I've supplied to your army are but crude versions of the ones we'll forge after the forces of nature are finally vanquished."

Aelrion balled his bare-skinned forepaws. "Why did you even summon me here, Galdreth? Not to advise you on how to use the piece of time, clearly. You'll wield it recklessly no matter my objections. You already have!"

Galdreth peered intently at his equal. "I summoned you here because you're the key to the doors of victory, so the threads have revealed." Aelrion sucked in a deep breath as Galdreth explained himself. "The South, my homeland, is completely overrun, and your Northern Kingdom is crumbling despite our recent counterattacks. Very soon we'll be broken and scattered by the combined might of the enemy, but if you swallow the piece of time and claim its potential, you can return mankind to a state of unrivaled dominance. I've glimpsed other, more obscure roads to triumph, but this one was by far the clearest."

Aelrion scowled and snarled at the ground. "There must be another way."

"There is, but we would be gambling the fate of humanity if we don't make the easy choice." Galdreth gave Aelrion a pleading look. "If *you* don't make the easy choice."

"Is there a chance I'll fail even if I do consume the piece of time?" Aelrion asked in a trembling voice.

Silversong repeated the Forgotten One's question to himself. Even now, was there still a chance he could fail?

"There's always the chance of failure," Galdreth confirmed, crossing his forelimbs under his chest. "But the opportunity is too great not to take. We're the final remnants of humanity, Aelrion, and I'm offering you the means of returning us to glory. Make your choice."

Aelrion approached the golden circle in wary steps, his eyes squinting at the diverging pathways in the shine, all spreading across the delicate fabric of existence. They converged, spidered away, looped, and led to different ends. The reluctant Forgotten One gazed deeper. "I see my future. I swallow the piece of time, and all hope fades. The threads suffocate my sanity. Too many possibilities. Too many clouded futures. My inaction destroys us all. The beasts have won. Our kingdoms erode, and all memory of humanity drowns under a new primal age." His eyes darted to a stiff-faced Galdreth. "You lied to me! I don't lead humanity to victory! The weapon drives me insane, and I doom us all in the process!"

Galdreth studied Aelrion as if his outraged reaction hadn't happened. "Keep looking."

Aelrion peered at another road winding above the golden circle. "A false victory for the beasts. They think they've won until I shatter their hopes. Humanity returns to an age that had forgotten it. We're hunted as we strive to bring mankind back to its former days. A portal to the heavens themselves opens to swallow me whole." He reached out to stroke the piece of time. "There's a wolf… in the sun…? And it's burning, but not dying… never dying." Aelrion found Silversong hiding behind the threads and gasped, forepaws lifting to his chest as if to put pressure on a wound, but there was nothing there but cool metal.

Galdreth eyed Aelrion like a vulture waiting for its prey to die of thirst in a blistering desert.

Aelrion quivered, but not in fear. "Your weapon is evil, and I won't accept its lies! Wield it if you must, Galdreth, but I'll lead my people to victory without being swayed by forces I can't control."

For a moment even the constant noise of the expanse quieted itself almost in anticipation of Galdreth's response.

"So be it." Galdreth stepped forward in quick strides and clutched the golden circle. Aelrion veered in the opposite direction and stormed off as the Forgotten One in deep green opened his mouth and swallowed the piece of time. Silversong merged into the faint aura surrounding the lone vessel. "It's done. The circumstances are met. Our hope for victory is rekindled. You may save us yet, Aelrion."

Time slowed to a still point, and everything tensed until existence itself was about to splinter. The golden circle collapsed in on itself and expanded again, snapping Silversong into the present, into his own mortal shell. The shine coming from inside his stomach dimmed. He linked unseen threads to every chunk of stone the Heretic had flung in his direction, the weaves tightening, keeping the projectiles suspended in the air. Countless potential futures bloomed and decayed in the time it took Silversong to blink once; he could feel certain seams binding reality together, feel them tremble at his regard like subjects awaiting orders from a tyrannical master. He could immerse himself in the aura he emitted and affect the matter within it. He'd already done it. By freezing the circular stream of time, everyone and everything stayed still as if stuck in ice. The wolves and their snarling and frightened faces, the rain of metal and stone above, the fire in the singular eye of the protector, its risen forepaw aimed directly at his head—all of it had stopped in the stilled whirlpool of time's winding strands. The power was immense, but he couldn't reach so far as to influence distant things.

He gritted his teeth at the sharp jab of pain in his skull. The migraine worsened the longer he sustained the stoppage. He struggled forward on shaky limbs until he stood before Frostpaw's terrified face. More spikes stabbed his brain and twisted deep, forcing him to relinquish control over the essence of time. The threads resumed their steady motion.

A shower of stone crashed around the protector as it bellowed again. The exiles yowled and barked, and the Heretic backed away from Silversong, green eyes bulging in sheer panic.

Silversong grinned at his enemy's defeat. "You should've killed me the moment I was brought to you, scatfur."

Wrath and fear battled for dominance over the Heretic's expression, but the imminent danger saved him from attempting a foolish assault. The protector, maddened by its failure to protect, released another roar so loud even Rime let out a whimper, the ground thundering beneath him. The spires and buildings tipped over, some crashing into each other as the ceiling above cracked like a breaking sheet of ice. Falling stones drummed a terrible rhythm. The behemoth's eye blazed wildly, its untamed fury fueled by a flickering heart. All wolves tucked their tails and ran as if death itself were reaching out to smother their lives.

The Drowned Titan's voice was almost a relief amid the destruction and the chaos. **"Run, little one! Run!"**

CHAPTER 23

✦

The Heart of the Mountains

Flesh and bones burned to ash. A fierce humming shuddered the ground as another huge beam of searing orange flame blasted out of the protector's eye, incinerating a party of exiles fleeing along a wide, beaten lane. Stone turned to liquid fire, engulfing the surrounding buildings and swallowing all in its wake.

The enormous body of black crystal loomed over the survivors, examining each until its glare settled on Silversong. It let out another terrible roar.

"Sorry, but I had to eat it," Silversong whined to the giant, but doubted his apology would have the desired effect.

Chunks of debris landed everywhere and pummelled the old structures still standing into sprays of grey. The Heretic glanced at Rime and his remaining exiles and howled. "Flee to the edge of the expanse! There's an entrance above the steps we descended! Hurry!"

Rime's gaze darted from his master to Silversong. "But the piece of time! He—!"

"We'll tear it out of him after we escape!" The Heretic stayed far out of reach of Silversong's aura. "Move! Before the ruin devours us all!"

The Heretic and his followers sprinted around a corner away from Silversong. The colossus bellowed once more, demanding the return of the weapon it was tasked to protect. Potential futures where Silversong stayed there gawking like a stupid pigeon flashed in his head, all of them ending in unpleasant deaths.

"Time to go!" He nosed Frostpaw's shoulder and pursued the exiles, the aura blooming from within his stomach shifting fluidly to wherever he moved, encompassing a wide area.

"You're crazy, Silversong! Absolutely insane!" Frostpaw yapped, falling in from behind.

They ran in the direction the exiles had gone, avoiding a hail of stone and collapsing constructs. Silversong's migraine slowly faded, encouraging the temptation to use the powers of time again. The heated blood roaring in his ears muffled the pounding of his heart, and his vision narrowed itself on the road ahead. His surroundings blurred out of focus as if he were in a tunnel leading only forward.

The impact of the giant's heavy steps pushed him beyond a speed he once thought impossible to achieve. Frostpaw struggled to keep up, and Silversong connected himself to the stirred air around the lieutenant, willing it to aid his strides. Frostpaw thanked Silversong, the two racing side by side amid the destruction.

The protector collided against one of the more stable structures, reducing the obstacle into a shower of solid clay. They rounded another corner as one of the fractured pieces landed atop an exile, who yelped and struggled underneath.

The Heretic smacked a forepaw on the ground, and the fallen wedge lifted itself, but it was too late. The protector stomped on the crushed exile, ramming his body into the ground. Silversong's gut knotted itself as the giant prepared another eye-blast, aiming it at Ripper and his group a few paces in front of the Heretic. Futures branched out like lichen before Silversong's eyes, some clear, some uncertain and foggy. He caught Frostpaw's tail between his teeth, stopping the lieutenant before he ran where a falling boulder was about to crash.

The Heretic charged toward Ripper and the others, bringing his forepaws inward. Two thick buildings on either side of him moved at a blurry speed to block the searing beam of the protector before it extinguished its helpless prey.

"MASTER!" Rime yowled and hurried to the Heretic's side.

The shield of combined stone lasted for only a breath. The beam melted through its heavy layers, but the makeshift bulwark bought enough time for Ripper and the others to flee out of danger. Rime pushed the Heretic aside mere moments before the eye-blast drilled through the remainder of the shield, liquefying the ground where Ironwrath had been standing.

"You boulder-headed brute!" the Heretic growled, eyes leaden, body shaking. "You could've gotten yourself killed!"

"And I would again, to save you." Rime pulled his master up, the confession appearing to lend Ironwrath the strength he needed to cling to life. "You promised us salvation, and I won't allow death to keep you from fulfilling your promise."

Silversong thought about attacking the two of them while they were distracted, but the ground was too fragile where they crouched, and too many possibilities in time's threads led to his abrupt end if he took the gamble.

Ironwrath's eyes widened, the look of shock foreign to his face. "Stubborn fool. I should've listened to you about the Whistle-Wind pup. He's made things a lot more complicated." The two-legged giant scanned its smoky surroundings, searching for the one who'd swallowed time. It prepared its pursuit, unsure now who to chase.

"Quit staring like a petrified owl and come on!" Frostpaw barked.

"Right!" Silversong hurried after Frostpaw.

They sprinted parallel to the exiles, separated by a row of crumbling columns. Silversong's enemies were barely out of reach, time's aura scraping their fur, not enough for him to weave the unseen threads around their bodies. The protector launched itself into the air, blocky forelimb extended, and punched straight through a solid barrier, its foundations collapsing atop another exile. Ironwrath and Rime turned alongside Ripper and the others onto another lane. Frostpaw followed his target, pace quickening. The possible futures blurred themselves again as another pulsing migraine made Silversong wince.

The giant caught up to an exhausted Blackroot and kicked him into the air. It thrust a forelimb upward, using the momentum of the strike to launch itself off the floor. An instant later, it faced the poor mongrel midair and smacked him to the ground. Silversong cringed at the splattering sound of the impact, the exile's body lying a couple leaps away—a squished puddle of blood, bone, and fur. The Heretic's army was nearly halved now. Still a formidable force, but a crippled one.

The behemoth touched ground some distance behind Silversong. He clenched his jaws as tremors vibrated through the entire ruin. Frostpaw at his side, he turned the corner of another building, narrowly avoiding the orange beam melting their previous lane into molten stone. In the clearing, Rime stood at the edge of a pit, counting the surviving exiles as they passed by him.

A vision of Frostpaw pushing himself and Rime into the pit jolted Silversong's head up, but he failed to prevent the future he'd glimpsed. As sudden as an unexpected wave, Frostpaw crashed into his mother's killer.

"NO! WAIT!" Silversong barked all too late. He tried to make time go backwards, but the unseen motion refused to move in the opposite direction.

Frostpaw and Rime tumbled over the rim of the square pit, the protruding white gemstones breaking their momentum until they landed at the bottom. Silversong jumped into the crater, hopping from crystal to crystal as he carefully made his way to where the two wolves fought. A falling boulder smashed onto the pit's floor, disrupting Rime's balance.

Again, Silversong tried reversing the course of time. Pain exploded across his brain, and he bumped into an invisible barrier on every attempt to go against one of the rules binding existence together.

From within, memories tied to the golden circle spoke to him. *"Some rules you just can't break. Time flows only forward."*

Frostpaw, you complete gullwit! Silversong's heart rapped against his burning chest as he prepared to save the idiot lieutenant from the fate of a martyr.

Fragments of stone rained everywhere, drumming to the deafening chorus of the protector above, but Frostpaw faced the Heretic's second-in-command as if everything weren't collapsing all around. He crouched, ready to pounce. "Get up, murderer! Now you pay for your crimes."

Rime pushed himself up and snarled, spewing a spray of saliva in front of him. "Reckless pup! You've no idea of the true story between Cindersky and me. If it weren't for the Wolven Code, our hearts would've been as one, and your mother would've still been alive."

Multiple futures all ending in Frostpaw's death flowed through Silversong's thoughts. He descended faster, taking care not to stumble on one of the smooth crystals.

"You're not worthy of speaking the name of the one you deceived and seduced!" Frostpaw charged the large exile. "I'll bring justice to her and my mother! And I'll finally atone for my mistake!"

Rime leaped to the side and used his teeth to reopen the wound on Frostpaw's shoulder. He yowled as Rime tossed him against one of the protruding gemstones. "If your wretched mother hadn't found us, everything would've been fine! But her inquisitive, zealous nature got the better of her, and she paid the ultimate price for it in the end. If she hadn't threatened to have Cindersky executed—" Rime froze, shock spreading across his face. He growled curses under his breath before refocusing his hatred on Frostpaw. "Now you'll join your mother in the hereafter. Give her my sincerest regards!"

"Fallen Titan take you!" Frostpaw shook off his injury and rushed Rime in a blind rage. The two collided, and the exile bit Frostpaw's throat, but the River-Stream lieutenant returned the deadly attacks. Rime used his greater weight to topple Frostpaw, forcing him onto his spine. He tucked his head as Rime stood over him, sharp teeth aimed at his exposed belly.

Frostpaw placed his forepaws on Rime's chest and for some reason, the exile squealed and convulsed. "Did you forget I can force the water inside you to obey me?!"

Blood! He's controlling Rime's blood! Silversong was nearly at the bottom, the aura of time barely brushing the two wolves.

"NOW BOIL!" Frostpaw barked.

Rime released Frostpaw and recoiled, wheezing raggedly, fear scent wafting.

Frostpaw rolled over and stood up, launching himself at the murderer. Rime easily sidestepped the assault and tore out clumps of fur and flesh from his attacker's side, taking care not to allow his blood to be controlled again. He pushed Frostpaw to the rugged floor and picked up a severed shard of crystal in his mouth, its glinting point aimed at Frostpaw's throat. Rime motioned the sliver to a downward thrust.

"FROSTPAW!" Silversong yelped, the reach of the aura finally enveloping Rime and Frostpaw alike. He tightened the threads around the exile and froze him in place, jumping onto his shoulders and biting him in vulnerable places. "You won't touch him ever again!"

The migraine returned. Fine spikes slowly impaled Silversong's brain, urging him to release the invisible fetters binding Rime. The exile's mouth curled into a snarl as he released the shard. Teeth bared, he shook Silversong off him and scurried away until he was out of the aura's reach. Silversong helped Frostpaw up, and the two growled at the vile killer.

Rime laughed until it appeared to pain him. "Isn't this adorable? A Whistle-Wind scamp and a River-Stream flea fighting together against the big bad exile." He dug his claws into the ground. "My master is far too trusting at times… but no matter. Even without the piece of time to wield, he'll still shatter the Wolven Code and unite the Four Territories as one. You could've witnessed a glorious future rise, but instead you chose to remain on the side of oppression."

"You're wrong." Silversong braced himself as more debris landed into the pit. "I'll win us a better future. One where the Wolven Code is amended and the Four Territories are brought together through peace and understanding rather than by force."

Silversong lunged at Rime alongside Frostpaw, ready to freeze the exile again and deliver the killing blows. Rime vaulted over a protruding crystal, fleeing up the pit, leaping from gemstone to gemstone and out of the aura's reach. He turned and released a grating grunt. "You'll rot within the Mountainmouth forever, scatfurs."

"Coward!" Frostpaw started climbing after Rime, wincing as his reopened wound squeezed out more blood. The ground rumbled furiously at the constant bellows of the behemoth stomping above.

A gigantic chunk of the ceiling plummeted into the pit, breaking many of the jutting gemstones along the way. Silversong sprinted, the currents stirred by his motions ready to aid his coming leap. He sprang high into the air and scrambled onto one of the broken crystals beside Frostpaw, flinching at the deafening impact below. The protector's roar echoed clearly through the chaos. To Frostpaw's dismay, Rime disappeared over the edge of the crater. Silversong jumped and climbed until he too pulled himself out of the hole alongside his friend. Panting away their exhaustion, they chose a cracked road to flee on. Justice would have to wait.

The shadowy figure loomed at the far end of the breaking expanse and climbed up the huge ledges of stone, chasing the small, escaping exiles who hurried through a large opening at the very top. Silversong and Frostpaw pursued Rime toward the steps, their panting quickly turning to dry wheezes.

They reached the steep incline and followed Rime up and up and up until the black exile scrambled over the rim. Silversong could barely feel his limbs now as he climbed the fracturing ascent, finding little nooks in the breaking stone to use as toeholds. He strained for every breath, Frostpaw trailing him two steps below, eyes distant. The lieutenant slipped, but Silversong tensed the threads of his aura around his friend to prevent him from losing balance. Silversong ignored the sharp pain skewering his head and fought the temptation to faint. He had to look after Frostpaw. He couldn't let him die. Not here. Not now.

A gaping tear rifted the underground kingdom, growing wider and wider until all the buildings and constructs still standing leaned and dropped into darkness, devoured by the earth's ravenous throat. Silversong took one final look at the dying memory of a forgotten time before helping Frostpaw climb the remaining steps. Side by side, they passed through the exit and started up the bowels of the mountains.

They tracked the exiles through tunnels and crumbling rooms, entering freezing pathways of bronze and charging into slanted corridors on the brink of collapse. Silversong led the way up more steps, a few winding, others straight, some breaking behind as the roaring of the protector shook the entire ruin.

Into a cluttered chamber of clear tubes and dangerous-looking contraptions, they ran. The Heretic crouched beside his lieutenant at the very end, bristling alongside their surviving subordinates. The behemoth prepared to incinerate its targets, but a pair of exiles jumped off a ledge overlooking the protector and bit at its eye. Their teeth snapped against the unyielding surface, but they never stopped their frantic strikes. The giant released a low, humming growl, iris brightening until it fired a blinding beam, instantly vaporizing the two nuisances.

The orange trail of searing flame came onto Ironwrath, but he bounded out of the way as the beam melted the stone behind him, creating a gap leading into another chamber. The Heretic barked, ordering his exiles to flee through the improvised exit. Rime led the way as his master smacked the ground, willing sharp pieces of metal to launch themselves at the giant, but it swatted the lances aside without effort. Ironwrath whirled around and escaped.

The behemoth smashed through the rocky layer above the gap, and Silversong shuddered at the damage it would inflict on the Four Territories should it leave the Mountainmouth. He saw it all so clearly—wolves crushed, bones smoking, loved ones burning, forests reduced to ash. How would Ironwrath have stopped it if he'd swallowed the piece of time instead?

Silversong and Frostpaw stuck to the road of destruction, taking care not to get noticed by the ruthless colossus. They found themselves in a familiar lengthy hallway, and Silversong realized he was in the corridor tied to the place where the Heretic had ordered him to bite Frostpaw. They stalked the protector as it thudded up another flight of steps, eye blazing bright the moment before it fired.

They turned the corner, and Silversong stopped to gape at the closed entrance of reddish stone melting into white-hot liquid. The exiles barely dodged the deadly beam, leaping over the now-melted door. Silversong and Frostpaw scampered up the steps and into another familiar place, the giant stomping after its prey. Glowing mushrooms and translucent slugs infested a burrow on one side of the chamber, and on the other, wide ledges descended to a yawning abyss in which platforms dangled from an unseen roof. Directly to the front, between the legs of the protector, the exiles ran.

The Heretic and his army continued into the corridor of stone effigies, the giant preparing another charge. They were closer to the exit now!

"Frostpaw!" Silversong halted the lieutenant, ignoring his own exhaustion. "The behemoth is after me. I can't let it leave the Mountainmouth!"

Frostpaw worked a disbelieving sound out of his mouth. "There's no way we can possibly beat it, Silversong! Even if you have the piece of time now!"

Silversong studied the abyss and the dangling platforms. "I think I can beat it." He scried the future and saw two possibilities diverge in opposite directions. It could go either way; he could defeat the giant or be buried here forever. "Go, Frostpaw! I'm not letting this monster loose on the Four Territories!"

Frostpaw's head darted from the fleeing exiles to Silversong.

"HEY!" Silversong barked, willing time's strings to fasten themselves around the protector. "You big old lumbering oaf! I'm here! I swallowed the piece of time! I'm who you're looking for!

OW!" A wave of pain washed over his skull, and he let go of the threads. He would have to learn how to control them better.

The giant stopped in its tracks and turned around, humming a deep growl.

Silversong charged toward the great chasm, buying time for Frostpaw to escape.

"Oh, Motherwolf's milk!" Frostpaw cursed and followed Silversong before he could protest. "Whatever crazy idea you got, you'll need me to look after your rump."

"I'll look after it myself, thanks!" Silversong grunted.

"Too late. We're stuck together now." Frostpaw caught up to him. They pushed on their haunches and jumped onto a hanging platform, moving swiftly from one to another.

As planned, the giant switched targets and launched itself into the bottomless expanse, landing on one of the suspended surfaces, the chains holding it in place straining, but not snapping.

"Pricklethorn!" Silversong swore, the claws of frozen dread sinking ever deeper into his chest as every possible future winked out of focus. "Why won't it break?!"

A sudden spark of understanding flashed in Frostpaw's eyes. "Oh, I see. Great plan!"

"It would be if it worked!" Silversong gulped as the protector prepared to fire. The two leaped onto a higher platform, evading a blinding orange line that melted their previous surface into oblivion.

"That's it!" The heat of the blast singed Silversong's fur as another idea popped into his head. "Frostpaw! Distract it! Now!"

"Distract it?!" Frostpaw barked as if he couldn't believe Silversong's orders. "Maybe it *was* a bad idea to follow you."

Without time to argue, Silversong hopped onto a lower platform, Frostpaw howling for the protector's attention. It worked, and while Silversong jumped his way closer and closer to the crystal monster, Frostpaw sprang from surface to surface, the burning beams missing him by a hair.

Silversong landed on the protector's platform unnoticed and looked up at the enormous construct. Its heart blazed in imitation of the sun's fury, and its light frightened all shadows into flickering, formless shapes. As it prepared to strike at Frostpaw again, Silversong tightened the threads of time around the giant, holding it there. He released it at the start of a migraine, but the act was enough to steal the monster's attention. It bellowed in anger and glared at Silversong, ready to unleash fiery death. The instant it did, Silversong used all his remaining strength to leap onto a higher platform. The behemoth wasn't quick enough to avert its gaze, and the beam it fired incinerated the surface it stood on, burning it to cinders.

The mountainous body of black crystal plummeted into the hungry chasm, roaring in defeat. Huge, inky tentacles rose to claim it, and the Drowned Titan's voice echoed from deep below. "At last! The Heart of the Mountains is MINE! I AM FREE!"

A blinding inferno lit up the darkness. Tongues of scorching red flame licked the stony bowels of the mountains, and crackling embers drifted to the breaking ceiling. A loud explosion sparked tremors throughout the cavernous deeps, and everything caved in. Silversong panicked as the heat of the fire warmed his soon-to-be blistering flesh.

From falling platform to falling platform, the two wolves bounded. Silversong made use of his lithe shape and feeble weight to move up to even ground. Frostpaw struggled at his tail, but Silversong grabbed him by the scruff and saved him from the fractured roof plunging into the flaming void. Silversong heaved and pulled Frostpaw onto the swaying steps, scuttling up them before they too splintered and broke.

Silversong hardened the outer layers of his aura, forcing his willpower to dampen the worsening headache. The falling debris that otherwise would've crushed him simply bounced off time's tightened threads as he and Frostpaw ran side by side, determined to survive the dying of the mountains. They dashed through a room of shattered effigies and scurried up inclines drenched in shadow, Silversong's stomach barely able to contain its contents. They ran and ran until fresh air greeted their parched throats. At their tails, a hail of rubble rained, and just as it caught up to them, they exploded out into the open and hurled themselves onto the cool, snowy ground, rasping as exhaustion finally claimed its deserved victory.

Silversong let go of his influence over time and rolled over. The silvery sliver of the moon and the blinking stars above was like seeing old friends after an eternity of solitude. He relished the taste of outside air as Frostpaw lay panting beside him. The surging river, the hooting of distant owls, the chirping of insects, the shifting of the forest, the mellow whistling of the breeze—all of it stunned the senses.

Behind him, fallen rubble blocked the entrance to the Mountainmouth, its final breath a cloud of heated dust slowly fading into the purple sky. The sound of a gargantuan wave at the far end of the ridge lessened into a hushing echo.

Silversong got up, a stream of saliva drowning his tongue. Hot vomit gurgled up his throat, and he retched, releasing it all in front of him, grimacing at the bitter, stinging taste. For a moment, he feared he might've expelled the golden circle from his stomach, but he still sensed it turning within him. He lapped up clean water from the ice on the ground, swallowing the frigid liquid in hopes of banishing the foulness.

The satisfied voice of the Drowned Titan writhed into his ears. **"Thank you, little one. As promised, the favour shall be returned one day. But for now, it's time I remind the denizens of the sea who truly rules over its endless tides. I suggest you make use of your borrowed power before your enemy plots a way to remove it from you. Be wary of his persistence. Be wary of new threats rising from within. Be wary of yourself and who you trust. The storm hasn't yet cleared. Farewell, Silversong of Whistle-Wind."**

Silversong ambled over to Frostpaw and licked the wound on his shoulder. "We did it. We stopped the Heretic. For now, at least."

The lieutenant sat under the shining stars, drooping like a blade of grass touched by early frost. His head stayed low, and his eyes locked themselves on his own quivering forepaws. "You may have won, but I failed."

CHAPTER 24

✦

Out of a Distant Memory

"I failed," Frostpaw whispered again, lifting his gaze to the heavens. "I'm sorry, mother."

Silversong rested his head on Frostpaw's shoulder as the gentle spray of the coursing river sprinkled their coats. "Rime, he killed your mother after she found out about him and the Flame-Heart member. It's why you were so eager to enter the Mountainmouth. You wanted to avenge her above all else." The lieutenant swallowed a whimper. "Oh, Frostpaw…" Silversong whined.

Frostpaw clenched his teeth and ran his claws through the layers of snowy ice. "It's my fault she died." Silversong broadened his eyes at the confession, an uncertain weight pushing his heart low. He removed his head from the lieutenant's smooth fur and managed but a confused stare. "The night it happened," Frostpaw continued, "I woke up from a bad dream and padded into her lair." He released a bitter chuckle. "I can't even remember why I was so scared. All I remember was the need for her comfort."

Silversong listened, ears poking the air as Frostpaw explained himself. "I woke her up, and she did exactly as all mothers should do. She gave me all the love and care I needed to vanquish my fears. Maybe if I'd fallen asleep earlier, she wouldn't have noticed Tiderunner—Rime—sneaking away from the den. Maybe she wouldn't have followed him all the way into Flame-Heart grounds and confronted him. Maybe she wouldn't have—"

"It's not your fault, Frostpaw." Silversong nuzzled his friend on the cheek. How could Frostpaw blame himself for something so out of his control? It shattered Silversong's heart. "It's not! You were only a pup."

"My father blamed me for her death." Frostpaw's whimper cut clean through the chirping of distant crickets. "And my siblings followed his example. I'm happy they did, or else I would've never realized the extent of my mistake."

Silversong couldn't imagine how anyone could blame a pup for the crime of another. He licked Frostpaw on the snout, but the lieutenant never acknowledged it. "Frostpaw, listen to me. It's not your fault."

"My mother was a brave lieutenant," Frostpaw gulped on a couple more whimpers. "She smiled whenever I tried to impress her and taught me how to chase prey. And she lived by the Wolven Code like no other." He stretched out his head and nestled it under Silversong's throat. "Sometimes I smell her scent in my dreams, and I hope I wake up to her smile so she can remind me I'm not alone."

"It's okay, Frostpaw." Silversong couldn't think of anything else to whine. "I'm here. You're not alone."

Frostpaw's mother wouldn't have appreciated me being this close to her son, Silversong reflected on her apparent devotion to the Wolven Code. *Does Frostpaw realize this?*

"After Rime confessed his crimes to us, after he explained how he seduced an innocent member of Flame-Heart and murdered—" Frostpaw couldn't finish it. "I never understood how at fault I really was until my family started blaming me."

Silversong wanted to comfort Frostpaw until no more sorrow remained. "Don't blame yourself. Please don't." The reminder of Silversong's den getting destroyed by Rime reopened unseen scars. He pictured every packmate the exiles had killed, pictured the broken corpses and terrified expressions. The essence of time churned within him. "Whatever happens, I won't let the exiles claim another victory. By Motherwolf, I swear it."

Frostpaw removed his head from under Silversong's throat and peered into his eyes. The lieutenant worked a fragile look of determination onto his face.

Roads leading to futures where Silversong reigned victorious over his enemies shone wherever he looked. He focused on them to keep the migraines at bay. *I already beat you once, Ironwrath, and I'll do it again. The weapon you would've wielded against us is mine to wield against you! And once you're truly defeated, I'll lead the Four Territories into a future you never could've imagined.*

Other futures hid in the shadows of the good ones—futures where the Heretic, despite having his weapon stolen, caused pain and devastation to the Four Territories, ruining each beyond repair. *But I won't let it happen!*

The dawning sun burned crimson streaks across strips of creamy clouds. The sky glowed softly in welcome of the morning yet to come, and the stars muted their shine as the moon dipped toward its slumber, fleeing the waking of its eternal rival. Silversong blinked, and in the brief darkness before his eyes opened, he saw himself wagging his tail in front of a group of familiar wolves. They waited for him below the ridge, in the Songwoods. Someone from a warmer time awaited him too, but he couldn't get a good glimpse at whoever it was.

"Frostpaw!" Silversong nosed the distant-eyed lieutenant, causing a startle. "We should start heading to your den. We've got a lot to report to our Chiefs."

Frostpaw whined in agreement, managing to at least hide some of his sorrow and regret for now. He and Silversong descended the rocky incline, following the river's tumultuous beginning. They landed on the grass still grey under the scarlet sky and hurried toward the looming forest, Silversong pursuing the invisible trail leading to the wolves he'd glimpsed.

Doubt flooded through him, but he pressed forward regardless, deciding it would be better to worry about the Heretic after the upcoming reunion. Alongside Frostpaw, he hopped into the forest still reluctant to wake, immersing himself in its earthy scents. He padded into a small glade where yellow flowers leaned over the dew-ridden undergrowth and stopped there, obeying intuition.

Frostpaw panted and halted beside him. "Why're we stopping?"

Silversong planted his forepaws into the moist soil, heartbeat racing as insects chirped their melodious tunes. "They're almost here."

"Who's almost here?!" Frostpaw crouched into a defensive stance, ears flattened and tail stiff. "Silversong?"

"Shh…"

"Don't *shush* me!" Frostpaw woofed. "Quit being all cryptic and—" Frostpaw sniffed, catching the scent of approaching wolves. His hackles hardened.

Hazel and Palesquall charged into the clearing, mouths wide open and eyes bulging. "There he is!" Hazel barked. "See? My nose is never wrong!"

A grey-furred stranger leaped into the glade, bright-eyed and scarred in many places. He was a bit larger than Frostpaw in size. "This is him?"

Palesquall looked over his shoulder at the newcomer and stretched his head out. "Oh, it's him all right."

"Hey." Silversong beamed, tail brushing the flowers.

"*Hey*?" Hazel's forehead protruded over fiery green eyes. "REALLY?!" she yapped and charged him. Of course, Silversong had foreseen her reaction to him suddenly showing up here, but the better outcome would be to let Hazel have her way and not resist. She knocked him to the ground and growled. Frostpaw backed away, his stunned face morphing into an awkward look. "Sun scorch me, if I weren't so angry at myself for letting the River-Stream oaf freeze me to a tree, I would bite your tail off and stuff it in your mouth!"

"And I would give a bone to witness it!" Palesquall grunted. "Why did you leave us, Silversong?! We could've helped you!"

"You could've gotten yourselves killed, you mean!" Silversong barked, remembering the futures shown to him by the reflections in the maze of madness. "Even if having you two by my side would've made things easier, I would've never accepted the possibility of losing either of you."

Hazel's fur stiffened into fine spikes, and she backed off as if finally sensing the strange aura radiating from Silversong. He got up slowly. He had a lot of explaining to do.

"He's as stubborn as you described him to be," the grey stranger grunted. "I guess it's a strong trait in the family."

The aura of time enveloped the grey one, and the threads making it up branched out to reveal former events of his life: a chase through a wicked forest, roots entangling him, black clouds brewing, savage eyes watching, a flash of crooked lightning, a chain of mountains breaking…

Frostpaw's voice pulled Silversong to the here and now. "Hazel, Palesquall, what happened after we left? I assume you made it safely to my den?"

Silversong pointed his nose at the newcomer who clearly wasn't a River-Stream wolf. "And who's this?"

Hazel flashed Frostpaw an indignant grimace, refusing to even humor Silversong's question until she gave the lieutenant a piece of her mind. "After our prisons melted, we hurried to the River-Stream den. Chief Amberstorm and the others arrived soon after, and there was a lengthy meeting where the higher-ranking wolves of our two territories discussed plans of action. Having us all kicked out or executed were options proposed, by the way!" She gave Frostpaw her signature sneer, making him peer off to the side.

Air gusted out of Palesquall's nose. "Good thing the River-Stream wolves weren't in the mood to boil us all alive. It was decided we would join forces and launch an assault on the Mountainmouth tomorrow—which is now today, actually. We volunteered to be the scouting party by the way. The main army is probably still preparing at the den."

Bad timing. They just missed the Heretic. Silversong cursed silently.

The burly grey male stepped forward. "Yesterday evening, *we* also arrived at the Saltshore." He flicked his thick tail up and displayed it proudly. "The Great Chain may be broken, but under the Warden's leadership, the surviving sentinels have reformed, and we remain strong as ever!"

Renewed hope stirred in Silversong's bones, and a feeling of weightlessness swept over him. The softest breeze could've carried him away.

Frostpaw sucked in a surprised breath and bowed his head respectfully. "You're a sentinel?!"

The grey wolf faced him, and he tensed. "I am. Those of my order are helping your packmates prepare for the assault on the Mountainmouth as we speak. They'll be leaving as soon as the sun crests the forest."

The piece of time seemed to vibrate inside Silversong. "Now's probably a good time to mention—"

"Silversong!" Hazel barked loud enough for it to tremble Silversong's eardrums. "Don't you EVER abandon us again! You did it TWICE now, and I don't think I could forgive you if you did it a third time!"

"I won't have to." Silversong grinned and licked her on the mouth, loosening her glare. "I won, Hazel! I beat the Heretic! He failed to claim the weapon at the core of the Mountainmouth."

The sentinel's ears perked up. "He's… dead?"

"No," Silversong admitted, knowing the answer crumpled the wishes of everyone present. "Dozens of his followers died in the Mountainmouth, but him, Rime, and many others escaped. At least the Heretic is beaten and on the run for now."

"*For now* isn't good enough," stated the sentinel. "He won't accept defeat, trust me. We tried killing him many times after he took control over the Furtherlands, after he became a threat to us, but he always eluded even our sharpest hunters. I reckon he's already plotting vengeance against you if you truly thwarted his plans in the underground ruin."

"Oh, great!" Palesquall shivered. "Another thing to worry about."

Silversong lifted himself to a proud stance. "Oh, he's definitely coming for me. And I'll be waiting for him." He tightened the threads of time, smirking at the startled wolves before him. "Don't worry. He'll think twice about attacking us openly again." He loosened his grasp on the aura, dismissing the motions only he could see. He focused on the here and now, steering his eyes away from the future.

Frostpaw gave him an uncertain look, and his other friends exchanged curious glances.

The sentinel broke the silence, his confident voice commanding everyone to pay attention. "We've all been briefed by Palesquall about the Heretic's ambition to wield a piece of time against us. You're telling me you stopped him from claiming it? How? We heard the mountains growling before the day dawned. We thought they may have buried you alive in their rage."

"I stopped him all right." Silversong's smile reached his ears. "You're not going to believe—"

A sweet, pleasant, familiar voice out of a distant memory compelled a tingle to slide along Silversong's spine. "Greyhail? Where are you? I think I found tracks belonging to—"

She emerged like a luminous spirit out of the shadows and stopped beside the grey sentinel. Silversong thought his heart would leap out of his body. The weightlessness returned, and countless butterflies fluttered about his stomach as a bubbling heat streamed through his veins. There she was, silver fur rippling in the breeze, green eyes fixed on him, her smile so loving it could've cured the deepest sadness. "Silversong?"

"SWIFTSTORM!" he barked and rushed straight to her, nothing but bliss driving him closer to her smile.

"We probably should've mentioned his sister was alive," Palesquall mumbled to Hazel. "Oops."

Silversong collided into Swiftstorm and licked her face as if it were the cool water of an oasis amid a sweltering desert. He took in her new scent, his tail making a whole assortment of chaotic movements. Everything dissolved until the only thing remaining was a fizzing sensation of pure joy.

Swiftstorm returned the gestures of love. "It's good to see you too, Silversong. I never doubted you were alive!"

"I… I was scared you were dead." He failed to express himself further and chose to remain in her embrace instead. He detected dozens of bruises and a couple healed gashes along her body, but otherwise, she was the same old Swiftstorm he remembered from their time spent together as rookies.

"Yeah, I was scared I was dead too," Swiftstorm sighed, still smiling as she glanced at the other sentinel. "But the big oaf here commanded the stone of the Great Chain to shelter us from its own collapse."

"You're welcome, by the way." Greyhail smirked.

Bright futures where Silversong and his sister thrived like blooming flowers spread across his vision, and he returned every nuzzle she gave out. Nothing could ever go wrong again! His sister was still alive! And together, they would defeat the remnants of the Heretic's horde.

Greyhail walked over to Swiftstorm. "We should start heading to the River-Stream den. Your brother claims he thwarted the enemy, but the Heretic isn't fully beaten yet. Calling off the assault on the Mountainmouth and refocusing our efforts should be our top priority. The longer we stay here, the more we give the Heretic time to recover from his defeat." He eyed Silversong like a fox watching a squirrel. "You'll have to explain everything in detail to us along the way. Can you make it to the Saltshore without resting? If we move at a trotting pace, we'll get there before the army heads out."

Swiftstorm's presence gave Silversong the encouragement he needed. The weariness in his bones and the hunger cramping his gut weren't enough to smother his determination.

"Good," Greyhail grunted. "You've got a lot of explaining to do. I suggest you ready yourself for a lengthy interrogation once we arrive at the Saltshore. Odds are you'll be as popular as one of the founders of the Four Territories whenever we get there."

Swiftstorm groaned grimly. "It's true. Everyone has so many questions, and the Warden above all others. I think it's high time you met her."

Silversong stood motionless, and a chill washed over him to reveal his concern to all who looked. He tried peering into the future, but the blank cloudiness of his anxiety prevented him from doing so. After turning to Frostpaw, to his packmates, and seeing their reassuring faces, Silversong breathed out and calmed his worry. He would get through this. He wasn't alone. Not anymore.

"Come, brother." Swiftstorm nudged him on the side. "I'm sure mother and father can't wait to see you."

"Bet they couldn't keep their tails still once they saw you." Silversong loosed a shaky laugh.

"Oh, if only you were there to see how father charged into me. Can't say I've ever been so embarrassed before." She aimed a glare at Greyhail, who chuckled under his breath.

"Sounds exactly like him." Guilt squeezed Silversong's heart. His parents must be so stressed right now. He sighed, already preparing himself for an awkward reunion. "Guess I should expect a similar treatment."

"Oh, if I were them, I would sit on you until you swore not to go on any stupid adventures ever again!" Hazel's claws raked the earth. "Motherwolf's mercy, even Palesquall has never made me this angry before." She shook her head in exasperation.

"An achievement in and of itself." Palesquall barked a laugh and beamed at her. "Don't worry, Hazel. You'll have plenty of time to be angry at him while we make our way to the River-Stream den."

Hazel's scowl disappeared, and she too finally laughed, if only a little. "I don't think there's enough time in the whole universe to scold Silversong properly." She licked her fangs. "But I'll certainly try."

Under the stretching sun, Silversong gazed at the fading stars. The golden circle stirred inside him, sending vibrations through every bone and every muscle. The strands making up the reach of his aura quivered at his regard. *And now the true storm begins.*

Frostpaw, who'd stayed oddly silent throughout the whole reunion, came beside Silversong and offered him an unsteady smile, eyes sometimes darting to the watching wolves. Silversong nudged his new friend on the cheek, pushing away whatever was making him act so funny all of a sudden. It worked, and Frostpaw grinned like a perky pup.

Surrounded by his friends and his sister, Silversong started forward, ready to meet the challenges of fate head-on. "Let the storm come." He flexed the threads of time bound to his command. "Let it rain its hardest!"

EPILOGUE

The Storm

Rime winced at the pulsing wounds given to him by the Whistle-Wind pup and his vengeful companion. Their misplaced sense of righteousness was almost amusing.

Before him struggled a young watersnout doe who'd been all too curious about a group of mangy wolves passing through the dreadful woods of River-Stream. The lithe beast screeched as rotting roots coiled around its throat, their sharp ends tunneling into its scaly flesh and severing its arteries. Rime drowned himself in the rage and hate festering inside him—an oozing boil always on the verge of popping. It fueled his cruelty as he willed the corruption of the Fallen Titan into his surroundings. A final, ragged breath escaped out of the doe's mouth before the roots returned to the earth to poison the willows they belonged to.

"You should be grateful death brings the end of your pain," Rime whined to the twitching corpse, the corruption in his heart sinking deeper than mere flesh. "Some of us aren't so fortunate." He thought he heard the phantom chuckle of a crackling voice, but he decided against humoring the baleful presence forever bound to him.

He picked up the watersnout by its seaweed mane and dragged it through the forest, the sun warming the scars all over him, cooking them alive, but he'd suffered far worse pains. The lavender tendrils of the willows tickled his hackles and tempted him to order their immediate decay. The putrid boil within him pulsed harder, acknowledging the presence of the Fallen Titan, but he ignored it for now and continued through the leaning grass, padding into a small clearing and dropping the doe before his subordinates.

Ripper and the others snapped to attention and rushed toward the carcass, looking to Rime for permission to dig in. Ripper stopped and sniffed, the sour scent of his anxiety curling Rime's nostrils. "I've finished reporting to the master. There're sentinels lurking about the River-Stream forest, Rime! They've reformed under the Warden! She's still alive!"

"Good," Rime grunted bluntly. "Now she can witness the destruction of everything she swore to uphold." His response did nothing to dissuade Ripper's uncertainty. "We've already accounted for the possibility of the surviving sentinels rising up from their defeat, Ripper."

"But not for the Whistle-Wind pup and the *thing* he did." Ripper shivered, not even wanting to admit the consequence of Ironwrath's foolishness. "The master hasn't given us any orders since we escaped the underground ruin. You have to speak to him! We're getting restless here! He can't intend for us to give up! Not after we've come so far!"

The blood-red sun singed the edges of the narrow clouds. Rime swayed his tail side to side. "You've nothing to worry about, Ripper. Our master hasn't given up. He's only accounting for the… complication."

May the Fallen Titan violate the little lamb's soul! The boil ruptured, and Rime sensed his inner corruption leaking into the ground, the roots below absorbing the foulness like water. *I'll tear off his hide while he screams for mercy! And I'll force his little friend to witness it all!* The lavender strands of the surrounding willows withered into brown tendrils, and his subordinates backed off, allowing him some room. Flies swarmed the doe's carcass, drawn to the taint of its wounds. Already they laid countless eggs within the gashes.

"Where is he, Ripper?" Rime snarled. "Where's our master now?"

"On one of the knolls close to here." Ripper pointed his tail in the direction he meant, the action swift as if he wanted to get rid of Rime as quickly as possible. He couldn't fault his subordinate's fear; it was wise to feel uncomfortable in the presence of the Fallen Titan's vessel.

"I think it's time we talked." Rime started toward the stretch of hillocks rising like grey pustules out of the willowy woods. "Satisfy your stomach while you can. I'll return shortly."

Morning rays of crimson filtered through the ugly branches and pliant leaves as Rime made his way in silent anger up one of the knolls dotting the woods. He wanted so badly to leave this dreadful place in ruin! Even the overly sweet odours here struck a nerve. Ironwrath's distinct scent was almost a relief to smell. There he sat, gazing toward Flame-Heart Territory, its blood-coloured leaves barely visible beyond plains of rolling grass.

Ironwrath seemed older in the daylight, his blanched coat revealing his true age. Rime strode forward and stopped beside him, eyes unable to look away from the Flame-Heart grounds. His tail lashed the swaying blades.

I wonder if she still remembers me. I hope I convinced everyone of her innocence. If anything happened to her… no. She has to be safe. Something fluttered around Rime's heart—a feeling he thought he'd forsaken ever since banishment, ever since his old name was stripped from him by the Warden. But now the almost alien feeling resurfaced like weeds once cut to the stems.

"You'll see her again soon enough, Rime," Ironwrath grunted, steady eyes unblinking.

Rime almost grinned, tail swishing faster. "You've decided then? We go to war?"

Ironwrath inclined his head up to face him. "The little lamb has forced it upon us. I'd wished to destroy the Wolven Code and unite the Four Territories through quicker means, but my sense of mercy has betrayed me, and now we'll all pay the price for it. I hope you can forgive my foolishness."

"We'll have to be careful not to let the silver pup wield time against us." Rime shuddered at the idea of losing everything to the petulant scamp.

Ironwrath's forepaws trembled, and the earth beneath him rumbled. "He doesn't have the focus required to properly wield the powers of time. He only understands the basics of its functions and not its true potential. The Empress revealed to me more than just the location of the weapon. She taught me about its workings and complexities. Silversong is like an eagle who only yesterday learned how to fly. Sooner or later, he'll pluck out his own feathers and plummet to the ground."

Rime growled and gritted his teeth. Everything would've gone so smoothly if Ironwrath hadn't given Silversong a chance to prove his loyalties to a higher cause. How could Ironwrath have ever trusted him to see the truth? "And how do you propose we beat him now?"

"We'll stress his resolve little by little, adding more and more pressure until he shatters." The quaking below Ironwrath intensified. "We'll take everything from him and leave him a vacant, hopeless shell whose failures are too heavy to bear. And once he relinquishes the power he stole from me, I'll use it to bring about the future I promised you all."

Rime dragged his claws through the soil, feeling his oozing hate seep into the riled earth. He basked in the filthiness of the disease inside him, the putrid power of a once-noble being. He let it consume him entirely from bone to spirit. "The Fallen Titan's strength is yours to command, master."

Ironwrath craned his head toward the blistering sun—a flaming eye foretelling a bloody future. "A new war is upon us, and we'll win it no matter the choices we're forced to make."

The clouds above turned black and reached for the sun, smothering the day before it had fully dawned. Rime funneled all his hatred into the dying heavens. *It's time I returned my pain to the Four Territories. I'll conjured a storm they won't ever forget.*

THE RING OF REALMS

THE REALM OF LIGHT

THE PRIMAL REALM

THE FORGOTTEN REALM

THE MYSTICAL REALM

THE SPIRIT REALM

THE GREAT WILDERNESS

THE VOID

THE MORTAL REALM

The journey continues in

CHE CHREADS OF
CIME

Book Two of

A WOLF IN THE SUN

PREVIEW:

The Threads of Time

Chapter 1

The Warden

Sunlight pushed through the breaking clouds to illuminate the shocked faces of the wolves staring at Silversong.

"YOU WHAT?!" Hazel and Palesquall barked at the same time.

Swiftstorm and Greyhail exchanged a look of concern for Silversong's sanity. Frostpaw stayed put a few steps away from the others, eyes bouncing between Silversong and the ground.

The piece of time turned within Silversong's body as he watched a stray hummingbird hovering over a blue flower. He tensed the winding threads only he could see, wrapping them around the small creature and freezing it midair. Removed from the currents of time, the hummingbird stayed still as if encased in ice. A cool breeze gusted through the woods and carried on its trail an array of broad leaves. He captured those too.

Gasps came out of every mouth save Frostpaw's. Silversong repeated himself. "I swallowed the piece of time before the Heretic could claim it, and now I have its powers."

Palesquall nosed one of the leaves frozen in time's embrace, moving it through the air. Through the threads. "Whoa…"

Whoa was right. From Silversong's perspective, it looked like Palesquall was pushing a small island through an ever-flowing river. Even after consuming the piece of time, it proved an immense struggle to understand its workings. None of the things Silversong could now do should be possible, and yet they were. He fought to keep the beginning of a headache at bay. He needed to study the weapon more. He needed to master it if he had any hopes of defeating the Heretic once and for all.

Swiftstorm's wide eyes remained locked on him throughout the display. "Brother…"

Silversong turned to his sister, and the swell of joy warming his heart influenced the invisible threads rotating around her. If he squinted at them, he could make out glimpses of her potential futures. They branched out and revealed wildly different fates, good and bad, and piecing together the circumstances leading to each individual outcome seemed a lofty task. The weapon, spent as it was over the eons, would require much focus to master.

Tiny thorns pressed into his brain, and he flinched, letting go of the tightened threads and allowing them to resume their steady course. The hummingbird glided from one flower to another, oblivious to its previous entrapment, and the once stilled leaves drifted downward much to Palesquall's disappointment. Silversong padded to his sister and bathed in her scent, nuzzling her concerned face. She smelled of home, of family, of something that should never have been lost.

Greyhail watched him close by, eyes lit by the glint of opportunity. "We must get you to the Warden as soon as possible. She needs to know how exactly this weapon functions."

Hazel studied the leaves freed from their unmoving state. "Why must you keep plunging into dangerous situations, Silversong? Palesquall told me all about your audience with the Empress of Spiders, and now this?!"

His sister failed to conceal a shiver. She'd obviously heard this tale from Palesquall too.

Wait until you learn about all the other dangers I faced.

Silversong thought it best not to mention his other audiences with equally murderous Titans. "Look, I—"

"Can you see the future?" Palesquall prodded. "Can you let me know when I'll finally be promoted to lieutenant? I'm looking forward to bossing Hazel around all day."

Hazel nudged him on the cheek. "In your dreams, gullwit."

"You can freeze objects in time," Greyhail began, tail swishing in a controlled manner. "But what else is possible, I wonder?" His suppressed excitement was almost unnerving.

"Can you go back?" Swiftstorm's whine carried the weight of deep regret. "If we can stop the Heretic before he uses Rime to break the Great Chain—"

The wolves hurled swarms of other questions at Silversong to the point where it became impossible to keep track of them all. Within him, the piece of time stirred, urging him to tie its threads around every yapping mouth.

Frostpaw, who'd stayed silent so far, barked loud enough to frighten a soaring eagle. "That's enough! Silversong can answer all your questions once we're safe at my den. Speaking of… shouldn't we get there before an army of wolves departs to the Mountainmouth?"

The startled wolves all turned to the River-Stream lieutenant, realizing they'd gotten carried away. Silversong blinked his thanks to Frostpaw, but his new friend only returned a blank stare like they hadn't just faced death itself together.

Before Silversong's mood could be dragged down further, Greyhail spoke up. "You're right. We'll have all the answers we need in due course. Let's keep moving."

They maintained a trotting pace through the waking forest as summer's heat boiled away the final wisps of a foul storm that hadn't had the chance to rain its fury. Silversong remained at Swiftstorm's side, reminiscing about younger days before the Warden had separated them. It was his way of blocking out the gossip about his new powers.

"I hope it wasn't too difficult for you when the Warden chose me to become a sentinel." Guilt trickled into his sister's tone.

Bitterness flooded Silversong's stomach as he tried to stamp out the memory of him howling his sorrow to the sky following Swiftstorm's departure. "The Warden could've at least given us more time to say goodbye to you. Mother and father tried pretending they were all right for my sake, but I saw through it. For the following seasons, we couldn't even mention your name without wishing we'd done more to stall the Warden from taking you away."

Swiftstorm lowered her ears and head. "I'm sorry. I also remember the awful feeling of leaving Wind's Rest. The crushing weight of knowing I might never see you all again haunted me for a long while." She sighed, and Greyhail licked her face as a gesture of comfort. "Good thing I had you there to distract me," she teased, earning her a smirk.

Silversong stared at the passing ground, at the ants battling for measly crumbs under the shade of the trees. "No. I'm the one who should apologize. It must've been way harder for you being separated from all your packmates. I can't even imagine how scared I would've been if I'd taken your place. I don't think I could've survived all the challenges I'm sure you faced."

To his surprise, his sister only laughed. "You were one of the reasons I became the sentinel I am today, Silversong. Mother and father too. Without you three, I would've been food for the exiles by now." Silversong tilted his head, his confusion met by a tender smile. "All throughout my training, I had your encouraging faces ingrained in my thoughts. The need to protect those I loved far outmatched the pain of every hardship I had to suffer. Even though it was unlikely, I had faith I would see you all again. I knew everything would by all right in the end."

Silversong returned his sister's smile. "Looks like you were right." The piece of time vibrated as if in warning. The threat of chaos and destruction was still out there, but he put aside his worry for now and enjoyed his sister's company while Hazel and Palesquall laughed about something from behind.

"Your sister is one of the strongest sentinels I've ever had the pleasure of knowing," Greyhail grunted at Swiftstorm's other side. "She's saved me more times than I can count. There's a reason the exiles fear her, and it's the same reason the Warden chose her. She'll do anything to defend the Four Territories, even if it demands the ultimate sacrifice."

My sister is the best sentinel ever! Silversong beamed, tail wagging and chest kindling a fuzzy heat. Another future flashed in the threads surrounding her. It passed too quickly for him to make out any meaningful details, but he could've sworn Swiftstorm had been smiling and staring lovingly at someone as she soaked in a pool of her own blood.

Swiftstorm must've caught on to Silversong's concern. "Hey, what's wrong?"

"Someone's coming." Frostpaw halted at the front of the group, tail going stiff. He sniffed the air some more.

Silversong dismissed the vision. Brief as it had been, it was probably among one of the more unlikely outcomes. Still, he had to be careful. He wouldn't let anyone harm his sister. Not when he had the power to save her.

Anxiety bubbled in his core as he studied the new scents drifting his way. They clearly belonged to wolves, some strong and tangy, others more mellow and sweet, but all brought a sense of familiarity he couldn't quite explain. They reminded him of his sister, and of the one who took her from him all those seasons ago. He honed his focus and attempted to search the near future for answers.

"It's her." Greyhail tensed.

Swiftstorm's ears perked up, stopping the trotting wolves.

"We stopped," Palesquall yipped obliviously. "Why've we stopped?"

"Use your nose for once, bug-brain," Hazel snapped. "I think it's the Warden."

Palesquall finally caught on to the unmistakable presence of approaching wolves. "Oh."

Silversong padded up to Frostpaw, who took one look at him and backed off. It was like Silversong's heart had been strangled by thorny vines. Why was the lieutenant suddenly so scared of being close to him?!

Did I do something to offend you? Silversong frowned, but Frostpaw refused to meet his gaze, turning every which way but at his friend. It's like you're pretending I'm a complete stranger all of a sudden.

Before Silversong could confront the lieutenant, the new scents intensified, and a shuffling in the nearby bushes announced the newcomers.

Swiftstorm dipped her head to whisper into Silversong's ear. "If she wanted to, the Warden could've snuck up on us, and we would've been blind to her approach until she was directly in front of our eyes. She can be silent as a butterfly."

Silversong wondered why the piece of time hadn't warned him about the Warden's approach. It seemed the weapon chose what to reveal and what to withhold at random.

There must be a way to make it more precise. Maybe it just needs to get used to me.

Greyhail flicked his tail beside Swiftstorm. "Despite her age, the Warden is as fierce in battle as she is cunning. Don't for a moment underestimate her power, Silversong. She can make the toughest Chiefs whimper in fear if she thinks they're acting out of line. I've seen her reduce the meanest of exiles into sniveling mongrels, and never has she tasted defeat in a duel."

Greyhail's embellishment of the Warden certainly had an effect on Hazel and Palesquall. Tucked away behind Swiftstorm, their tails shook against their bellies. Frostpaw froze where he stood, every strand of fur lifting like a quill.

Out of the shadows she came, fur so white not even the snows of winter could compare. Her gaze encompassed them all as more sentinels appeared behind her, battle-hardened and showing not an inkling of emotion. The Warden's stance was elegant and deadly. It looked like she could spring into battle at a moment's notice. Her pale eyes descended on Silversong, devoid of any kindness. They drilled into him, but he looked away before they dug too deep. Staring at a ghost wouldn't have been as unsettling! He let an icy chill slide across his spine as he recalled the first time he'd seen her. She was as intimidating then as she was now. If anyone could beat the Heretic in a one-on-one fight, it was her. Silversong would bet his life on it.

The Warden's voice, deep and smooth in spite of her age, cut cleanly through all lesser sounds. "You are Silversong, are you not?"

"Yes, ma'am," Silversong answered instantly, pouring all the respect he could muster into his tone. Her station demanded as much. He tucked his tail as far as it could go but met her gaze confidently. How would she react when he revealed his triumph over the Heretic? Would she see him as a threat?

"I thought so." The Warden's tail swished slowly as the mean-looking sentinels surrounded his friends, forming a perimeter in case of an attack. Although they were deep in River-Stream Territory, the Warden quite plainly wouldn't take any chances where the Heretic was concerned. "Swiftstorm has mentioned you on countless occasions, and after hearing about your recent endeavours, I grew eager to finally meet you."

Silversong gulped as the weight of all he'd done crashed onto his shoulders. "I, uhm…"

"Ma'am," Swiftstorm came to his defense, "we found him earlier this morning, and we were on our way to the Saltshore in hopes of intercepting your army before they—"

"It's curious how fate rewards those faithful to the Wolven Code." The Warden craned her head skyward, and even the clouds seemed eager to flee her regard. "I had a feeling something was amiss, and so I delayed the advance of my army until I could be sure no threat would hinder our assault on the Mountainmouth. I set out to join your scouting party, and here we are. Siblings reunited, a wayward lieutenant found safe, and the Heretic thwarted for the time being. An accurate assessment, is it not?"

Silversong gasped, and the golden circle lurched in his belly. "How did you—"

"After you've interrogated as many wolves as I have, you'll learn to piece together clues in a very accurate manner." The Warden's voice was constant like a stream—no, a river—that carved through earth and stone without pause. "If I hadn't learned of the exiles willingly giving themselves to the Fallen Titan's corruption in an attempt to wield it against us, the Heretic would've launched his assault on the Four Territories before the Wise-Wolves even gave you your name, and he would've succeeded too. Indeed, I stalled their invasion for as long as I could. Unfortunately, I failed to predict just how powerful the Heretic's prized lackey had become in his mastery over the corruption. An oversight I pray shall haunt me to my dying day."

The Warden let her confession burrow into the heads of everyone present. "Now, our current situation is made rather obvious. Your eyes wouldn't be as confident as they are now if my nemesis had claimed the weapon he sought, so either you prevented the Heretic from consuming the piece of time, or you beat him at his own game and ate it yourself. I'm willing to bet on the latter, judging by your untroubled scent, not to mention you're emitting a subtle aura I can't quite describe. I'll also venture to say that the Heretic isn't fully vanquished, or you would all be far more jovial."

Frostpaw shifted from paw to paw, fear-struck eyes darting from Silversong to the Warden.

The leader of the sentinels loosed a quick grunt, frightening Frostpaw even more. "Your unlikely ally is as afraid of you as he is of me, or should I say, he's afraid of the thing inside you."

The lieutenant made no sound, and the Warden took this as confirmation. Silversong wasn't convinced. There was another reason for Frostpaw's fright. Another reason why he stood far from his friend.

Silversong thought about explaining his actions here and now before the anticipation got too high, but the Warden allowed none of it, barking a declaration. "You'll reveal to me everything about your journey once we're all gathered at the Saltshore and no sooner. I'll escort you there to save time. These old bones need the exercise. Take heart, my wolves, my soldiers. Stay true to the Wolven Code. Condemn those who break it, and we'll overcome any obstacle. Move out!"

The sentinels howled in unison and began their stride toward the River-Stream den. Hazel and Palesquall pursued them submissively, as did Frostpaw. One look from Swiftstorm was all it took to get Silversong moving, but the uneasy sensation gripping his insides slowed his pace.

Condemn those who break it. Silversong and Frostpaw had broken many rules in the Wolven Code. But surely the Warden would forgive their infractions after they'd achieved so much.

Doubt plagued his thoughts. He closed his eyes and tried forcing the piece of time to reveal the inevitable outcome of his code-breaking. He cursed under his breath. As if to spite him, his own anxiety had beckoned a sheet of opaque fog to hide the future. He needed a clear head to properly use the weapon. He would have to try again later.

He clenched his teeth at the acknowledgment of another threat to the Four Territories. This one was far more sinister and hid in plain sight, masquerading itself as a blessing when in truth it was a curse constricting the freedom of every soul. A chain preventing the Four Territories from becoming their strongest selves.

Silversong lifted his eyes to the Warden—the embodiment and enforcer of the Wolven Code.

Credit: Sharmila Chowdhury

About the Author

Coltrane Seesequasis is a young fantasy writer of Willow Cree heritage who grew up in Gatineau, Quebec. He first began his writing journey on long bus rides to school where he would alleviate the boredom by daydreaming of fantastical worlds, noble heroes, and unwavering villains. Eventually, he put those ideas to paper and started writing stories of his own with the hopes that they would one day morph into something more than just a passion. *Secrets of Stone* is his debut novel and the first book of a planned four-book series that follows the adventures of the young wolf Silversong. Inspired by a love of nature as well as myths and folklore that challenge the limits of creativity, Coltrane Seesequasis joins a new generation of writers, adding his voice to the immersive genre of fantasy.